A PLACE WE BELONG

DEANNA R. ADAMS

A PLACE WE BELONG Copyright © 2024 by Deanna R. Adams. All rights reserved. No part of this book may be reproduced in any form without permission from the author, except by a reviewer who may quote brief passages in a review, or article.

First Printing, 2024

Author's Note

This book is a work of fiction. Although clearly, I was inspired by a few characters who were a part of Cleveland's history, most notably, Eliot Ness and his last two wives. However, my main character, Lydia Swanson, and other supportive characters, along with certain events, and all dialogue, are products of my imagination.

I was inspired by several events in Cleveland's history, particularly the time period when Eliot served as Safety Director from 1935 – 1942. I've taken some creative license to allow myself to tell the story that I wanted to tell. For example, where I mention the Harvard Club bust, the real one took place in 1936, rather than the time I noted in 1940. That said, Eliot did get into a car accident in 1942, after he and Evaline had been drinking. Due to his leaving the scene of the accident, it ultimately led to his leaving the city of Cleveland. He did return in 1947 and ran for mayor, but was defeated by the incumbent, Thomas Burke.

It's also true that in the 1930s, Cleveland, then the fifth largest city in the nation, had one of the worst U.S. traffic-fatality records of all the major cities in America. And because of organized crime activity, as well as corruption within the police departments, Cleveland was considered the most dangerous city in America. By 1938, however, Ness had orchestrated huge improvements in both the police and fire departments, and as a result, decreased crime and traffic fatalities so much that Cleveland then won the National Safety Council's title of "Safest Large City in America." Yes, Ness did that in just five years.

As an author who loves history, I tried to stay true to who Eliot truly was, according to experts, and accounts by those who knew him. While one expert insists that Eliot did not drink much and was not a womanizer, other credible accounts say otherwise. I chose to represent him somewhere in between. Either way, it hardly matters as I fell in love with the man, his integrity, and all he did for Cleveland. He will remain a hero in my eyes, and I hope you find him as dashing as Lydia found him in these pages.

And here's a little secret: I had no idea I was going to write about the dark history of some adoption practices in the 1930s and 40s, or more specifically, The Tennessee Children's Home Society. But once I read about this Memphis orphanage, I knew I had a deeper story. When I write fiction, I always want a true purpose for telling a particular story and bring to light an important part of history, whatever it may be. This book, my fourth novel, is no exception.

And while I have taken some creative license to write this novel, I've saved a few interesting factual tidbits for the Afterword, along with a Readers Club Guide for Book Clubs. As they contain some spoilers, I ask that you please complete the book before you read.

I should add that I've always been intrigued by the art form that was Burlesque in the 1930s and '40s – the elaborate costumes, the big colorful fans, the dance and theater of it all. Those women worked hard at their craft and broke barriers for themselves in the entertainment industry and I wrote about them with much respect.

This book is my tribute to the great Eliot Ness, who also broke barriers and made a lasting impact on my favorite city, Cleveland, Ohio. For true Eliot Ness fans, I wanted to reveal the real man vs. his "Hollywood" persona. The real man was a lot more interesting, actually, and I thank Rebecca McFarland (see Afterword), and the Cleveland Police Museum, for honoring the legacy of the man, and not the myth. I hope you find this story that merges fact with fiction most entertaining, as I did in the writing of it.

Below are some books I used in my research for this novel, including those that feature the disturbing role that Georgia Tann played in history. I highly recommend these books.

The Show Girl, by Nicola Harrison

A Kiss from Mr. Fitzgerald, by Natasha Lester

Feuding Fan Dancers, by Leslie Zemeckis

Rust Belt Burlesque, by Erin O'Brien and Bob Perkoski

Eliot Ness: The Real Story, by Paul W. Heimel

Eliot Ness: The Rise and Fall of an American Hero, by Douglas Perry

Orphan Train, by Christina Baker Kline

Before We Were Yours, by Lisa Wingate

The Baby Thief: The Untold Story of Georgia Tann, the Baby Seller Who Corrupted Adoption, by Barbara Bisantz Raymond

Before and After, by Judy Christie and Lisa Wingate

"In this moving tale of friendship, family, and love, Adams' fictionalized story of Eliot Ness, set in Cleveland, is a saga that will capture both your heart and soul. A compelling glimpse of history, a measure of hope during a time of trouble, rich period detail, and characters that come alive on the page. *To Whom We Belong* is a satisfying and enjoyable read. I highly recommend!"

- **Abby L. Vandiver,** *USA Today* **bestselling and author of** *Where Wild Peaches Grow*

"In 1935, Eliot Ness was tapped to clean up Cleveland, Ohio, the most dangerous city in the nation. Not only has Deanna Adams captured the excitement, the tension and fear of that era, she's added a fabulous tale of missing persons and a corrupt adoption ring. When her protagonist, a burlesque queen enlists Ness to find her sister, all hell breaks loose. Read this once for the tension-filled story, and again, for the well-crafted description of a bygone era."

- **Don Bruns,** *USA Today* **bestselling author, and editor of** *Back In Black,* **including a new Jack Reacher Story**

ADVANCE PRAISE FOR *A PLACE WE BELONG*

"Adams's characters are sharply drawn, realistically complicated, and heartbreakingly believable. Her plot is sophisticated and well-paced. Don't miss this page-turner."

- Mary Ellis, *USA Today* bestselling author of *The Quaker and the Rebel*

"With Deanna Adams' new novel, *A Place We Belong*, Northeast Ohio's first lady of rock & roll fiction takes readers back in time to the early 1940s, when post-Untouchables lawman, Eliot Ness, was tasked with cleaning up Cleveland's corrupt safety forces. Fun, fascinating, and filled with the details of a time when Cleveland was the fifth-largest city in the country, Adams serves up a noir-ish thriller that gives readers a generous look into a world of streetcars, city pubs, romance, and mystery."

– Scott Lax, author of the novels, *The Year That Trembled* and *Vengeance Follows, and the play, 1970*

PRAISE FOR THE NOVELS OF

DEANNA ADAMS

"In *Peggy Sue Got Pregnant*, Adams hits all the right notes in this roman a' clef that now joins a select group of good rock and roll novels." – Ron Antonucci, Editor and Book Critic

"*Peggy Sue Got Pregnant* is a trip back to the historic beginnings of rock 'n roll. This book is for rock lovers, but also anyone who has ever loved, or whose love has gone untold. A masterpiece of emotion." – Paula Balish, Cleveland Disc Jockey, CBS Radio/WNCX ClassicRock

"*Scoundrels & Dreamers* is a trip down memory lane for music-loving children of the 1980s. But the music is just a soundtrack to a darker tale about family, children, the power of love and the power of art. Great Read." - Laura DeMarco, *Plain Dealer* Arts & Entertainment Reporter

"*The Truth About Justyce* is the third volume in Adams' generational fiction series, and her first YA crossover. The story works well as a stand-alone, with necessary information revealed in manageable pieces, and the ultimate resolutions of Justyce's and Dylan's many conflicts are both realistic and satisfying." - *Kirkus Reviews*

"*The Truth About Justyce* is an engaging story of self-discovery and first love with a '90s grunge soundtrack." - Reedsy Discovery

"In her novels, Deanna writes about untamed girls who grow to be undaunted women." – *The News-Herald*

Also By Deanna R. Adams

NOVELS

Peggy Sue Got Pregnant

Scoundrels & Dreamers

The Truth about Justyce

NONFICTION

Rock 'n Roll and the Cleveland Connection

Cleveland's Rock and Roll Roots

Cleveland's Rock and Roll Venues

Confessions of a Not-So-Good Catholic Girl

The Writer's GPS: A Guide to Writing & Selling Your Book

Dedication

To all those children from so long ago who never knew where they belonged.

I hope you found your place in life.

It's not what happens to you, but how you react to it that matters.

- Epictetus

Act One

September 10, 1997
Lake View Cemetery, Cleveland, Ohio

I was the first to arrive.
 I sat on the cast iron bench, straight and still as the monuments surrounding me, gazing at the splendid flowers, grand oaks, and Japanese maples when the thought crossed my mind. Were our life paths chosen? Or were they destined? Those times when things worked out as we'd planned, against all the times when they didn't. And yet, looking back, it had all worked out pretty well.
 All except for Eliot Ness.
 "Make sure I get there before the crowd," I'd told my driver, Edward. I needed time alone with Eliot, or at least his spirit. Time I'd been robbed of once he left Cleveland for good. I'd gotten my hair dyed back to my famous peachy blonde shade, had my nails done a bright coral, and wore a chiffon dress, blue, of course, that I'd picked up at Saks Fifth Avenue.
 I wanted to look nice for him.

He deserved to be here, where other city luminaries rested. Like the Rockefellers and the Garfields. And now, the Nesses. Here, in this serene lagoon before me, Eliot's ashes would be placed for all eternity.

I hadn't been surprised when I heard, back in '57, that Eliot had died of a heart attack. That man always kept his emotions inside. Untouchable. Many times I wanted to tell him that crime fighters were often their own worst enemy. But it was never my place. He belonged to someone else.

He always belonged to someone else.

I'd told him once that keeping his feelings buried wasn't good for him, but he had shrugged it off. Like he did that last day I saw him. A little shrug, a kiss on the cheek, was all I'd gotten. My final memory. Considering what we'd been through together, I deserved more. And so had he.

Poor man's been dead forty years and just now being put to rest, for God's sakes. Closing my eyes, I let out a sigh thinking how nice it was of that librarian to insist that Eliot and his dear ones receive a decent burial. After he, his son, and last wife all died, their ashes were kept by an unidentified relative. But that person finally understood that Eliot belonged to the people. The people of Cleveland. They had even named a damn beer after him. That gave me a chuckle. Eliot always preferred scotch.

I still couldn't believe the Eliot Ness I knew had become such an American folk hero. The books, the TV series, the movie with that handsome Kevin Costner. All done without his say-so.

All done without my say-so.

I'd been kept out of that book his so-called friend had written. Sure, I could have spoken up a number of times. But sometimes it's best to let sleeping dogs lie.

A Place We Belong

"Most of the people coming didn't even know you, the real man," I whispered to the sky, nodding to the clouds. Sunshine would not be fitting today.

A day that made me also think of Mother. I never did find out where the woman was buried. As a young girl, I hadn't known where to start. Besides, once life took all those turns, it didn't seem to matter anymore.

I recalled when she'd get mad, Mother would say to me and my sister, "I'll knock you into next week." Then one awful, life-changing day, she did.

That sudden slump to the kitchen floor flung us girls into another life. Separate lives, for years. Until Eliot agreed to help me find Tess, which catapulted a chain of events that no one could have predicted.

Destiny?

I shifted in the hard seat wishing I'd brought my ass pillow, as I called it. I always had a bony derriere, but luckily my other endowments had given me a pretty good living. At least for a time.

Out of the corner of my eye, I saw the stretch of cars approaching, pushing away old thoughts. Turning slightly, I watched the caravan wind slowly down the road, coming my direction.

The cars lurched to a stop. Doors squeaked open, doors slammed shut. The chirping of birds seemed to announce his arrival. A cardinal landed on the edge of my bench, just for a moment, then took flight. As I watched it go, a faint breeze brushed my cheek. Soft, warm, comforting. I placed my hand there, lightly, not wanting to smudge my rouge.

He's here.

I lifted my head and gave him a little wink, like I used to in the old days.

After all, old habits die hard.

1.

Cleveland, August 1940

*S*ex and crime can be great motivators. I learned that soon after I started this gig. It's one of the things Eliot and I had in common. We were both meshed in the forbidden fruit business.

As I dipped and twirled on the makeshift stage, my eyes veered toward the front door. If rumors were true, Eliot Ness, the famous crime-fighter and city safety director, would be stopping in for lunch. I'd seen him here before, but he was always surrounded by important men so I could never approach him. But today was going to be different. I wasn't going to chicken out this time.

And I was dressed for the occasion. All dolled up in my sequined, strapless blue gown with elbow-length white gloves and feather boa. But damn, it was hot. So stinkin' hot, the sequins stuck to my skin, making me wish I could take off more than allowed.

Thank God I'd left the corset, fishnets, and heavy ostrich fans—items more fitting after dark—back in my dressing room a few blocks over. I wasn't performing on my usual stage but in a corner of the room where businessmen, political men, cops, lawyers, mobsters (especially mobsters) came on a regular basis. "Roxy Wednesday" was a hit at the Theatrical Grille Restaurant, thanks to me, Lydia Swanson. Better known as Blue Satin Doll.

Strip steak was the blue-plate special of the day. I could appreciate the gag but didn't have to like it. I was more than some afternoon delight. Not one of those loose, pay-me-in-cash type broads. I was classy—strictly entertainment. And I'd make damn sure the man who just walked in knew it too.

I spotted him the minute he entered, and it nearly threw me off.

The lunch crowd was sparse, probably due to the heat, so despite the dim lighting and swirling cigarette smoke, I could make out every face. Still, even in a packed house, no one missed the presence of the man who had all of Cleveland in a tizzy, including me.

Normally he wore a boring brown suit with pricey looking tie but today's heat had him in a simple tan shirt, neatly pressed trousers. I stole a few peeks from behind my boa, saw him pony up to the bar. Nerves crept through my insides as I watched him remove his trademark gray fedora and set it down on the wooden bar top. His Brylcreemed hair was slick, his middle part straight as a race track.

Like me, Eliot had a moniker besides his real one. Many, including some law officials, called him the "Boy Scout." I heard he hated it.

The instant my first act was done, I tossed the boa and gloves on the chair, sashayed across the hazy room, past the long bar and made my way to the corner barstool, thankfully next to the big swirling fan. Eliot was sitting next to Big Joe, who immediately made the introduction. I took a deep breath, smiled sweetly and shook his hand. "How nice to meet you, Mr. Ness."

He smiled, just as sweetly. "Please, call me Eliot."

"Eliot, it is." I flashed my big Irish eyes—I couldn't help myself.

I had to fight the urge to toy with him. I wasn't the only gal in town who had a little crush on the handsome law enforcer, but I was different from the others. Sure, my occupation made me stand out, perhaps warrant some extra attention, but I had more in mind than being some hussy on this man's arm.

That's not to say I wouldn't love a piece of him, I'm only human. Even if he was an older man of thirty-seven, he had that certain something that appealed to the ladies. Still, my main interest in this top official was more of a business nature. Besides, he was married—worse yet, a newlywed (second time around, no less)—so getting his attention in that form was futile. Any man worth his salt didn't stray till at least the second year. I may be only twenty-two but I'd become a fast learner of life working as a burlesque queen.

I turned to Joe. "Sweetie, could you get me a Jack 'n Coke, please?"

"Coming right up, Lydia." His thick hand flagged down Albert, the weathered old barkeep who'd worked here since probably my first moment on earth.

Big Joe was the bouncer at the Roxy Theater, where I'd been dancing since my mama died. He served as my personal bodyguard and always accompanied me to the Theatrical. After all, you never knew when some sloppy drunkard (and there was usually one, even at noon) might decide it was okay to put his grimy paws where they shouldn't be. That unfortunate soul would quickly be met with a large bear clutch to the back of his neck, dragging him on a little guided tour of the back alley. It happened with less frequency now, thanks to word-of-mouth, so I had a soft spot for Joe.

Eliot stood and waved his hand toward the stool. "I imagine you could use a minute to sit." Everyone knew Eliot was a gentleman, but his words were more telling than his actions. Any gentleman would give up his seat for a lady, but this one didn't do it as a mere polite gesture. His comment showed straight up that this fella understood the working girl.

I shifted my gown slightly and slid onto the offered seat. While Joe babbled on, something about the bust at the

Harvard Club, I glanced around, rather enjoying the envious looks from the few women in the place and listened for an opening. I waited patiently for my drink, and my opportunity. My glass arrived first. In ladylike fashion, I sipped it slowly, purposefully. The syrupy liquid soothed my insides, summoned my confidence. I was more than ready. I'd rehearsed it for days.

"So, Lydia, you from around here?" That resonant, self-assured voice tugged at my insecurities, but I was used to the question. A lot of burly girls lived in other cities. Like Sally Rand and Ann Corio, who spent much of their careers flitting from one town to another. Traveling the wheel, they called it. Those were the girls who made the real money. But living out of a suitcase was not my cup of tea. I preferred a home base.

"Westside? Eastside?" His eyes, a merging of blue and gray, penetrated my own. Despite the hot blush I knew was adding to my rouge, I couldn't look away. He took a swig of his drink not taking those eyes off me. It was a bit unnerving.

"Oh, I'm a Westside girl."

"Is that right? What part?"

"Lakewood."

"Why, we're practically neighbors."

"You don't say?" I took another dainty sip to quash my burst of glee. Practically neighbors? Maybe he really would be willing, feel obliged even, to help me. Setting the glass down, I noticed his beverage was in a tall pop glass, no fruit. Ginger ale. "No drinking on the job, I presume?"

He shook his head, just slightly.

What must he think of me, then? Drinking in the early afternoon *and* while working? I slyly pushed my glass to the side as I opened my mouth to begin my prepared speech. "I was hoping to have a few minutes to ask—"

A dark-haired woman, wearing a mustard-yellow polka-dot dress and crooked smile, pushed herself between us.

Damn.

"Well, if it isn't the big man himself." The lady said it like she didn't like him.

Well over six-foot tall, Joe towered over the woman. "Thelma, why don't you take your mouth and swagger elsewhere."

Thelma? The only woman I knew of with that name belonged to Angelo Parrisi from the Mayfield Road Mob. His girl.

Thelma raised her head, inhaled smoke from her silver cigarette holder, then met his gaze for an uncomfortable second before glaring at Eliot and stomping off.

Big Joe scanned the room as if checking for Angelo and his boys before shifting his attention to me. "Looks like your fans are getting anxious."

I turned toward the crowd in front of the stage. He was right. The room had filled up, the voices louder. "Oh jeez. That time already?" I leaned in to read Eliot's watch. An Omega. I knew the brand. Bill, the man who thought he owned me but didn't, had one just like it.

"Excuse me, Mr. . . . er, Eliot. I do want to talk to you, it's rather important."

Big Joe's hand pressed on my back as I heard the announcer paging me.

"And now folks, it's time once again for our delightful star of the show! Blue Satin Doll, come ooooon uuuup."

"If it's important to you, it's important to me." Eliot said as he patted my hand, holding it there a three full Mississippis. Was he flirting? Hard to tell. "Call me anytime," he added. Full of respect. That alone could make a girl melt like chocolate in the sun.

Feeling a hot blush, I turned away and spotted my glass, still half-full. I was tempted to let it be, but I was parched. I gulped it down.

The hell with dainty, I was who I was.

Meandering through the crowd back to the stage floor, I felt a rush of giddiness. Something resembling hope.

Now what? Did he actually mean I could call him at his workplace? Now that we were acquainted, was that acceptable?

Maybe I wouldn't have to. Maybe he'd make his way down the street one night to catch my Roxy act. I knew he would enjoy it. Married or not.

I danced the next set in a daze, thinking Eliot Ness might just be my savior. There was more to this man that met the eye, or his reputation. More than his status as one who refused bribes from gangsters like Al Capone. More than his leadership qualities that helped clean up our fair city. And certainly more than the man who had known failure. People still taunted him for not snagging the notorious serial killer that had Clevelanders so frightened a few years back. Still, he'd accomplished a lot in his six years here. Like fighting organized crime, reorganizing the police and fire units, getting traffic lights installed to reduce traffic fatalities. That all was nothing to sneeze at.

*E*liot was gone by the time my show was done, and with him went my expectations. Ever since I'd decided to seek his help in finding my sister, I couldn't keep my mind on nothing else. I had to get him alone, explain the whole story, beg for his help. And yet, the perfect opportunity had passed me by. Doubt seized me quickly. What if even the great law enforcer, with all his connections, couldn't help me? What if he was just too busy to help me? Or worse, what if he simply wouldn't want to? Still, even if he turned me down, better to know than keep those elusive dreams alive.

Hope can be such a bitch.

2.

*T*rudging upstairs to the dressing room, I changed into street clothes—black slacks, sleeveless white linen blouse with the ruffle down the front. I was strapping on my Mary Janes when the door opened so abruptly I nearly lost my balance.

"Hey, Doll."

Bill.

Son-of-a bitch.

I stood back up and with hands on hips, threw him a look. "Closed doors are for knockin'."

He was out of uniform, which surprised me. I remember him saying he'd switched to day shift. He drew me into him before I could protest. "I've missed you."

His peppermint breath felt cool on my face, but I didn't welcome it. He'd been calling me so much I'd been thinking of changing my number, but that wouldn't do a bit of good. Bill knew where I lived. Knew it well.

I pulled away. "I told you I needed a break."

"I'd say a month is break enough. Come on, lemme take you home."

That was tempting only because I hated taking the streetcar. "Why aren't you at work?"

"I put in a lot of hours last week, needed a day off." There it was, those puppy dog eyes. The eyes that often made me say yes when I meant to say no.

Why did he have to look so damned much like Clark Gable, complete with that come-hither grin? Our first date had been to see *Gone with the Wind*, and at times I'd teasingly call him Clark. But only when feeling romantic.

A Place We Belong

Which wasn't now.

A trickle of sweat formed on my brows, and I swiped at it. "Bill, I'm too hot to argue with ya, I'm in no mood." In the last two hours, my emotions had gone from anticipation to anxiety to excitement to disappointment, and now, annoyance. A lot for one day. I felt like Mama always did. Hot and bothered.

Helen strode in just then but stopped on a dime. "Oh! Officer Baker. I'm sorry to interrupt."

"You're not interruptin' nothing, Helen. Mr. Baker was just leaving." I leaned into the mirror just to avoid looking at the goon. Besides, I could use a touch-up.

I began applying my daytime lipstick, "Natural Rose," and caught his reflection. Not happy. *Good.*

Bill lit a cigarette, snapped the lighter shut. "Suit yourself, Lydia."

I sneered at his departing image in the glass, then swung around. "So, Helen." I squeezed the woman's hand to let her know all was okay. "If you're done, we can ride home together."

Helen had worked the Theatrical's kitchen for years, doing everything from making the salads to whipping up desserts. If it wasn't for her and Frank, I might still be living in that crappy jalopy, or worse. As soon as Helen learned I was homeless, an orphan, they sublet the upstairs apartment of their duplex to me. In the years I'd been there, they'd only raised the rent once, and at forty dollars a month, including utilities, it was still a bargain.

I threw my arm around the older woman's plump shoulder, and we walked out into the stifling heat. Four nights a week I worked at the Roxy, so this afternoon gig was perfect. I danced from noon till two, then off the rest of the day. And today was a new day, indeed. Tossing Bill from my life, I felt emboldened for the first time in a long while.

I'd planned on going to the market later but now all I wanted was to go home and cuddle with Spencer, my sweet cocker spaniel I'd named after Spencer Tracy. My boss, George gifted me with him when I became the club's featured performer. The other girls had those fluffy toy things—Chows, Pekingese, Pomeranians—I was glad he hadn't chosen one of those. I didn't want to be a cliché. At least no more than I already was.

Helen and I stepped off the streetcar, silently grateful our house was just a block away. Today was not a day to walk far in this heat. But relief gave way to exasperation the minute we turned down Central Avenue. As we approached the house, I caught sight of Bill's stocky frame. He was there on the porch, hands in pockets, pacing.

"Aw, damn it to hell." I stopped right there in the middle of the sidewalk. "That man cannot take a hint." Instinct told me to run the other way, but there's no place to run when you're involved with a copper. Especially a dirty one.

I took in a breath as Helen linked my arm in hers. As close a friend as Helen Sabo was, she tried staying out of my business, but she was also protective of me. We reached the house and as we climbed up the front steps, Helen stayed next to me like an armed guard.

I gave her a nudge. "Go on, it's fine."

She squinted at me, not sure I meant it until I nodded a second time. She went in then, but not without slamming the screen door behind her.

I was determined to stand my ground before noticing that here was the meek Bill, the guy I had fallen for.

"What's goin' on with you, Lyddy? What'd I do that you're acting this way?" His eyes were moist. Yeah, he thought he was such a tough guy. "We had a good thing going, you and me."

A Place We Belong

I gave a frustrated sigh. "You're so smart, you should've figured it out by now." I set my pocketbook on the porch swing, crossed my arms. "I may not have the most respectable job, but I do have ethics and you . . ." I stared straight at him, raised a brow. "I heard you don't."

He looked away, smashed his cig in the metal ashtray nearby. "What ya hear?"

I didn't want to have this conversation, but then, maybe it would make him go away. "That you're one of those crooked cops Eliot Ness despises." I kept my arms crossed in case he tried holding my hands. He always wanted to touch me when we fought. "The kind that takes bribes."

His expression stayed neutral but I caught his face tighten. "Who you been talkin' to?"

"Bill." I wiped away a limp curl from my forehead. "It doesn't matter, I just don't love you, okay? It boils down to that." A twinge of guilt caught my throat. Despite it all, I didn't want to hurt him, but it appeared necessary. I pointed to his green Buick. "Now please leave, I got things to do."

I whipped around, and like Helen, banged the door behind me. Leaning against it, I placed my hands to my chest, trying to calm my racing heart. He always got to me, one way of another.

After a minute, I turned and peeked through the ruffled curtains.

He was gone.

3.

*T*wo weeks passed before I saw Eliot again. I'd just finished my Friday night show when Kitty grabbed my arm in the hallway. "Hey, guess who's here?"

I shrugged. It could be anyone. Celebrities came by on a regular basis to see us girls. Why, just a few weeks ago, I met Frank Sinatra. I kept a signed photograph of me and him in my dressing room, where I was headed now.

I gave her a side glance, kept walking. "Better not be Bill." Kitty was my best friend and knew what was up.

Grabbing my shoulders, she made me face her. "No. It's Eliot Ness! He asked to see you." She was practically bouncing in her T-straps.

George appeared behind Kitty. "And he's a busy man so don't keep him waiting." In other words, keep Mr. Ness on the premises as long as possible. He drank the best scotch and was a good tipper.

I winked at him. "Whatever you say, Boss," and breezed past him so fast I was sure a few blue feathers dusted his shoulders.

Rushing to my room the size of a closet, I placed my big fan in the corner, stripped off the fishnets, then gently pulled off the pasties. I squeezed my breasts into a navy lace bra, threw on a silk blouse—a nice sequined number that revealed just a hint of my bulging assets—and tight black skirt. I gladly wiped off the stage makeup and floozy red rouge, applied a soft coral lipstick, but kept the fake lashes, which gave my eyes more expression. But oh lord, my hair was a fright. I sometimes regretted not wearing a short bob that was all the rage and easier to manage, but I never wanted to follow fashion. Then I'd be like everybody else.

Besides, my shoulder-length ginger hair was as popular as my stage outfits. Depending on the act, I'd wear it in tight waves, in a snood, or simply attach a big flower the color of whatever fan I was using that night. The downside was, longer hair required maintenance and despite the sticky spray, my thick mane was often disheveled by show's end. Which was definitely the case now.

"Need some help?" Kitty could read my mind, I swear. Luckily, she liked to think of herself as a beautician on the side.

I'd already pulled out the bobby pins and did my standard "flip and fluff"—bending over and brushing my locks upside down to get out the spray, then flipping back up. Kitty grabbed my brush and swooped my hair to the side of my forehead, ala Greta Garbo, tucked the rest behind my ears, and stabbed in a rhinestone hair comb to secure wayward strands.

"He's alone too," Kitty added, "so maybe you'll finally get to have that talk."

"Right. Fingers crossed." Kitty was the only one I'd confided my troubles to. Being a woman of Asian descent and having escaped cruel bigotry growing up in San Francisco, the gal knew all about the lemons life can throw at you.

"Better make it quick, you know he won't be alone for long."

True enough. No one left that man alone, male or female. Standing now, I stepped away to get a full look at myself. "Good?"

Kitty leaned in and whispered in my ear. "Cat's meow."

I checked my pocketbook, making sure the emerald glass marble was safe and secure in the inside pocket. It was part of the story I would tell him. Clasping the purse shut, I spun around and blew my friend an air kiss. "Wish me luck."

It was after midnight now and the place was dark and packed with regulars, making it hard to navigate between the round tables to get to the back bar. Spotting him in the back (he obviously liked corners), I kept my focus and ambled my way through the smoky room.

He stood when he saw me approach. I extended my hand, hoping he wouldn't feel my nerves. "Eliot, what a pleasant surprise."

The new young bartender, Tony, stood watching us, ignoring the row of drinkers with half to empty glasses.

"Would you like something, Miss Swanson?"

I hesitated until I saw the amber liquid in Eliot's rocks glass. No ginger ale tonight. What a relief. "Yes, please."

"Jack 'n Coke, right?" Eliot asked before Tony had a chance.

I couldn't hide my astonishment. "Why, sweet of you to remember," I said, cracking a smile. "However, I think I'd rather enjoy a good gin martini tonight. With a lemon twist."

He smiled back. "Tony, a gin martini for the lady," laying down a crisp dollar bill. "And don't forget the twist."

I took the seat next to him. He looked happy to see me, which was an added thrill. "Thank you for stopping in."

He waited until Tony was out of earshot. "I came on business, just a lookout."

My thrill collapsed like a punctured balloon. So he wasn't here to see me, necessarily. I hid my disappointment with another little grin. As if he'd read my mind, he added, "However, it appears all clear so I'm off the clock and—" he swiveled his barstool to face me, "now, we can visit."

"Wonderful." I took a sip before going on. "I've heard so much about you, Eliot, it's nice to meet the real thing." I squished up my face. "Oh, that didn't come out quite right, did it?"

"I know what you meant." He offered a cigarette. Lucky Strike. I preferred Chesterfields but I took it. "Your reputation precedes you as well," he said with a mischievous grin as he lit my smoke. "Though not half as flamboyant as mine."

My drink arrived and I raised my drink, clinked his glass. "Touché."

"I suspect, Miss Lydia, we do have this in common. We are more than our personas suggest."

In that brief second, I felt more understood than I had in years. And each time he referred to me as "Miss Lydia," I sat up a little straighter.

He pushed his empty glass forward and Tony was back in a flash. It surprised me how fast the man could drink, yet he appeared completely sober. "It seemed you had something to ask me that day at the Theatrical. I'm intrigued."

Here we go. "Yes, I've been wanting to talk to you for some time." I took another sip of courage. "But I know you're a busy man. I don't want to intrude on your work."

"I'll be the judge of that. What is it you need?"

The hootin' and hollerin' was rising. Blanche was beginning her act. The one known for flashing more than what was legal. I didn't like that George allowed it. I tried hard to be more tease than sleaze and girls like Blanche could take us all down the gutter.

"Eliot, could we perhaps go somewhere else to talk?"

He, too, noticed the growing ruckus. "Next door?" He was referring to a tavern called The Little Bar.

"Oh, Eliot, that's just as crowded on a Friday night. Besides, no respectable woman goes into that place." I smiled, adding, "Yes, I fully recognize the irony, but I'm a classy broad."

He grinned back. "Indeed, you are." The affirmation warmed him to me all the more.

"Ya know, there's a cute little Irish pub called Sullivan's, between Lakewood and Bay Village."

"I know the place." His eyes darted around the room, as if checking to be sure he hadn't missed whoever he'd come looking for. Satisfied, he polished off his scotch. "That'll be fine. You need a lift?"

"I'd appreciate that," grateful I didn't have to ask. "I do hate taking the streetcar at night."

"You don't have someone driving you home at this hour?"

"Not usually. In bad weather, George will take me, or his son, Johnny, when he's here."

"That's nonsense." He slid a half dollar toward Tony's end of the bar then took my hand to help me off the barstool. "A lady should not be using public transportation after dark."

"Don't have a choice," I said, flattered by his concern. "While I could probably afford a car—" My voice trailed off, looking into those blue-gray eyes. I couldn't lie to him. Didn't want to. "I'm afraid I've never learned to drive."

He started to say something but the howls grew louder, as they always did when only drunks remained. We beat it to the exit, and he led me around the back where his black Chrysler Sedan sat away from the other vehicles. I may not drive one, but I knew my cars, thanks to Daddy's obsession. Before he high-tailed it out of our lives.

As the car turned down East Ninth Street toward the lake, conversation was at a standstill. I cranked the window down slightly and almost mentioned how nice the evening breeze was, but talk of weather bored me to tears. I shifted in my seat, just to make some noise. "Does your radio work?"

Eliot glanced over at me as if, for a second, he'd forgotten I was there. Maybe he wasn't used to having other women in his car, being married and all. Both of those thoughts made me feel a twinge uncomfortable. Maybe this wasn't a good idea.

"I love that big band station they have on 'round this time of night," I said, "I don't get to hear it too often by the time I get home."

"Another reason you need to stop taking the streetcar this late." He leaned toward the console. "What station?"

"Here. You drive." I fiddled with the dial. "I'll find the music."

We listened to a Glenn Miller song, then Tommy Dorsey's "I'll Never Smile Again" came on. "That's about the saddest song I've ever heard." I was tempted to change it, but then, it gave us something to talk about, like how Sinatra left Harry James for Dorsey's band.

Despite it being a Friday night, Sullivan's was dead, with only two men at the bar. Eliot seemed relieved at that and I had to wonder if he felt awkward being here with the likes of me. I did enjoy my job but my occupation sometimes made me feel inferior to those outside the business. He led us to a small round table toward the back. "Take a seat, I'll get our drinks."

"Just a Coca Cola for me." I knew better than to have another drink and still be able to tell him what I needed to. I leaned back in the chair and took a few deep breaths. I still felt anxious being with him, but the different atmosphere helped. The pub was a lovely drinking establishment. Dark, cozy and quiet, even when busy. Unlike other bars where folks went to dance and get rowdy, people came to Dan Sullivan's place to unwind. To talk.

Eliot returned with two Cokes. "No fun drinking alone." I smiled, though I was sure that wasn't always the case.

After chatting about the upcoming election, agreeing that Roosevelt was a shoo-in, Eliot asked again what was on my mind.

I paused, trying to recall the speech I'd memorized weeks ago. Eliot would be one of few to know what was eating me up inside, but he'd be the most important. I'd been watching him carefully—his mannerisms, how flawlessly he wore his clothes, his dark hair always slick and perfect. He always appeared thoughtful, like his mind never shut off. I needed someone like him.

But opening up this can of worms had me questioning the whole idea. If he agreed to look into this, might whatever he discover destroy me? Was it better to never know?

I pressed my lips together. No, there was nothing worse than the not-knowing. It had been five years, I had to do something before time made it impossible. And Eliot Ness's reputation for getting things done was known throughout the Midwest. I'd read about his work in Chicago. How he'd formed a team of men called, "The Untouchables," because they refused to take bribes, be it from criminals, or crooked law enforcers. Now he was doing the same for Cleveland with a new team of Untouchables, aiming to eliminate rampant crime in one of the most populated cities in the country. He'd even unveiled corruption in his own police department, which led to several convictions of high-ranking officers and had others on alert—like my snake of an ex-boyfriend.

I knew Eliot had his hands full, but I was desperate. And he was just the kind of guy who I was certain would help out a woman haunted by her past.

"Eliot, you know so many people. You can find out things regular people have no access to . . ." I stared into his eyes to show how serious I was. "And well, I'm hoping you could help me with a most difficult problem." I looked back down, suddenly shy. "I don't know where else to turn, it's . . . so complicated—"

My eyes caught the time on my silver watch, half past one. Damn. This promised to be a long conversation. "It's late. I imagine your wife's wondering where you are by now." I very much wanted to be respectful of the woman. If I were her, a husband being out this late would surely get my goat.

"It's fine, she understands the business I'm in. Please. Talk to me."

The sincerity in his eyes gave me a lump in my throat. "Well, okay." I sucked in a breath. "I guess it's best to start at the beginning."

4.

I did not, however, start at the beginning. Which would be when our son-of-a bitchen father took off for places unknown. No need to start there.

And so, I recounted the trauma of watching my mother slump to the kitchen floor, me and Tess rushing to the neighbors, and how Mrs. McDowell and some ladies from the local church conducted a funeral of sorts in our house.

"So many details about those two days I don't recall, though I still have nightmares of seeing my mother lying in that wooden box in our living room," I said with a shiver.

Eliot nodded. "I can imagine. But of course, funeral homes are expensive."

"Yes, though someone must have helped with burial expenses," I said, staring at my Coke glass. "And someone made the decision that we girls needn't know where they took our mother. To "spare" us, I overheard someone say." I felt the anger boil up. "No one ever told us where she ended up. With no money, I imagine she's in an unmarked plot somewhere."

I told him about staying overnight at the McDowells, and how two ladies showed up the next day. "They were stern-looking women—surely not kind church ladies—who said that Tess and I had to go with them. One of them said we were 'Wards of the Court,' without explaining what the hell that meant."

Did I have to tell him all this? I wasn't sure but my mouth spewed on. "I remember it was dark when we arrived at the orphanage. They put us in a room with a bunch of other kids. We slept on a cot in a corner."

A Place We Belong

Eliot leaned to the side, pulled out a handkerchief from his trouser pocket, and handed it to me. I hadn't realized I needed it. I dabbed my eyes and forced myself to keep going. Eliot had to understand all of it. Because then, how could he refuse me?

"The next day, we were whisked off to separate rooms. A week later, they told me Tess was going to a foster home, due to overcrowding. I remember a heavy-set woman in ugly brown clothing walking me down the hall so I could say goodbye." My eyes, as usual, began tearing up. "She just stood there. No facial expression whatsoever, as tears streamed down our faces. When they told Tess it was time to go, she did not go quietly. She started kicking and screaming and I wanted to yell at her to stop. She was just making it worse. And if I fussed, too, those people might punish us both—how, I didn't know—but it was clear, there was nothing either of us could do to change what was happening. The woman had a good grip on her and pushed her through the door."

I stopped to take a sip. Without alcohol, the pop was sickeningly sweet.

"I just stood there frozen, completely dazed. Yes, I was scared, but I did think they'd eventually bring us back together. Why wouldn't they? We were sisters. We had no one else." I shook my head. "God, I was so young and naïve. I simply assumed they couldn't possibly separate us forever . . .

But they could. And they did."

I felt like I'd just ended a session with a psychologist and wondered if Eliot was now sorry he'd asked about it. "I'm sorry about me rambling on, you didn't need to hear all those details, but . . ."

"No, it's important. I thoroughly understand your situation now."

I sat back, exhausted. "Oh, Eliot, you look as tired as I feel. We can talk more another time. I think we both need to call it a night." There was more to tell, but for now, I'd told enough.

As we walked to his car, I realized I hadn't asked him the one big question. "I want you to know that I have asked around through the years, but no one would help me find out what happened to my sister." I stopped beside his car, looked straight at him. The moonlight illuminated his face. And in that soft expression, I had my answer.

He opened the passenger door but before I got in, he reached for his wallet and handed me a card. "Here's my private business line. Hang on to it."

I went to take it and our fingers touched. We smiled, and let go simultaneously. "Thank you, Eliot."

Then, to lighten the moment, I stuffed the card inside my brassiere and flashed him a big ol' grin.

Neither of us spoke on the way home and yet, it wasn't uncomfortable. Quite the opposite. I felt I had a comrade in arms. I had shared a part of my soul with him and he had understood. In fact, he seemed to know about that festering hole that can eat away at you, bit by bit. How he knew, he didn't say. He didn't have to. I knew it that night. I knew he had been there too. Maybe he still was.

***

Never in my wildest dreams had I planned on getting into my present line of work. In fact, as a young girl, I never gave much thought to my future. Why would I? Little girls were brought up to have dreams of marriage and children, so I merely assumed that was my fate. Still, I always felt a yearning for more. Of what, I was never sure. I pondered the only acceptable occupations—teacher, nurse, clerical worker, beautician, telephone operator—but none of those appealed to me, or suspect I'd be any good at. I barely got by in school. I had no desire spending life in a classroom. I cringed at the sight of blood. And unlike Kitty, I felt no joy from dressing hair. For a time, I dreamed of being a novelist like Agatha Christie, or Margaret Mitchell. *Gone with the Wind* was still my favorite book. Or perhaps I'd be a dancer, like Ginger Rogers. But reality hit the minute Daddy walked out and our mother was forced to become the sole breadwinner.

I learned right then and there that dreams were just that. Illusions.

Mother began emphasizing, nearly every day it seemed, the importance of independence. She urged us to work hard in school and get jobs as soon as we could to make our own way in the world. "Never rely on a man," became her mantra.

We relied on her as our sole caregiver until she was suddenly gone, leaving us kids with not a pot to piss in. No home, no options, no control in life.

It wasn't her fault. The poor woman hadn't planned on a heart attack at the outrageous age of forty-seven. Hell, no. She'd been busy raising me and Tess, who, at thirteen, was already a pistol.

It was all Daddy's fault. Two years before life came to a screeching halt, the son-of-a-bitch just walked out, with not so much as a dollar or a glance back. Our mother's death should not have been surprising, though. She'd been overworked, underpaid, full of anxiety, and extra pounds. All because of him. I still hated the man for that.

The rest of the story, which I hadn't told Eliot, was what happened after Tess left.

The minute my sister disappeared behind that door— her screams still echoing down the hall— the women came back for me. But not before I spotted the emerald marble on the floor in the corner of the room. *Marbles*. The last game we'd played before Mother up and died. Tess must've taken the cloth pouch with her when we'd left the house. My sister loved that game, but more so, she loved to gaze at the colored designs of the circular glass balls.

I scooped it up quick and tucked it into my bra. I vowed that no one would take it from me. It was a gift. All that I had left.

At first, the people in charge told me I'd be able to visit her "soon" but several weeks went by and I demanded answers that never came. "Where'd you take my sister? I need to see her!"

Finally, they got tired of me asking and the woman who had taken Tess away said, matter-of-factly, that she was being adopted.

"What d'ya mean? That's impossible!" I didn't know much, really nothing about fostering and adopting, but it didn't seem that it would be so quick, or as simple as that.

"Don't you worry now, it's for the best," the awful woman said. "Your sister will be well cared for." Then she turned and stalked away.

"Why are you doing this? It's not right—you have to take me to my sister!" I yelled so loud that two men appeared out of nowhere, grabbed my arms and dragged me to a smaller room as I screamed just like Tess had done, though I knew better.

Once locked in the room where all the girls slept, exhaustion took over. Lying on a cold cot, I punched the bare pillow and wept so hard, I nearly choked on my own saliva.

I had to find a way out. I had to find her.

I'd made friends with a young girl about Tess's age, Flora. One night, we made a plan. Once a week, they let us take showers after dinner, with a woman standing guard, watching us leave single-file, back to the sleeping room. I made sure I was the last girl and when Flora stepped out of line, the woman (we never knew their names) went to grab her, giving me time to make a run for it, out the back door. Of course, that sounded an alarm. But I was already long gone.

I'd been hearing trains rumbling past since I'd gotten there so I bee-lined straight toward the woods to the tracks. There, I hid among the bushes until I heard the sound of freedom, and train-hopped back to Cleveland.

I knew how to do it. The McDowells had once helped out a hobo, a girl of all things, who had left an impression. In the few days she had stayed with the family, I became fascinated by Patsy's free-spirited life and quizzed her about her travels. Her last night there, she told me about how she "rode the rails."

"Ya hang near a station and as the train slows, you jump on. Then ya look for an empty car towards the back." She said circus people did it all the time.

It had been just a fantasy to me, I never dreamed I'd actually have to do it one day. Thinking back on it, it was one of the reasons I believe there must be a God. He doesn't give you info like that without reason.

I had chosen a good night to hop that empty train car. It didn't go too fast through the whole trip so I wasn't scared about jumping off when the time came. When I spotted the station I knew was closest to my neighborhood, I braced myself for courage and leapt. I landed on the gravel, which cut into my pants, but I'd made it.

When I got to our old rental house, the doors were locked. I peeked in the window and to my shock, everything was gone. The house was bare as bones. What had happened to all our stuff? Mother's things? Her beloved doll collection? Our toys, clothes? Our damn furniture?

My legs gave out then, and I sat on the porch floor bawling my eyes out until I got up and walked around and saw that Mother's beat-to-shit Ford sedan was still parked in the back of the drive. Abandoned, like us. I crawled inside and cried myself to sleep. I dreamed that night that my family was whole again, and life was normal. But it had only been a dream.

The next morning I spotted Mary McDowell in the backyard playing with their old Beagle and called her over. Mary was so happy to see me, and being twelve, was only too happy to keep a secret. She brought me a pillow and blanket and all the leftovers she could manage to stash into a paper bag each day. She also snuck me into their house whenever her mother went shopping while the dad was at work so that I could wash up.

But nights were the worst. I couldn't stop the thoughts running through my brain, like that locomotive I'd hopped. Images of our disintegrated family, our good-for-nothing father who had ruined everything.

I was now a true orphan. Every night, I lied there in that dark back seat, stomach tight, haunted by so many images. And where was Tess all this time? Something was wrong. Nothing made sense. Who would suddenly adopt a bratty thirteen-year-old? A teenager instead of a cute baby? It didn't feel right to me, but I was powerless to do anything about it. Sure, I'd thought if Mary told her folks, maybe they'd take me in, like they did Patsy. But then I remembered them being there near Mother's casket in our living room and they'd said nothing. They let those people take us away.

I had to make my own way in the world, like Mama had, but hadn't the slightest clue as to how. What kind of job could I possibly get? Who would hire a young girl like me? Jobs for teenagers were next to impossible to find. Just like my missing sister.

But God worked in mysterious ways. Mary was the one who ripped out the ad in her father's newspaper and showed it to me as we sat in the backseat of that ol' rusty car.

Roxy Theater Looking for Talent. No experience necessary!

A Place We Belong

"I hear these girls make a ton of money," Mary had said. The photos made the work look glamourous. "But I'm only seventeen," I reminded her. But my new savior had an answer to that, too. "Just lie," she said. "You're tall—and stacked—you can easily pass for eighteen."

Then came the gavel. "You gotta leave anyway. I heard Mother telling her friend on the phone that the landlord's been comin' around to get your house ready to rent again. Probably tow away this car too. If you get caught, they'll just take ya back to that place." Her face dropped. "And I could get in real trouble for helpin' ya."

Just thinking about going back to that hellhole cinched the deal. I'd do anything to keep that from happening. And I sure didn't want Mary to get into trouble, she'd been too good to me. Plus, I was backseat sore and sick to death of cold, scrappy leftovers. "Aw, hell, mize well give it shot." After all, I did love to dance.

We had to wait for Mary's mother to go grocery shopping again so I could use the telephone. Mary and I practiced in her living room, speaking in low, sexy voices, like May West. We'd ended up giggling every time. But then, it was now or never. We hovered over the black phone as Mary recited the number in the paper and I dialed with shaky fingers.

"Roxy Theater." The voice sounded no-nonsense, which got my heart racing even more.

"Yes, I'm, uh, calling . . . I'm interested in the ad you have for a job as a, uh, chorus girl." Mary told me they called some of them that. That girl seemed to know a lot for her age.

"Good, I need some girls right away." The man sounded in a hurry. "Come in tomorrow, noon, and audition."

Audition? How was I to do that? The pictures showed women with skimpy get-ups but weren't totally naked, so I felt better about that, but how much was I supposed to take off?

Just my bra? Certainly not panties! Did I have to sing while doing it? What kind of dancing was expected?

"Oh jeez, I can't do this, Mary," I said after hanging up. "I don't know a thing 'bout what to do."

Mary waved my fear away. "Don't worry, we'll practice. We'll come up with something." Mary demonstrated by showing how to move my hips and act sexy. "See? Just fake it, is all."

"Maybe *you* should be the one trying out." I laughed, trying my best to make light of the crazy situation.

"Nah, I'm just a kid, and I look it too. Besides, I don't have your boobs." She took her hands and scooped up her barely there breasts. "And they don't jiggle like yours do." We giggled again. "Big bouncy boobs are all they really care about."

I asked how she knew so much about all this and she told me how she'd been bored one day from playing outside and snuck into her parents' bedroom. It was a snow day and her folks had to go to the market, leaving their only daughter home alone. Mary decided to rustle through the closet, and way in the back on her father's side, there was a stack of what her mother would call "dirty magazines." Naked women all looking happy to be photographed.

"So it must be fun and like I said, you're perfect for it."

My face grew red just thinking about it, but what choice did I have?

"Just relax and do it," Mary urged. "You don't hafta take off all your clothes, just to your undies." Seeing my face, Mary put a hand on my shoulder, like a wise old soul. "Wanna go back to that orphanage?"

And there it was. The god awful truth.

Next morning, I stepped onto the streetcar wearing one of Mrs. McDowell's fancy dinner dresses and high heels, ignoring some of the looks I got. The dress was a little big, except in the chest area, and the shoes were snug, but the outfit was good enough for my mission. Mary had copped her mother's tube of "Tango Red" lipstick and a ribbon to tie in my wild scarlet hair, then gave me a hug for luck and sent me on my way.

5.

It took no time at all to get there, but a lot more time to go in. I stood outside clutching the small handbag Mary had also found in the closet, and stared up at the big marque of the most famous burlesque house in all of the Midwest. Or so the ad had read.

Finally, I took in a huge breath, straightened my posture, sucked in my tummy, and opened the side entrance like the man had told me. And walked in like I owned the place. It was time to start my new life.

I couldn't believe how dark it was inside. You'd never know it was daylight on the other side of that door. It was smoky too. A layer of hazy tobacco fogs swirled through the room.

Two men were standing by a table talking about something or other when I sauntered over in my grown-up heels. "Excuse me, Sir." My mouth was so parched from nerves, I could barely eke out the words.

The heavy set one with the wireless glasses looked over at me. "Yes?"

"Uh, I'm here to," I swallowed, "audition for—"

"Wait, you?" He stamped out his smoke, eyed me again. "How old are you?"

That was it. He had my number. I didn't belong here. "Eighteen, sir."

He let out a husky laugh. "Yeah, they all are."

"No, it's true. I just turned eighteen last week. I swear." I had to stand my ground.

"Ya know, your face is so honest, I almost believe ya." He pointed to the steps on the side of the stage. "Go on up there, let's see what you got."

Before I lost her nerve, I climbed up. My stomach started churning and I felt my knees quiver, like a newborn filly trying to get itself right. I thought about sprinting right out that door, but then what? I needed money to eat, a place to live. I couldn't rely on Mary much longer. I couldn't live in that old beater till I came of age. I still had three months to go.

"Come on, young lady, we don't have all day."

Suddenly came music playing overhead, with lots of drum beats, just urging me to do those bumps and grinds that Mary had shown me.

I started to move. The music helped me forget about the trembling. The man had turned away, talking to the other man again, not paying any attention. I decided to have a little fun with it. Ham it up, what the hell? I followed the music and moved like I was already one of them.

I shut my eyes, unzipped the dress, then flinching, kicked it to the side revealing the only bra I owned, dirty and yellow from wear, same as my panties. I kept on the shoes because Mary said these girls all danced with their heels on. Plus, it made me feel older, womanly.

I swayed and wiggled, shimmied and twirled, and pretended I was someone else. Finally, the man looked up and asked, "Okay, let's hear ya sing."

The question threw me. "Sing? I'm sorry sir, I do love to sing, but I'm . . . I'm afraid I'm not very good at it." I grabbed the dress to cover myself.

"Well, then." He rubbed his chin. "To be a chorus girl, you gotta sing." He shook his head like I lacked a brain. Then he peered at me more intently. "So that's not going to work."

"No!" The word tumbled out before I could think. He gave me a look that dared me to talk back. The other man had left, leaving just the two of us. I zipped up best I could and rushed down the steps. "I'm sorry, forgive me, Mr. . . . Sir. Please. I have to have this job. I'm . . .." I stopped in front of him, bowed my head, feelings of shame flooding my insides. "I'm homeless, sir. It's true. My parents are dead and I'm alone. I had to borrow money for the streetcar." I had no choice but to be honest with him. Gruff as he appeared, I somehow felt that he might have a soft side. "I've got no real skills to do much. Do you know where else I might find some kind of work?" Maybe he could at least help me with that.

He scratched his head, gave me this fatherly look. "Every one of you girls got a sob story."

My heart pounded in my chest. Where would I go from here? I was now more scared than I'd been on that stage taking my clothes off.

"I don't mean to be callous, young lady, it's just a fact. Some of you gals had to grow up way too soon. Damn shame." He lit a cigar with a match, flicked the stick in the nearby green glass ashtray.

I didn't want to hear any more. "Yeah, well, thanks anyway." I turned to leave.

"Where ya going?"

I spun back around. "Sir?"

"You need a job and I need another girl." He extended his hand. "And don't call me sir. It's George, owner of this fine establishment." His grin was like a beaming light to my soul. "We'll have to start ya as a burly girl right off the bat. *But*," he emphasized with an index finger pointing at me. "Till you earn it, you'll get chorus girl pay rate. And you'll go on first, before the others."

I was still hung up on the term. "Burly, sir?"

He stared at me. "You really *are* green, aren't ya?" His lips hung onto that cigar. "Hope you're a fast learner. Be here tomorrow. One o'clock sharp." I wanted to hug him but didn't dare. "I'll take your skinny bones to lunch and you can meet Betty. She'll teach ya everything you need to know. You can start next Tuesday, it's a slow night."

He turned to go but kept talking as he walked away. "You got some work to do, kid, so ya better practice a hellava lot. And get more relaxed, or you won't last a week."

The next day, Buxom Betty took me shopping—on George's dime—to this little shop on E. Fourth Street, where they, and some prostitutes I would later learn, got a lot of their fancy things. It was there I found my first ostrich fan, and six-foot long feather boa. Betty gave me pointers about the business and let me stay at her place.

"So watcha gonna call yourself?" she asked. "You'll want something that looks good on a marquee."

Funny, that was the easy part. I thought about my favorite color. I thought about my mother's satin pillowcase that she would sometimes let me lay on when I was a child. And I thought, because I would never forget, of my doll collection that I missed so terribly.

The following week, after hours and hours of concentrated work, I sauntered on the stage using all my new training, a powder blue fan, feigned confidence, and my own imagination.

That night, Lydia Swanson became Blue Satin Doll.

6.

*C*rane's Bookstore was just up the street from where I lived. I loved to walk there, even in the winter. The store's name honored the bird, with its image gracing the overhead sign. But it's also for the owner, Dottie Crane, a spinster who seemed proud of her single status at an age when all hope for a husband was long gone. "I'm in my late forties and can come and go as I please," she often boasted. "Don't hafta answer to no one. It's a wonderful life."

I wasn't convinced. I loved my freedom too, but deep down, I didn't want to be alone forever. Not that I ached for children but there's something appealing about a man coming home on a regular basis. And yet the more men I meet, the more I wondered if the man of my dreams even existed.

Clearly, Dottie had never met a guy that was up to snuff, either. But then, pickins were slim when you never ventured further than your own backyard. The woman lived above the bookstore and employed no staff so her business was her life, and she seemed perfectly content about it. Her constant companions were two tuxedo cats, Puss and Boots, who were given free rein through the shop, adding to the store's charm.

I spent many of my Mondays off in the comfort of books. They took me away from reality, got me through the worst of times. Today, I headed to Crane's with a special purpose in mind. I was anxious to get a copy of a book Eliot had said he loved. It thrilled me, his mention of books. Bill Baker didn't know Hemingway from Faulkner.

A Place We Belong

"Morning, Dottie," I called out, though the tiny bell above the entrance had already announced my arrival.

The distinctive smell of books hit me as soon as I stepped in, giving me a sense of calm. The quiet exhilaration I felt here was such a deviation from the showbiz life.

Dottie was high up on the ladder, reaching over a row of paperback books. "Oh, hey there, be down in a jiff."

I never knew what books I'd end up taking home and that was half the fun. Every corner of my living space was filled with books of all kinds, though I had yet to find books as good as *Gone With the Wind* and *Tender is the Night*. Just last week, Helen, had come upstairs to borrow one. She gasped at the stacks of books throughout my apartment.

"My word," Helen had said, "why do you keep all these books if you've already read them?"

Her reaction wasn't surprising. Helen scrimped and saved on everything she bought, mostly due to Frank, her cheapskate husband, though we never called him that out loud. Frank was sure another Depression was right around the corner.

Sure, I could've just gone to the library but my schedule allowed little time to get through a book very quickly, no matter how I loved it. Besides, I hated paying overdue fines for something I had to give back. Simpler just to keep it. Helen could at least relate to that logic.

I headed straight for the hardback novels and started browsing. Dottie climbed down and headed toward me. "Did'ya hear Willa Cather's new book is out? It's called *Sapphira and the Slave Girl*, I bet you'd like it."

"Slave girl? Ooo, I don't much like the sound of that," I sneered. "But you know I love her books, so I'll take a look." If Dottie was recommending it, it was a safe bet.

I knelt down to pat Boots's black-and-white head. "Actually I'm looking for a book called . . . oh darn, I thought

37

for sure I'd remember the title." The cat rubbed against me as I tried remembering what Eliot had said. "Something-something Falcon?"

Dottie squinted. "*Maltese Falcon*?"

"Yes. That's it."

"Hmm. Since when do you go for detective novels?"

I had to laugh. Dottie knew I got a kick out of smutty romance books, along with the classics. True, I didn't go much for detective stories, not even the ever-popular Agatha Christie books. Though I was fascinated as everyone else reading how the author disappeared for eleven days only to re-emerge with no knowledge of where she'd been. I always figured she just needed some time from the madness of losing her mother, then having her husband dump her for his secretary. That would take any woman for a mental spin.

Realizing Dottie was awaiting my response, I gave a shrug. "Just thought I'd change it up a bit."

"Well, let's see. I may have one copy left." Dottie walked over to the other aisle and yelled out. "Got it."

I nearly clapped with excitement. After doing meticulous work sewing sequins on my latest outfit, kicking back with a good novel—one that Eliot enjoyed—sounded heavenly. I hoped that reading something about the work Eliot did might give me better insight into the man himself.

While Dottie rang up my purchases, I glanced outside. "Oh no, it's pouring out there." I never carried an umbrella, just a rain bonnet in my pocketbook. But now I was more worried about the books than getting my hair wet.

"Ugh, such a dreary day," Dottie sighed. "Business is sure to be slow today. Why don't you stay awhile till it lets up?" She pointed to a big blue chair in the corner. "You're welcome to sit over there and read."

"Wonderful! I've got no place to be, except to grab some groceries later. Thank you."

A Place We Belong

Dottie brought me a plate of Fig Newtons and a lovely cup of Ovaltine and I spent a glorious afternoon surrounded by books, cats, and delicious refreshments.

***

*E*very chance I got that week, I dived into the lives of Sam Spade and that Brigid woman. By Thursday, I was nearly done and hated having to tear myself away to get to work. I arrived there in the nick of time, the characters still on my mind as I began my act.

Then, just a few sashaying movements later, all hell broke loose.

7.

*E*ach night has its own personality, like characters in a play. I've learned to judge the atmosphere by a number of things—animated chatter versus quiet conversation, crude talk versus respectful exchanges, clinking of glasses versus scraping of chairs—and on particularly rowdy nights—loud shouts followed by punches and the occasional overturned table. I did love my job, though there were indeed times I longed for boring nine-to-five office work. Thursday could be as rambunctious as Fridays, when businessmen liked to get a head start on the weekend revelry.

Through the dark haze of cigarette and cigar smoke, I rarely saw the faces of my audience past the front row but could always get a feel for the crowd. A lively, appreciative audience could bring out the best of our performances. But a night such as this, with its restless energy, raised voices echoing throughout, could be distracting. In those times, I relied on instinct.

Something was up.

I knew this even before stepping on stage. All the way from my dressing room I could hear the booming, throated laughter vibrating the thin walls. The night's comedian, an older fellow known for crude language, off-color jokes, and bawdy sexual content, was getting the boisterous customers all worked up. The men, most likely Mob regulars, were full of piss and vinegar, that much was clear. I knew I better cook with gas tonight and be ever watchful.

A Place We Belong

I'd already been informed there was a celebrity in the house. My ten o'clock show would be in the presence of an important congressman from the Carolinas. I'd heard he was eager to meet me backstage after the show, which meant having drinks with him. I truly hated when politicians, especially out-of-state, mysterious ones, wanted my personal attention. "That's part of your job, Lydia, don't ever forget that," George reminded me early on. "Well it shouldn't be," I snapped back, arguing that I gave enough of myself in my performances. I shouldn't have to do anything other than that.

How naïve I'd been back then.

When the lights grew dim and the laughter died down, my name was announced and in honor of the Southern congressman, I sashayed out wearing a peach-colored Southern Belle outfit with full skirt, fluffy sleeves and large floppy hat—a replica of the doll I was holding, similar to one from Mama's collection that disappeared soon as she did.

Moseying over to the side of the stage, I placed the Baby Doll on the table. It was an act I'd begun at the start of my career when I was a scared, shaky, inexperienced teenager. Using props kept my nerves at bay, helped me feel less alone up there on stage. I had figured—wrongly, of course—that the presence of theatrical objects would distract the men from constantly gawking at my body.

But this act was always a hit. As I'd methodically remove each item of clothing—hat, gloves, and frilly top—I'd waddle over and do the same with the doll, flinging the items with exaggerated dramatics, rolling of the eyes, Betty Boop giggle, and the audience ate it up. One thing about this profession, I soon discovered, it allowed for a little fun. And how I loved it when my creativity was rewarded with enthusiastic cheers.

This may not have been the job I would've chosen for myself as a little girl, but thanks to that god-forsaken

41

orphanage, the job had chosen me. And I was determined to make the most of it, and never end up in a vulnerable position again. There were merits to being a burlesque queen, including a decent wage for a woman. I'd been a quick study and happily discovered I had a flair for entertainment.

And a natural talent for reading a room.

Normally, I danced across every inch of the stage, making sure that wherever the customers sat, they wouldn't miss a dip, shimmy, or shake. But the "honorable" statesman's table was front and center, so I had to spend more time in that spot. A few times our eyes met and I didn't like what I saw. He was a big man, thinning hair, bushy eyebrows, but it was his hard expression that rattled me. He was a goon. I could spot his type a mile away.

I set the parasol down, grabbed my feathered fan and began my finale all the while racking my brain, thinking up some way to get out of meeting this creep backstage. I knew the drill. He'd show up backstage, shake my hand respectfully, insist on taking me out on the town, buy me drinks laced with compliments. He would then suggest a "nightcap" in his hotel room where he'd offer me a "nice dividend" to sleep with him. Like I was a prostitute. That was the part of the job I hated. The assumption that I could be bought.

That'll be the day.

I was at the part where I loosened a string to undo the big hoop. That's when I felt the mood shift. The room, the chatter, the din got louder, angrier. The heat of the lights was making me sweat. The howls of amusement turned to catcalls, with loud drunken voices egging me to "take it all off." I heard the word, bitch. It ticked me off, but I had to ignore it and avert my gaze away from the congressman's dark eyes.

I was bending down to give them one last cleavage peep when a gunshot exploded through the air, jolting me so hard, the front snap of my bra popped loose. Everyone jumped

A Place We Belong

at once, screaming and scrambling for the exit. Before I had a chance to move, two strong hands gripped my waist from behind, lifting me up and off the stage. I squirmed like a wild cat, my heart racing. Was this man trying to kidnap me? Had I been the target? "Let me g—"

"It's me."

I strained my neck enough to see it was Big Joe. Of course. He always put me first, before anything else in the club. When we reached the narrow hallway, he set me down but didn't release the firm grasp on my arm. Someone flicked on the lights and there I was without my fancy fan, just panty bottoms and pasties.

Adrenalin pumped through me as Joe pulled me past my dressing room. "Wait! Where're we going? I need to get some clothes on," I screamed, automatically putting my free hand over my breasts. Funny how I could be comfortable half-naked on stage, yet off-stage, I felt exposed.

We headed toward the backdoor exit. Others had the same idea. A pack of men scrambled out the door and Joe pivoted back around. No way could I be vulnerable to the raucous men that made up this night's crowd. As we turned a corner, Joe lightened his grip and I managed to break, bolting back towards my room. I scooped up my floral satin robe off the chaise lounge and wrapped it around me, then snatched my beaded clutch before Joe caught up. When he did, someone was with him.

Eliot.

"What are you doin' here?" The sight of him instantly calmed me, if only for a second. Before I got an answer, he and Joe hoisted me up. I had no choice but to go along.

Joe led us down the stairwell, pushing open the emergency exit.

"My car's over here," Eliot called out.

43

In half a second, I was plopped into the passenger's seat of Eliot's sedan. Big Joe long gone. Eliot swung around to the driver's side, hit the gas and the car swerved through a back alley.

"What the hell is happening?" I asked, but again I was ignored. He weaved through more backstreets before speeding down East Ninth. "Eliot?" I placed my hand on his arm. "Am I in danger?"

That got his attention. He glanced over at me. I noticed then that I was sitting on the sash of my negligee. I tugged it out and secured myself tightly in a bow.

"No, not you. Though you needed to get out of there."

"I need a smoke is what I need." Despite his assurance that I wasn't the target, I still felt jittery. I fumbled through my handbag. "Ah, hell, I'm out."

As Eliot hit the west Shoreway, he dug in his shirt pocket, tapped out two Lucky's on the steering wheel, then lit both, handing one to me.

"Thank you," I said, taking a good long puff, despite not liking his brand. "Now, will you tell me what's going on? And how'd you know to be there in the first place?"

The corner of his mouth lifted ever-so-slightly. "A little birdie told me there might be trouble. The congressman has some enemies."

"Not surprising." I raised my brows. "Mob-related?"

"Less you know, the better."

"Is he dead?"

"Not that I've heard." He flicked his ash out the valance wing window. "I'll be dropping you off, then making the rounds."

I stared at him. Like Joe, he had put me first. Before everything else that was happening.

I rolled my window all the way down, hoping the cool night air against my face might alleviate the flush of my cheeks.

44

A Place We Belong

Why was I blushing? He was a gentleman after all. Gentlemen do these kinds of things. Put women first. No big deal. I blew out the cigarette smoke, sorting my thoughts. His actions could be just out of sheer politeness. Then again, since sharing some of my past, I felt we had this secret bond. Palpable, yet unspoken.

*B*ill was there when Eliot walked me up the porch.
Son-of-a-bitch.
I caught both men's expression. Deadpan surprise.
"Evening, Mr. Baker," Eliot said, eyeing him like a target.
"Mr. Ness." Bill's gaze flashed to me.
They know each other?
The outside light cast a shadow between the men. "You both have a good night." Eliot said with a tip of his felt hat before turning and heading to his car.

Ignoring Bill, I chased Eliot down the drive, a whiff of the honeysuckle bush breezing past me, heightening my emotions. When he reached the car door, I touched his arm.

"I really appreciate what you did, Eliot." I wanted to say more but the words wouldn't come.

I couldn't read his expression, but his manner had changed from the ride over. "Don't mention it. It's my job." His eyes flickered to my chest so briefly I wondered if I'd imagine it. "You're trembling, better get inside."

Once again, I felt more naked than I actually was. And chilly in the night air. Though I doubted it was the sole reason I was quivering. My head was pounding too. "Be careful, okay? Hope things—"

Eliot had shut the car door, started the engine. With a quick wave, he pulled away. I let my words dissolve in the wind.

I watched his car disappear round the corner. Turning toward my house, I ached to go inside and collapse. But there

45

was Bill, still on my damn porch. Standing, smoking, waiting. Not taking his eyes off of me.

Great, just great, I whispered. Tired as I was, I still had him to deal with.

I dragged my feet up the steps. "I'm exhausted, Bill. I just want to go in and collapse."

He blocked the doorway. "I was worried about you, Lydia. I heard the news in my car and rushed over." He bent forward, the smell of whiskey nauseating me. "But apparently you were in good hands." He glared at my breasts. The robe had loosened a bit.

"Don't start." I reached for the front door, but he stopped me, grabbed my wrist.

"You sleeping with him?"

"Oh, for god's sakes, Bill, get the fuck off my porch."

He backed away, as if struck. "I thought we meant something to each other, Lyd."

I shook my head. "Just go. Please. I've had enough for one night."

I slammed the door behind me, bolted the lock, slid to the floor, my head between my knees, I allowed the tears to choke out. It had been so long since I'd bawled out loud.

"Lydia, you all right, honey?" The hand was so light on my shoulders, I jumped. "Oh. Helen."

"I'm sorry if I startled you."

My robe was completely undone now, exposing my gem panties, my bare, bejeweled breasts. I closed the robe with my fists.

"You look frazzled. What happened?"

"A shoot-out at the ol' corral," I said with a faint smirk.

"Good lord, anyone hurt?"

"I don't know, Helen, I just wanna go lie down."

"Of course, dear, anything you need?"

Helen took my arm and helped me up. Even though I said no, Helen followed me up the stairs. Once in my apartment, the sight of Spencer curled up on the bed was heaven sent. I plopped down beside him.

"We'll talk tomorrow," Helen whispered, as she covered me up with the handmade quilt she'd made for me last Christmas.

I was fast asleep before I could respond.

8.

The *Cleveland Press* played out the night's episode on the front pages the next day. Frank was reading the story aloud to Helen when I entered the kitchen. Although I had a kitchenette in my place, I often joined them for coffee and morning chats.

"Apparently it was just a warning shot," Frank was saying. "to *encourage* the congressman to leave town, and quick."

"So no one was hurt?" I asked, glancing over his shoulder.

"Nah, but like I've been saying, Lydia, wish you'd consider another occupation." Frank said, ignoring Helen's warning look.

"And like *I've* been saying, Frank, I like my job," I retorted, taking the stoneware mug filled with coffee from Helen. "Not to mention, there's nowhere else that would pay me that kind of money."

"You're so rich, maybe we should raise your rent," Frank said, but with a grin.

I pulled out a chair to sit between them, catching Helen's foot kick Frank's ankle under the table. "Aw, come on, Frankie," I patted his arm like pacifying a child. "A girl's gotta make a living. And you know, if I was forced to move out due to skyrocketing bills, you'd be crying in your beer missing me." I gave him a wide smile.

"You got me there, my girl," he laughed, rising from his chair. I always won that argument. "Okay, ladies, I'm off. Gonna check out Ray's new car before I go to work." Frank Sabo worked second shift at the General Electric lighting plant.

A Place We Belong

Their colossal grandfather clock chimed from the other room, an incessant eleven times. The damn thing struck every quarter-hour, twice at the half-hour, three times at the third quarter-hour. Then, at the top of every hour, the full dong effect. It unnerved me, though it never seemed to bother my landlords.

"Oh my, didn't realize it's that time already," Helen said after the last chime. "I gotta get going myself, you know how Fridays are."

I did indeed. The Theatrical regulars came streaming in early to start the weekend with their three-martini lunches. It was quite a sight at times. The cops conversing along the right side of the wall, while mobsters leaned against the left side. It was one of the few establishments they shared with mutual respect. There were some on the right, however, who crossed loyalties and those were the ones Eliot had his eye on.

"Be careful today." Helen gave me a quick hug.

"Always am." I waved to her, thinking how futile that statement was. You could only be so careful when your job was entertaining a bunch of drunken, horny men. Even with Big Joe around, things could get out of hand. Nights like last were a perfect example. Made me wonder if maybe I *should* consider getting out of the business.

But then, I didn't know how to do anything else.

I picked up the newspaper and finished the article. Eliot's presence hadn't been mentioned and that didn't surprise me. I'd already learned that he liked to remain behind the scenes. Though that was often impossible. Eliot Ness was a town celebrity, whether he liked it or not.

I got up to wash out my cup, thinking of the business card I kept on top of my dresser. Since confiding in him about Tess, I began to feel confused. While I believed he would help me, he never said how he planned to do it. Maybe he had to think on it more. Maybe he was already looking into things. We of course hadn't mentioned it last night with all the craziness going on, but I had to wonder what came next, and how long would it be to know more. Did he give me his card so I would make the next move?

I needed to know how he planned to proceed. And there was also the matter of Bill. I recalled Eliot's demeanor when he'd left last night, and it bothered me. He obviously thought Bill and I were an item, and given the looks they'd exchanged, Eliot had to know that Bill was one of those cops who took bribes. I hated the thought that Eliot might put me in that same scheming category. Would he believe me if I told him I hadn't known about Bill's extracurricular activities until just a few months back? And that when I did find out, I immediately dumped his ass?

So much I wanted to talk to Eliot about. And that required another personal meeting. Could I rustle up the nerve to phone Eliot at his office?

As I stared out the kitchen window, a cardinal flew right up to it and looked me straight on, giving me a start. Mother always said when you see a cardinal close by, a deceased family member was saying hello. "Hi, Mama. Yes, I'm trying to find Tess. I will find her, I promise."

The minute I said that, I wanted to take it back. How could I possibly promise something that was so uncertain?

Now I *had* to follow through. I made up my mind right then that I'd push Eliot more. Yes, the man was busy but I knew that he now cared about me, and that had to work to my advantage.

With that determined thought, the bird flew away. I returned to my room and a hungry Spencer was all over me. "Okay, okay." I poured out his food, and as I listened to my dog wolfing down his breakfast, I took Eliot's card, plopped on my bed, leaned against my headboard and memorized the number.

A Place We Belong

But just as before, the doubts began to swirl. Maybe he hadn't been in touch because he'd changed his mind. After all, because of Bill, he had to think I was linked to the kind of people he abhorred.

I knew I had to set him straight and the only way to remedy that was to call and persuade him to meet up where no one could interrupt us. But where? Few recognized me in public, but most anyone could spot Eliot Ness a mile away. Even at Sullivan's. To make things worse, if we did happen to be seen together pretty much anywhere, the rumors would fly. A married man spending time with a Roxy girl was just the thing to set tongues a'waggin' and newspapers flying off stands.

Spencer's scratching at the door interrupted my thoughts.

"I know, I know, sweetie." Dogs were so needy. I got up and tucked the card in the small slot inside my purse, opened my chest of drawer to get the green marble. I'd keep that with me too. For luck.

I grabbed my coat and his leash. Thankfully I was already dressed, hair brushed, foundation and eye cream applied, so if I ran into a neighbor, I wouldn't die of embarrassment.

I hadn't counted on the light drizzle and was instantly sorry I hadn't worn my rain bonnet. We were both relieved when Spencer did his business in record time. We rushed upstairs, and as I dug in my coat pocket for my key, I heard the phone ringing on the other side of the door. I hated missing calls because you always wondered who had been on the other end. And in this case, my thoughts naturally flew to Eliot.

I stuck the key in the lock, pushed through the door and ran to grab the receiver. "Hello?"

"Hey, girl, I've got fun news." Kitty. My swift disappointment wasn't lost on me. "Listen to this. There's a huge outdoor party happening at the Bennett's place tomorrow night. I know it's last minute but I haven't a thing to wear and I'm free all day and I need your expert fashion sense." The girl was positively giddy. "Please say you're up for a little shopping spree today?"

This *was* exciting news. The Bennett's were a well-to-do couple who owned one of the most popular dance halls in Cleveland. Their massive Euclid Avenue home boasted a large ballroom where they hosted a number of charity events, as well as a backyard swimming pool. Their beautiful garden had even been featured in all the Cleveland newspapers. Their parties were legendary, yet I, nor Kitty, had ever attended one. It wasn't every day a Burly girl was on the prestigious guest list. Unless it was to perform.

"What's the occasion? Who invited you?"

"Gary. You know the guy I told ya about? He's still asking me out and I'm still turning him down, but guess he figures if I get drunk enough at the party he can lead me astray," she said, laughing.

"Gary Bruno? Isn't he part of the Mayfield gang?" Although I knew many guys in the Mob, I steered clear of them in social situations. Especially after that party in '37 when one of the Roxy girls was accidentally shot during a raid.

"Well, sure, but he's harmless."

"Yeah, of course he is," I chuckled. I wasn't surprised by Kitty's nonchalance. Being a few years older, the girl had been around more than a few blocks. Which made her a wise best friend.

"I told him I was bringing a friend, so he'd know straight up I wasn't his date. He was fine with it. And get this, he's pickin' us up at the club in his shiny black Cadillac. How 'bout that? He's got the secret password for entry too. They're calling it a Roaring '40s End-of-Summer Bash. Everyone's

A Place We Belong

supposed to dress up like the Roarin' '20s. We need to get us some flapper clothes."

"But tomorrow's so soon."

"That's okay, I figure we'll hit Fran's Dress Shop, she's got all those great outfits. We'll grab some chic hats and stockings too. And if by chance we don't find just the thing, there's that fabric shop on Detroit Avenue. I can sew up something quick as a bunny in an emergency. Oh, Lyd, it's gonna be a grand time."

"Sounds like it and I'm glad you called. After last night's fiasco, I am definitely up for some fun. But you know you have to wait for me till I get off." My last show came after hers and didn't start until eleven. Luckily, our acts lasted only fifteen minutes, tops.

"No problem. I told Gary not to get us till 11:30. You can change in a flash."

I laughed, "Ha, we'll see. But sure. Parties don't get interesting till after midnight anyway."

"You ain' lyin' there, girl."

"Okie, dokey, count me in." I glanced out the window. "Looks like it's clearing up outside. I'll bundle up and take a stroll." Kitty had a car, but I preferred to walk. With a pair of comfortable shoes, I could leisurely walk the mile or so with no problem. "Meet you at Fran's at noon." I'd be sure to take a bonnet this time, just in case.

I hung up the phone feeling foolish that I had hoped the call was from Eliot. I'd nearly tripped over my dog trying to catch it before it stopped ringing. Besides the obvious reason I shouldn't care was the fact that he didn't even have my number and it wasn't listed in the phone book. Then again, I knew Eliot could get it if he wanted to.

Shaking off thoughts of the married safety director, I switched my enthusiasm toward the upcoming party. I already owned some pretty garish outfits, but those were for the stage.

53

Hopefully, I could find something decorative and classy. Something fun and flirty, glittery and tight, like Daisy in *The Great Gatsby*.

An hour later, I found that and more at the dress shop. As soon as we entered, my eyes popped seeing a mannequin wearing a sleeveless black-and-gold sequined number with fringe at the knee. I grabbed it off the rack and headed straight to the dressing room. "This is perfect," I called out as I squeezed into it, then opened the door for Kitty could see.

"Oooo, good and tight," Kitty nodded her approval. "Shows off those boobs nicely."

"Wow, you look like Jean Harlow in *The Red-Headed Woman*," Fran added.

"Really?" I smiled at my friends. "Okay then, I'll take it."

But when I went to pull the dress off, I called from the room. "Help! I can't get out of it." I jumped up and down, pulling and yanking, almost strangling myself in the process.

Kitty and Fran rushed back in, and each took a side to help me wrangle out of it. "Thank goodness it has some stretch to it," Kitty said, and we all started giggling like teenagers.

Once freed, I agreed the dress may be a bit tight, but I did look great in it, so I really had no choice but to make it mine. Though, my teeth clenched at the price tag. But who knew what handsome bigwigs I might meet at the party? After being with Bill the past two years, I was ready for a nice, successful, man to sweep me off my feet. And while the dress just might do the job, I wondered if I'd have to call the fire department to get me out of it after a night of eating and drinking.

Kitty's dress had the opposite problem. One size too big. But with her seamstress abilities, she could make it just as snug and look amazing. I loved her, but often felt insecure around her. And who wouldn't? Kitty, with her thick mane of

A Place We Belong

black hair and striking brown eyes. Like a modern version of Madame Butterfly, her dark exotic looks could turn heads without lifting a painted fingernail. So much so that when she got in the biz, her stage name came easily: Queen Butterfly. While I was known for my fan dances, Kitty used bright butterfly "wings" to seduce her audience.

We hit pay dirt at another store, finding everything we needed to complete our outfits. Gemstone drop earrings, black stockings, a feathered hat for Kitty, and rhinestone choker for me. All very Roaring '20s. We were confident we'd be the talk of the party.

As with most of our shopping ventures, we stopped at Woolworth's Luncheonette. It was past the lunchtime hour, so we easily found two empty stools at the counter. But one look at the menu presented a slight conundrum.

"Jeez Louise, there's not a damn thing I can eat if I'm to fit into that dress tonight." I sighed. "No way can I risk a bloating episode. Ordering those juicy hot dogs inside buttery buns is not a possibility."

We settled on splitting a bacon-and-tomato sandwich, and instead of our favorite shakes, we ordered iced tea. It would be worth the sacrifice.

9.

*O*ur Saturday night show went off without a hitch—and without gun shots. The minute we were done, Kitty and I changed into our party attire and rushed out the front door of The Roxy, skirting past the eyeballs of the few men smoking in the foyer. Gary's gleaming Caddy was right on time.

We crammed into the front seat, and twenty minutes later, Gary was pulling into the long circular drive. I squeezed Kitty's hand when I caught sight of the massive house. While it wasn't as big as some others along what was once called, Millionaire's Row, it was substantial, with large white stone pillars and lavish gardens.

The interior was equally lavish—that was obvious the second the butler swung open the door to greet us in the grand entranceway. The two-story foyer had a gleaming crystal chandelier, carved vaulted ceiling and plush furnishings. I was still gazing at the ceiling when Kitty snuggled against me. "Great Gatsby indeed," she whispered.

"Oh yes, we *do* belong here," I said with a wink. *Least I'd like to think so.*

Contrary to what some uppity ups assumed, burlesque girls could easily fit in and mingle with high society. Despite the fact we were often shunned, dismissed as "loose women." But not tonight. Tonight, Blue Satin Doll and Queen Butterfly were received like royalty.

We headed first to the powder room to check our faces and hair. I was seated in a skirted vanity chair while Kitty was refastening one of my errant curls when a woman stepped in wearing a sequined flapper dress and beaded headpiece that matched a long beaded necklace. She looked like one of the

A Place We Belong

fashion models I often saw in *Photoplay* magazine. Her chestnut hair was slicked back in an artful chignon, her chiseled face dusted with powder and a touch of red lipstick. She gave me a poised expression as our eyes met. My immediate thought was, how could one wear such little makeup, and a loose-fitting dress that revealed nothing and still look so sultry and sexy? In comparison, Kitty, in her bust-enhancing getup, and I, in my corset dress, appeared more on the tawdry side.

The woman didn't head to the commode but instead stood there, observing us.

"Oh, sorry, would you like more room?" I scooted over a bit, away from the small circular mirror. "For a mansion, this bathroom is surprisingly small."

"Well, it's just the ensuite," the woman answered, attempting to straighten the headpiece that didn't need correction. "The others are much larger, of course."

My eyes shifted to Kitty, who raised hers ever-so-slightly. I suddenly felt uneasy, like maybe we didn't belong here, after all. I popped my compact inside my clutch.

"We're done here anyway," Kitty said dryly.

We high-tailed it out of there and headed to the ballroom where Gary was waiting. "Ladies, what's your fancy?" He waved a hand toward the waiter walking around with a tray of drinks. "The special tonight is the Gin Rickey."

"I'll take something simple, gin and tonic is fine," I said, scanning the room filled with fringe flapper dresses, pearl string necklaces, striped three-piece suits, and Panama hats.

Kitty ordered an Old Fashioned and Gary marched us around, introducing us to all the typical high-society partiers—business owners, politicos, high rollers, and a few theater workers. I was pleased to see several people from various Short Vincent establishments. The good, and the bad, including "Mushy," Theatrical Grille's notorious owner who everyone knew had Mob connections.

A lively soiree of music, dancing and animated conversations kept us basking in it all. We were particularly gaga over meeting the illustrious John Kenley, who had begun his theatrical career as a Burlesque performer and choreographer, and now worked as assistant to famed producer, Lee Shubert. His friendly presence made me feel comfortable.

As we moved on in different directions, the sister of the owner of a downtown clothing store stopped me and kept me prisoner to her chatter. She didn't take a breath, not even while grabbing the arm of the waiter to snatch up another cocktail. I was ready for another, too, but this wasn't a place where one got sloppy. I wanted to prove that showgirls could be refined, vowing to remain at least halfway sober.

I'd long lost track of what the woman rattled on about but couldn't very well appear rude, so I just kept nodding and grinning, mentally planning a polite escape. Casually scanning the room, I spotted the chic woman from the ladies' room. My opening. I placed a hand lightly on the woman's shoulder and feigned apology. "Oh, dear. Millie, is it? I'm so sorry, but there's an old friend across the way and I must go over and say hello." If I offended this one, my reputation among this circle would be doomed. "Let's continue later, shall we?" I swiveled away before Millie could stop me.

As I made my way through the crowd, I kept my focus on the lady I had been so intrigued by. She was encircled in a small group, her hand snuggling the arm of a gentleman in a simple brown suit and black fedora. Their backs were turned, but as I inched closer, the gentleman's manner, the confident way he stood, looked familiar. I was just a few feet away from the couple when I recognized the back of his head. *Oh, no. No.* A hot rush slid up my spine. What to do now? Continue on and greet them as planned? Pivot and slink away? Just as I decided on the latter, the man's head turned to the left. He spotted me. His face showed surprise, but he recovered quickly, gave me a little nod.

Was that his wife attached to his arm? Of course, it shouldn't matter. If I was going to let him help me, I knew I needed to get over this shameful attraction I had for Eliot Ness.

"Cocktail, ma'am?"

I faced the tray man and grabbed the first drink within reach. "Thank you," I uttered, then skittered away fast as I could.

When I reached the outdoor patio, the warm September breeze was a welcome embrace. The party lights above sparkled on the pool water, making the courtyard look like some kind of wonderland. I glanced around, hoping to find Kitty in the sea of people. I took a sip from my drink and nearly choked. It was a sickening mix of sweet and sour. As I tried to stifle a cough, a man from behind me laughed.

"Don't like the Bee's Knee's?"

I shook my head and turned to see Eliot standing there. Lucky Strike in one hand, rocks glass in the other, which I knew contained scotch.

I allowed a slight smile. "That's what this is called?" I glanced down at my dainty coupe glass. "What's in it, gasoline?"

"I believe it's gin, lemon and honey."

That was it. I hated honey. "Hmm, I normally like gin, but this is god awful," I made a face and laughed.

"You here alone?"

"Oh no." How embarrassing that he even thought that. "I'm here with my friends, Kitty and Gary, but somehow I've lost them. So many people here."

"Always is at these things. My wife likes to come. She's a fashion illustrator at Higbee's. Has many friends in the arts."

"Oh. I thought she might be in the fashion industry. I happened to meet her in the powder room. Lovely woman." I took another sip of the dreadful concoction. "Oh, by the way, I just finished reading *Maltese Falcon*." The last person I wanted to talk about was his wife. "I don't think I've ever read a book so fast. Finished in a couple of days."

"Glad you liked it," he said, giving me his full attention despite the babble surrounding us. "Did you hear they're making a movie of it? Humphrey Bogart is playing Sam Spade."

"Oh! I love Bogie!" I jumped a bit with excitement, stopping short of spilling my drink all over that nice blue shirt of his. Blue, like the blue in his bluish-gray eyes. "I'll be sure to watch for it. Do you know who'll play Brigid?"

I didn't much care at this point, too busy debating if I should bring up the matter of Tess since no one was around. Until there was.

"There you are!" Kitty's lofty voice shook me out of my own head.

"Oh, hey, Kitty." I noticed Gary had a good paw on her waist.

"Your friends?" Eliot's face tensed.

"Yes." I immediately realized my mistake. Eliot had to know who Gary Bruno was.

Damn. First, Crooked Bill. Now Mobster Gary. My stomach turned sour and I knew it wasn't from my drink.

I felt guilty for being sorry she'd found me. I decided to act like I didn't know the man whose hand was now rubbing my friend's back. "Oh, and, uh, it's Gary, right?" I said, lamely, turning to make a sham introduction. "Of course, you must know Mr.—"

But Mr. Ness was no longer there.

"Lyd?" Kitty was looking at me strangely. "You have too much of the sauce? You know Gary's name."

"Of course, I just—"

"Gary, would you excuse us a moment?" Kitty yanked me over by the shrubbery. "What's the matter with you?"

"You kiddin'? Gary's a mobster and I didn't want Eliot to know that I—we—socialize with him." I peeked out through the bush searching for where Eliot had gone. "Apparently the minute he saw Gary, he skedaddled." My heart sank. "Oh, Kitty he must think I'm horrible." I whispered to ensure no one overheard. "*And* guess what? That high-class lady we met in the powder room?" I pointed back to the revelry. "None other than his wife."

"No shit?" Kitty pulled on my arm. "Well, don't worry about it now, we need to get back." She shot me a look. "And don't be gettin' all high and mighty 'bout who we are seen with." She took a puff from her cigarette holder and blew out a perfect smoke ring—one of her great talents. "You best get over that li'l crush you got goin' on, or it's sure to land you in hot water."

I wanted to defend myself, but I knew Kitty was right. When they dropped me off at my house, I ended up sitting on the porch swing pondering my friend's words, wishing my life wasn't so complicated. I stayed there so long, I fell asleep and woke up sore, and steamed. On so many levels.

The only saving grace was that I had stretched out my party dress enough to manage to get out of it without calling for help. A small grace, but something.

10.

*N*ormally autumn was my favorite season, but this year I began reevaluating my life. Eliot was my only hope in finding Tess, and here I was, already messing up my chances. Weeks had passed since that party, and I hadn't seen hide nor hair of him. Seeing me with a crooked cop and a known gangster in a matter of a month had to be the reason he'd stopped showing up at the Roxy, or even his favorite haunt, The Theatrical. He knew where I lived, yet he never appeared there, either. It was clear he was avoiding me. Which meant he must have changed his mind about helping me.

The reality of the situation was causing me such despair that it was beginning to affect my work. And George had noticed. He summoned me after my show last week when half the crowd left before it was over.

"Hey Doll." Many people called me Doll because of my stage name, but George usually said it with affection. Not this time. "That was a pretty lackluster performance and it's not the first time lately." He lifted my chin and looked at me direct. "Whatever's happening in your life, don't bring it on stage. That doesn't cut it from our main gal." When it came to money, that was the bottom line. "Ya better put more pizazz back in or I'll have to demote you."

Ah, hell. As if things weren't bad enough already. Other than the out-of-town acts that regularly came through, there were just four fulltime girls on the roster, and the main girl was paid more in salary. I needed it, not only for rent and other debts, but those flamboyant costumes of mine aren't cheap. I'd begun to make my own costumes to save money but even at that, the fabrics of silk, satin and metallic threads were expensive, along with materials, and all the rhinestones and such, added up to a small fortune. All that aside, bottom line, I needed to stay on top.

In the meantime, Bill was attempting to rekindle our snuffed-out affair.

He showed up after my Friday night show, and feeling down, I thought, *the hell with it*, and allowed him to buy me an after-work thirst quencher. By my third cocktail, Bill had softened my reserve as he displayed all the charms I had once fallen for, making me laugh, which came easily at closing time.

Bill wasn't as rough and tough as he wanted people to believe. I'd met him when he came to the Roxy for a birthday celebration of one of his fellow officers. He was nice looking with light brown hair, deep-set brown eyes and manly physique. And the perfect gentleman. He bought me and Kitty drinks after the show, lit our cigarettes, told us jokes. He also drove us home and when he walked me to my door, he had simply said goodnight. No kiss, not even a handshake. At first, I found that refreshing. With most dates I went on, the men's sole purpose was getting to the heavy petting part, often wanting, sometimes demanding, more. I'd begun to wonder if I deliberately chose them like that. Or, based on what I did for a living, did they simply assume I was an easy catch?

When Bill repeated the hands-off manner the next time he took me home, with not so much as a peck on the cheek, I figured maybe he wasn't attracted to me. That intrigued me all the more. It gave me a challenge. Whenever he came to the nightclub, I made a point to ask him to take me home. The third time proved the charm. I invited him up to my place and before long, he embraced me with such gusto that it ignited a flame in me that had long been dormant.

I soon learned that he had an older unmarried sister who had been crippled in a car accident some years before, and he had become her main caregiver with the exception of a housemaid. Hearing him speak of it endeared me to him even more. He was not only a gentleman, he took care of family. To me, with no family left, that meant everything.

Our relationship was a heated one, both physically and emotionally. After months of fun and excitement, Bill began to show another side. He started referring to my occupation a bit too much, and in a negative manner, reminding me why he really shouldn't be seeing me, or be seen with me. "It looks bad, ya know, a police officer dating a strip-teaser." Oh, how I hated that term. They had started using it more and more in advertisements and it made me cringe. Burlesque was a theatrical art form that went back centuries. And to ignore the choreography, the beautiful, elaborate outfits and refer to us merely as "strip-teasers" was a downright insult.

The profession did get a respectable boost when Florenz Ziegfeld created his Ziegfeld Follies shows. But then Morton Minsky and brothers added their own provocative brand of burlesque in Manhattan, which ultimately turned it into a "dirty" profession.

So whenever Bill questioned our relationship based on what I did for a living, we'd argue and he'd leave in a huff. Then a few days later, he would show back up at my doorstep. We'd talk and he'd say all the right things, we'd make love, and all would be forgiven.

I wanted more, but more never came. I longed for a man I could learn about new adventures, the arts and whatnot. But each time I tried to have an intelligent conversation with this man about books or movies or artwork I admired, he'd change the subject. He wasn't a bit interested.

I began seeing other things too. A temper, for one. And despite him claiming that he understood me and knew the ways of my profession (such as flirting with important men to keep them spending money at the Roxy), his face burned red when any man approached me or eyed me with interest. More than a few times I caught his car driving slowly by my house as if I was bringing these men home. He was checking up on me and it grated on my nerves.

So when Kitty told me last July what she'd discovered about him, my passion for Bill disintegrated like sawdust. Kitty had been talking to a man at a bar, who'd had a few too many and started bragging how his gambling business was thriving, thanks to his friendships with a couple of cops.

"I got him to tell me who these friends of his were," Kitty had said. "And I quote—'Oh, you know the one, the guy who's screwing your girlfriend. Name's Bill.' 'Course I asked his last name and at first he wouldn't say. So I spit out, Baker? He looked away then and muttered, 'You didn't hear that from me, Toots.'"

Kitty then added, "The guy said everyone in the field, as he called it, knew Bill and a coupla other coppers who charge a high fee for their silence but it's worth it 'cause it's good protection from the slammer . . . another direct quote."

That meant if *everyone* knew about Bill, so did Eliot Ness.

I'd been furious at the news. I may not be all innocent, but he was a dirty cop. Dating him made me dirty too. I promised myself to never let Bill Baker darken my doorstep again.

And I'd stayed true to that vow all these months. But damn if booze and lust didn't get in the way. I'd been so miserable about my feelings for Eliot that I threw all caution to the wind. On the way home, my alcohol-fueled body snuggled up to Bill as he drove, telling myself that he wasn't so bad.

Maybe he was all I was worthy of. What made me so high-and-mighty, thinking I deserved better? Why would I—a girl who appeared as window dressing and sultry in nightlife

65

entertainment ads—rate a more decent, honorable kind of fella?

It was clear that Eliot's vanishing act had wormed its way into my psyche, reminding me exactly what I was, and not what I often imagined myself to be. In my heart, I envisioned myself an educated woman (I was an avid reader, after all), a good friend to the few I had, kind to animals . . . a good person.

Yet, what Eliot obviously saw was a promiscuous woman with questionable ethics who danced half-naked in front of men, socialized with them after hours, and most likely entertained them in her bed.

And now I'd gone and proved it by sleeping with Bill again. To make things worse, he didn't even stay to cuddle afterward, saying he had to get home. My head ached that morning, but it was nothing close to the ache in my soul. How could I possibly do my Saturday show when that required confidence and I was hating myself for what I'd done.

Soon as I arrived at work, Kitty saw right through me. "Whatever is the matter with you, Lyd?" She placed a hand on my face. "You haven't been yourself for weeks."

"I make terrible decisions," I said, eyes getting moist. "Let's talk later." I had yet to tell her of my conversation with Eliot about Tess, but what would be the point now?

Still, I felt a great need to confide in someone and she was my best friend. Pretty much my only friend.

Kitty helped me get ready, pumped up my self-esteem with kind words, and it somehow did the trick. My show wasn't great, but better than they had been.

Afterward, we went out for late-night burgers at Otto Moser's, a snug place with decent food and walls lined with celebrity photos and theatrical playbills. After some small talk, I set down my half-eaten sandwich on the plate and sighed. "I know I've been a mess, Kitty, but I didn't want to talk about it because nothing can change it, but I could use to sound off a bit." I stopped to light a cigarette.

"You talkin' about Ness?"

"No. Yes . . . Well, it's not everything. Like I said, the whole thing's useless." I updated her on getting Eliot to agree to help me and how nothing had happened since. "With him knowing about Bill and, well, us being with Gary at the party, I'm afraid he's turned tail." I waved my smoke away and watched it merge with the rest of the hazy cloud in the air. "He hasn't shown his face anywhere in weeks now. He obviously doesn't want anything to do with me."

"You don't know that." Kitty had wolfed down her meal, then took a sip of her ginger ale. I was glad we weren't drinking so we could discuss this with sober minds. "And just so ya know, me and Gary are getting along real good so you might have to get used to it."

"I'm sorry. It's just that I'm afraid my associations with Bill and Gary has put the nail in the coffin, far as Eliot getting involved in my problems." I put a hand on her wrist. "Please don't be offended. It's nothing to do with you."

Kitty shook her head. "You think Eliot Ness is that shallow? I mean, I know he's fought criminals during Prohibition and spent years goin' after Al Capone, but Jesus, we're just two nice working gals, and in our profession, it stands to reason we'd have some contact with a few seedy characters."

"Exactly." I stamped out my smoke. "And that's it in a nutshell."

"I don't believe it is." Kitty tapped the table for emphasis. "I have more faith in the guy than that. I rather like him."

"You've never even met him, Kit. He didn't even give me the chance to introduce you that night."

"I know. I guess reading about him and what you've told me about him makes me feel like I know him." She let out a weighty breath. "Look, I know he'll help you with Tess if you give him a chance. And the only way to change his opinion of you, if that's what you're worried about, is to let him get to know the real Lydia Swanson. You have his number, call him, for god's sakes. Worst that can happen is he'll continue to ignore you. It wouldn't be any worse than what you're goin' through now, right?"

I couldn't deny the logic in that. We got up to leave and I gave her a squeeze. "Thanks, Kitty. You've made me feel much better."

Then I confided something else to her. I told her about the cardinal and the promise I'd made to my mother.

I had to keep trying.

I waited till Tuesday. Surely I couldn't bother him on a Sunday, and Mondays were probably filled with meetings or something. I laid in bed wide awake that morning, waiting for the clock to reach a decent hour, rehearsing a new speech that would sway him back on the track that led to Tess.

At nine-o-five, I pulled myself up, summoned all my nerve, picked up the living room phone and dialed. I'd let it ring three, maybe four, times. Any longer, I would know he was busy, and I'd be interrupting him, which would start it all off on the wrong foot.

On the third ring, he picked up. "Hello?" I bit my lip. "*Hello?*"

"Eliot. It's Lydia."

"Lydia, nice to hear from you." His voice sounded pleased.

"Oh, I'm glad. I was afraid you wouldn't want to talk to me anymore."

A Place We Belong

The pause made me more nervous. "Why would you think that?"

"Well... I don't know, I haven't seen you at the clubs. Or heard from you. You know, about my sister." I wanted to cut straight to the chase.

Turned out, Eliot had just been busy. He told me he'd been working overtime, had barely even been home the past few weeks. "I'm just wrapping up an investigation," he said, "And I sure could use to see a pretty, friendly face."

Hmmm. Did he mean pretty *and* friendly, or just pretty friendly? I decided it was the first.

"I apologize. I do want to delve into it, but I need a bit more information, if possible. While I have you on the phone, can we try and meet up again?" I suppressed a burst of delight. He still cared about my plight. "Would you be free for lunch later this week?"

"Oh yes. I'd love that." And just like that, the perfect place sprung to mind. "And this might sound strange, but when I need to get away from everything, I take a long walk along the gardens at the Lake View Cemetery. The grounds are truly lovely, especially in fall."

He said he'd been there a few times, and so, we made plans to meet on Thursday at noon in front of the Wade Memorial Chapel. I offered to make a bag lunch for us and imagined us taking a leisurely stroll, having lunch by the nearby pond, getting to know more about each other.

It seemed almost too perfect.

11.

I was surprised to see George at my Wednesday Theatrical show, but then again, I shouldn't have been. He was checking up on me, concerned that I may have lost my touch, based on weeks of bland performances. But that was no longer a problem. My glum mood had lifted almost instantly since talking to Eliot.

I amped up my moves to show my boss I was still the girl every man wanted to see. And it paid off with rousing applause and shouts for more.

"More? Y'all want more?" I teased my fans. I began singing "Puttin' on the Ritz," my favorite number by Fred Astaire. I only knew the first two verses so ended with the ever-popular Betty Boop phrase, "Boop-Oop-a-Doop!" The crowd ate it up.

And so did George. I was back in his good graces.

Afterward, I rewarded myself by going to Fran's Dress Shop and buying a delightful, belted tea-length lace dress, a bright lilac shade that would be lovely for an afternoon among colorful fall gardens. Most women would wear it to a fancy dinner party, not a cemetery, but it looked good on me, and I wanted to look extra nice. As I approached the counter, I spotted an ivory feather tea-party fascinator hat. "Oh Fran, I must have this too."

I was too excited about my purchases to care that I had to lug the big bag onto the streetcar. When I got home, I took little Spencey for a brisk walk, made myself a delicious BLT, then settled down with a new book. It was turning out to be a great day.

Then the phone rang. "Well, hello, Miss Lydia."

Eliot? He did have my number!

"Why, hello, Mr. Crime Fighter," I purred, feeling giddy. "What brings me the pleasure of hearing from such a busy, important man?"

"Well . . ."

Oh dear, his voice had suddenly turned sullen. I bit my lip. Perhaps I'd taken the jovial teasing too far.

"I'm afraid I have to cancel our lunch meeting."

"Oh?"

"Evaline wants me to take a few days off and drive down to Columbus to see an old friend of hers." I heard the click of a lighter before he continued. "I owe it to her after being away from home so much lately. I hope you understand."

"Why, of course, I do." I winced. I felt like a tramp, feeling as I did about someone else's husband.

"I'll give you a ring when I get back. I'm sure you're very anxious about your sister and I really do want to help."

"I know you do, Eliot, and I very much appreciate it." I tried to hide my disappointment. *It's been five years. A few more days sure won't make a difference.*

As soon as we hung up, that helpless sense of despair returned in full force. I sat on the edge of my bed, letting the tears come. Maybe it wasn't meant to be, me finding Tess. Aside from this awful attraction I had for this man, he represented hope for me. Yet, just when I'd think the ball will start rolling, something got in the way. His work, his wife . . . maybe I was barking up the wrong tree.

By now, Tess was an adult woman, almost eighteen. I'd missed so much of her life. My little sister could be married, maybe even with a baby of her own. Or, God forbid—forgive me, she could be dead. Who knows? For five long years, so many thoughts haunted me. Where had those people taken her? Were her adoptive parents decent people with money who had given her a good life with a nice home and opportunities for a happy future? That had been my constant prayer.

But what if those people were more sinister, taking her to make a workhorse out of her, or worse . . . I knew those things happened.

Dear God, will I ever know the truth?

I rose to get a tissue from the bathroom and when the phone rang again, I made a dash toward it. Maybe Eliot had changed his mind.

"Hey, Lydia."

Damn. "Hello, Bill."

"I got tonight off, how'd ya like to catch a movie? I see *His Girl, Friday* with Cary Grant is playing at the Detroit Theater."

I sighed. That did sound fun. Bill knew I loved going to the movies. And that I loved Cary Grant.

Anything was better than sitting home alone, with all the "what ifs" playing over in my head. And when it came to any possibility of romance, I had few options.

Besides, in my present state of mind, it wasn't good to stay home and sulk. "Okay." I sighed. "What time you gettin' me?"

And so, despite myself, I sat there in the darkened theater with a man who truly cared about me, was a good kisser—and had no wife—and accepted my fate.

That evening, and four straight ones after, I lied in my crooked cop's arms, feeling spent after long sessions of making love. Every one of those nights, he whispered in my ear that he would never leave me. That I was his girl. *That he would give me anything I wanted.*

But he was wrong. There was one thing I wanted more than anything, and Bill couldn't make it happen.

That much was clear early on. Over pillow-talk one night early in our relationship, I confided in him about my sister. Surely, being a cop, I thought Bill could help. He expressed sympathy but told me there was little anyone could do under the circumstances and quickly abandoned any effort.

"So I should just give up?" I yelled, then begged him to at least try. But he never followed through. It was something that always stuck with me. How he'd dismissed my heartbreak. How the world seemed to have dismissed my heartbreak. The not-knowing was tearing my insides, eating me away like a slow growing cancer.

Bill was not what I needed. I knew that. He was no special agent. No chief investigator. No Untouchable. There was only one man who had the means, the experience, the smarts, to find my sister. I had no choice but to pursue him. Despite my little crush, I could not, would not, give up on my mission.

Just as I was ready to call him, Eliot rang me up, and again, we made plans.

"Can we meet me tomorrow at that chapel there, after my Theatrical show?" That gave me the rest of the afternoon and the evening free. Surely, in a quiet environment, with no one else we knew around, we could discuss strategies. We agreed to meet at three o'clock.

I got there late because the streetcar only ran every two hours. Walking up the hill towards him, clutching a big brown deli bag, I noticed that his Brooks Brothers dark navy suit happened to go well against my lilac dress. And I was glad he hadn't worn his hat. I liked seeing his whole face, and that ever-straight part.

"I hope you like roast beef sandwiches and potato salad," I said, greeting him. "I had to wait a bit for the car, so I snuck into the delicatessen around the corner." I gave him a sheepish grin. "Seeing how I forgot to make our lunch before I left this morning."

In truth, I hadn't forgotten at all. I just wasn't much of a cook, or lunch packer.

"Roast beef happens to be my favorite. How did you know?"

"Lucky guess," I answered with a delighted shrug. Luck, indeed.

We stood and smoked a cigarette outside before going into the chapel. I leaned against one of the tall white columns, gazing out at the surroundings. There was a nip in the air but the October sun was warm and bright, for which I was grateful since I hadn't brought a wrap.

We chatted about the fall foliage and what a perfect day it was. "I do love it here. The quiet, the loveliness, it gives me a rare moment of peace." I smiled.

He nodded and smiled back. He seemed more relaxed today than other times. Almost content. "Shall we go in?"

We snuffed out our butts in the tall ashtray provided, and with a hand on my lower back, he led me through the grand bronze doors.

Once inside, I pointed to the large stained-glass window facing us. "Isn't it amazing? It's Tiffany glass. It's called "The Flight of Souls." We paused at the center of the room to take it all in.

"Incredible. I've never been inside." He said it as if wondering why he hadn't. "It certainly gives one pause."

Finally, a man who could appreciate the arts. "See the mosaic on this wall?" I asked, gesturing. "It symbolizes the prophecy and the law of the Old Testament." I gave him a moment to process the intricacy of it. Then I placed my hands lightly on his shoulders and turned him to the other side. "And over here . . . that wall signifies the fulfillment of the Prophets' laws through Christianity." I added a few more facts that I'd learn from a book I'd read.

"Hmm." He turned to me with raised brow. "You're quite knowledgeable about all this. You could be a tour guide."

I laughed because I had once thought of doing just that. To escape the sometimes craziness of my profession. But even as the notion crossed my mind, I knew I would dearly miss Blue Satin Doll.

"Like I said, I come here fairly often," I answered nonchalantly.

As we stepped out from the darkened room, the stream of sunshine felt blinding. I tipped my fascinator more at an angle to fight off the glare. "That chapel is probably my favorite place anywhere. It's just so inspiring. Peaceful," I said as we walked along.

He stopped for a second, looked at me direct. "That's the second time you used that word, peace. I imagine you don't get much of that at work."

Before I could respond, he added, "Or is there something else bothering you?"

My thoughts immediately went to Bill. Yeah, he was bothering me alright. And I was letting him. And it had given me no satisfaction. I didn't love Bill. Yet when we were together, he made me feel like I was important, like I mattered. At least to someone.

Apparently my remorse, my guilt, showed. And yet, that was one subject that was definitely off limits. I didn't respond, just kept walking.

We strolled along in silence. He seemed to grasp that I wasn't yet ready to bring up the business of Tess. Just having him next to me, marveling at the bright, vibrant trees and gardens was enough, for now.

We explored the Garfield Monument, which was rich with gold mosaics and marble, gorgeous stained-glass windows, and magnificent red granite columns. When Eliot admitted he had never been up to the top of the temple, I perked up. "Then let's go," I said, lightly taking his hand, leading him toward the stairway. I failed to tell him there were sixty-four steps to the outside balcony.

Halfway up, I turned behind to see that he wasn't following me with the same enthusiasm. "Eliot?"

"I'm coming," he said, mixing a laugh with heavy breathing. "Guess I should be doing more calisthenics."

Being a dancer, regular walker, and well, much younger than my companion, I hadn't given the long climb a thought. But Eliot couldn't hide his huffin' and puffin.' Reminding me that he was an older man. Nearly old enough to be my father. Oh, dear, I did not want to think about that. *Dear God, what if he had a heart attack? And in my company?*

Shaking off such thoughts, I slowed my steps so he could keep up, and at last, we reached the top.

Leaning on a rail, we gazed out at the picturesque scenery. "They say you can see forty miles away." I pointed over to the sight before us. "Look out there. See Lake Erie?"

By now, he had caught his breath. "Sure do." His enthusiasm had also returned. "This was certainly worth the trudge. The view is spectacular."

I caught him gazing at me instead of the view. The crease in his eyes made them almost twinkle.

Blushing, I looked away. And so did he.

12.

We continued on, chatting and marveling at the grand statues, reading the headstones, learning about the historic people buried there; like John D. Rockefeller, President James Garfield, and others who had made such an impact on the city.

"Look at this, Eliot, isn't it striking?" I stood gazing at the large bronze sculpture of a crying angel, the word Haserot at the bottom. "It's the Haserot Angel. Of the Haserot canned foods family dynasty. Most people call it the 'Weeping Angel.'"

"I can see why," Eliot leaned closer. "Actually looks like tears, dark tears. Haunting."

Caught up in the moment, and the chill in the air, I slipped my arm through his. It was such a natural response, I didn't think that it might not be appropriate until it was done. I went to gently slide it away when he squeezed my hand, encouraging me to leave it there.

When we reached the lagoon, we walked toward the bench overlooking the water. "Ready for some lunch?" I asked, lifting up my impromptu offering.

"I am," he said, guiding me to sit. "I thought you might be tired by now, carrying that brown sack around." His chuckle warmed my heart.

"Ha, don'cha think it goes well with my beige pocketbook?" I lifted the bag with a little smirk.

As I pulled out the wrapped hoagies, I realized my blunder. "Oh, shoot. I am such a dope. I completely forgot something for us to drink."

"Not to worry, young lady, Eliot Ness is on it." He dug his hand into his jacket pocket. "Will this do?" He pulled out a pack of Black Jack gum. "A stick of gum always quenches my thirst."

"Ah. Always prepared, like a Boy Scout."

I cringed as soon as the words left my mouth. Eliot knew the mobsters called him a Boy Scout behind his back. I quickly backtracked. "I love that gum—and it can double as dessert," I said lightheartedly, leaning into his shoulder.

Luckily, he grinned. "Good thinking."

I laid out the napkins, glad I had the deli clerk cut the sandwiches into small sections so I could eat daintily. I didn't want to feel self-conscious eating in front of him.

"By the way, don't ever call yourself a dope," he said, interrupting my thoughts. "You're an intelligent woman, anyone can see that."

I wanted to hug him. It wasn't often that I received compliments that weren't about my body, or my act. "Why, thank you. That's nice to hear."

We sat enjoying the sandwiches, gazing at the surroundings and I pointed to a lovely magnolia bush. "We had magnolias like that in our front yard when I was a kid. They're beautiful, aren't they?" Without waiting for an answer, I asked, "Did you have a happy childhood, Eliot?"

He shrugged, like he never thought about it much. "It was pretty normal, I guess. I was the baby of the family, and my brothers and sisters teased me a lot. Called me a Mama's boy. But then, my father was gone much of the time. Left early in the morning, returned late at night. He owned a bakery."

"No kidding?" I perked up at the coincidence. "My mother worked at Hough Bakery!" I loved that we had this in common, and after some talk about our favorite baked goods, I managed to ask him about other things I was curious about.

"So tell me, how'd you get into this business of yours?"

He hesitated, staring into the water. "I guess I'd been wanting to get into police or detective work since I was a kid but didn't think I had it in me." He gave a sheepish grin. "When I got the job as a prohibition agent chasing bootleggers, I hadn't a clue what I was gettin' into. When you're young, you want to change the world, even though you've yet to understand it."

"Oh, but you did change it, Eliot, you definitely made an impact on the underworld with your Untouchables."

He threw me a cynical look. "You've been reading too many papers."

My eyebrows lifted. Since meeting him, that's exactly what I'd been doing. I had visited the library several times to research him and his days in Chicago. And I kept up on all the local news reports. Not just his work with city crime, but also how he'd ordered hundreds of traffic lights to reduce car accidents and it had made a major difference in auto deaths. Eliot Ness was touted constantly for being the best security chief Cleveland ever had.

"Now wait," I argued. "You've made a huge difference since you've been here. And that was no small potatoes busting Capone and his thugs. Everybody knows that."

"Humph," he scoffed. "We gave him some trouble, sure, but never got him convicted for all the things he had his hands in. Frustrated the hell outta me. The guy could weasel his way out of anything. Especially because he had half the town in his back pocket. He knew what he was doing and he was ruthless."

We'd finished eating by then and he offered me a smoke, which I took. Lucky Strikes were growing on me.

He lit my cigarette. "As you may know, he finally went up the river for tax evasion, of all things," he continued, "The least of his crimes." The snap of his Zippo echoed in the air.

I wished I could wipe away the bitterness he obviously felt, but before I could say anything positive, he went on.

"I'll admit, I did love the rush of excitement that came with being on the guy's tail all the time. Kept him on his toes." It was nice to hear pride in his voice. "I like making the bad guys squirm. But nothing beats getting them locked up." He took a drag, then stared at the burning ember. "I'll admit it was rough, and at times, dangerous work. You have to be on your game at all times. I'm afraid my biggest missions have eluded me."

"How so?"

"Well, besides that crap with Capone, those unsolved Kingsbury Run killings will haunt me till I crack it, or die trying. Whichever comes first."

I shuddered. I did not want to talk about those ghastly butcherings while sitting in a cemetery. But it confirmed that he possessed the exact trait needed to solve my own life mystery. "I'd like to hear more about your career highlights," I said, hoping to defer him from those horrific crimes.

He shook his head. "Enough about me. Tell me more about that home you and your sister were placed in."

I waited for a few people to pass by, some stopping to observe the pond and the surrounding sculptures and greenery. Finally, we had the place to ourselves.

And I was ready. I touched on my younger years and our parents, which turned into the revelation of my father's abandonment and mother's death, and then, to the last day I saw Tess.

"There's just something fishy about it," I told him. "Why would they not tell me where they took her?" I managed to voice my long-held fears out loud. "Do you suppose if I'd stuck around longer, they would've told me? Maybe I left too soon . . ." I was always haunted by that emotional decision to flee.

He shook his head. "I doubt that would've made a difference. I agree, their actions are suspect. And you were there for weeks. If they'd planned on telling you, they would have done it when they informed you that she was to be adopted. Even though the files are private, you were sisters, you came in together. No, you're right. It doesn't sound logical."

On one hand, I was relieved that someone thought as I did. On the other hand, it scared the hell out of me. What in God's name happened to Tess?

"I don't want to be right." I could feel the tears dampening my cheeks. "I want to think their hearts were in a good place."

He put an arm around my shoulder and pulled me close. I leaned into his strong, comforting chest and we sat for a moment in silence. Then I looked up into his face. "Will you please help me, Eliot?" I needed a firm confirmation.

"I have to," he whispered, wiping away my tear. "I hate to see a lady cry."

I straightened up and wrapped my arms around him, squeezing him so tight I felt my breasts pressing against his chest. Embarrassed, I pulled away. "I'm sorry, I'm just so grateful."

"Don't ever be sorry, Lydia."

As I pulled out a tissue from my purse, Eliot retrieved a ballpoint pen and pocket-sized notepad and began asking me questions like Tess's birthdate, what she looked like . . . but when he asked me the name of the facility we'd been sent to, I couldn't recall the exact name.

"Let me see, I was in such shock the whole time I was there." I wiped a salty tear that touched my lips. "It was m-something." I racked my brain. "Moore? No. Murone, Mur . . . Murphy! That's it. Murphy's Home for Orphan Children. And it wasn't right in the city. I recall them driving us for awhile. It was outside of town."

A stark memory flashed to mind. "I remember this lovely portrait hanging in the dining hall. It was of a mother embracing a small child. I saw that tender picture every day and it broke my heart. I couldn't understand why they had it there. I'm sure it was meant to show that they cared and would help reunite families. But their actions spoke so differently. How cruel of them to taunt children with photographs of mothers when most had lost theirs."

"Like you and Tess."

I bowed my head, mourning my loss. "Yes. Like us."

I dug into my purse again and pulled out the little pouch with the emerald marble. "This is all I have of her. I keep it in my dresser drawer, but I wanted to show it to you. I know it sounds silly, but it's very special. It represents our last good time together, before our mother died. And everything changed."

He squeezed my hand. "Please know that I will do all I can to get to the bottom of this, and right away. She'll be eighteen in four months and when that happens, she could leave and go off on her own if she chooses. Could make her harder to find."

"My dream is that she'll come find me, but she'd have no idea where I am, either." I raised my eyebrows and gave a half laugh. "I'm quite sure she never dreamed that her big sis would become a burlesque dancer."

He squeezed my shoulder. "I suppose not, but you do make a grand one, lady."

My face softened. "Why, Eliot, I believe that's the nicest thing anyone has ever said to me." A sweet rush ran through me, like the solace of good wine. I hugged him again. I couldn't help myself. The gesture came as right as rain.

He straightened up and backed away as an older woman passed and gave us a disapproving look. Reminding us that public displays of affection were frowned upon.

A Place We Belong

Eliot returned to the matter at hand. "And you know, your sister may have taken the name of her adopted family. If indeed, she had one."

I cocked my head. "What do you mean, if she had one?"

"You have no proof that she was actually adopted. Sometimes those things fall through. I've heard of children being separated and their siblings not informed where they are sent. Sadly, it's fairly commonplace."

This certainly did not make me feel better.

He returned the notebook to the inside of his suit pocket. "Right now, we need to find out where they took her in the first place."

He stood now and extended his hand to pull me up from the bench. I discarded the wrappers in the nearby trash can and we continued on our way.

"Eliot? I hope this won't interfere with your other work."

"This is a job, like any other. I just have a different boss."

Boss. I hadn't thought about it in that sense. "Oh, and, of course, I'll pay you. How much do you charge?"

He squinted, though the sunlight was behind us. "Lydia, we are friends, are we not?"

I pursed my lips. "I like to think so."

"I will be honored to help you. Pro bono."

"Oh, no, that wouldn't be right."

"It's right in my book." He gave me a look that said it wasn't up to discussion.

"Oh, Eliot. I can't tell you what this means."

"You don't have to."

I put a hand to my chest. Yes, we really were friends. And maybe that was more special than being lovers. Less

83

complicated and—as I'd discovered through the years—oftentimes, more lasting.

Our final stop was to pay a visit to the gravesite of famous ballplayer, Ray Chapman, the Cleveland Indian's shortstop who had died from a fast pitch in 1920. That's when I learned that Eliot was a big baseball fan, and made a mental note. One more thing I now knew about him.

"Oh, my," he said glancing at his watch. "It's nearly five. I best be going. Evaline always has dinner for me when I'm not working late."

Of course she did. Oh, why did she have to be so perfect? Why couldn't she be an awful wife? And ugly?

"Gum?" He asked, handing me a stick.

"Oh yes. We forgot. Dessert." I smiled, taking it cheerfully.

"Come on, I'll drop you off."

It was the third time I had thanked him that day. I wouldn't have to take that damn streetcar again.

13.

A week later, I ran into Evaline Ness.

I'd been late going to Crane's Bookstore that Monday because I'd slept in on account of a date with Bill. My afternoon with Eliot had reinforced the fact that I had to settle for what I could get. Eliot was not available to me romantically and I couldn't waste time hoping and dreaming that he was. Much as I wished things could be different, I cherished the friendship we were developing. I had to be happy he was willing to help me. That had to be enough.

Still, I was a woman with needs. And with so many lugheads around me most of the time, Bill at least truly cared about me, had known me for more than a fleeting moment. I constantly told myself that despite those things I wasn't crazy about, Bill Baker had some redeeming qualities. Like, he did well in the love department. Including those little murmurs every girl loves to hear.

I need you. I want you. I love you . . .

It was better than nothing, I supposed.

As I walked into the shop, I saw that Dottie had it all adorned in Halloween decorations. I was not a fan of the holiday. As a little girl, I loved dressing up but now I felt I dressed up enough as it was. I didn't know why, but seeing people in masks and truly awful outfits sometimes unnerved me.

I headed straight to the table of new books when the little bell above the door chimed. I turned to see a statuesque woman step in, wearing a brown wool cape coat, accented with mink collar.

"Oh hello, Evaline." Dottie greeted.

I watched Evaline shake off her coat and saw that she was dressed simply underneath as well—black slacks and soft lime green sweater—yet still managing to look like a *Vogue* model.

As Dottie did with all her regulars in fall and winter, she took her coat and hung it on the rack for her. Apparently the woman planned on staying a bit, just like I often did. The quaint little corner towards the back, with those comfy chairs and refreshments, was ever popular. That Dottie was a smart business woman.

I got a whiff of Chanel No. 5 even from where she stood an aisle away. While most women adored that perfume, I preferred, or rather could more afford, Evening in Paris, which I discovered one day on the cosmetic counter at Higbee's—the very department store this woman, I now knew, worked as a fashion illustrator.

I scooted behind the nearest bookshelf and eavesdropped.

"Can I help you with something today, Eva?" asked Dottie, ever the salesperson.

"Well, as you know, I've been dabbling a bit in poetry and such," Evaline said, "but I'm steering more toward children's books. Of course, Eliot and I have no kids, but I think I'd like to try my hand at writing some books for them, which I could donate to my various charity functions."

"Oh, what a wonderful, thoughtful idea." Dottie said.

"Yes, I do think so too." Evaline patted her dark wavy hair, pinned back from her thin face. "However, I have to learn how to write one first so thought I'm pop in and peruse what you have and study up."

"Of course. Come right on over here."

I realized in that moment that I was hiding behind—just my luck—the children's bookshelves. I stifled a gasp.

But then, why should I hide? This presented an opportunity. I had wondered if Eliot had told his wife about our friendship. Only one way to find out.

I straightened my posture as the women approached. "Oh, Dottie, am I in the way?" And as I knew she would, Dottie introduced us.

"Evaline, this is one of my most regular customers, Lydia Swanson," Dottie said proudly. "Lydia, Evaline Ness."

"Yes, I know Evaline," I said with a genuine smile. Despite myself, I did admire the woman. "We met in the powder room at the Bennett's party a few months ago. How are you?" I extended my hand.

Mrs. Ness looked at me like she'd never seen me before. "Oh. We did, didn't we? I'm sorry, I attend so many functions, hard to keep track sometimes." She gave a weak laugh, along with a limp handshake. "Nice to see you—again."

She didn't know me from a hole in the wall. She had no clue who I was, nor did she care.

Evaline whipped around, turning her attention to the children's shelf.

I turned tail, too, feeling disgracefully snubbed, and headed for the door. It was the first time I'd ever left the shop without making a purchase.

I wasn't sure why the blasé treatment set me off. I should probably be glad the woman's ears didn't perk up at the mention of my name. Did I actually expect Evaline to say, "Oh, yes, Eliot has mentioned knowing you," or some such thing? And yet, I felt offended by her dismissal and decided I no longer gave a rat's ass about feeling guilty for my friendship with this woman's husband.

When I got home, I took Spencer for a chilly stroll down the street, thinking about my life, and I made two

87

decisions. First, that I needed both Eliot, and Bill, in my life. One may never be mine in the sense I desired, but he served me well as a friend, and who knows what he might find out about Tess? And Bill, well, he was a sure thing, so why *not* keep dating him? After all, I had nothing to do with his secret activities.

Okay, then, that's settled. I would keep them both.

My next decision was that Blue Satin Doll needed a fresh act. I would give my old pal Zorita a call for inspiration. She and I had met soon after I began working at the Roxy and she had arrived from Chicago to do a show. Her act, which involved dancing with a live eight-foot boa constrictor named Oscar, and indigo snake she called Elmer, had mesmerized everyone, including me. We became fast friends when I learned her real name was Kathryn, the same as my mother, and that she'd been born in Youngstown. Now, we were successful showgirls—though Zorita on a grander scale, both in national popularity, and income. Still, we shared a sisterhood that I only felt with one other girl, Kitty.

If anyone could help Blue Satin Doll jack up her game, it was the flamboyant Zorita. Though one thing was certain. It would most definitely not involve snakes.

I was walking up my drive when I heard a car pull in behind me. I swiveled around to see Bill opening the car door.

"Lyd, I tried calling you but then remembered it was dog-walking time," he said, all smiles.

"My, you're a chipper fella today."

"Yes, I am. Had me a real good day."

"How so?"

"Just never you mind, all you need to know is we've been invited to a grand private party at The Alpine for Halloween and we need to get us a costume."

A Place We Belong

Thinking about his "never you mind" response, I wanted to retort, "Maybe we can go as the showgirl and the crooked cop?" but bit my tongue.

"You know I don't care for Halloween."

"Aw, come on, it's gonna be at The Alpine. They got that good beer, and guess what? Frankie Yankovic's band is playin.'" He grabbed my hands and started polka-ing, right there in the drive, until Spencer's leash got us all tangled up.

I couldn't help but laugh.

"We can't miss this." He squeezed me against him. "Come on, whaddya say?" he purred, whispering in my ear. "It'll be a hoot."

Yes, it probably would be. "Ah, why the hell not," I said, defeated. "Maybe we can go as Bonnie and Clyde."

"Hey, now you're talkin'. Great idea." Grabbing my hand, he pulled me up the porch steps and into the house. "Come on, you can make me a drink inside."

We passed Helen in the hallway. "Hey, Helen, Bill tells me we have a Halloween party to go to Thursday night, can you please feed Spencey and take him out before bedtime? I'm sure it'll be a late evening."

"I can do that." She eyeballed me before breezing past us as if Bill wasn't there. Helen clearly wasn't happy about our reunion.

"You're a peach, Helen," I called out as the woman walked away.

Helen may not approve of everything I did, but she was loyal, and a true friend. And she and Frank treated my doggie like their own, giving me more freedom to go places and not worry about him.

I let go of Spencer's leash and he took off upstairs. Following behind, Bill gave me a pinch on my derriere and chased me up the steps. He most definitely was in a feisty mood.

89

As we sat on my red davenport nursing highballs, making a list of what we needed for our outfits, I was tempted to ask why he now felt we could go to a big shindig together. In the two years we'd dated, Bill hardly ever took me to places as public as The Alpine Village in Playhouse Square, where so many fat cats went. After all, heaven forbid someone recognize the blue blood with the infamous Blue Satin Doll. Even if he wasn't in uniform.

Instead I asked, "Why would the restaurant close on a midday week for a silly Halloween party?"

He leaned back, crossed his legs, took a sip of his whiskey and ginger. "Because, my dear, this is no silly *soiree*." I chuckled the way he emphasized the fancy word. "This is an invite-only party in the Eldorado Room upstairs. The restaurant will be open downstairs, but we'll be in the place where all the big celebs go when they're in town. Who knows who we'll see?"

He sounded more excited than I was about it and I was getting quite excited myself. "Oh, I've heard about that room. Bob Hope has been there, and Cab Calloway, even Fred Astaire and Frank Sinatra."

"That's right, Doll." He patted my knee. "Just remember who you're with."

Oh, that possessive streak again. But it didn't bother me this time because he was finally going to take me on his arm and let others know that he wasn't ashamed to be with me. A new step in our relationship.

"Aw, Bill, you know I'm your gal," I said and led him to my bedroom.

14.

We'd be late, of course. The party got underway at nine but my Thursday show wasn't until ten. I managed to sweet-talk George into being the first girl to go on instead of my normal time. That is, after I told him I had a great act for the Roxy Halloween show.

"I'm wearing a Bonnie Parker outfit 'cause me and Bill are going to a party afterward," I told him. "I'll come on stage in these '30s duds. I'm thinking of a sexy red beret (I doubted I could find one last minute but "thinking" wasn't the same as "having" so I wasn't lying), red silk scarf around my neck and I'll tuck a toy gun in my garter, under a snug brown pencil skirt." I raised my index finger. "*But* I sure as a hell not wearin' those god-awful Oxfords they say she wore. Anyway, I'll kick the night off real good, pave the way for the other girls. It'll be a show to remember, I promise." *And* I'd kill two birds with one stone, making it easy to hop right into Bill's car already dressed for the party.

I wondered what had changed Bill's attitude. Although my old feelings for him had returned, somewhat, this new public date had me curious. I didn't always trust his motives, but I didn't question him further and by the time we walked into the lavish upstairs ballroom dressed as the notorious bank robbers, I'd forgotten my doubts about him.

When we arrived, we were greeted by the restaurant owner, Herman, who startled me with his creepy oversized "old man" mask. I wanted to retreat immediately but Herman was already leading us to a table next to a marvelous spread, a banquet of all sorts of finger foods; shrimp cocktail, chicken salad stuffed tomatoes, roast beef, scalloped potatoes, and various kinds of gelatin desserts. We ate first to absorb the liquor we knew we'd consume, and when the band began playing those lively polka standards, Bill kept me on the floor until I was dizzy.

Especially after the group switched to flapper music and we danced the Charleston and Lindy Hop, which Bill and I were quite good at.

It was I who wore out first.

"You forget, ol' boy, I did a show tonight," I said, trying to catch my breath between numbers. "My feet are killin' me." I kicked off my four-inch heels and slid them under the table.

We sat it out as I gazed around the room at all the fun get-ups, and was glad we'd come. These things weren't so bad. I marveled at the creativity of the outfits as everyone was vying for the huge $50 prize for best costume.

Bill and I were gunning for that and looked every bit the part. As "Clyde," he wore a dark suit with brown necktie and brown fedora—and those awful oxford shoes. I'd found a brown beret at the dress shop and used Rit to dye it red. I hemmed my "Bonnie" skirt several inches above the knees and cut a little slit on the side, to reveal the play gun strapped to my thigh.

But soon I realized we didn't stand a chance at winning the grand prize. Some highlights included a man in an elaborate pirate suit, a woman in the best gypsy outfit I'd ever seen, and another dressed as Glenda the Witch from that fabulous movie, *Wizard of Oz*.

A Place We Belong

I then spotted a man who didn't looked dressed up at all. A man who looked like . . . Eliot? My heart quickened until he turned his head and I realized he was just dressed like him—razor straight part and all. Ha, to think someone had actually come "as" Eliot Ness. I couldn't wait to tell the real Eliot that he was so famous, he was now a Halloween costume. Then again, I hoped he didn't take offense to it. I knew by now that he preferred to remain in the background, no matter how many newspapers wrote about him.

Sitting near the buffet table meant seeing everyone in attendance. I could spot the hoity-toity ones at first glance and giggled under my breath when I recognized a few regulars from the Roxy—with wives who I knew had no idea their husbands had seen me half-naked.

One of those couples stopped at our table to say hello to Bill. The man was dressed as Clark Gable, she, as his actress wife, Carole Lombard. I didn't recognize them until I caught the woman's stern gaze. Ah yes, Mr. and Mrs. Kaplan. The councilman and his wife who'd tried to ban The Roxy last year, citing that its debauchery was ruining the fair city of Cleveland.

Having downed my third, or was it fourth, gin martini, I decided to have a little fun. I stood up and extended my hand, eyes fastened on the man. "Why, Sam Kaplan, I almost didn't know it was you, looking so dapper as Clark Gable, my favorite movie star," I purred. I then turned my attention to the Mrs. "And Clare, I finally get to meet you." I didn't bother with the formality of a handshake. "My, I admire you for going through the bother of dyeing your hair for just a li'l costume party. It almost looks natural."

The woman's round face turned color to match her husband's ripe tomato cheeks. She gave a little *hmph* sound under her breath as she tugged her husband's arm. "Dear, it's getting late, we must be going."

93

"Going? Why it's just after midnight." I leaned over and tapped Sam's arm. The one that wasn't hostage to his wife's grip. Even without shoes she towered over him. "Which reminds me, Sam, it's been much too long since you've been at the club." I waved my hand away dismissively, "we know you didn't mean all that fuss about us girls. You have a political career to worry about, after all." I learned in to whisper, but loud enough for the right effect. "I must say, though, we all sure miss you at the Roxy."

The band announced their final song and began playing, "Roll Out the Barrel." I pecked Sam's cheek. "Don't be a stranger now, ya hear?"

I spun toward Bill. "Come on, honey, I feel like dancing."

He didn't have a choice. The Kaplan's were gone in a flash and I was already sashaying to the beat so he'd look like a fool if he didn't join in.

"They should be playing the Doghouse Polka," I giggled in his ear as we took to the floor.

Bill wasn't amused. He went through the motions but his face was like an angry bulldog. As soon as the song ended, he took my arm forcefully. "Get your shoes, we're leaving."

"But the contest?"

He didn't respond, just kept pulling me toward the door. I wanted to fight him but that would not end well.

Once in the car, he let me have it. "What the fuck was that? How dare you embarrass me, in front of a city councilman yet. The only reason I took you was I got tired of us never going out, keepin' ya hidden like a, a mistress. I wanted us to be a real couple, you and me. Thought it'd be nice ... I'd never have taken you if I'd known you'd make a scene."

"A scene? That was hardly a *scene*. I was just putting them in their place. And I'm sure not gonna hide who I am for some hypocrites who have their heads up their ass. They almost got our place shut down, Bill. And he acts like he wasn't a regular customer—just to please that *holier-than-thou* wife of his."

I knew Clare had forced her husband's hand in "doing something" about the "immoral" Roxy. It ultimately went nowhere, but Blue Satin Doll had been named in an article about it, so no love was lost between us.

I sat with arms crossed the whole way home. Even the radio couldn't offset the tension. The awkward quiet forced me to reassess my behavior. As Bill pulled into my drive, I decided to make amends. "Okay, so maybe I overdid it a tad, but those people need to be taken down a notch or two."

He put the car in park but didn't shut it off. "It should not have been you."

"Why the hell not? I didn't see anyone else defending me. Then . . . or now." I leaned into him. "They hadn't tried to strip you of *your* job."

"Interesting choice of words, *Blue Satin Doll*." He wouldn't even look at me.

"Oh, go to hell, Bill."

I slammed the car door with brutal force and pounced up the steps.

15.

I laid in bed an hour after waking, my head throbbing, fighting an attack of the guilts. My brain was foggy, yet it failed to erase the night's events. I was glad Bill had taken me home when he did. Gladder still that he didn't stay over. Who knew how ugly things would've gotten if he had?

My bedside clock read ten-fifteen when I dragged myself out of bed. I had to tinkle and get some coffee and aspirin in me. I ambled downstairs in my PJs knowing Frank and Helen were already gone. I let Spencer out the back door to do his thing, and was grateful seeing that Helen had left the coffee pot on. *Bless these people.*

I made myself a piece of rye toast and grabbed the loose sections of the paper I knew Frank had already read. Tucking them under my arm, I trudged back upstairs with Spencer leading the way, and planned on staying in all day, until it was time for my Friday show.

In bed, I propped up my pillows and settled in. When I flipped open the front page, I sucked in a breath. The headline read, "Another Kingsbury Run Killing?" The article noted that a body of a female was found in a remote area where other victims had been found between 1935 and 1938. This one appeared to be that of a woman around seventeen or eighteen years of age.

Goosebumps prickled my skin. The last gruesome murder, the twelfth, had taken place nearly two years ago. In fact, they had a man in jail for it. Everyone thought it was over. Everyone except Eliot Ness. He thought they had the wrong man in jail. Could that be true? Was that evil killer still out there?

A Place We Belong

Ever since I had first read about the "torso murders," as they came to be called, I harbored an innate, and seemingly unnatural, fear. The same year the murders began was the same year Tess and I were separated. Could my sister have been one of those unidentified victims? The sensible part of my brain told me that chances were slim. Tess most likely had been adopted, just as I had been told. But the fanatical, distrusting part of my brain continued to question why anyone would adopt a teenager rather than a baby. Whenever I thought of that, it rattled me.

Even Eliot agreed the whole thing was odd, suggesting that maybe Tess hadn't been adopted at all. That perhaps she languished in an undesirable foster home. I knew there were people who took children in simply for the government handout. There were nights I couldn't sleep, as images of Tess being mistreated, even abused, played out in my head like a film reel. Still, if that were the case, I'd tell myself, my feisty sister would surely find a way to escape, like I had. But then what? Most runaway girls ended up on the streets for lack of means. Homeless, street people, or prostitutes.

Or victims of a madman . . .

My imagination ran overtime as I read about this latest victim. The familiar sense of dread and horrific fear pummeled my insides, shaking me to my core. Despite the unlikelihood, I couldn't stop it. In truth, Tess could be anywhere.

And so could the "Mad Butcher."

Fridays were not a good time to call Eliot—especially in light of this new development—but after a fitful night, I had to hear his reassuring voice.

I rushed to the phone and dialed his office. The second I heard his voice, all that I was feeling burst out of me. "Eliot, I'm so glad you answered. I just read the paper. I'm frightened. I never told you this but I've always had this awful fear about those murders. I get scared to death with worry that my sister could be a victim. I know it sounds crazy but—"

"Lydia, it's okay, I understand," he interrupted my rant. I was aware how anxious I must have sounded. "Please. Relax. It's not her."

"How do you know?"

"She's already been identified. It's the daughter of a local businessman," he said in a low voice. "They've just taken a man in, most likely a copycat killer. But please, Lydia, keep this under your belt, it hasn't been announced to reporters yet."

"Oh dear God." Heavy with relief, I sank into the chair. "I'm sorry I bothered you."

"I told you that you can call me anytime and I meant it. And since I have you on the phone, I do have some news related to your sister. It's not much so please don't get too hopeful, but the information is enough to keep moving forward."

I shot up. "Really? That's wonderful news." Despite his warning not to get my hopes up, it hopped on board.

"I'll try and stop by tonight. We can talk over a drink."

"Oh, yes, great, okay."

With renewed hope as my guide, I felt relaxed and confident about my next performance, knowing I remained on probation in George's eyes. I'd spent a small fortune on bigger, brighter colored fans to add to my collection. They not only caught folk's attention, but gave the element of surprise, enhancing the allure. Some nights I emerged on stage with brilliant yellow feathers, other times, bright red, pink, or purple. Tonight, my color was a dazzling emerald green.

Anxious to show off my new fans, I'd been disappointed by the sparse crowd. In the darkness, I couldn't see past the first tables, but could rate the crowd size based on the din in the room, the cheers and whistles. I suspected some were home, nursing hangovers, like I had earlier, from the

A Place We Belong

Halloween festivities. The bar was too far back to make out any of the customers there, either, so as soon as I got off stage, I changed clothes and headed straight to it.

As soon as I go there, Tony said, "I have a message for you. Your gentleman friend asked if you could wait an hour. He should be here by then."

We both knew who "he" was. I glanced at my watch. "Oh dear, it'll be closing time by then."

"No problem, Lydia, I've got nothing doin' tonight, I'll stay as long as you want me to."

"Oh, Tony, I must say, you are my favorite." I blew him a kiss ad took a seat at the end of the bar.

Although the club closed an hour after the last show, George often let a few special people stay after hours. And special meant the girls and their companions. This was our sanctuary. There was always a chance for trouble when one of us was recognized in other public bars in the heat of the night.

I only had to wait some twenty minutes before Eliot opened the side door. I grinned. The man had access to any side door he wanted.

"Your usual, sir?" Tony asked as Eliot slid onto the stool next to me and saw my glass. "No, I think I'd like a Jack 'n Coke too." His eyes met mine. "I thought you only drank that on Wednesday afternoons."

"I like to change it up. Besides, unlike martinis, I don't get too tipsy with just a couple of these." I winced, recalling the night before.

Eliot reached into his top pocket, pulled out a sleek black leather cigarette case, flipped it open and offered me one. Ever the gentleman, he lit mine first as Tony brought the drinks, immediately retreating to the far end of the bar to read a book. By now, the place was empty.

I waited patiently for Eliot to take a sip, then a drag from his smoke before I asked, "So tell me, what'd you find out?"

He placed his hand on my bare back—I was wearing a mauve Cashmere sweater that dipped low in the back—and spoke softly. "Murphy's Home, where you were sent when your mother died, shut down more than a year ago."

I held my breath. "And?"

He took another sip. "I'm looking into why."

"Oh." I leaned forward. "Wouldn't they have said why when it was announced? And what happened to the kids who were still there?"

"They claimed they had to close for financial reasons, but with the funding these places get, especially since the tail end of the Depression, doesn't make sense. Unless they were mismanaged, which certainly happens. I have to delve further, but it's what they did with the kids that's got my flags up. My source says most of them were taken to this other orphanage in Tennessee and I'm wondering why so far away. There are other places in Ohio, one right in the Cleveland area that take in children." He flicked his ash. "Outside of that, I did find there was no logical reason they should've separated you and your sister . . . the usual procedure in incidents like yours is that children suddenly orphaned generally go to a Home only until arrangements are made with other family members."

"That's just it. There are no relatives that I know of."

He nodded. "And in that case, those under eighteen would then be placed in someone else's home for fostering or adoption, as what happened with Tess." He blew out a puff of smoke that lingered above them in the dark air. "But seeing how you were almost eighteen, they could've kept you both there until then, when you could get a job and be Tess's legal guardian. That's what's rather suspicious about it."

"Oh, Eliot, I'm so scared. What if whatever happened to Tess is awful?"

He laid his hand on top of mine, which began to shake. "There's a good chance she was adopted by a wonderful family and has lived a happy life. Never give up thinking that." His focus shifted to the bar top. "But I must tell you that, on the other hand, the outcome might be upsetting. I want to warn you now." He sounded like he was talking from experience. "Just know that we're on this road together and whatever we find out, we'll find out together." He drew me close and gazed into my eyes. "Whatever it is, Lydia, you need—and deserve—to know the truth. I promise I'll keep nothing from you." He leaned away but kept his gaze on me. "That is, if you're truly ready for anything I may find."

My stomach tightened. "I might never be ready. But I don't have a choice. I have to know." I gulped down the last of my watered-down drink. "Hey, Tony, I think I'll have one of your perfect gin martinis."

I turned back to Eliot. "Let's change the subject, shall we?" I propped my chin up with folded hands and leaned into him. "Tell me more about your time with Capone, or something about when you were the prohibition agent for the Treasury Department. Bet you've enough stories to fill a book." I'd read everything I could about him and his escapades and was anxious to hear some directly from him.

"Water under the bridge." He squished out his cig, like he was killing an insect. I got the hint. "Tell me more about you. What were you like growing up?"

I laughed. "My, that entails a lot."

"Well, for starters, did you like to dance when you were little? You have a real talent, you know."

I tried to hide my surprise. Had he been watching me perform more often than I'd thought?

"Every little girl loves to dance, of course, but believe me, I never thought I was stage material. But a girl's gotta make a living." I took a long drag, blew out the smoke with a sigh. "I mean a girl like me." My eyes flashed toward the stage. "There's no knight-in-shining armor who's going to swoop me up and take me away from all this . . . and live happily ever after."

Eliot looked at me side eyed. "Something tells me that is not what you'd really want, anyway."

The shock of his statement threw me for a loop. "What makes you say that?"

"You're too vibrant. Being a stay-at-home housewife doesn't suit you. You'd get bored, restless. You'd need broader interests."

"Hmm . . . you do have a point." I shrugged. "Though I probably should get a more respectable job." I gave him a little smile.

He took my hand, rubbed my fingers with his thumb. "Lydia. You should never feel you have to defend your occupation. You're beautiful at what you do." For a second there, I thought he might kiss me.

"But you've only seen me a coupla times."

"You think I just started coming here since we met?" he said, a twinkle in his eyes. "I wasn't a regular, but every red-blooded man in the city knows of the captivating, enchanting Fan Dancer." He peered down at his glass. "Personally, I'm partial to the aqua feathers."

I covered my giggle with my hand seeing his boyish expression. "Well, now, I'll have to remember that." I licked my lips, savoring the sweet taste of gin. The martini was making my head swirl. Or maybe it was something else.

He threw his head back and laughed so loud, it echoed in the empty room. And his right hand remained in mine. I squeezed it. "Could it possibly be that we met just over three months ago?" I didn't wait for him to answer. "Sometimes I feel like we've always known each other. I'm so comfortable, feel so safe with you." I felt my eyes get misty. "I'm so glad we've become friends."

It was hard to tell in the dim lighting, but I thought he looked a little sentimental too. He lifted my hand and kissed it, making me shudder. Then he lifted his glass. "A toast. To us. To our growing friendship and the upcoming journey we have started on."

We clinked glasses, and with that, we downed our drinks and called it a night. The clock on the bar wall read a quarter to two.

16.

*K*itty and Gary had been going hot and heavy for six months so he became a front-and-center regular for Queen Butterfly's show and often stayed for Blue Satin Doll's act as well. I didn't mind. He and his cronies were always enthusiastic and I enjoyed playing it up a bit more for them.

All of us girls had to work the night before Thanksgiving. Most married fellows were noticeably absent since their wives demanded their husbands be home to prepare for the big family gathering. We girls called this, "Bachelor Night," and made sure to make it special. At the finale, we'd come out on stage together for a dance, complete with high headpieces, wearing just our tassels and bikinis. A real crowd pleaser.

But sometimes, these single boys went too far in their appreciation. Like the time an excited young man jumped on stage and kissed Violet Blaze, a nervous young girl just starting out, before Big Joe lifted him up and out the door. Violet quit soon after.

Tonight, it was all Gary's fault. He came in with four other men, dressed like the gangsters they were. They claimed their usual table, but as I observed on the sidelines, they had pushed the table up so close, they were practically on stage themselves.

As usual, I came on after Kitty, so Gary and his thugs were already half in the bag. My act this night involved me shimmying to the edge of the stage to do a little peekaboo from behind my massive rainbow feather fans. I'd give the men a quick flash of my "naked" physique that was actually clad in a nude body stocking. This caused the men to whoop it up more.

A Place We Belong

I was almost done so I ignored the man who threw his tie onto the stage and yelled, "Put that around your hot tits, baby."

I just kept going, concentrating on my dips, twirls and turns. I had dramatically tossed my rhinestone bra to the side but my breasts were hidden by vibrant feathers. While I focused on wrapping up my act—a deaf ear to the catcalls—I ventured too far forward and as I approached the front, one of the men bent over and grabbed my ankle. I tried jerking it away, but he had a good hold and lifted my leg up so high, my silver high-heel pump went flying. And so did I. I swooped to the floor, and as I tried to break my fall, I let go of my fans. I pulled myself up in the most ladylike manner possible as the crowd jumped to its feet yelling obscenities and tossing chairs through the air.

"Let's go." Big Joe ordered, helping me up. "Off stage now!"

Grabbing my fan, I spotted Bill by the gangster's table. He had the man who attacked me in a head lock. He was punching his face. I did as I was told and hightailed it to the stage exit. In my haste, I smacked straight into Kitty in the hallway. "Oh my God, it's crazy out there."

"Hon, it's time to skedaddle."

We raced to the dressing room where I threw on street clothes fast as I could, grabbed my bag and fur coat, and together we rushed out the back door. I didn't have time to tell Kitty just what I thought about her boyfriend just then.

We headed down to Otto Moser's, hopefully, for some peace and quiet. "Sorry, ladies, we're closing," the man at the door told us. I looked at my watch. It was just after eleven. "You guys stay open till one." He gave me a quizzical look. "Lady, don'cha know it's a holiday tomorrow? You gals should be home baking bread or somethin'."

"We're showgirls, fella, not homemakers." I pivoted, took Kitty by the arm and we headed toward the Theatrical. That place was sure to be open.

On the way, Kitty laughed, "And here, we were gonna be good girls and not drink tonight. Guess we're not meant for sobriety and a clean domestic life."

"Oh, hell with that. I've got nothing going on tomorrow 'cept dinner with Frank and Helen late afternoon." I swung the door open, and the sound of merriment hit us both in the face. The place was packed. I bobbed my head toward the bar. "Let's get sloshed."

"I see an empty booth." Kitty yelled over the chattering and the sound of Tommy Dorsey's *Boogie Woogie* on the jukebox. "I'll go grab it."

I ambled up to get my order when a voice creeped up my neck. "Well, if it isn't the one and only Blue Satin Dollface." I swiveled to see a short chunky man. I eyed him up and down. "Sorry, I don't know you."

"Well, everyone knows you, doll face, can I buy ya a drink?"

"No, I can afford my own, thank you." If he called me "doll face" one more time, I was going to let him have it.

I turned back, pulled out a five-dollar bill from my purse and waved it in the air to get the barkeep's attention. Of all nights for me not to remember his name. But money worked better, and the man was there in a flash. "Two gin highballs, please." It was no night to weave martinis through this crowd.

When the bartender returned with the drinks, another voice spoke from behind. "I'll get that."

I knew the voice before I even turned around. I was surprised that I was actually glad to see him. We'd both had enough time apart to cool off since the Kaplan episode. "Thanks, Bill. How ya been?"

A Place We Belong

He grabbed the drinks and followed me to the booth, where I plopped next to Kitty. Sitting across from him, I noticed Bill's puffed cheeks and swollen red eye. "So, what's the other guy look like?"

He screwed up his injured face. "He would've looked a lot worse if my buddy hadn't broke it up and hauled his ass to jail." He took my hand and squeezed it. "Had to defend my girl." He turned his head and looked dead on at Kitty. "What the hell you doin' with a guy like that?"

"Bill's got a point," I piped in. "I don't like him or his crowd."

"Huh." She glared at me. "You sure liked him all these months they were giving our place such great business."

"It's a good thing we were there tonight," Bill interrupted my opportunity to say more. "We've been tailing them for awhile 'cause we know those crooks are up to no good. Some nasty rumors going 'round about their activities. I'd steer clear of him if I were you."

Kitty shot up from her seat. "You're not me." She chugged down her drink, then slammed down her glass. "And you're one to talk, Bill Baker. Rumors been goin' around about *you* for months. Only, they're not rumors."

I watched her disappear out the door, wondering now if Bill was still up to his dirty tricks. But I wasn't in the mood to get into it. I'd had enough drama for one night. And the thought of taking the streetcar home alone on Thanksgiving Eve depressed the hell out of me. When we finished our drinks, I asked, "Will you take me home, Bill?"

"Sure thing, Doll."

"Bill?" I said as we walked out into the frigid air. "Don't call me Doll."

"But I always—"

The drunken man's "Doll Face" rang in my ears. "Not anymore."

107

*B*ill woke me up with a hand rubbing along the curve of my body. "Morning, baby," he whispered. "Say, how 'bout you making us a nice Thanksgiving dinner, just the two of us?"

I stretched out and stared at his face. I did always like those deep-set eyes. "I think I'd like that."

I had bought a small turkey for me and Spencer but lacked some fixings for a traditional Thanksgiving dinner. I put on my robe and crept downstairs, dreading to change plans with my landlords and then, have the gall to borrow ingredients.

"Happy Thanksgiving." I gave them each a hug. "I hope you don't mind, but Bill and I were talking, and we haven't made a dinner at home together since, oh, I don't know, last winter?"

"This isn't his home."

"Helen, that's not like you." I regretted telling Helen about Bill, but we were broke up at the time. And that was then and this was now.

Helen didn't respond, just got busy putting my requested items in a shopping bag.

"Thank you." I gave her another tight squeeze. "I'll make it up to you, I promise. I'll make you and Frank my special apple pie I know you love." On that high note, I headed up the stairs.

As I prepared the turkey and placed it in the oven, Bill helped with the side dishes. We whiled away the hours by playing cards until it was time to check the bird. I was mashing potatoes in a bowl when the phone rang. Wiping my hands on my apron, I grabbed it.

"Lydia, it's Eliot," he said soon as I answered.

I could feel my face heat up and turned away from the kitchen doorway. "Yes?" I tried sounding aloof as I tugged the phone cord further around the corner while thinking what I would tell Bill when I hung up.

"Pardon me for calling. I know it's a holiday and all, and I do hope I'm not interrupting anything, but I have some more information for you and tomorrow's the only day I'll have available through the next week." He stopped. "Can we meet somewhere before you go to work?"

"Ah, sure. Of course." I felt a presence hovering over me, then Bill's hot breath on my neck.

"How 'bout a late lunch at Sullivan's? Say two o'clock?"

It was perfect. I hadn't been there since we'd spent that nice evening there last summer. I could spend the afternoon with him before getting to The Roxy by five. "That'll be fine. Thank you for calling."

As I replaced the receiver, Bill turned around to face me. "That was a man's voice."

"It was just a friend, Bill. I'm allowed to have friends."

His face was now redder than my own. "Not if it's our fair city director."

I walked past him. I wanted to say it was none of his business but bit my tongue. "I have to check on dinner."

He snatched my wrist. "No. Tell me what's going on with you two."

Just then a lightbulb went off. Bill had only seen Eliot at my place just that once, months ago. What did he know, or think he knew?

I jerked my hand away. "Have you been spying on me, Bill?"

"Don't have to. I have friends."

I couldn't believe it. He actually had people following me?

"Look, he's helping me with something that means a lot to me. It's business." I didn't dare tell him that I sought

Eliot's help about Tess after he himself had abandoned it. "I'm not ready to talk about it. With you or anyone else." I rushed back to the kitchen, hoping that would end this conversation. How foolish I was.

"Oh, so now you and Mr. Ness have a *secret?*"

I returned to my potatoes, not wanting to fight. But then he said, "I noticed your boy scout wasn't anywhere to be found last night when you needed him. But I was. Then again, he does have a wife to tend to."

My whole body throbbed with rage. How *dare* him. I scooped my hand into the steaming mashed potatoes and flung the gob right into his face. "Get the fuck outta my house."

He raised his hand to strike me, but must've thought better of it. He grabbed the kitchen tea towel, wiped his face. "This isn't over . . . *Doll*," he spat out before slamming the door so hard the whole house shook.

17.

*N*ot one to waste good food, I shoveled my plate like a starving child until my stomach was bloated and sore. I was so enraged I hadn't even felt my burned hand until I took Spencer for a walk and the leash jabbed into my palm. Once back inside, I wrapped it with a cool rag, but it failed to cool my head.

All night a dozen scenes flashed through my mind like a bad, disjointed play. Mental images flitted from Bill to Eliot to my now uneasy friendship with Kitty. Then, to the past. Of Tess, my mother, my father. . .

It had been a long time since I allowed myself to think of my father, but there it was, haunting me. I had purposely, maybe subconsciously, erased him from my mind but now I speculated on what, exactly, had caused him to leave. Dad worked second-shift at General Electric Plant, and although he often stopped at a bar afterward, he always came home. Always there in the morning, always attentive to his wife and daughters.

Until he wasn't.

I recalled the argument as if it were yesterday. Tess was eleven, I'd just turned fifteen. Cracklings of thunderstorms had kept us up, so we sat crossed-legged on the bedroom floor playing Jacks, then Marbles, way past our bedtime. Even if we'd been asleep, the slamming of the backscreen door from the gusty wind would've announced Father's arrival. And with it, our parent's escalating voices. Tess and I crept down the steps and huddled under the stairwell, as we often did when we knew some drama was about to take place. It was the only way to get information since our folks believed in the mantra "children should be seen and not heard."

"What'd you do with that money?" Mother's shrill tone hurt our ears.

"You know we can't trust the banks, it's in a safe place. I got it handled. Not your concern."

The slight slur in his speech made it clear that Dad had been hitting the sauce, as Mama would say. This was not surprising. The Great Depression had caused many fathers to sedate themselves with drink.

"*Not my concern?*" Mother hissed, perhaps aware their anger was as loud and forceful as the howling wind.

"I'm done with this conversation."

"No. Tell me! We need that money *now*."

That's when we heard the slap. We looked at each other with wide eyes. I grabbed Tess's hand and we scrambled up to our room.

"Get in bed," I whispered, pulling a blanket over her. "Stay here. Don't move an inch. I'll be back."

I had to know if Mother was alright. I snuck back downstairs, but my mother met me halfway there. "What're you doin' up, Lydia?" Even in the darkened stairway, I could tell she'd been crying.

"I, uh, was comforting Tess . . . the storm scared her."

Mother turned me around by my shoulders. "Get back up there. Everything's okay, just go to sleep now, ya hear?"

I did as told, and not hearing any more sounds in the house, I eventually fell asleep.

Two days later, Mother announced she had gotten a job at the bakery. The day after that, our telephone no longer worked. The day after that, our father disappeared.

At first, we all thought Dad would see the error in his ways and return. When Mother had gotten the bakery job, I figured she'd been determined to show her husband that we didn't need him. Soon enough, it became clear that he didn't need us.

I barely slept. As light streamed through my lace curtains, a wet nose greeted me. Spencer's bladder always dictated my morning schedule. I pushed him away. "Leave me alone, lie down," I yelled. I knew I was cranky but how would I function all day and into the night if I didn't get back to sleep?

My dog's head plopped down on the edge of the bed, his sad eyes staring up at me. *Ah, hell.* I pulled myself up and Spencer sprang off the bed. I shuffled to the bathroom, my pet at my heels, and gasped when I caught myself in the mirror.

I looked a total rag. *Dear Lord, I should really cancel my meeting with Eliot.*

No. I couldn't. He'd said he had information for me, and nothing was going to keep me from hearing it. My stomach still ached and my frayed nerves didn't make it better, but there was one thing that was sure to make me feel, and look, better.

At precisely nine o'clock, I dialed Betty's Beauty Salon, crossing my fingers they had a last-minute appointment. Luck was on my side when Betty said they could fit me in at noon. I nearly jumped for joy. A shampoo-and-set and updo took just over an hour. I could hop on the streetcar and make it to Sullivan's right on time, if not early.

I entered the tavern at ten minutes to two, wearing a dark blue swing dress with sweetheart neckline and flutter sleeves, pearl clip-on earrings, and silver T-strap kitten heels. And because it was darn cold, I was wrapped in my muskrat coat. I might have been a bit overdressed for an afternoon in the Irish pub, but better to be overdressed than understated.

There were only a few customers left from the lunch crowd, but all eyes turned when I stepped into the place. I hadn't really meant to draw such attention, I simply was trying to feel better after my sleepless night. At least that's what I told myself.

I spotted Eliot, waving me over to the same table we'd shared months before. Funny how I no longer felt tired anymore.

He greeted me with a quick peck on the cheek.

"Eliot, you saved our table," I winked before sitting across from him.

"Of course. Pays to have connections," he winked back. *Oh, why do you have to be so darn charming?*

"Would you like a bite to eat?"

"Oh, yes. I'm famished." I not only was no longer tired, my appetite had returned as well.

We ate turkey sandwiches and sipped on Cokes talking at first about topics like the weather, and the exciting news that Judy Garland was playing at the Theatrical during the Christmas holidays. He mentioned that his brother, Charles, was coming for a visit and he and Evaline were hosting a party Saturday night. I liked that he talked of his family to me but I also knew there'd be no invitation for me to attend the grand festivities on the famous houseboat on the lake.

A moment later, Eliot surprised me by mentioning the elephant in the room. "I want to apologize for calling you at your home yesterday."

I looked up from my food.

"I could tell I was interrupting something, I could hear it in your voice. I hope my calling didn't cause you any trouble."

I pushed my plate away. "Bill's an asshole."

"Oh." He lit a smoke. He was finished eating too. "I wasn't aware you were still seeing him." Yet his face, and tone in his voice, sounded like he was very aware.

My face grew hot. I should not even be talking to Eliot about my complicated romantic life.

He must've read my thoughts. "I'm sorry, what you do in your personal life is not any of my business."

I weighed that sentence. It may have been technically true, but it didn't feel true. There was something about this man that made me want to tell him everything. Every thought, every emotion, every problem.

The place had emptied out, so I didn't have to worry about nosy eyes or ears. "Eliot? Do you know about Bill's uh, dealings?"

In the back of my mind I worried I shouldn't speak of it. It could cause problems for Bill, and even though I was mad at him I still cared about him.

He averted my gaze. "I can't talk about what I know."

"Then you do know." I nodded. "When I first learned of it, I was furious. But in time, well, I gave him a pass because he has an invalid sister he cares for. So there's expenses—doctor bills, prescription pills, nursing care . . . he's got a lot to deal with."

Why was I defending him? I sat forward. "It's wrong, I know that. But I honestly thought it was only when he was in a pinch. When I confronted him about it months ago, he told me he was back on the straight and narrow. And I believed him." I straightened my posture. "I don't anymore."

Eliot leaned in as well. "Lydia, once someone starts dealing with those men, there is no stepping back. He's—" He scrunched his face. "Never mind. Again, I can't talk of it. It'd be unethical."

"Yes, of course. I understand. We're good friends but I would never want you to step over the line."

He glanced down at his watch. "I don't have a lot of time and I do want to tell you what I've learned so far."

In other words, no more Bill talk. Fine with me.

He pointed to my soda. "Ready for something stronger in that?"

"Thought you'd never ask." I grinned and pushed my glass forward. I didn't know what to expect, but a good shot could only help.

He got up to get two Jack 'n Cokes, then sat and waited till I took a few sips before he began. Then he leaned down and picked up a folder from the floor. "I've been looking into that place in Memphis. The owner of Murphy's Home, where you and your sister were, was apparently friends with the woman who runs The Tennessee Children's Home Society." The name meant nothing to me.

He opened the folder that looked like it held some twenty pages. "Seems there's been a surprising amount of children taken to Memphis to live until they got adopted. Though some have been there for a while."

"Does that involve older kids, like Tess?"

"The oldest I've been able to find out about was eleven. That girl came from Murphy's and was soon adopted by a wealthy couple. I've heard some folks actually prefer older children because babies and toddlers are a lot more work. So there is hope that Tess was given to a couple such as that."

I pursed my lips. Eleven, okay, but a girl practically fourteen? "Eliot, I've given this much thought. Even went to the libraries to find out more—though there was little to go on, that's for sure. I can believe a kind couple wanting to help out and foster a child, but adopt them so soon? Without even knowing the child?" I sighed. "Seems doubtful."

He bowed his head. "I know and yes, it is difficult to research. I've discovered these places aren't good at keeping records. I suspect they discard the paperwork once the child is fostered or adopted."

He showed me the papers with names, dates, and official looking stamps.

"How'd you get these?"

"I have a friend who works for the FBI in Chicago. These are copies." He threw me a half grin. "Don't worry, they're all legal documents. Public domain."

"I believe you, but . . ." I stared at the papers. "What does it all mean?"

"That's the million-dollar question. I've heard some so-called Homes are heavy into the baby selling business, making alarming amounts of money in these dealings."

"*What?*"

"Oh, most of them are legal. But whenever big money's involved, you often find some rats under the surface. Greed occurs in every walk of life, Lydia, and while I admit finding these children a home with family is often better than growing up in these places, there doesn't seem to be much background checking on the people involved. And no follow-up on the children's welfare once they leave the premises. Worst yet, there's no real criteria needed to take in a child, except having the money to fork over." He paused before adding, "The amount of funds taken can be quite exorbitant. People are basically profiting from orphan children's misfortunes."

I shut my eyes. "I can't imagine anyone doing such a thing."

"Terrible thought, isn't it?" He gazed into his drink. "I've always wanted children myself so I have a soft spot in that regard."

My eyes shot open. "Can I ask . . . why then, you don't have kids? You would make a wonderful father."

"My first wife and I really tried," he said to his glass. "She wanted a baby even more than I did. Guess it wasn't to be. Probably a good thing since the marriage didn't last."

Before I brought up the next obvious question, he answered it for me. "Evaline's not that interested in having children." He suddenly looked sad. "She likes working outside the home. She likes our lifestyle as it is."

Which meant, I knew, being popular with the city's movers-and-shakers, and hosting fancy parties. I thought back to the woman's conversation with Dottie that day in the bookstore. Evaline never said she wanted kids, just that she wanted to write books for her "various charity functions."

My heart ached for Eliot, but I was touched that he'd confided in me something so personal. He was opening up to me more and more, which meant he trusted me, which meant everything.

He smacked the folder closed. "Back to the matter at hand. I'm not saying all those agencies are not on the up-and-up, but Murphy's and this Memphis institute seems questionable. My Chicago friend, Howard, has his suspicions too. His college-age son is friends with a boy who spent over a year at the Tennessee facility. I talked to him on the telephone the other day. Bobby was seven at the time and recalls at least three children he knew who were there one day, gone the next. He said he'd look for them at breakfast, then lunch, but never saw them again. When he asked about them, he was simply told that they were gone, or been adopted, or moved to a new boarding home. He hadn't given it much thought at the time, accepting that adults don't tell kids anything anyway. He didn't question it further and, of course, life went on . . .

"So they must make the exchanges late at night, and you have to wonder, why not in the daytime? Why awaken a child to take their leave in the dark of the night?"

I opened my mouth to speak but he quickly added. "Another thing I found is the Memphis woman is politically connected, and then some. Her father's a judge, with a rather shady reputation. That doesn't prove unscrupulous behavior, but I've seen a lot of dirty dealings in my time. Enough to get a sense about such things. They say where there's smoke, there's fire, and I say, where there's a chance for easy money, there's crooks."

I finished my drink, feeling defeated. Did this really have anything to do with Tess? He said himself the oldest child there was younger than my sister, so it made little sense that anyone would take her in, especially since she had an older sister who would soon be considered an adult.

When I voiced these thoughts out loud, Eliot shrugged, "Perhaps that little fact wasn't mentioned to the higher-ups. Even if Tess told them, it may not have made a difference if they thought they could place her somewhere." He stopped, catching her grimace. "I'm sorry, but when it comes to people like that, money is the end game."

He took my hand and squeezed it. "Or maybe there was a caring couple who had hearts of gold and wanted to help a young girl with no parents."

Tears made their way down my cheek. "Are there really good people like that in this world, Eliot?"

"Without a doubt. I've seen it with my own eyes." His smile felt like salve on a wound. "Please don't worry. Whatever it takes, my dear girl, we'll get to the bottom of it." He leaned over and kissed the hand he held. "We'll find her, Lydia, I promise."

As much as I wanted to believe him, I knew even the great Eliot Ness was only human.

18.

I went through the weekend in a daze, absorbing what Eliot had told me. I was convinced now that there really was something underhanded about Tess's departure—which made me heartsick, and angry at myself.

How could I have let all this time go on without fighting harder for answers? Done more to find her? Why had I eventually given up?

Then I remembered why.

During that first year we were separated, I *had* tried. I asked anyone I thought might have a clue as to what could've happened to my sister. Where could those people have taken her? It surely didn't help that I had no photos of her so I hand-drew her image, best I could, complete with colored pencils for hair and eye color, and showed it to people I met in the neighborhood shops, at Dottie's bookstore, the meat market . . . to anyone I felt might know something or give me some direction on how to proceed with my plight. No luck.

I'd gone to the police station and filed a missing person's report. Once a week, I'd call them for possible updates and the responses went from a nice "sorry," to a curt "no," to an aggravated "Lady, we'll call you if we find out anything." One nice copper took the time to hear me out, then said that if Tess was moved to another orphanage, that was a typical procedure and so, she wasn't considered missing. That news alone should've shattered all my hope. But hope is a stubborn lover.

I'd been working at the Roxy for several months when I met a security guard who I thought could help me and told him of my desperate search. The man, while feigning

A Place We Belong

sympathy, told me the police had a lot of business on their plates. It was 1935, after all, Cleveland was the sixth largest city in the country—and the most dangerous. There was organized crime, a rampant amount of thefts, and, most notoriously, the discovery of what turned out to be the first of those torso murders. The department was overwhelmed, he'd said. It was then that I first heard the name, Eliot Ness, who was brought in to clean up the town.

Soon, I resigned myself that if the police couldn't help me, no one could. But then I met Bill and confided in him, thinking he could surely help. When he told me there was nothing to be done, I forced myself to give up. Tess was gone and no one else cared. Over time, I grew numb to it, like the ghost of a missing limb. There, but essentially gone.

But the more I read about Eliot, the more hope wormed its way back in. Why not ask him for help and see what happens? And now I had the famous G-man on my case. He had made it his own personal mission to help me. How could I not love him for that?

Of course, that itself was becoming a problem. The more we were together, the more it became obvious there was more going on between us. Every touch we shared sent chills through me, with an ache that was physically painful. A hot spark we couldn't deny—but had to. When he'd kissed my hand that night, it took all the discipline I could muster not to turn that motion into a passionate kiss on the lips. But I'd kept my wits about me. An affair was the last thing either of us needed. No matter how appealing the very thought of that was, I had to keep my feelings in check.

I knew he was fighting the same battle. He showed it by the lingering way he often looked at me. And yet, to cross that line would mean to risk what we had now. This cherished friendship. I only hoped we'd be able to keep that bubbling passion from bursting to the surface like a volcano.

121

After my Wednesday Theatrical show, I ran into Cliff, who always tried to buy me drinks or offer to take me to the movies. I'd repeatedly told him that I didn't date customers. But I hadn't seen him in a while and, as we struck up a conversation, he again asked me to have a drink with him. This time I accepted. Why not stay for a cocktail with a nice-looking man? I wasn't bound to anyone and had nowhere else to be.

I stayed for dinner and had one too many, so Cliff drove me home so I wouldn't have to take public transportation. Thankfully, he didn't argue when I said good night on the porch and gave him a quick peck on the cheek. I rushed upstairs knowing it was long past time to take Spencer out. The poor thing's bladder would be ready to burst.

Feeling tipsy, I fumbled in my pocketbook for my key, but the second I gripped the knob, I knew the door wasn't locked. Had I forgotten to lock it? I was always so careful about that.

Then I noticed the split wooden door frame. My skin prickled. I swung the door open, afraid to go in. I called out to Spencer but he did not greet me as usual.

"Spencer baby, where are you?" My fear for him outweighed my fear of all else. I dashed to the bedroom.

My top dresser drawers had been rummaged through and my mattress was cockeyed, as if the culprits thought maybe I had money or something hidden underneath it. My focus shifted when I heard Spencer's whimpering. He was curled up in the corner, obviously frightened. I scooped him up and felt him shaking. "Oh, my poor baby." Whatever had happened, it most likely had occurred fairly recently. I needed to scat. Protective arms around my dog, I ran out the door and down the stairs.

"Frank. Helen," I called out, banging on their door.

A Place We Belong

I pounded incessantly until reason told me they couldn't possibly be home. I was scared to go back upstairs but logic told me no one would still be there. Burglars, if that's who it was, did not remain on the premises once they got what they wanted. Or hadn't found it.

Spencer jumped out of my arms and ran to the back door, reminding me why I was anxious to go home in the first place. I flicked on the back light, and as I grabbed the knob to turn it, I noticed that too was left unlocked. So that's how the bastards made their getaway. Spencer ran outside before I could grab him, and I panicked, praying no one was hiding behind the tree Spencer decided to use. "Hurry up, baby," I yelled, trying not to sound as frightened as I felt. One thing I knew was that you should never appear vulnerable among criminals.

Like the good dog he was, he ran back to my side as soon as he was done and I scooped him up, locking the door behind me.

Back upstairs, my dog safe in my arms, I ran to the kitchen and grabbed my sharpest knife, just in case, then checked all the closets and underneath my bed. I saw no one, and found nothing missing. My hidden hundred dollar bill for emergencies still in its envelope, tucked under wool skirts in my bottom drawer. They'd been through the top drawers, so they must have left quickly before going through the rest. Perhaps they heard my footsteps on the front porch and skedaddled out the back. My head filled with different scenarios.

This didn't feel like a burglary. After all, what could they possibly want from my upstairs apartment that they knew they wouldn't find by breaking into the first floor, clearly the easier of the two?

Whoever had been in my apartment wanted something they thought I had. Or did they just want to scare me? But why? And who would *they* be, anyway?

I locked the door, including the chain that Bill, interestingly enough, had suggested I get a year ago. He had used it as another dig to my profession. "With what you do for a living, Lyd, men can get a little crazy and follow you home."

Still a bit shaky, I opened my top kitchen cabinet and pulled out a bottle of Jack Daniels Old No. 7, filled a glass of ice, poured it half full to calm my nerves. I wanted to turn on the radio but wanted to keep an ear open for strange noises. The more I sat and thought about it, the more I felt violated. I needed to know who had done this, and why. Another good swig and I figured it out.

Eliot's words came to me like a vision. "Once someone starts dealing with those men, there is no stepping back." He'd said it in relation to Bill's involvement with the mobsters that ruled Cleveland.

Bill.

He had just been here last week. After the night he'd gotten into a fight with them, sticking up for me. He had hurt one of their men. Despite his being in cahoots with them, he was still a cop. The enemy. Didn't Bill realize he couldn't play both sides?

I needed to talk to Eliot. I wouldn't be able to sleep until I did.

I threw back the rest of the whisky and grabbed the big city phone book, praying he was listed.

My finger ran through the list of names. N...N-a...N-e—s! There it was. Ness, E. I staggered a bit on my way to the phone, sat on my bed and fought to keep my fingers steady as I dialed. *Please, answer. Please be home.*

The woman's voice jolted me. *This is wrong. Hang up!* But I didn't. I wouldn't let rational thoughts disrupt my mad quest.

"Oh. Evaline. It's Lydia Swanson, I need to speak to Eliot. It's an emergency." It was when my words hit the air that I wondered if his wife would have even remembered meeting me.

I heard a muffled exchange before Eliot got on the line. "Lydia, what is it?"

"Oh, Eliot. My place just got broken into. I don't know what to do, how I'll be able to sleep. I think I need some protection."

"Did you call the police?"

I shook my head. "No, Bill will get involved, and I'm afraid he's why the men broke in. He roughed up one of them last week. You know, the night before Thanksgiving." I hated to even bring that up. "I was . . . hoping you could come over just to check out everything here." I wanted to add that I was genuinely scared, but I didn't want to admit it.

"Is anything missing?"

"Not that I see, but my bedroom's a mess. They were obviously looking for something. Or maybe just wanted to scare me . . . And they did." No sense in denying it.

His voice lowered to a whisper. "I'm afraid I can't come. It's just not possible. I'm sorry. Isn't there someone else you could call?"

My heart sank. Kitty would be off with Gary. My landlord's car had not come down the drive. I was completely alone. I hated feeling so vulnerable. It wasn't like me.

"No, there isn't."

There was a pause at the end of the line. *He's considering. He'll come, he won't let me down.* "Eliot?"

125

"I'm truly sorry, Lydia. Maybe I can send someone over?" I felt his frustrated sigh more than heard it. "I might have a friend who can help—"

I sank on my bed. "No, no. Don't do that." Now I felt foolish. And the thought of another stranger in my house unnerved me.

The bedroom clock showed half past eight. My head was clearing of its fogginess and my wits slowly returned. Did I really expect Eliot to leave his wife and run to me? Sure, he'd told me I could call him anytime. But at his office. He never meant his home. His *married* home. I had crossed the line. *Oh, God, what have I done?*

I spoke as calmly as I could. "I'm sorry, Eliot. I shouldn't have called." I flinched with embarrassment. "I'm just so beside myself, and alone. My landlords aren't home and well, I'm sorry," I repeated. "I've no right to call your house. It's just that, we're so close and I need you so badly right now." I choked back tears. "But I understand. I'll just wait till Frank and Helen get home."

"I'll call you first thing tomorrow."

I took in a deep, accepting, breath. "Okay. I won't do it again, I promise."

It was then that I heard a distinct click on the line and thought he'd hung up, but then, as an afterthought he asked, "Did you try Kitty?"

"No. I guess it's worth a try."

"Good night, Lydia."

"G'night. And thank—"

He hung up before I finished.

I set the receiver down and flopped against my pillow, exhausted and full of despair, on several levels. Spencer jumped on my chest and licked my face. At least I had someone who understood how I felt. Who loved me. I let the tears flow now. After awhile, I sat back up, gathered the energy to try

A Place We Belong

Kitty. Despite our differences about Gary, she was still my best friend.

She answered on the second ring. I immediately told her what happened, and before I had a chance to ask, she said, "I'll be right over."

For the next two hours, we sat at my small kitchen table and while I made myself some coffee, Kitty polished off the Jack Daniels. I soon confessed about the shameful thing I'd done by calling Eliot's home.

"I can't believe I did that."

"Oh, hon, it's completely understandable. Don't be so hard on yourself."

That did make me feel a tinge better. She knew me so well. "I guess I wasn't thinking straight." And there was something else that was bothering me. "But you know somethin', Kit?"

"What?"

"I'm wondering . . . do well-to-do people have more than one phone in their house?"

"I imagine they do. Why?"

"I heard this click when I was talking to Eliot, towards the end of our conversation. Like when someone hangs up before you? That clicking sound? But he hadn't hung up, he asked me about calling you. Then he said goodnight and I heard it again. That time he had hung up." I reached across the table for one of her smokes since I'd smoked the last of mine after that dreaded call to him. "Do you suppose it's possible, given the fact they probably have two phones in different rooms, that Evaline might have been listening on the other line?"

Kitty gave me a smirk. "Hon, I think you can bet your sweet ass on it." She placed her cigarette in the ashtray, leaned forward, fists on her thighs. "If I was a wife, that's the first thing I'd do if another woman called my husband." She saw

127

the stricken look on my face and sat back with a sigh. "Aw, Lyddy, I'm sorry. That came out way harsher than I meant."

"No, you're right. I shouldn't have done that. I was half-drunk, and you saw my bedroom. I was kinda in shock. But I know, that's no excuse. Oh, Kitty, I've made such a mess of things."

Just then, I heard Frank and Helen's car pull up the drive and we rushed downstairs to tell them what happened. When Kitty decided to go home, I was relieved when they offered me and Spencer their sofa bed. I wasn't ready to be alone.

I woke up still feeling uneasy, but grateful I had Kitty, Frank and Mary in my life. Until I found Tess, they were the only family I had.

But now, I greatly feared that my terrible actions last night may have caused me Eliot's friendship—and any hope of finding my sister.

A Place We Belong

19.

*"H*ere, have a shot of this." Kitty held up two short glasses, sticking one of them in front of my nose. We were in the dressing room getting ready for our Saturday night show. I took a whiff, glanced at the bottle's label on Kitty's vanity.
"Macallan Scotch?"
"Macallan *Twelve*."
"Holey, Moley, Kit, this stuff's expensive."
"You betcha," Kitty tapped the glasses. "Cheers."
Scotch wasn't my favorite, but I downed it for the sake of camaraderie. I surprised myself by not wincing as the warm liquid flowed down my pipes. "Where'd you get it?" I croaked.
"Where you think? Gary. We're goin' to the Terrace Club to see Dino Martini tonight."
"Who?"
"You know, that real looker who sings in the Sammy Watkins Orchestra."
I nodded, recalling an article I'd read on the singer. He was a local boy named Dino Crocetti, but called himself, Dino Martini. I loved the fun moniker.
Kitty gave me a big hug and whispered in my ear. "Come on out with us, okay? Gary has a real good-lookin' fella I just know you'd like."
It was the third time Kitty had asked me to go out since my place was ransacked, and I was still hurting over my stupid behavior with Eliot. Although he had, indeed, followed through on his promise to call the next day, it had been a strained conversation. It ended with him saying that he and his team had gotten word on something going down real soon and it would take up all his time over the next few weeks.

In other words, don't expect to hear from him.

And I hadn't.

But I had heard from Bill, who called wondering how I was.

"I'll tell you how I am," I spat, proceeding to give him the details of the break-in.

"Lydia, why didn't you call me?"

"Because we are not together, and I'm convinced whoever was digging around my things had something to do with you. Nothing turned up missing so I think they just wanted to scare me after your little tussle with them. I think they followed you that night to my place so they'd know where I live."

He grew quiet. Then, "Well, after that Halloween party, it's well known that you and me are an item." I heard the heavy sigh through the phone lines. "I know I need to break off my association with them so I told them I wouldn't be giving them any more tip-offs. They're not happy."

"Well, what'd you expect?" You know there's no breaking away from those thugs," I said, mimicking Eliot.

After his profound apology, I let it be known I wanted nothing to do with him either. Ever again.

And now I was ready for some fun. Kitty assured me this guy, this blind date, was not a gangster but an old friend of Gary's sister, who hated her brother's lifestyle and so, the man was surely "clean."

Right now, anything sounded better than spending another Saturday night alone. "Okay, okay, what the hell." I smiled at my excitable friend.

"That's the spirit, honey." She pinched my cheek. "I just want you to be happy again, ya know?"

"I know." I turned her around to help secure her butterfly wings. "But I'm beginning to think happiness isn't in the cards for me."

A Place We Belong

"You stop that right now!" Kitty swiveled back around, practically smacking me in the face with her wings. "You just need to find yourself a good man. And who knows? This guy tonight could be the one." She took another swig, this time straight from the bottle, to "get the party started" and dashed out to do her act.

I sat in her makeup chair hoping Kitty was right, but highly doubting it. I thought Bill had been a good man until I learned otherwise. And then, there was the man I could never have. And yet, I needed him if I were to ever be united with my sister.

Before I knew it, Kitty had returned from the stage, startling me. "Hey, you're on."

Already? How had I missed my cue? I hadn't heard or even seen the baggy pants comedian come down the hall. "Oh, shit." I grabbed my fans as Kitty tapped my derriere. "Packed house tonight. Give 'em hell. And don't forget you gotta date later."

I reached for the scotch bottle just like my friend had and tossed it back before rushing on stage and giving the crowd their money's worth.

The Terrace Club was a bit of a drive for city folks, located outside the county line, but worth the trip for the well-to-do and the well-connected. I knew all about this club, known for expensive steaks, renowned big bands, fancy cocktails named after sports figures, and bigger comedians than those who played burlesque houses. The place attracted anyone who liked to drink, dance, eat and mingle, but there was another part that regulars preferred to keep under wraps. "The Club" had an underground following for its gambling operations with rows of slot machines, a private bar, and other closet goings-ons that only the privileged were privy to. Being in the rural part of town made it a tad easier for the club to stay out of newspapers, and often times, court dockets. Although the club had been busted a few times for illegal practices, the owner and silent partners often skirted any real consequences. Rumor had it that the proprietor was generous to public officials' coffers so any charges were quickly and quietly dropped, or severely reduced.

The illegal activities took place quite literally behind closed doors, a dancer had told me. The only way to get to the parlor was through the back of the kitchen with a secret door that had been used since Prohibition days. Only those accompanied by a member were allowed in.

The minute our foursome was seated at one of the best tables, Kitty and I excused ourselves to the ladies' room. "So whaddya think of your date?" Kitty asked the minute we saw it was unoccupied.

"Kinda early to tell but I will say you were right. He's a handsome one. And Antonio sure is a sexy name," I laughed, raising my brows. "Seems like a decent enough fella."

"Yeah, and ya know, it could be worse. I could've set you up with Switch—they call him that 'cause he always carries a switch blade," Kitty snickered. "*And* with a paunch and balding hair . . . not someone you'd wanna take to bed." She had a ha-ha kind of laugh that always made me chuckle too.

"I imagine not. *Especially* if he carries a blade." I gave her this wide eye expression that made us both giggle. I was already feeling better than I had in some time.

A blast of horns playing "In the Mood," hit the air the minute we opened the door to return to our dates. We did samba movements all the way to our table, much to the men's delight.

Antonio did all the right things. He pulled out the chair for me, complimented me on my red sequined dress, and kept me entertained with stories of his travels abroad. He never said how he had the means to travel so much, and I didn't ask. I was simply happy to be here, enjoying a night on the town with someone who made me forget my troubles.

"I hear Dino sings at the Hollenden Hotel too," Kitty yelled over the music, gazing at the dark-haired male vocalist.

The Hollanden Hotel was on the Short Vincent entertainment strip, just a block from the Roxy. Their lounge, the Vogue Room, featured a stream of singers and orchestras, from up-and-comers to the real famous. "Really? I saw Lena Horne there. That gal is terrific, so sultry and classy."

"Did I hear you girls talkin' 'bout sultry and classy?" Antonio leaned in. "You must be talking about yourselves."

"Oh, aren't you the charming one," Kitty hummed, voicing her obvious approval. It was a welcome compliment from others often attached to us, usually to the tune of catcalls.

After a delightful dinner, my date took my hand and led me to the dance floor, where we stayed for several numbers. The orchestra played one of my favorites, "Begin the Beguine," then the gorgeous crooner stepped in and sang a song I wasn't familiar with, but his deep, smooth baritone soothed me. Just as we were ready to take a break, the band went into "Sunrise Serenade," a song perfect for slow dancing.

I started to walk off the dance floor, but Antonio pulled me back into him, so close I could smell his aftershave. "We can't stop now," he whispered. I responded by melting into his arms. I laid my head on his shoulder, closed my eyes and basked in a peace I hadn't felt in so long.

The song was almost over when I lifted my head, opened my eyes to gaze at my attractive date. The place had filled up and as I gazed around, I noticed something else. Merged in the sea of faces, I could've sworn I spotted Bill. I sucked in a breath.

"Something wrong?" Antonio was looking at me, reading my startled face.

'No, no, I'm just . . . in awe of this place."

133

Sensing my distraction, he asked, "Wanna take a break?"

I nodded, and as he guided me to the table, I fought the urge to glance over my shoulder. Who cared if he was here? We got back just as Kitty and Gary were getting up. "Time to hit the slots," Kitty said, grabbing her beaded clutch.

"Hold up, we're right behind ya." Antonio gulped down his drink, then reached for my hand.

A man dressed in a dark blue pinstriped suit approached us. "Welcome to the swankiest joint in town, folks," he boasted, slapping Antonio on the back and giving me a crooked grin. "Why, hello, beautiful." He took my hand and kissed it before I could yank it away.

"Hands off there, Blackie, this one's mine." Antonio's smile didn't meet his eyes.

The man let go of my hand. "No disrespect intended, Anton. But you know I always appreciate a good-lookin' doll." His eyes took in my whole body like I was a shiny Cadillac.

I opened my mouth to give him a piece of my mind but clamped it just in time. I'd learned not to ruffle highfalutin feathers.

"Lydia, meet Black Jack McNeil."

Ah, the owner of the club, infamous womanizer, and friend to the Cleveland Mob Gang. *Good thing I'd kept my trap shut.*

Antonio placed his palm on the small of my back. It was a casual gesture but smacked of possessiveness, emphasizing his "this one's mine" message. It rankled me. What was it about men, who, after all these centuries, still acted like cavemen sometimes?

"How do you do," I said, politely.

"Better now that we've met," he said with a city slicker grin. "You're quite a dish." His eyes went to my breasts when

A Place We Belong

he added, "Wait a minute. I recognize you. You're a Roxy girl, ain't ya?"

Shit. I forced a bright smile. "Yes I am," refusing to be made to feel like it was a bad thing. I was proud of Blue Satin Doll.

Antonio thankfully intervened. "Nice seein' ya, Black, we're off to try our luck."

"Looks like you've already got that in spades." The man's sneer gave me the willies.

As "Black" walked away, Antonio whispered in a dark tone. "That man doesn't always know his place," grabbing me and leading me away. "But you don't want to piss him off. If ya know what I mean."

I nodded but my mind was elsewhere. The crowd had thinned as more and more headed to the back room, allowing me a clear view of that face talking with another man.

No mistake, it was Bill. As if he'd sensed my eyes on him, he turned his head and our eyes met. He did not look happy to see me, and quickly glanced away. "Come on, m'lady," Antonio urged me toward the kitchen door. "We'll hit the craps table first. I gotta feeling you're my lucky charm."

I wondered if Bill would follow but we were moving too fast. As we rushed through the kitchen, the big band sounds faded away, replaced by the clanging of pots and pans and animated chatter among the chefs, paying no attention to several of us passing through. We reached what looked like a closet door where a burly man gave Antonio a knowing look and swung it open for us. I now knew Kitty had lied. Antonio was a mobster, like the rest of them.

A whir of noise hit the moment we entered. There was action everywhere. For a room filled with illegal activity, the room was far from discreet. The folks at the craps table were hollering back and forth, the full bar was surrounded by people cheering and laughing, the chimes and dings of slot machines,

135

and in one corner of the room, a couple having a time of it necking, as if there was no one else around. I had been to my share of shot-and-beer bars as well as swanky joints, but this almost seemed like a brothel. I immediately felt uncomfortable.

"Hey," Antonio said, pulling me to the left, "there's an open spot over there," pointing to a Blackjack table. "See, you're already my lucky girl." He reached into the inside of his jacket pocket and yanked out a wad of money. All twenties. "Wanna get in on it?"

I shook my head." I'll just watch for now."

He pressed his lips hard on mine. "Even better. You just stand here lookin' pretty, babycakes."

Jesus, enough of the compliments. Stupid men. Such comments never used to bother me but since knowing Eliot, I knew what it was like to be treated like a lady. I had held out hope that this Antonio might be someone I'd want to keep dating but he'd blown it with that one demeaning word. The term, babycakes, shut my feelings as quickly as a door slam.

I waited till Antonio was immersed in the game before slipping away to look for Kitty. If he didn't like it, too bad. I wasn't about to be anyone's trinket, lucky or otherwise.

I meandered my way through the noisy crowd and spotted Kitty and Gary at the bar. I was almost there when someone grabbed my arm and spun me around. "What the hell ya doin' here, Lydia?"

Bill looked furious, but he had no right. I jerked away. "Take your hands off me. I'm not your woman, remember?"

"You need to leave. You gotta get outta here. *Now.*"

"No! Get away from me." I pushed his chest. "I'm havin' a good time and I can be anywhere I please. *And* with anyone I want."

"Lyd, you don't get it. Now's not the time to be stubborn." He yanked my arm again and this time it hurt. "Come on—"

"No! Leave me alone."

"Don't fight me, Lydia."

I raised a hand to slap him but never hit its mark. An ear-piercing noise suddenly erupted from the other side of that kitchen door. I knew immediately what that sound was. A gunshot.

20.

*T*he room burst into chaos. People scattered in all directions, screaming in terror. Men flipped over the Blackjack and poker tables and suddenly they were regular tables you'd find anywhere. Another gunshot propelled me to duck quickly, gripping an over-turned chair. My mind screamed *run like the others*, but my body froze in fear against the pounding, shouting, and thunderous racket. I turned just in time to see the back door fly open, and like a mirage in the haze of smoke, Eliot and his Untouchables burst in, all except Eliot holding up guns. "Everyone stay where you are," one of the men demanded.

I realized then that I knew no one around me. Antonio, Gary and Kitty, even Bill, had disappeared. Right behind me, I heard the clamping of handcuffs. Still hovering, I watched a man being led away. I couldn't move, my eyes searching for anyone familiar when a cold hand gripped my wrist. "Ow!" I screeched as a man forced me to stand. He kept a good hold on me as he reached for those hard metal restraints. "Hey! Wait, I didn't do any—"

"Not her." Eliot gave the man a sharp look. "Get her out now, tell Paul to take her home."

The man didn't question the order, he merely led me out the same doorway they had broken down, where another man was waiting in a big blue Plymouth. A door opened and I, gladly, slid into the passenger seat with the stranger.

On the way to my place, I asked the driver what was happening. Was it a rival gang war? I knew things had been heating up between the Mayfield and the Cleveland Gangs. Or was it just a gambling bust? I stopped asking questions seeing the set jaw of this man named Paul. He wasn't giving up anything.

The minute I got in my door, I tried calling Kitty, again and again, but there was never an answer. Did they go to Gary's place? Probably not if he was one of the men they were after.

How I wished I had his number, but then, he was probably behind bars, along with Antonio, most likely. And maybe Kitty too? I dearly hoped she'd somehow escaped. But if she had, where was she?

I wondered, too, about Bill. Why had he been there? Which side had he been on? The cops or the gangsters?

I tossed and turned all night, my mind replaying the events over and over. As the sun came up, I was still too frazzled to sleep a wink. I got out of bed and camped by the window on alert for the paperboy. The second I spotted him weaving through the snow-covered streets on his rusty old bicycle, I threw my coat over my nightgown. The ringing of the phone stopped me midstride. I grabbed it on the first ring. "Kitty?"

"No, it's Eliot."

"Oh, Eliot, I was just going down to get the paper, what all happened last night, what's the latest?"

"Lydia, I need to tell you something." His voice was deeper than usual. Hoarse. It didn't even sound like him.

I braced myself. "What is it?" Oh, God, something happened to Kitty.

"I'm not sure it made the morning edition, but I wanted you to know before you read about it."

I held my breath. "What?"

I heard him sigh heavily. "It's your friend. Bill. He was shot."

"Shot? Oh no, what hospital is he in?" I would get dressed right away and go see him, if they'd let me in. I knew they often only allowed family, depending on a patient's condition. I thought about Bill's sister. Should I check on her? Maybe I could get Frank to take me there, it would be quicker than the streetcar.

"I'm sorry to tell you this on the phone," Eliot went on, interrupting my stream of thoughts. "I wish I could tell you in person, but we've got our hands full at the department."

He hesitated enough to make my heart beat faster. "I'm afraid Bill didn't make it. He died on the way to the hospital."

My hand flew to my mouth as I sucked in air.

"I wanted you to know before they announced it. He and one of the gang members got hit in the crossfire."

So many scenarios flashed through my head, but only one image stuck. Of me yelling at him. Of me pushing him away.

He'd been trying to save me. And I had screamed at him, fought with him. And now he was dead. "He tried to get me to leave right before it all hit the fan. He knew what was coming."

"Yes, we all did."

"Wait, was Bill there to stop the gang war?" I knew that despite everything, Bill Baker was a cop first.

"Yes. He was supposed to case the joint, get word to us through our two-way radio, then get out before anything went down." Another pause. "He didn't get out in time."

Because of me. "Oh God, Eliot. He tried to warn me, but I pulled away from him. I refused to go with him. I was so wrong."

"Don't think that. I'm sure you had your reasons—" His voice moved away from the phone. "Hold on."

I heard whispering and knew he'd cupped the receiver. "I have to go. I'll call you when I can." The click was so swift I didn't have a chance to thank him for calling.

I clutched the phone, listening to the silence on the other end. I hung up and dropped into the nearby chair. Bill

A Place We Belong

was dead? He had put himself in jeopardy to protect me. He'd lost his life trying to save mine.

The regret I felt was unlike anything I had ever experienced. How would I be able to live with myself knowing the last conversation that man had was with me yelling at him?

Sometime later, I pulled myself off the chair, took a sponge bath and forced myself to put on makeup and wrap my hair, stiff with last night's hairspray, into a scarf.

I needed to see Frank and Helen. I needed their comfort. And I needed to get a hold of that paper.

Rushing downstairs, I feared the details I was about to read. But more so, I was worried about Kitty. I'd never been terribly religious—our parents rarely took us to church—but now I found myself praying with each descending step. I knocked on their door, smelling the homey scent of bacon that gave me an odd sense of calm. A hint of normalcy in a shattered world.

Frank was already in his usual spot, eyes buried in section A.

"Come on in, honey," Helen greeted. "Coffee's on and I have fresh Danish from that new bakery down the street."

I flew passed her. "Oh, Frank, please, I need to see that section."

He gave me a quizzical look.

"I was there," I announced. "And it was horrible—"

He let the paper fall to the table. "You were at the Terrace Club last night?"

"Yes, and . . ." my eyes tearing up. "I need to see it."

Helen's eyes flashed to Frank. She set down a plate for me, but I shook my head. "I can't eat a thing."

She started to protest but my expression clammed her up. "Bill was killed last night." I sank into the kitchen chair next to Frank and cupped my face with my hands. Helen wrapped her arms around me, giving me permission to pour

141

my heart out to the only people who would understand how conflicted I felt. When I ran out of words, Helen handed me tissues and Frank slid the paper over to me.

The headline was like a slap. Stark black letters on the upper fold of page one. I took in a big breath and began to read as Helen stood over me, protective hands on my shoulders.

Shoot Out at Terrace Club Leaves Two Dead
It wasn't a lucky night for illegal gamblers in the backroom of the Terrace Club last evening. While patrons enjoyed the sounds of the Watkins orchestra, an intense war was playing out behind the scenes between rival mobsters; The Mayfield Gang, and the Cleveland Gang, ultimately resulting in a police raid and a round of gunfire.

At 11:32 p.m. patrol officers led by safety director, Eliot Ness, busted down a back door with crowbars and axes, just after gunshots were fired by one of the gang members. It's been reported that Ness and his men had been investigating the growing tensions between the gangs and were aware of a possible confrontation taking place at the nightclub.

Federal, state and local police rounded up seven members of both Mob organizations. Two of the men arrested were on Ness's most-wanted list. Other suspected accomplices managed to escape, along with many illegal gamblers.

In addition, two city policemen, long suspected of covering up and cavorting with members of the Mayfield Mob, were arrested, along with four prominent businessmen for illegal gambling. Two females, popular

A Place We Belong

burlesque dancers at the Roxy Theater, were also in attendance but were not arrested.

Two men were pronounced dead on arrival at Huron Road Hospital. One was a Cleveland police officer, the other is believed to be a member of the Mayfield Gang. Names of those killed are being withheld until family is notified. The Terrace Club will be closed until further notice.

I threw the paper on the table. "Of course, they had to include a line about us, didn't they?" Many would know that the "two burlesque dancers" were Kitty and I since we were well known.

"At least it seems Kitty got out okay." I glanced at Helen. "But I haven't heard from her and that concerns me." I breathed a sigh of relief that she wasn't in the slammer, but then, where was she? I fell back against the vinyl dinette chair the color of sunshine. "I can't believe this has happened."

"I'm terribly sorry about Bill," Helen said.

Funny how people's attitude changes in death. "Why? You didn't even like him," I snapped. The emotions of the night, coupled with no sleep, had gotten the best of me.

"While that may be true," Helen answered. "I never wished the man any harm."

"I know," I sighed. "I'm sorry. I guess I'm just in shock." I wiped my face with my fingers. "And exhausted. I'm going back upstairs. Try and get some sleep."

But sleep wouldn't come. I wondered about Kitty, was heartsick about Bill, and I couldn't help speculate how Eliot felt about seeing me at the club that night. He had saved me from being arrested, but at what cost?

The ringing of the phone jerked me out of a daze. I tripped over the heels I'd left by the bed and hobbled to the receiver. "Hello?"

143

"Lyd, it's Kitty."

"Oh my word, where are you?"

"At an *undisclosed location*," she said with a light laugh. "Gary got word right before they busted down the door. I looked for you, but he was dragging me out the side door. Thank God, you're okay too."

"Yeah, thanks to Eliot. They were about to cuff me when he stopped them." I lowered my head. "Did you hear about Bill?"

"Just now, on the radio . . . I'm so sorry, sweetie."

I told her about our encounter. How awful I had been. "He was just so insistent, Kit, and I misread it. I thought he was being jealous and demanding, as usual—" I stretched the cord enough to sit on my bed, watching snow flurries get heavier outside my window. "But I don't wanna talk about it anymore. Say, why didn't you call me sooner?"

"We weren't by a phone. We had to find a safe place until he's sure the heat's off. He's waiting to get word that the Feds aren't in search of him and he thinks I should stay under the radar, too, least for a few days. I just called George to get the new girl to take my shift this week. By then, I should be able to come home."

"Yes, best to be safe. And wait'll you see the paper. They just *had* to say that Roxy girls were there. Least they were kind enough not to use our names."

"Already heard that too. First thing outta George's mouth. I'll warn ya now, he's up in arms about us being linked to the Mob."

I let out a laugh. "Oh, for heaven's sakes. Everyone knows we see our share of racketeers in the place. If he's so worried about his rep, why's he own a damn burlesque house?"

"That's our George. Hey, I gotta run. I'll call ya tomorrow with any updates."

I barely got the goodbye out before the line went dead.

Knowing Kitty was okay, my thoughts returned to Eliot. I remembered him telling me that something was "going down real soon." He had to have been talking about the raid. If he had known I'd be there, he would have warned me not to go. And Bill might still be alive.

But it did no good to ponder the What Ifs. It would only make me crazy.

The next day I went to see Bill's sister to offer my condolences in person. It was an awkward visit, to say the least. When the woman suggested that I not attend the service since many of Bill's colleagues would be there, what could I do but comply? I couldn't even be mad. It was what I deserved, given my well-known occupation.

The day of his funeral, I stayed in bed mourning Bill in private, questioning everything about our relationship. Had I been too hard on him? Had I loved him more than I ever admitted? Maybe I should get out of this crazy business if I stood any chance at being respected, taken seriously.

By afternoon, I forced myself up to do chores, hoping to keep dark thoughts at bay. I dusted shelves, swept rugs, folded laundry, cleaned my whole damn apartment. After placing the last pair of my stockings into the chest of drawers, I poured myself a glass of cheap whiskey, then swore out loud, realizing I had just one cigarette left and was out of matches. I put the cig to my mouth, went over to the gas range, turned on the fire, and bent down to light it, nearly catching my hair on fire.

I stood puffing away, looking out the front window. The glistening snow was much too pretty, too bright, for my dismal feelings. I watched the children across the street, throwing snowballs, making angels, attempting to make a snowman. Their joyful, innocent attempts at play brought tears to my eyes.

How I missed my easy, uncomplicated, childhood.

21.

*T*he next night, the Roxy was filled to capacity. If George had any qualms about the Mob link, he'd be sure to get over it once the money was counted. I never liked sticking around on crowded nights, but after my act, Big Joe came to my dressing room door. "Hey, Lyd, some fella at one of the back tables been askin' questions about ya. I've been keeping my eye on him. Seems harmless but thought you might wanna take a peek 'round the corner. See if you know the guy."

That was Joe for ya. Ever-watchful, but always gave me the lead. It was probably one of the Stage Door Johnnies who'd wait for us girls to leave, then bug us for personal attention. You never knew if it was some slimeball wanting to get in on my action, or just a shy guy who simply wanted an autograph.

I grabbed my coat and bag and headed to the lounge area with Joe right behind.

"He's at the bar now, over there," Joe pointed to a man in a long wool overcoat. I could see his profile in the darkened room. Brown wavy hair, dark framed glasses, sharp nose. He was giving Tony a slip of paper.

The nose gave him away. My heart nearly sunk to the floor. I felt my skin crawl, like an invasion of tiny, dirty roaches.

"Recognize him?"

I couldn't answer. Just stood there, staring. I couldn't believe it. How would he even know I was here? But then, I answered my own question. My face and body was always plastered in the local paper's Friday entertainment section.

"Hey." Joe's beefy hand on my back made me flinch. "You okay?"

"What kind of questions was he askin'?" I watched the man take the last swig of what looked like an Old Fashioned. He always did like the whiskey.

"Tony said he wanted to know how long you worked here. Asked if you were married, so could be one to watch."

Married? *That's* what he wondered about?

I was trying to calm myself when the man set his empty glass down and headed for the exit.

"Guess ya don't wanna talk to him, huh?"

My mind told me to run after him, but my body stayed paralyzed.

I watched the man walk out the door.

This might be my last chance. He might never come back. I found my legs and forced myself to go after him, but George interrupted me midstride. "Lydia, wait! I got your pay here, and we need to have a li'l discussion about last night and what you plan to—"

"Not now, George," I said, pushing him aside.

But he caught my arm. "Hey now, not so fast. Don't be getting all uppity with me. Show some respect for a guy who gives you a pretty good living—"

"Let me go," I spit out. He looked shocked. I never talked to George like that but I had no time to explain. I brushed past him and pushed through the door. Squinting in the dark, I searched left and right for a man who had suddenly vanished like an evaporated illusion. For the second time in my life.

I stamped my foot. "Damn it!" I may not have been ready to face him but now I'd lost any chance at answers that had been haunting me since I was fifteen years old.

"When you're ready to leave, I'll take you home." I heard Joe's gentle tone, like he felt my anguish.

I turned and leaned into his hefty chest. "Oh Joe, do you know who that man was?"

"Not a clue." His chest vibrated against my forehead.

I looked up at him, tears streaking my painted face. "That was my son-of-a-bitchen father."

As we walked back inside, Tony called me over. "Hey, Lydia, this man left you a note."

I couldn't get to him fast enough. When he handed me the folded slip of paper, my hands were shaking so that I had to use the bartop to steady them. I spotted the ashtray in front of where he'd stood. A smashed out Camel. His brand.

Tony and Joe went about their jobs of closing up while I held the note in my hands. Unfolding it, I anticipated an explanation. An apology. A way to contact him to make amends.

I got none of those.

Lydia - Your a disgrace to the Swanson family name. Guess I shoulda stuck around - Raised ya decent. Maybe someday you'll see the air of your ways. Too late now. Hope Tess turned out better.

A frigid chill passed through me, cold as a block of ice. "You bastard!" I yelled out. "How *dare* you?" *He* had been the cause of it all. As soon as things got difficult, the chicken shit took off and I had to make my own way. We all had to make our own way. Mama died making our own way. All I wanted now was to see that man come back so I could pummel him with my fists until he cried out for mercy.

Joe and Tony shot me a look and asked in unison. "You okay?"

"Just take me home," I told Joe, who didn't ask any more questions.

A Place We Belong

Anger turned to devastation by the time I got home. Even though I'd ripped the note to pieces and threw it in the trash on the way out, the words festered in my psyche. After all, if my own father thought I was shameful, how would any other man in my life think different? If my own father felt no love for me, maybe I wasn't lovable. The very thought gave me an awful tightening in my chest. I fought the urge to bawl my eyes out, but it hurt like the dickens. I was sorry the man had ever stepped foot in the place. I'd been better off not knowing he was still around. Better to think of him as dead.

Snow had turned to icy slush the next day. The sound of hail pounding the gutters had lasted through the night, giving me yet another restless sleep. I had to put on full gear—heavy coat, galoshes, rain bonnet—just to go to the mailbox. Walking briskly along the driveway, I grabbed the small stack of parcels, rolled it under my arm, and once back inside, dropped the pile on my kitchen table. I'd go through it later when I returned from the market.

But as the envelopes fell flat on the Formica surface, a letter caught my eye. I didn't recognize the penmanship, and there was no return address, which was odd. Although neatly written, it didn't have the familiar feminine slant. This was a man's cursive, I was certain.

I pulled out a chair, sat down and ripped it open, sensing something, though I didn't know what. The second I unfolded the piece of paper, my eyes moved straight to the bottom of the letter. *Sincerely, Eliot.*

Oh, hell. This would not be good.

Dear Miss Lydia,

First, I'd like to apologize for not being in touch sooner. As you know, recent developments have required my

149

utmost attention. Surely, you have read the papers and although I am pleased with the arrest of many we'd been after, my feelings are conflicted concerning your friend, Bill. Naturally, it's always a disappointment when we find fraud and dishonestly among those with whom we hold trust. But in the end, Bill stepped up and did his job and helped us nab those characters. I hope you take some comfort in that.

There is yet another development that I must address to you, and the reason for this letter, in lieu of a phone call or personal visit. I'm afraid Evaline is extremely upset upon discovering your profession, combined of course with learning of our close friendship. You see, she became suspicious when you, a woman she doesn't know, called our home asking to speak with me. I'm afraid she took it upon herself to listen in on our extension that night you called so distraught – though it was understandable.

Just as I'd suspected. Evaline had indeed listened in on our private conversation. I felt just as I did that night I'd call. Violated. I tried in vain to recall all I had said to him that night, but that was impossible. I'd been a tad inebriated, and scared.

My hand gripped the paper so hard, it crinkled.

Her extravagant suspicions - which I assured her were unfounded - has made it impossible for me to defend the growing rumors about the nature of our relationship.

Rumors? Who was doing the talking? The only ones who knew about our meetings were bartender Tony, and Kitty, my closest friend. And maybe Joe. None of them would've started rumors. But then, there were always strangers lurking about wherever we were.

A Place We Belong

Why the hell can't folks mind their own darn business?

Once again, I am very sorry about your loss. I truly am. That should never have happened. However, and unfortunately, it does not help that you are often in the company of the sort of people I work hard at protecting our fair city from. You of course are free to associate with whomever you wish but given my position - and the fact I may decide to run for mayor in the future - I have to be quite careful about the elements that surround me.

The elements that surround him? That didn't sound at all like Eliot. I envisioned Evaline standing over his head with a shotgun as he wrote.

I do hope, and I believe, that you can understand that.

The dreadful words were becoming blurry, causing a nagging pounding in my brain.

Now concerning your sister, he went on. *While I cannot dive further into this case for the reasons just mentioned, I hope you will be comforted to know that I can seek out a trusted employee who I'm sure will agree to take over for me as a personal favor. So the pro bono promise still stands.*

No! He can't do this to me. I didn't want a stranger involved in such a personal matter.

Please know that I care for you deeply but I cannot in good conscience risk my career, or naturally, my marriage.

*I hope you'll keep the memories we have shared close to your heart, as I will - with great affection.
Sincerely, Eliot*

Act Two

22.

I read the letter again to let it sink in. *I wasn't fit to be friends with the likes of Eliot Ness?* I knew for a fact that he had an array of assorted acquaintances and friends from every walk of life—businessmen, salesmen, radio and newspaper men, factory men, even garbage men and shoeshine boys . . .

And what was that comment about running for mayor one day? That had to be Eveline's doing. I distinctly recalled Eliot telling me that although some have suggested he run for office, he did not want a political job. He was happy with what he was doing.

The thought of Evaline's influence on him made my blood boil, but then, damn it, she was his wife, she was allowed. So, this was it. There'd be no more lunch dates, no more drinks together, no more interesting conversations. Worst of all, he'd just ripped apart any chance I had at finding Tess. It completely broke my heart—more than losing my poor excuse for a father.

Why was everything falling to pieces?

When the phone rang, I immediately thought it might be Eliot. Maybe he'd had second thoughts. I hated myself for hoping, but I rushed into the living room and snatched up the receiver mid-ring. "Hello?"

"Hey, whacha doin'?"

Not Eliot. Hope was becoming my worst deceiver. "Kitty! Are you back?"

"Yep, got in yesterday and back at work tonight."

"Oh, thank God. I need you. I'm just beside myself." I told her about Eliot's letter. The latest on my father could wait another time. "In fact, let me get it, I'll read it to you."

Hearing the words out loud only made it worse. "I'm no good, Kit. Being seen with me can ruin his life, can you believe it?" I wound the phone cord so tight around my fingers it almost stopped the blood flow. "All these damn men just love to see us dance in front of them and buy us drinks in hopes of getting laid, but be *friends* with such women? Oh no, that's a crime."

"Aw, Lyddy, I'm so sorry, that's not right." Her voice rose. "Forget him. He's just like the rest of them. Let's you and me go shopping, whaddya say?"

"If it includes cocktails, count me in."

When Kitty suggested Sullivan's for lunch, I almost declined, but decided right then and there, I had to live my life without damn memories. And besides, I liked the place. Plus, I'd be with someone who always made me feel good about myself.

After a successful shopping spree, we found a table by the front door and set our packages in the corner by the window. We ordered gin and tonics and agreed to split a sandwich.

"I feel so betrayed," I said, still wrestling with the fact that Eliot would actually hand over my private mission to someone else. "I don't want some stranger knowing my private business. It's too delicate. And yet, at the same time, I need help where I can get it. Been so long since Tess has been gone. I can't stand it anymore."

"I know, kiddo," she said, patting my hand. "But I'm sure Eliot would choose someone with all the ethics that he has. Make everything on the QT too." She paused to tap out a cigarette from her pouch. "Maybe it's better this way. I think you're way too hung up on the guy, truth be told, and when it comes to married men, that outcome is never good."

A Place We Belong

It hurt to hear, but I knew she was right. "I know. My head tells me that too, but oh, my heart . . . he and I have such a deep connection. I can't even explain it."

Our thoughts lingered in the air just as a tall darkhaired woman with a red fox fur stole snaked around her collar, threw open the door and moseyed her way toward us. "What's shakin,' girls?"

"Zorita!" We screamed at once. "What brings you to town?" I was first to ask.

"Spotted you two in the window. I got me a gig at The Cameo in Akron. I'm booked there tonight and tomorrow." She set her gigantic purse on the floor next to our packages. "A li'l birdy told me I might find you gals here."

I glanced at Kitty. "I told George what we were doing in case he needed me in early. You know how undependable that new girl is." I shifted back to Zorita. "Don't know why he hires those young things. We end up coverin' their asses."

Zorita took a seat between us. "Yeah, they don't make 'em like us anymore," she said, flagging down the waitress.

"You ain't whistling Dixie." Kitty struck a match and finally lit the cigarette she'd been holding.

I laughed at the absurdity. It sounded like we were gossipy middle-age ladies when in truth, Kitty was twenty-six, and Zorita, just twenty-three, a year older than I was. The new dancer was eighteen—same age as we all were when we started in the business. Yet, we always took our jobs seriously, too desperate to mess up. Now, with the fame of Gypsy Rose Lee, the incorrigible Sally Rand, and other girls who'd gone national, the new ones seemed to be in it for the "fame and glory." Little did they know it wasn't all it was cracked up to be. The resilient ones caught on quick and thrived in their environment. Others got hitched within a year's time and started spitting out babies like a fertility machine. The weaker

155

ones got into drink and drugs, or other questionable antics, which often shortened their career.

Girls like Kitty, Zorita and I got wise to the world early on and became smart, independent women who were able to support ourselves and, for the most part, we liked it that way. But yes, we often did feel beyond our years because of it.

Zorita ordered a vodka "straight up" and the three of us spent the next hour catching up. I sometimes envied Zorita's greater fame and fortune, though I knew the gal worked hard. She was never in the same city for more than a week or two, spent most of her time traveling the circuit playing high-profile places. She was also featured in most of the International Exhibitions in big cities like San Francisco, San Diego, Chicago, New York and Cleveland—where I first watched in awe as she performed with those huge snakes that became her calling card. She amazed everyone with how she handled them, both expertly and sensuously.

That summer of '36, and the following year when we worked together, had cemented our friendship. We'd spent many nights drinking after hours, flirting with men at various establishments, and sharing the stories of our lives.

Once over drinks, Zorita revealed that she'd been adopted, which caught my attention. I learned that Zorita's father died when she was four, her adopted mother remarried and she began getting abused "in every way." It raised more fears in me as to what Tess might be going through, which made my nightmares worse.

Zorita told me how she married at fifteen, just to escape. "Of course that little set up didn't last long, seeing how I wouldn't put up with his shit, but it did teach me to be self-reliant. I worked as a cigarette girl at the New York State Fair and saw my first burlie show and said, that's for me!"

Now she was as big as those stars we all admired. Kitty especially loved Josephine Baker, who became a Ziegfeld

A Place We Belong

Follies star despite her dark skin, proving to an Asian girl like Kitty that dreams could come true if you were determined. You just had to change your negatives into positives. Turn your differences into your own unique persona.

But Zorita sometimes took that approach too far. She often made enemies with bosses and colleagues alike. She'd been arrested many times for "indecent exposure" and lately had been cited for "animal cruelty." She was called out for taping her snake's mouth shut and was recently spotted walking her slithering companion on a leash down a New York city street. All adding fuel to her exotic reputation. Zorita was a character, for sure, but she was true to herself and all the girls in the biz admired that.

Because Zorita was a real hoot, we had a grand time seeing our "snake girl" before she was to go back to New York City's famous Minsky's club. The stories and laughter exchanged kept me from my depressed thoughts.

The following weeks were a different story. It was Christmastime and everywhere I went were sights that reminded me, with staggering clarity, how truly alone I was. All those fancy gift ideas and children's toys in department store windows, the sixty-foot tall, lavishly decorated spruce tree inside Sterling Lindner's, the scores of happy parents with excitable children standing in line to see Santa . . . families making memories.

Growing up, Christmas had been my favorite season, but for the past five years, I dreaded December with every fiber of my being. The holidays filled my head with images of my mother taking me and Tess shopping downtown, of sitting on Santa's lap, smiling happily for a snapshot, of baking cookies and pies and fruit cakes. Of my father bringing home a live tree each year, bragging for days how he haggled the best deal out of the salesmen. And, of course, Christmas dinner, where the

157

table offered a feast of turkey, glazed ham, sweet potatoes, cranberry sauce, and of course, pumpkin pie.

How I missed having a family.

All the pomp and circumstance brought my mood crashing down. I couldn't even visit Frank and Helen without feeling sad looking at their living room tree with its festive lights, array of ornaments, and sparkling icicle tinsel, hearing the older couple buzz about all the preparations they needed to do. And Kitty, she was busy with Gary, enjoying all the romance of the season.

The worst was hearing those ever-present songs. There was no avoiding them. On the radio, in the department stores, blasting out neighborhood windows, and through the sound of carolers, whose voices echoed into my room upstairs. So much so that the melodies rang in my head as I'd try to fall asleep. The sounds of "Winter Wonderland," "Jingle Bells" and "Silent Night" filled me with such melancholy, it was hard getting out of bed each day.

Especially after Eliot called to tell me that the man he had in mind to help my cause wouldn't be available until after the new year. It seemed everyone had something important going on in their lives. I was alone.

23.

As Christmas loomed closer, I felt dead inside. Even Spencer gave me no joy so I had Helen take him "until the holidays passed" as I was in no shape to care for him. I stayed in bed bawling for two straight days. I couldn't eat, nor did I listen to the radio, thus avoiding those damn cheery-ass songs. I slept. And slept some more.

On Christmas Eve, the phone rang three times before noon. I let it ring off the hook as I stayed in bed under the covers. I hated what my life had become. I hated that I missed Eliot, knowing I had no right to.

Another round of chimes through my lifeless apartment was the last straw. They had to be wrong numbers, which I got fairly often, and I'd had enough. Not having eaten in who knows how long, it took all the energy I could muster to make it to the incessant black machine and when I reached it, I yanked the cord straight out of the wall, then dragged myself to the bathroom.

I did my business, washed my hands, looked up in the mirror and was horrified at the image gazing back at me. What a sight I was. Not only was my face all puffy, but my green eyes were streaked with red lines and so glassy from crying I was surprised I could see at all. My nightgown was a wrinkled mess and needed a good washing too. I took it off and threw it in the hamper, grabbed my blue Chenille robe from the hook on the door and tied it around me. I had just one more day to be back at work. I had to do something with this awful face. I still needed to make a living and I couldn't upset George or disappoint my fans.

But in my heart of hearts, I hardly cared.

I grabbed the jar of cold cream and, as I smeared it on my face, I thought about how I ended up so alone. Whatever would become of me? *I can't go on.*

I slid down the bathroom wall until I hit the floor, where I stayed sobbing, wanting to die. Even when they had taken Tess away, I'd kept hope in my heart. But these past few months had wiped away any hope I ever had. Because of my actions, I'd lost a cherished friendship of the man who had kept my hope alive. Without him, who would right all the wrongs made by people who stripped children from their families?

And there was Bill. The man had been flawed, yes, but oh, so passionate. I now believed he had been the only man in my life who had truly loved me.

I remained on the cold tile floor, head dangled between my legs, mesmerized by the black-and-while hexagonal design of the linoleum. I couldn't stop weeping, rolling the toilet paper from its holder until there was none left, just a soppy mess surrounding me.

The sudden hard rap on my apartment door gave me a jolt. Then, I heard the squeak of it opening.

I straightened up, fearing the intruders were back. I leaned in, ear against the bathroom door, paralyzed.

"Lydia, are you in here?" At first I thought it must be Frank, who had a key, but it didn't sound like him.

The voice came closer, and louder. "Lydia!"

Oh, dear Lord. I knew that deep, resonate tone. I shot up, grabbed my hairbrush from the basket on my vanity and raked through my tangles best I could.

"If you don't answer me, I'm breaking down this door." Could it really be Eliot, or was it mere wishful thinking?

"Yes. I'm here," I called out, turning on the faucet. "Be out in a sec."

A Place We Belong

I looked up in the mirror. The brush had hardly helped. I shut my eyes. No use trying to make myself look good at this point.

I brushed my teeth, splashed my face, and dried it with a towel that had been on the rack three days. Ugh. Opening the medicine cabinet, I snatched the powder puff and made a quick attempt to at least smell better.

I had barely opened the door when he grabbed me and held me tight. "God, I was so worried about you. Why wouldn't you answer your phone?"

"That was you?" *Was I dreaming?* I took in the manly scent of him as he kept me wrapped in his arms.

He stepped back to look at me, lifted my chin and stared into my red swollen eyes. "You really had me scared."

Me? *I* had scared the rough and tough Eliot Ness? It seemed impossible, yet his face showed intense worry.

My head flopped into his chest like a ragdoll. "Oh Eliot, I'm so sorry, I'm such a mess."

"Come, sit." He threw off his heavy coat and laid it on the back of my recliner before guiding me to the sofa. He wore a starched lime-colored shirt and tan pants with a perfect crease down the front. I had a hard time envisioning the exquisite Evaline slaving over a hot iron. Maybe they had a maid.

Once we were seated, Eliot placed my hands in his. "Talk to me."

I shook my head. "I'm sorry, the holidays just get to me." I couldn't look at him, choosing the floor instead.

"I've been calling since yesterday." He let go of my hand but kept his gaze on me. "I wanted to see you . . . apologize for my inexcusable behavior. I'm sincerely sorry, I know how disappointed you must be that I was going to abandon your search." *Disappointed? Your letter shattered me.*

He straightened his posture. "I shouldn't let other people influence me." *Was he talking about his wife? Someone else?* "I promise you, I will never do that again."

Filled with surprise, and relief, I whispered, "I've missed you." It came out before I could swallow it back.

That made him blush. He cleared his throat. "I came by to tell you that I've made arrangements to leave work for a week, right after the holidays. I'll be going to Memphis to see what I can find out about that orphanage."

I sprang off the couch, immediately dizzy from the effort, but I didn't care. "You're back on the case?"

He stood up too, seeing me sway, and grabbed my shoulders. "Yes, I am. And I don't plan to quit until we get some answers." Before I could respond, he added, "I'm doing it for you, yes, but also because it needs to be investigated. I'm doing it for those children too."

What a good man he was. "Thank you from us all." I swung my arms around him and squeezed him tight.

A second into the embrace, I realized my satin belt had come loose and my bare breasts were squashed up against his knit shirt. He must have realized it at the same time and we both stepped back as I quickly retied my robe, my face hot as Satan's pitchfork. "Sorry."

He smiled, watching my every movement. "Don't be sorry, Lydia. You are a beautiful woman. I have nothing but respect for you."

We gazed at each other and the world stopped. Gently, slowly, he grabbed my waist, now decently wrapped in the Chenille, and pulled me close. He lifted one hand up to caress my cheek, his eyes not leaving mine, penetrating my very soul. My heart beat wildly wondering what would happen next. He came within inches of my face, his other hand cupping the back of my head, guiding me to him, and suddenly his lips were on mine.

A Place We Belong

It was the kind of tender kiss I'd only dreamed about. One I had never experienced. Soft, yet filled with longing. Dare I say love? The kiss deepened and soon our arms were wrapped tightly around each other until we could barely breathe. My head was spinning, thinking thoughts I never knew were possible. But maybe they were.

The knock on the door made us both jump out of our skins and we instantly withdrew.

I cleared my voice before speaking. "Who is it?"

"Lydia, it's Helen, are you alright?"

Eliot smoothed his rumpled shirt, fingers combing his mussed hair. "I should leave," he whispered.

I held up my index finger. "Helen? I'm getting ready to take a bath, can I come down and see you when I'm done?"

"Oh, yes, of course. Just making sure you're okay. You haven't been down for breakfast in two days, I was concerned."

"I'm fine. I'll see you later." I called out, then listened as the footsteps faded.

Eliot and I glanced back at each other, no doubt wondering how to proceed after such an intimate moment. I didn't want to ruin the mood, but reality smacked me in the face. "Eliot, I treasure what we have. And I am ever so grateful you changed your mind about helping me. But—" I tried to calm the tremble in my voice, "I don't want to muddle up your career, or your marriage." I looked away. "You were right in your letter. About the risks. I care for you so much, I'd hate to cause you any trouble." I couldn't believe I was saying it, but any other direction could be disastrous for us both.

He drew me back into him and whispered, "I've been in much worse trouble, my girl. But yes, you are a client. Actually, my favorite one." His face softened. "You're also a dear friend and I'll continue helping you." He sighed. "And in doing so, yes, I agree we must keep it on a professional level."

So that was that. How I wished it didn't have to be that way but I'd sacrifice anything to find my sister. I held out my hand. "Friends, then?"

He shook it, then lifted it to his face. So close to his lips I could feel his warm breath. "I'm still allowed to kiss your hand, though. Correct?"

I laughed. "Why, certainly, my gallant man. All the true gentlemen do it."

"I'm glad you agree." He kissed the top of my hand so lightly I barely felt it. Then he turned toward the door. "Merry Christmas, Miss Lydia."

"Merry Christmas, Eliot." I watched him grab his overcoat, turn for a moment to flash his renowned grin, then shut the door behind him.

I went to the window to watch him leave, wondering if my landlords had spotted him here. Chances were they hadn't, as I now saw that his Sedan was not in the driveway, but that he had parked three houses away.

24.

*T*hanks to my reunion with Eliot, a few good nights at the club, and substantial holidays tips—the only time George allowed it—I managed to get through the maze of the holidays better than expected. I began feeling whole again, back in control. I even drummed up a new act to start 1941 off right.

And as promised, Eliot left for Memphis the first chance he got. I had looked it up and knew that it would take him around twelve hours to drive there. He called Sunday morning and promised to phone me when he arrived. "But then, you probably won't hear from me till I get back. I imagine whatever I find, if anything, will be best discussed over a good drink when I return."

I smiled into the receiver. "At least one." I felt such joy that they were back on track.

On Monday, I had a conversation with Helen.

I'd been ready to go out the door to the five-and-dime to pick up some makeup and a few household items when Helen stopped me. "Oh, Lydia," she called out from the hallway. "I've been meaning to talk with you. Gotta minute?"

I let out a sigh. There was no such thing as a minute with Helen. We'd go from talking about the weather, to the latest news concerning our jobs, to real fears that America was going to get into the war in Europe. "A minute" often turned into an hour. That meant I would miss the streetcar and the next one didn't come until noon. Which meant my being late to the bookstore, which meant I might end up missing the call from Eliot, saying he had arrived in Memphis safe and sound.

Helen caught me glance at my watch. "It's awful slushy out. How 'bout after a quick cup of coffee and I can take you wherever you need to go. You know it's my day off, and Frank left me the car."

How could I say no? I followed her into her kitchen.

Turns out, of all the topics to discuss, she decided to go straight to the topic of Mr. Eliot Ness.

For all I knew, Helen was not aware of my friendship with the lawman. I hadn't told her that I'd summoned him to find my sister, fearing what this opinionated woman would have to say about that. Only Kitty knew Eliot was helping me, though I had yet to update her on recent developments, too afraid to jinx it. I didn't want to risk speaking too soon or I'd be knocking on wood like a tapping woodpecker.

I hadn't seen Helen since the lovely Christmas dinner I had with them. They'd invited me over for New Year's Eve to listen to Guy Lombardo's radio show but I had worked late and ended up closing The Theatrical to get lost in the crowd with the other lonely showgirls.

Helen poured me a steaming cup of Maxwell House. "I've been wrestling with myself whether to even bring this up, but you're like a daughter to me and I care about you, so I decided I simply must."

This start of a tête-à-tête is never good.

"I don't want to appear nosy, but I couldn't help wondering about the presence of our city safety director in your apartment that day I came by. When you swooshed me away."

I nearly spit out the sip of my coffee. "Swooshed? I didn't *swoosh*."

Helen was sitting across from me, giving me a "*come on now*" look she usually reserved for her husband.

I felt trapped. And yet, this was Helen, after all. The woman who had given me a home when I had none, a woman who, I agreed, treated me like a daughter. "Oh, Helen, I guess it's time I let you in on it."

A Place We Belong

The poor woman gasped. Like her worst suspicions had just been confirmed.

I couldn't help but laugh. "No, no, it's not like that."

The woman looked doubtful. "You told me that day that you were getting ready to take a bath but I know that man, a married man, mind you, was there with you." She drew in a breath, exhaled loudly. "I saw him leave through the back entrance."

I couldn't keep the hot flush from coloring my face, like I'd been caught in the act of some lurid activity. Sure, it almost came to that, but it didn't. We had handled what had transpired between us with dignity, maturity and—damn it—self-control.

"Aw, Helen, I know it must've looked bad. But don't be jumping to conclusions." *Although the daydream was nice.* I got up to refill our cups just for something to do. "Look, I am very aware of his marital status. *And don't need to be reminded, thank you very much.* I just wasn't ready to tell you yet. But I also don't want you thinking ill of either of us—

I sat back down. "Eliot and I have been friends for awhile now. And guess what?" I felt excitement surge through me, just being able to tell someone. "Eliot is working on finding my sister, Tess."

Helen got up, circled around the metal table and gave me a hug. "Well, I'll be. That is hopeful news." I went on to tell Helen everything. How I asked him for his help and that he accepted and was on his way to Memphis that very moment to investigate. "I do hope he finds her."

"Oh, me too. The sweet man has vowed not to stop till he has, but I don't know what he'll uncover, and that scares me."

"Have faith, dear. That's all you can do." She placed a hand on her chest for emphasis. You're gonna find her. I feel it in my heart."

This lifted my hopes considerably. Helen's been known to be a little clairvoyant.

"From your lips to God ears."

"But honey, be careful." She looked at me dead on and I knew what, or rather, who, she was referring to.

I gave her a tight squeeze, loving that she cared so much that she worried I might get hurt.

We placed our cups in the sink and instead of shopping nearby, Helen suggested we go downtown to run our errands. The bookstore could wait another day.

At the lunch counter at Woolworth's, we managed to snag two seats together. And just as we were finishing our sandwiches, we heard a familiar voice.

"Hey, fancy seeing you two here." Kitty had the kind of voice that carried so we knew she was there before we turned and saw her. "I was gonna call when I got home."

Thankfully what she said next was several decibels lower. "Boy, do I have some hot gossip for you." She pointed a long red fingernail in my direction. The place had emptied since we'd gotten there allowing Kitty to hop on the swivel stool next to Helen, who offered to switch seats. "Thanks. What I gotta say is sort of private."

Helen caught the hint. "I know I'm the old lady here," she said as we both began to politely protest. "Don't worry. I just remembered I have to get some socks for Frank. He's always getting holes in them, and being a working girl, I've got no time to darn."

"I hear ya, Helen," Kitty said, with a high-pitched laugh. I laughed, too, because Kitty had no inkling about darning socks, or what it was like to be a housewife. Though, if things kept going with her and Gary, she just might find out. And wouldn't that be sad? I still didn't like the guy.

The minute Helen walked away, Kitty revealed her secret news. "So get this. Remember my cousin, Donna? You

A Place We Belong

know, the one going to the Cleveland Art Institute? Well, they're doing this life-drawing course and she decided to be a model—a *nude* model." She raised a thick lined brow, arched like a cathedral.

The waitress came by and asked if she'd like something. "Yeah, sure, I'll take a Coke," just to get her out of the way. "Now this is where it gets interesting . . . guess who's taking the class?"

I knew this was rhetorical, so didn't answer, just tilted my head with interest.

"Evaline Ness." More raised brows. "Donna recognized her from that newspaper feature they did on her and Eliot last month."

Ah, yes. It was the cover story in the Sunday magazine supplement called, "How the Nesses Won Cleveland." All about the celebrated couple—their magnificent life in their Bay Village beach house, his triumphs over Cleveland crime, and his lovely, accomplished wife, who was making a name for herself as an ad illustrator for Higbee's. The article included several pictures of the happy couple. I'd read it over several nights, like a fabled bedtime story.

It made sense that Evaline, a renowned arts supporter, would be interested in taking a drawing class, but I couldn't quite envision the ever-elegant woman sitting in a hardback chair in a classroom for hours, staring at another woman with no clothes on, taking in every detail as she sketched her.

While I considered the scene, Kitty said, "Oh, it gets better." Her Coke had arrived by then, and so had Helen, bag of socks in hand.

"That was fast," Kitty said, looking at her like one would an unwelcome fruit fly, which embarrassed me. Yet, I was dying to know what else she had to tell me.

"Helen, would you mind terribly if I caught a ride with Kitty? She wants to hit the bookstore and I'd like to go along."

169

Lucky for me, Helen was a jewel. "Sure. I'm running late anyway, should've started dinner an hour ago."

The second after our goodbye, Kitty resumed. "So. After the class, Evaline comes up to her and asks her if she'd like to go for a coffee." She took a sip of her drink to lengthen the suspense, I could tell. "Now. Did I happen to mention that Donna goes, uh, the other way?"

This was getting more interesting by the minute. "No. You did not."

Kitty looked around to make sure no one was in hearing distance. "So they've met a couple times after that, but Donna was getting nervous about it because well, the woman *is* married to Cleveland's biggest hero and the scandal could have dire consequences for everyone."

I wasn't a prude by any means. I knew of such women. A few years ago, one of the Roxy dancers started getting too suggestive with some of the girls who didn't go "that way." It created such a commotion that George ended up firing her.

Still. The discriminating Evaline? Both ways? "I find that a bit hard to fathom," I said.

"Perhaps, but I spent an hour on the phone with Donna and got more details. She said Eva—that's what she goes by in the class—told her not to worry about their *friendship*. That Eliot was beginning to suspect she was seeing another man because her attention to him has been lagging of late. So apparently the hot flames are blowing another direction," Kitty giggled at her own joke. They were both having a bit of fun at Eliot's wife's expense. "Guess they had a big tiff coupla weeks ago," Kitty said as she dug in her clutch to pay for her Coke. "Gotta wonder how a man would feel if his wife was attracted to another woman. Talk about a big ol' slap to the ego."

As Kitty talked, I was doing a timeline in my head. Couple of weeks ago? That was just around the time Eliot had showed up at my place. Coincidence? Who knew? But I wasn't about to further flame any fans, and it was not a conversation I wished to have with him. It was sensitive and certainly not something he needed to hear from me.

Kitty checked her watch. "Say, we better hit it if we're to make the three o'clock trolley."

I spent the rest of day, and into the night, thinking about the state of Eliot's marriage. While I vowed not to tell him what I knew, I was anxious to hear from him. And that he had arrived safely in Memphis.

But the phone remained silent.

25.

I'd been dreaming of dancing when the phone chimed, startling me awake.

"Good morning, Lydia." I smiled in my dazed state. I loved hearing him say my name. "Hope it's not too early to call."

I glanced at my bedside clock. Seven forty-five. "Not at all. Are you there?"

"Yes. I arrived late last night, too late to call." He said that he'd found a Howard Johnson's, just down the street from the Tennessee Children's Home Society. "I'll be heading there after breakfast, do some snooping around."

I stifled a snicker. A man of Eliot's caliber using the word *snooping*.

We chatted some more before he had to go. Truthfully, so did I. I'd purchased a gorgeous multi-layered ostrich fan that spanned nearly seven feet, so there was a lot more practice needed to handle it properly. The fan was so heavy it was taking days to learn how to maneuver it while allowing some peek-a-boo moments through the performance. I couldn't wait to try it out on my audience, then later tell Eliot to come see my new act. The feathers were white with aqua tips, Eliot's favorite color, so my new fan dance would be, secretly, in his honor.

Eliot called again a few days later to tell me he'd made some headway, knowing I needed to hear that. "I discovered some interesting things about this woman who runs the place." He didn't elaborate but added that he wanted to dig further into it before heading home. I kept busy in the meantime, sewing up new costumes to go with my various fans. The days crawled, but finally the following Thursday, Eliot showed up at the Roxy.

As usual, the bright stage lights veiled the audience in darkness, yet I sensed Eliot's presence. The minute I wrapped up my performance, I changed and headed to the lounge.

Sure enough, there he was. In his typical corner, smoking and nursing a Cutty Sark.

"I thought you might be here." I gave him a quick peck on the cheek.

"Did you now?" He grinned so wide, his dimple deepened. "Have a seat. What're you havin'?"

It was a slow night, as most Januarys were, so Tony stood awaiting my order.

"I think I'd like a nice Bordeaux."

Eliot chuckled. "One thing about you," he said as Tony went to get it, "you're never boring, right down to your ever-changing drinks." His grin grew wider. "Which seems to be based on your mood . . . are we in a pensive mood tonight?"

"Well, before I saw your handsome face, it was restless and eager . . . to see that handsome face." I let out a nervous sigh. "Wine calms me and I'm thinking I need to be calm for whatever news you may have for me."

He nodded, regarding me over the lip of his glass as he took a drink. It seemed he was getting his thoughts together as he lit my cigarette, then one for himself. I stayed silent as Tony returned. "Enjoy the wine, Lydia," Tony said, "I hear this vintage won't be so easily available with all that's going on in France these days."

Bringing up current events and talk of war generally sparked much banter about Americans getting involved and whether that was right or wrong, but tonight Eliot and I had more immediate topics to discuss. Fortunately, Tony was not one to hover, and since it was closing time, the place was clearing out.

Eliot lifted his drink. "Let's do a toast. To this journey we have found ourselves on." Was that a good sign? I recalled this same toast not that long ago.

I took a hearty sip. "Sounds like the journey gets deeper? Please. Tell me everything. Start from the very moment you stepped into that Home. What was it like?" My nerves made my voice squeak.

This man was the kind that paid attention to details, so I absorbed every one. He began by telling me how he had called and gotten an appointment with the director. "Since I knew the agency catered to the rich, I told her that I represented a well-known couple interested in adopting. She, of course, said she was available the next day."

He described the Home as a large three-story brick house, similar to others in the upper-class neighborhood. "I was first greeted by a woman in a nurse's uniform, then waited in this rather garish, red upholstery chair for a good twenty minutes before another woman entered and introduced herself as the director, a Miss Georgia Tann."

She was a big woman, he told me, built and dressed more like a man. "A woman who took pride in her mission, as she'd called it. She'd boasted that her business was a large one, with a waiting list of couples as far away as Canada." He stopped, took in a breath. "Oddly, she showed no emotion when she spoke of the children. She had, what I would say, a prepared speech at the ready. Complete with details, such as the quick turn-around, implying that if a couple wants a blue-eyed, blond haired child, they best act quickly before they get snapped up."

"Snapped Up? Wow. Sounds a bit cold, wouldn't you say?"

"Indeed." He smashed out his butt into the already filled ashtray. "Though I suppose the line of business she's in, probably best to remain detached."

"How could anyone be so detached when it comes to the lives of innocent children?" I caught his face then, remembering his desire to someday be a father, though his wife, as he had mentioned, wasn't interested in starting a family.

My mind swirled. Part of me wished to play the devil's advocate. The woman did sound like a cold fish, yet maybe she forced back her emotions to do her job. Maybe she really wanted to do right by the children, even if she did cater to the rich. After all, those were the ones who had the means to provide a quality home life. The thought that a good family had taken in Tess eased my fears. Or maybe the wine had taken effect.

Eliot interrupted my thoughts. "Miss Tann claims she gives the orphaned children a better chance at life by giving them to high-bred people. But it's clear what she really means is she sells them to people she calls, the higher type." His face hardened. "*And* for exorbitant fees. She took great delight in adding that some of her clients were in the film industry, and that she was currently working with Joan Crawford, yes, the actress, who's interested in adopting one, maybe two, of her charges."

So much for devil's advocate. "Wait. Did you tell her who you were? What you do?"

He shook his head. "People tend to clam up when you say you're a part of law enforcement and come around asking questions." He stopped to light my cigarette. I always seemed to smoke more around him. "I did tell her I hadn't been forthcoming on the phone, which she didn't like, let me tell you. I said I was there on your behalf. That I was Samuel Swanson, your father's younger brother and looking for information about my niece. I added that I'd been overseas in the army when your mother died and no one at the Cleveland adoption facility knew you had family left."

175

"Oh, that sounds plausible."

"Yes, but it didn't seem like she bought the story. I had to pull out all the stops, be as charming as possible."

"Well, that comes natural with you."

That produced a slight grin but it left quickly. "I told her I didn't get the information about my sister-in-law's death until it was too late. You two were already gone. Now, to address her next obvious question, I said since your father disappeared years before, you never knew much about me so naturally you never thought to mention an uncle to the agency. Especially since you had no idea they would separate you and your sister."

He swiveled his stool towards me so that our eyes met. "I mentioned that when the Murphy Home closed up suddenly, there was a paper trail showing many of the children were sent to her institution. That got her attention. I caught a look, faint as it was, but there. When you're doing something that could be considered unethical, to say the least, and there's a paper trail, it tends to make people nervous. Plus, this way, *I* wasn't the threat, the real threat was that someone else could be breathing down her neck. If in fact, she had something to hide. And I believe she does."

Oh, God, what did this all mean?

"I told her the girl's name was Tess Swanson, that she was thirteen in 1935, the time she would've been sent there. I described her as you did for me: tall for her age, shoulder-length, wavy brown hair, big round eyes—

"That's when she straightened her posture and said, 'Oh. I think I remember that girl.' "

I clutched my chest. "Oh Eliot."

"Let me go on." He gave my hand a gentle tap, causing my fears to ratchet up again. "She admitted she once had a girl with that description, adding that she rarely took in teenagers. I asked if she had a file on the girl, to make sure it was her. She said that since she only sent children to good homes, record-keeping wasn't necessary. That's a big red flag I plan to dig into." His lips tightened. "She said the girl had been there about two weeks when she happened to be talking to a couple, good people, she quickly added. Acquaintances of her father, who, you'll recall, is a local judge." His frown worried me. "The couple traveled a lot and were looking for a nanny for their ten-year-old daughter.

Was this a good thing? My mind was reeling.

He lit yet another cigarette. "When I called you last Friday saying I was remaining a few more days, it was because I was making arrangements to meet that couple."

"Are you serious?" My voice rose so loud, Tony glanced up, but stayed in his place. "How'd you find out who they were? Did you meet with them? Is it her? How could you keep this from me for nearly a week?"

"I couldn't give you any more details then. I didn't want to get your hopes up in case it turned out to be nothing."

A knowing chill crept up my spine. "But it turned out to be something. Didn't it, Eliot?"

"Yes." He grabbed his glass and polished off his drink.

26.

*T*ony, looking haggard, returned and asked if we could possibly say goodnight as he had to go home and begin all over again tomorrow.

"Oh, I'm so sorry, Ton. Yes, of course." I stamped out my cigarette, leaned across the bartop to peck his cheek. "But thank you. This meeting means a lot to me."

"It's fine, Lyd. You know I'd do anything for you, but I really am bushed."

While Eliot paid our tab, adding a good-sized tip, I glanced at my watch. We had no clocks in the place so there'd be no reminder for husbands to rush on home. Almost two in the morning. Eliot wore a watch too, but he showed no sign of caring. Were the rumors true that he and Evaline were on the outs?

One matter at a time, I told myself.

Once we settled in Eliot's Chrysler, Eliot turned up the heat. But instead of going anywhere, he simply continued his story as we sat with our heavy coats in the roomy front seat.

Georgia Tann, he continued, had told him that she had not talked to the couple since Tess left there, but said that she would get their number from her father. "I didn't trust that, of course, but managed to get her to tell me they lived somewhere in Kentucky, along the Ohio River. She gave their last names—Ginart. With that being a somewhat rare surname, I had the means to find out where they were and decided to simply show up at their door."

Having learned the couple lived outside of Louisville, a small town called Mockingbird Valley, he detoured there,

A Place We Belong

settling into a nearby motel to plan his strategy for that Sunday. "I considered all scenarios so I'd be able to react in the right fashion, get information they may not want to offer.

"I do know a few things about adoption services and their outcomes, that adoptive families often keep their secrets close to the vest. In many cases, the adoptive parents prefer to live as if the biological parents did not exist. You have to wonder how someone would handle an older child who knew of her past."

I had a sudden thought. "Do you think they told her something happened to me in order to keep her from running back home?"

"That would be anyone's guess. I don't know the answer to that, but I do have other useful information for you."

I desperately wanted another cig, but my hands were trembling so, I couldn't get a good grip to pull one from my pack. I thought of asking Eliot, but he was too engaged with his story, and so was I. I pulled off my leather gloves, stuffed them into my pockets, and sat with clasped fingers tight in my lap.

He stared at the dashboard as he spoke. "I took a bus to their residence rather than a car they could identify, and I only had a short walk from the stop. The weather cooperated too. Not terribly cold that day. As I got closer, I could only hope they'd be there and not off on some winter holiday, as folks like that often do."

He shifted uncomfortably. "I tried to time it well, figuring if they were church-goers, they might be home after two. Their home was nice, quite large. Whatever the man did for a living, he was doing well. I rang the doorbell and a young girl answered. At first, I thought it might be Tess, but this one's hair was blonde."

"Their daughter?"

"Yes. I guessed she must be around fifteen now. Instead of asking for her parents, I asked for her older sister, not using a name in case they had it legally changed in the adoption."

"Right. Calling her Tess might shut them down immediately."

"Precisely."

Although I'd asked for, wanted, every detail so I could envision the whole scenario, my heart pounded so hard in my chest I feared I might not live to hear it all.

Sensing my anxiety, Eliot quickly went on. "She gave me a suspicious look, asked right away who I was. I told her I was from the census bureau. Explained it in case she didn't know what that was. I gave her a reassuring smile and she seemed to relax. I asked her name, she said, Susie, and how many were in the family unit. She replied, three. That threw me. I pulled out formal looking papers from my briefcase and bluffed that records showed there were four in the last census. Two female children. The girl nodded and said, yes, her oldest sister. I asked her name." He reached for my hand, met my eyes. "It was Theresa."

I let out a gasp. "Oh God." Goosebumps crawled up my skin. I wrapped my coat tighter around me.

"I remembered you told me her full name, so I was encouraged. The girl said Tess moved five months ago to New York. I asked where in New York, she looked at me strange and said, New York City, as if that was the only one in the state," he snickered and I did too. "I started to ask the address, saying I needed it to complete the family record, hoping she'd give it, when a car pulled in the driveway. The Ginarts were home.

He looked at me with tired eyes. "I came clean then."

"What?"

"Sort of," he grinned. "Naturally when the older couple walked up to the house, they were suspicious."

"I can imagine."

"I told them the same story I did to Georgia and that I hoped to share with Tess that her real sister was looking for her. I asked for a forwarding address, but the mother shook her head and said they didn't know where she was."

I was feeling faint. "Would you mind opening the window a tad, I think I need fresh air."

He rolled the window down a crack. "That's when Susie gave me a dirty look and disappeared. I guess I deserved that. I *had* tricked her."

"How did the parents take your news?"

"They asked me to leave. They claimed they hadn't had any contact with the girl since she left. Said that she'd turned out to be more trouble than . . . she stopped at that point, but the implication was clear."

That nagged me. But it also made me smile. My sister was still feisty. "Oh my Lord, I am so relieved she's okay. She's alive!" Once that sunk in, I added, "But I have to wonder what she's been through. Why would she leave and go to a big city like New York? Why would she not come home? "

"We're getting closer to finding out." Eliot finally pulled out his pack of Luckys, lit two, handing one to me. "Next stop is a trip to New York, though I may not be able to get away for another month."

"Oh, Eliot, you'd be willing to do that? Wouldn't that be a shot in the dark? "

"I told you I've committed to this, and I meant it."

I snuggled closer to him. It was an intimate gesture in the confines of a car but I felt so close to him. "Have I told you, you're my hero? You've given me such hope. Thank you for going through all this for me, and others."

He cleared his throat and softly said, "I think it's time we get you home." He kissed my forehead, then started up the car.

I scooted back to my side and gazed out the window. We stayed quiet on the ride to my place. When he pulled in, I knew he was tired and needed to get home, but I could no longer keep my curiosity at bay.

"I'm sorry, Eliot, but I have to ask you something before you go. A personal question." I could see his facial features under the streetlight at the end of the drive. He was beat but still he answered. "Of course."

"That letter you wrote me." I shifted a little in my seat. "Did Evaline put you up to writing it? I'm sorry, I need to know, what's changed since that letter? At the risk of prying, are you and Eveline having problems? You don't seem very happy lately." I looked away, embarrassed for asking.

His head fell to his chest. "I'm really beat, Lydia, can hardly keep my eyes open. Can we talk about this another time?" His tone suggested that I butt out, and I was instantly sorry I'd brought it up.

"Never mind, I'm sorry. Go get some sleep."

I yanked the door handle. "I can't thank you enough for what you've done, Eliot. It means everything to me." I stepped out of his car and didn't turn back around until I heard his tires pull out of the drive.

27.

*O*nce inside, my thoughts turned to what weighed heaviest in my heart. Tess would be eighteen in a few weeks, so young to be living in the Big Apple. That city can harbor a lot of danger. Whatever was she doing there? Was she an aspiring actress working as a waitress until she was discovered? A secretary in an office high up in one of those tall buildings? Or had she found the man of her dreams and was living as a happy homemaker?

I had doubts about that last thought. I recalled my sister's rebellious streak, how Father would call her a little spitfire. I couldn't envision her settling for a life of catering to a husband and children. Like me, Tess would want more.

That was good. The world could eat young, naïve girls alive. If you were tough, didn't take crap from anyone, you could survive. For the first time since I'd lost her, I felt renewed confidence that whatever she might have endured these past years, Tess was a survivor.

A full two weeks went by before I heard from Eliot, but that wasn't surprising. According to the papers, after nabbing much of the crime syndicate, and reforming the police department, he and the county sheriff were busy conducting raids on other gambling houses. The last article I'd read had praised their tactics, declaring the public much safer in the years that Eliot Ness had been in charge.

He called on a Monday night. We discussed the snowstorm that had blown past during the weekend, and how our days had gone. Then his tone grew serious.

"You asked me about Evaline and the letter I wrote, so I will tell you," he began. "I admit, we've gotten into a few bouts concerning you. She read the papers about the Terrace raid, where it mentioned the Roxy. She wanted to know if you were one of the girls at the bust. I told her the truth, trying to be reasonable, adding that I had not known you'd be there. She thought I let you off the hook because she believes we have a relationship. The kind we do not have . . .

"One night, she admitted listening in on our conversation that night you called."

I knew it!

"She'd been drinking, we both had, and she went off on this jealous tirade. She repeated everything you had said on the phone. About us being close, that I was the first person you thought to call. That you needed me—

"I tried telling her there was nothing going on between us, that you were a client. Of course she didn't believe me, given," he paused, "forgive me, your occupation." I wondered if telling me this on the phone made it easier for him than in person.

I couldn't help feeling angry. The woman was being judgmental, like all the rest of them. I wanted to tell him right then about his wife's supposed dalliance with another woman but bit my tongue. Now was not the time. I would keep that little tidbit in my back pocket, for the right time. Or maybe never. I wouldn't want to hurt him just to get back at her.

"I want to be honest with you, Lydia. She told me she felt I was risking my career, my reputation, our marriage . . . and forced my hand."

"Oh, Eliot, I am so sorry I made waves."

"Not your fault." He breathed so heavy into the phone, I could almost smell the scotch through the wires. "I'm not guilty of a damn thing. You mean something to me, Lydia, I don't want to give up our friendship. The minute I sent that letter, it bothered me so much that I had to explain. When I couldn't get a hold of you for two days, I started to panic."

"And you broke into my house and found me crying on my bathroom floor."

"Well, I didn't exactly break in."

"Maybe so," I'd been so distraught, didn't even think about locking the door." I shook my head, recalling the real break-in just weeks before.

I turned my thoughts to his words, *You mean something to me*. No matter what happened, I would always have that.

"There's another reason I called," he added.

"Yes?"

"It appears I'll be able to take a week off soon. I'd like to take that trip to New York." I heard the snap of his cigarette lighter. "It's a big city but I have some ideas on places Tess might be staying at. It's a crapshoot, but I'm used to those. I was wondering if you'd like to come along. I'd hate to find her without you there."

I sprung from my bed. "Seriously? You're not toying with me, are ya?"

"I would never toy with you."

"Aw, now isn't that a shame?" I teased. "You think we'll really find her, Eliot?"

"We're sure as hell gonna try."

I hung up and twirled until I was dizzy. I just may find Tess after all! And in New York City! Ever since I began my career, I'd heard all the exciting stories of performing on stage at all the glitzy high-class nightclubs, like Minsky's, Zorita favorite place, where she and other girls made a big name for themselves. If I'd had more nerve when I was eighteen, I, too, would've gone there to try my luck, but I'd been too green. And once I'd established myself at the Roxy, I was happy where I was. George, Kitty, Big Joe and Tony were people who really cared about me.

Did Tess have those kinds of people surrounding her, in such a big city as that? I prayed in my heart that she did.

I flopped back on my bed, pulling my blanket up to my neck. I couldn't sleep now if I tried. I closed my eyes and imagined reuniting with my baby sister, in the big, wonderful city that was New York.

A Place We Belong

28.

*F*or the rest of the week, I could think of nothing else. My deep hope that we would find Tess consumed me. What would it be like to see her again after nearly six years? I had even dreamed that we'd found her living in a fancy house, like the one Eliot had described that her adoptive family lived in. The minute we laid eyes on each other, we ran and embraced. The hug felt so real, the emotion of it jerked me awake. I woke with tears on my face and laid there for a long time envisioning our reunion.

But I also had to walk into George's office and ask for time off. He had become like a surrogate father to me, though he never meddled in us girls' lives. It was part respect, but also, I believed he figured the less he knew about our pasts, the better. Now I wanted him to know the circumstances that led me to work for him. It was time he knew about Tess and how imperative this trip was to me. I sat him down and told him the whole story.

The only thing I left out was who I planned to go to the big city with.

"I've recently discovered information that she's living in New York," I said without elaborating. "I think I'm going to need two weeks off." *Who knew how long it would take?* I held my breath. "I know I'm not due for a vacation yet, and I rarely take more than one week a year as it is. I have Kitty on board to cover some hours and that new girl seems anxious to work her way up and this could be her chance." I added that it was also good timing. The ever-popular Rose Le Rose was coming for a special one-week appearance and when the wheel-circuit gals came to perform, I often got more time off anyway.

"This is the first real opportunity I've had to find her," I pleaded. How could he turn me down?

He took his glasses off to clean the lenses and without looking up said, "Lydia, you're a hard worker. And dependable. I've always appreciated that about you. We'll manage." Then to my great surprise, the man who rarely showed affection with his girls, stood, put a fatherly arm around me and squeezed. "Go find your sister."

*E*liot suggested we take the train. He didn't have to say that it would be too intimate to travel together by car, it was understood. I'd never traveled outside of Ohio and wondered how I should dress for such an important trip. Being February, I knew to pack winter attire, but what sort of wardrobe? Casual? Night-on-the town stuff? Knowing Eliot, we'd surely hit a couple of taverns during our stay so I packed several different outfits. Luckily, the weatherman on the radio had promised no snow for at least a few days. I'd be ready either way, choosing my best Mouton fur coat with mink hat and muff, perfect for travel.

And Spencer was all set too. When Frank and Helen agreed to take care of my dog once again, we both realized that he'd become too much for me, given my work and now, this mission. And so, I gave my baby to them, knowing I'd see him nearly as often, anyway. It was sad to know he'd no longer be mine, but I was comforted knowing he'd have a better, more attentive, home.

When we got to our seats in our private section, we sat facing each other so we could both enjoy a window seat, watching the world pass by. I smoothed my hand along the soft velvety upholstery, not quite believing I was here. The little tied-back curtains gave the car a homey feel, as if sitting in one's living room as the train shimmied us along through hills, valleys and small towns.

As the sun peeked through the wintery clouds, I recalled that time I rode the rails. I'd chose never to relive that horrible time but now, in this car with Eliot, it felt safe to reflect. I closed my eyes, feeling the rumbling of the tracks, recalling the scared lonely girl I had once been. I remembered thinking what would become of her. How would she manage all on her own, without a family, without a friend? Even then, it was as if it was happening to someone else.

I pulled my hands out of the warm muff and placed them in my lap. I looked down at my fingers that now wore fancy rings. I felt the softness of my fur coat hugging my legs. I patted my hair, now free from my cap, glad to know it was still pinned neatly in a soft chignon. I not only felt grown up in that moment, I felt a sense of pride.

I'd become more than the woman I had dared to dream about. I had managed my life pretty damn well, in spite of it all. I was independent, made my own money, made my own way in the world. I had everything I needed. Well, save for a man to call my own. Still, I was pleased with the successful life I'd built for myself. *The hell with you, my so-called father, I triumphed in spite of you.*

I almost told my train-hopping story to Eliot but got distracted by the beauty outside the window. I felt light-headed as the train curved along through Pennsylvania, and covered my mouth fearing my laugh was too loud.

Eliot gave a quizzical look. "What's so funny?"

"I don't know." I laughed again. "I'm just feeling a bit giddy." I leaned towards him. "Remember when you were a kid and would get butterflies in your stomach in anticipation of something?" I placed my hand on my abdomen. "It's like going to a birthday party."

I pulled out a cigarette from my pack. "Although I can't really see you as a child. Seems like you always had this mature worldliness about you."

It was his turn to chuckle. "I'm afraid you're just being biased. I was an awkward kid." As the train wheels churned, he told me more about growing up the youngest of five children. "I was a good boy, but an introvert. And a poor student."

"Oh, I find that hard to believe. You're a college graduate."

"I know, and I admit I'm proud of that accomplishment given my background." He too turned his attention toward the window. "It wasn't easy growing up."

"How so?"

He told me about growing up on the south side of Chicago, a neighborhood filled with poverty and crime. "Guess, that's how I learned some tough skills for my future position. Lucky for me, my older sister's husband, Alex, saw potential in me. He liked my inquisitive nature, thought I had good instincts." He shrugged. "I suppose he was right."

"Damn tootin' he was."

Eliot let out a belly laugh. "I think you mean, darn tootin.' "

"Oh, right. Well, damn seems more fitting." I gave a little smirk.

The porter appeared and told us it was nearing time to go to the dining area for dinner. Afterward, we spent time in the train bar before retiring to our respective cabins. Just after nine Tuesday morning, the train pulled into Grand Central Depot, which Eliot said was the largest train station in the world. In awe, I gawked at the sea of people everywhere.

"Stay close," he said as we stepped off the train and ascended the stairs. I could see how we could easily get separated. As we marched through the crowd, I caught glimpses of the fabulous building with its tall chandeliers, celestial ceiling, the big clock at the information center . . . it was all so grand.

The wind slapped my face the minute we walked outside, but I hardly minded. The city did not disappoint. I marveled at the buildings that seemed to touch the sky, the hustle and bustle of people walking briskly through the slushy sidewalk. Everyone seemed to have somewhere to go. It was downtown Cleveland times twenty.

"We'll need to hail a taxi," he said, pointing with his head since both hands carried the suitcases. It made us look like a couple. His left hand, holding onto his masculine leather cowhide valise, his right, clasping her pink floral one, which was undoubtedly heavier.

I slipped an arm through his as we walked down the busy street. "I've never been more excited in my life." I waved my free arm in the air.

He seemed excited too, and proud to have me on his arm. Feeling bold, I let go of him and waved my hand anxiously as a yellow cab approached.

"You're a natural," he beamed.

He had booked us separate rooms at the Hotel Bristol. Walking into the lobby, with its glittery gold, high ceiling and hanging portraits, was like walking into another world. At the reservation desk, the manager handed us our keys. I rubbed my fingers along its grooves. I had never stayed in a hotel.

"We're on the same floor but mine is around the corner."

"You've stayed here before?"

"Once. A long time ago."

The statement hung in the air. He had lived so much more than I had, or probably ever would.

We took the elevator to the seventh floor. "Lucky seven," Eliot joked, stopping at my room first. "We'll take it from here," he told the bellhop after tipping him with folded bills.

Eliot took the key out of my hand. "Allow me." When he opened the door, I let out a gasp. It was small but had the look of luxury I hadn't expected. There was a lovely double-sized bed covered with a shiny red quilt. The nightstand had a lovely brass lamp on it, alongside a phone, also with brass trim. The heavy gold drapes reminded me of the ones in *Gone with the Wind*. In a corner, there was a cherry wood desk with a hardback chair to sit in and write letters.

"This place is right up my alley," I squealed, pouncing on the bed, skirt, shoes, and all, like the child I suddenly felt I was. Then I hopped back up and gave Eliot a big squeeze. "I could absolutely live here."

"I've no doubt," he laughed his deep hearty laugh, squeezing me back. "I can see you being right at home here. And you'll especially enjoy the maid service."

"Oh, how you spoil me," I gushed, breaking from him to gaze out the window, which had a stunning view of the city. I hugged myself.

I gazed out at the skyline filled with big everything—buildings, billboards, church steeples—all the while feeling Eliot's tall presence behind me.

I don't know how long I stood there lost in thought when Eliot slipped his arms around my shoulders and whispered, "She's out there, Lydia. And we're going to find her."

My lips began to quiver. Somehow I believed that too. I had to.

I turned to see him glance at his watch. "I need to get to my room, make some calls. Go ahead and get settled. We'll have lunch somewhere, then tour Manhattan." How I loved the sound of that.

A Place We Belong

While I waited for his return, I unpacked and hung up my clothes because I hated to iron. Then I drew myself a luxurious beauty bath with my favorite SweetHeart soap that I had made sure to bring. Not wanting to languish too long, I got out in twenty minutes and wrapped myself in the soft terrycloth robe I'd found in the closet, with the fancy monogrammed logo.

An hour later, we were strolling down the city streets where street peddlers were selling their wares, everything from a variety of meats and fish to leather goods and more. We found a quaint Jewish-American café just a block from Times Square, where the smells of breads, meats and hot coffee wafted through the air. I suddenly realized I was famished.

The lunch crowd was beginning to thin, so we were able to get a window seat. While perusing the menu, Eliot said, "You can't really know the New York experience until you've had one of these," pointing to the picture of a large sandwich called, the Deep-Well. I read the description. Slices of pastrami, salami, and tongue on a warm onion roll.

"Tongue?" My face displayed my horror.

He let out a belly laugh. "Okay, maybe you're not ready for that just yet. How about a nice Pastrami on rye?"

I laughed back. "I think I'd like that better."

The sandwich was mammoth but I managed to devour every bite. We sat, ate, and people watched. We kept the conversation light, not knowing what we'd face tomorrow. Or the next day, or the next. So, no talk of Tess. No talk of work. No talk of *us*. Simply a serene and pleasurable moment in New York City.

We strolled all afternoon and window shopped while smelling roasted hot dogs from the vendors. "Would you like to hit Macy's?" Eliot pointed ahead to a grand building.

"Macy's!" I squealed. "Oh, what girl wouldn't?"

We visited each floor and when we reached the men's tie department, I said, "Oh, Eliot, look at all these ties. There must be literally hundreds here." I was amazed at the rows and rows of long ties, short ties, bow ties, thin ties, thick ties, and in every color and design imaginable.

"I'd like to get George a nice one for giving me the time off, but there are so many, I'm at a loss." I pulled him closer to the counter. "Come, help me decide. Pick out three of your favorites."

"Three?"

"I need to have a choice, and depends on the price." I tried for an innocent face since I'd already determined I would give Eliot the one he liked best.

He commented on what he did and didn't like, and it helped me know him even better. He spotted a red one that had a sensuous looking lady on it. "You gotta admit George'll like this one." We laughed in agreement.

"But I also want to give him one that would appeal to most any man. Something real nice."

I saw his interest brighten when he spotted a wide rayon green-and-gold Cravat-style tie. I wanted to give it to him right then but decided to wait.

By the time we returned to the hotel, my feet hurt like the dickens and my eyes itched with exhaustion. To my surprise, Eliot still looked wide awake and chipper.

But he did notice me lean against the door for balance. "Go on, unwind, take a nap. I'll come back at seven, take you to dinner at the Pink Elephant downstairs. I think you'll like it."

All I could do was nod. The minute the door was shut, I kicked off my shoes and plopped on the bed fully clothed. The next thing I knew, my room phone was ringing and it was getting dark outside.

"Ready for a scrumptious dinner, good cocktails and even better company?" He quipped.

"I can't believe I'm saying this, Eliot, but I'm worn out. I guess all the anticipation and the long trip, and all that walking caught up with me. I don't have an ounce of energy left. Plus, this wonderful bed is so warm and comfy, I simply can't pull myself out of it."

"I can understand that."

"Plus I wanna be fresh for tomorrow."

"Of course. Enjoy your room and I'll see you for breakfast."

After a full day of fun enjoying the sights, I couldn't wait for morning to begin the search for my sister.

"Goodnight, Eliot."

"Goodnight, Miss Lydia."

Even the noise of the city outside my window couldn't keep me awake.

29.

*N*ew York City offered several boarding houses and apartments for unmarried working girls at reasonable fees. We ventured out early on our mission, with Eliot's list of those at hand.

"If Tess came here alone," he told me, "she most likely would be staying at one of these places." But these places were not without their rules, Eliot said. Male guests are only permitted on the main floor or dining room with strict dress and conduct codes.

"Oh dear," I said, "I can't see Tess abiding by such stern regulations, especially now that she's of age. Like I've mentioned, she could be a pistol."

"So can you, my dear," he said with a wry grin. "And we have to start somewhere."

Yes, we did, and I had to trust Eliot's instinct that we would succeed finding the proverbial needle in a haystack. As we walked along the busy streets, I had to ask, "What if she came here with someone? She could be living god-knows where."

"Sure, that'll be a bigger challenge." He patted my back. "But one step at a time. Let's rule out the obvious first."

The first stop was The Webster Apartments, closest to our hotel. We agreed that he would do most of the talking because some of these places don't give information out freely. He was to be my uncle and state that we had made plans to meet my sister when I arrived.

It was a good plan and I tried to keep calm and not get all a-flutter at the very thought that they might find her. Yet my heart betrayed me and fluttered anyway as we climbed the concrete steps and into the building. The woman at the desk seemed preoccupied.

"Excuse me, ma'am, we're here to meet with Tess Swanson." The clerk looked up to see the handsome man before her and responded accordingly. Before he could go on with his prepared speech, she checked her ledger, shook her head. "I'm sorry, sir, I know of no one here by that name."

"Are you certain?" One thing about Eliot, he didn't take no for an answer right off the bat. "She may be using a different last name." We had discussed the possibility that she might be using her adopted surname. His face grew serious. "She's trying to steer clear of a man that's caused her trouble in the past."

The woman nodded, no doubt having heard that before. "I understand and I am sorry but there is no resident here by the first name of Tess or Theresa."

As we walked out the door, Eliot said, "One down, but more to go. Don't get discouraged." He gave me a soft smile. "We've only just begun."

That's what I was afraid of. We only had a few days.

We had to get buzzed into the next residence, but the response was the same. Eliot asked if perhaps a girl by that name had stayed there in the past. Again, the answer was no.

"At least her name isn't Jane," I remarked on the way out. "Can you imagine trying to find, say, a Jane Smith?"

Our next stop was too long to walk. "Cabs are expensive, we should take the streetcar." He said it with a half-grin, knowing my disdain for them.

"That's fine." I was game for anything today. "It's a *New York* streetcar." I winked, causing him to smile. I loved when he smiled.

The Martha Washington Hotel was impressive. Too much so. "I hadn't realized this housing unit was so upscale," Eliot said. I agreed. Most young girls would not be able to

197

afford a place like this. Unless, of course, they were in the New York City Burlesque profession.

Not only was Tess not living there, but they also had many women on a long waiting list. None with her name on it.

The Barbizon was another popular building for female residents. This, too, was fancy, but with a homey feel. My hopes raised that Tess might be living in one of these nice places after staying with the well-to-do Ginarts. We just had to find the right one.

I was surprised to learn that many young women came to this large city on their own. Apparently, I'd been sheltered more than I'd thought. We kept going throughout the afternoon, each time leaving disappointed. But neither of us wanted to take time for a long lunch so we grabbed a hot dog at one of the street stands. My high heels were making my feet feel like I was walking on nails, but I forced myself to keep moving without complaint.

After another hopeful place proved in vain, I finally gave in. "I can't do anymore today." Eliot looked over at me and his face softened. "I can see that and it's okay."

We stopped at a corner where I leaned against a building, took off my heels. "It's just so damn disheartening," I said, rubbing one foot, then another. "I'm ready for a good stiff drink, how 'bout you?"

We hopped back on the streetcar and made our way to Minsky's. After all, I couldn't be in New York without stopping there.

We sipped Manhattans because, as Eliot said, "When in Rome." We enjoyed both the baggy pants comedians and the afternoon show. The dancers were true showgirls, complete with elaborate headpieces. None of them used fans. Was I *passé* already?

Eliot leaned in. "Getting some new ideas?"

I laughed. "Actually, yes," giving him one of my signature winks.

After the second show, I asked the cocktail waitress why the girls didn't dance with fans. The woman just shrugged saying that while she'd heard of Sally Rand and Faith Bacon doing it, it hadn't caught on there.

"Well, if Sally Rand is still doing it, I'm in good company," I replied with a smile.

I was feeling tipsy by the time we headed out. Once outside, Eliot caught my arm and suggested we go for an early dinner at the Pink Elephant. "Sounds good. But first, let me change and fix my makeup and hair. *And* put on better shoes."

When I got to my room, I plopped down on the bed and dialed Kitty. I felt a need to talk to a girlfriend. After expressing distress at not finding even a clue to Tess's whereabouts, Kitty commiserated, then said, "Are you at least having some fun, sweetie? Is New York everything they say?"

"Oh, that it is," I said, "It's like a whole other world and—"

"So..." Kitty interrupted. "What are you and the big guy gonna do the rest of the night?" Her tone was obvious.

"If you're insinuating what I think you are, that's the question of the hour," I said, letting out a little laugh. I felt a bit wicked just thinking of the possibilities. "We *are* getting along fabulously, but I tell ya, the strain of everything, including being with him, is kinda getting to me. I got tipsy just after a few drinks."

"Oh my, that could be trouble. But do try and make the best of it. You know what they say, when the cat's away..."

"Oh you're terrible," I laughed again, "I gotta run, girl, keep the place going while I'm gone."

"Sure thing and call me tomorrow with an update."

Since arriving, my emotions had been skittering all over the place. Now, as I lined my eyelids and fluffed up my lashes,

199

I felt nothing but exhilaration. Tonight I had a New York "date" with the man of my dreams. The lure of the big bright city had me feeling reckless, indeed.

We met in the lobby and Eliot escorted me into the restaurant like we'd done it for years. I wore my best satin emerald-green cocktail dress that was just low-cut to be teasing, a favorite pearl necklace, a flared out skirt and shoes perfect for dancing. I had pulled my hair in an upsweep but allowed a few loose strands to linger playfully along my neck.

Eliot had made reservations for a table near a gorgeous white grand piano. As we were seated, I set my evening bag on the table, along with the narrow package I'd been carrying.

"So what's that you're holding?" he asked as he pulled out the chair for me.

As if he didn't know by the shape and size. I grinned like a child holding a forbidden toy. "I wanted to give you something as a token for my deepest appreciation," I said, handing it to him.

I was practically giddy watching him open it. "Aw, yes, my now-favorite tie." He gave a shy smile and immediately took off the more conservative one he wore, though it surely was a better match with his burgundy pin-striped suit.

"I do think the green-and-gold adds some needed pizzazz, don't you?" I joked.

"I do." Holding his new tie in his hand and looking proud as a peacock.

I scooted my chair closer. "Here, allow me."

When I was done, he ran his hand along the length. "How'd you learn to tie a tie so perfectly?"

"I'll never tell," I said, batting my eyes. I wouldn't mention my father this day. Or any day.

He let out a laugh that seemed to come all the way from his diaphragm. He leaned over and kissed my cheek. "Thank you. I will cherish it always."

"Well you should, you picked it out," I quipped. "Seriously, thank *you*, my sweet man, and dear friend. This trip means so much to me."

The waiter took our order—short ribs for me, steak for him—and the piano man began playing. Though I was hungry, I had a hard time eating more than a few bites. Eliot hadn't finished either when he walked up to make a song request. He returned and offered his hand.

"Shall I have this dance?"

"Of course." I got chills when I heard the beginning of "The Way You Look Tonight." "How'd you know I love this song?"

"I didn't." He grinned that wonderful grin. "It was just the first thing I thought of when you entered the lobby."

Again, he managed to make me feel like I was the only girl in his world. As we swayed along the floor, I wished the night would last forever. The joy in my heart trickled through every vein in my body—from the top of my head down to my toes. Tonight, I was a princess dancing with my prince.

In this exhilarating city, with this charming man in my arms, I knew this moment was fleeting. "You're a wonderful dancer, Mr. Ness."

"You're only as good as your partner." He said it lightly, but it intensified my emotions.

Returning to our seats, I found the nerve to ask what had been on my mind. "So what did you tell Evaline about this trip?" I took a good swig of my cocktail.

"I told her I had to go to New York on business, which is true. I was as honest as I could be considering how she feels about you." He straightened up in his chair, like he was being interrogated. Maybe I shouldn't have brought this up. "She knows not to question me further when it comes to business affairs."

That last word hung heavy in the air. I gulped down my drink, gazed into those blue-gray eyes and the words tumbled out. "Do you still love her?"

Somewhere inside my brain, I knew I was overstepping boundaries but that was the curse of too much liquor. It allowed your mouth to spill out what it normally held safe inside.

He didn't answer. He threw a twenty on the table and placed his hand on my arm. "Let's go outside. Take a walk."

"But it's freezing," I said, before realizing he wanted me to get some fresh air. It was clear that all the roller coaster of emotions had caught up with me. The drinks and my feelings for him had gone down all too easily.

Once outside, I knew better than to talk. I leaned heavy on his arm as we walked down the block. Through my blurry eyes, the city looked like a starry wonderland. The huge signs and bright marquee lights illuminated the entire block. Bright. Glittery. Surreal. Everything lit up, like a Christmas fairytale. There were noises of life everywhere. From the sound of beeping cars, music filtering out of nightclubs into the streets, the clatter of busy people . . . I understood why my showgirl friends loved it so.

I wanted to shout out to the stars all the sensations bursting through me, but Eliot's mood had changed.

"I'm sorry, Eliot, I shouldn't have brought up Evaline—"

"It's okay." We were both shivering without a coat. He was leading me back to the hotel. "Come on, let's get you to bed."

I couldn't help myself, I started giggling. "Yes, let's go to bed, Eliot." My arms were linked into his and my head leaned on his shoulder. I lifted my hand and rubbed his ear with my index finger. "You got such cute ears," I said, giggling again.

A Place We Belong

His head pulled away so slightly I wondered if it was on purpose or simply from the movement of walking.

In the elevator, I leaned into him. "Eliot, I'm sorry, I know I'm tipsy. Forgive me?" I went in for a kiss, pushing my ample breasts against him so he could feel what I had to offer.

To my delight, he kissed me back, with all the passion I had felt for him since the day we met. I heard the lift ding but held onto his lips. When the door opened, an older couple was staring at us. Eliot straightened and guided me out.

He helped get my key out of my evening bag. "You *are* coming in for a nightcap?" I pointed my finger into his chest, then leaned back against the door, pulling his new tie toward me for another kiss.

He kissed me back but drew away sooner than I'd wanted.

"Eliot? Don't you want to be with me?"

He gazed into my sluggish eyes. "I would like nothing more, Lydia." He looked misty, sorrowful, or was it just my drunken imagination? "But I will never take advantage of an intoxicated woman."

"That's too bad," I whispered, now sorrowful myself.

When he led me to the bed, I pulled him down with me. "I won't mind, you know. It'll be our li'l secret." I rubbed the side of his face. He blushed so much I could feel the heat. "Please Eliot?"

He kissed my forehead, then pulled himself off the bed. "I'll call you in the morning."

I laid there and watched the door softly shut. Leaving me alone and full of yearning.

30.

I awoke in a wrinkled dress, smudged makeup, and a head full of regret. As the night's activities replayed in my head, I hated myself for my errant behavior.

And yet, I couldn't help but regret that Eliot hadn't taken me up on my offer. *Why did he have to be such a damn gentleman?*

Besides my shameful behavior, I suffered from an awful hangover. What if we found Tess today by some stroke of luck? I'd hate having her see me for the first time in all these years, looking and feeling as bad as I did.

When the phone rang, I was afraid to answer, but what choice did I have? I had to face the music. "Hello, Eliot."

"How you feeling?"

"Oh God." I placed my hand on my forehead. "I am so embarrassed. My behavior was atrocious. Can you ever forgive me?"

I had to wait a full four Mississippis for his answer. Two too many. "Forget it. It's been a long two days for both of us and we had a few too many, I suppose. You ready for a good breakfast? We've got four more places to check out. Third day might be the charm."

His shift in tone, dry and distant, wounded me. I felt the urge to talk about what had occurred between us last night. I wanted to redeem myself somehow. But he was probably right to avoid such a discussion.

We met downstairs at eleven, giving me time to pull myself together and swallow a couple of aspirins in hopes to dissolve both my headache and my guilt.

A Place We Belong

I decided to have the hair of the dog with my bacon and eggs, and to my relief, the Bloody Mary worked wonders. By one o'clock, I was feeling close to my old self again. Despite being disappointed that we hadn't yet found Tess—and my embarrassment over my all-too-affectionate display the night before—I was having the best time of my life.

We were sitting in the back of the streetcar headed to our first stop of the day as Eliot made more plans for us. He was anxious to take me to the famous 21 Club, telling me the whole history of the biggest nightclub in New York. He also promised to take me to a Broadway show. "You can't be in New York without seeing at least one."

"That all sounds wonderful."

"That is, of course, if something else doesn't come up." Eliot still believed we might find her. I started to squeeze his hand but pulled it back. After last night, I was afraid to touch him.

I had read about the next residence on our list and felt we might have better luck with The Penington Friends House in Manhattan, if for no reason other than it allowed men to live there too. Tess always liked the boys. She'd even had a "boyfriend" in first grade, something everyone, except our father, had thought was "cute."

As we walked up the steps and opened the door to the Brownstone townhouse, I noticed it had just the right atmosphere that would suit my sister. We talked to the resident housemother, but the answer was the same. No.

Seeing my disappointment, the lady sighed. She leaned in so close, it startled me. "You Jewish? You don't look it."

My confused expression was her answer.

"I was gonna say she could be at The Clara de Hirsch Home. *It's a vocational school,* run by prominent German-Jewish women." The housemother waved her hand away. "But that's neither here nor there. They are non-sectarian. *They help young working gals, much like yourself, I presume." She gave me an appreciative nod, confirming I was properly dressed.* "You say she's not yet eighteen so it's entirely possible she may be there."

I thanked her with a fervent handshake. People like this kind woman, and Eliot, kept my hope alive. And boy, did I need it.

The Clara de Hirsch *Home reminded me of one of the big family homes from my old neighborhood, but as we entered, it was more like a hotel. The woman who rushed up to us looked every bit like* what she most likely was. A gatekeeper.

"May I help you?"

Eliot had his spiel down pat by now, but it didn't take long to hear the dreaded "no" yet again. This woman practically closed the door on our faces. Eliot seemed as frustrated as I felt. We had gone to eight different places in the last two days.

I let out an audible sigh. "I need a break," I said, descending the steps. Though I needed so much more than that. My hope was vanishing. Hope for everything I'd wanted so badly. "Maybe a nice lunch will help." I reminded him of a café we'd passed on the streetcar.

"Agree. It's a bit of a walk so if you're not up to that, I'll grab us a cab."

My legs were as heavy as my heart. I was about to opt for the cab when a young woman with pitch black hair came running after us. "Excuse me, I overheard you say back there you're lookin' for a girl named Tess?"

I sucked in a breath.

Eliot spoke before I had a chance to. "Yes, Tess Swanson. Brown hair and eyes, about eighteen. Do you know her?"

"Yes, that's her. She didn't stay long at Clara's but Miss Clyde's a stickler for our privacy. She won't tell nobody nothin'—even after they leave. Anyways, Tess moved out just after Christmas. Got this fancy job 'cross town."

I clutched my chest. "Do you know where that is? Where she's staying? I'm Lydia, her sister, and this is . . . a family friend, Eliot."

"Loretta." She shook my hand, then crossed her arms warding off the cold. She'd run out the door without a coat. "I don't know where she's living but far as I know, she's working as a waitress at the Black Cat. She seemed real excited about it."

Eliot raised his brows. "I imagine so. I've heard it's a swanky joint."

"When I overheard you ask about her, I got excited. She seemed so lonely. I really liked her, though she hasn't kept in touch since she left. For all I know, she could be gone from there by now. She didn't seem to know what she wanted in life. But then, do any of us?"

It was an odd comment. "We learn as we go, I guess," I answered. I noticed the girl's dark skin, though not as dark as the few negro women I knew. She must be mulatto, I determined. And quite pretty.

"Wait, you're her sister? She told me her sister was much younger."

Did I look that old already?

"I think she's referring to Susie," Eliot said, squeezing my shoulder.

"But that's not her—"

Eliot stopped me, looked back at Loretta. "Susie's a step-sister. Lydia is her real sister. They became separated when their mother died unexpectedly and she's been desperate to find her. Do you know anything else that might help us?"

"I'm sorry, like I said, she wasn't here long. And I haven't heard from her since, though I thought we were friends. I've been wanting to stop in to see her, but that place is beyond my means."

Eliot raised his brows. "How about you come with us, if you have time. We were just going to go somewhere for lunch, so we'll head there. If you'd like to join us. It's on me."

"Oh, I would love that." Her excitement faded quickly. "But I'm afraid I can't right now. I have a class later this afternoon—I go to a business college here."

"Well, maybe another time then. Here," Eliot pulled out his wallet and handed the girl his business card. "Also, we're staying at the Hotel Bristol. I'm in room 710. If you recall anything that could help us, please ring me up there."

"Me too." I searched in my handbag for a pen and paper. In my line of business, I learned being prepared was always handy. You never knew who you might come into contact with. I'd been able to meet some important people merely by exchanging personal info. "Please, give me your number. If we find her first, I'll be sure to let you know." It was a bit of a lie, of course. Who knew if Tess even wanted to see this girl again?

As I jotted down her number, Loretta looked up at me. "Hey, I just happened to think. I know Tess would be working nights because she said that's where you make the real money."

I smiled. "That sounds like my sister." Just speaking of her in the present and knowing for sure that Tess was alive brought tears to my eyes.

"So ya might want to wait a few hours to go there."

"That's a great tip, thank you." I normally did not hug strangers but I was so grateful to this Loretta.

As Eliot and I walked toward the trolley line, I clasped my gloved hand to my mouth, fighting a surge of giddiness. "Is this really happening?"

Eliot gave just a hint of a smile. "Remember, nothing is for sure. But lucky for us, Loretta ran after us."

A Place We Belong

We decided to go back to the hotel so I could freshen up. "I don't know what to wear," I said excitedly. "What do I *wear*?"

Eliot laughed. "I doubt your sister would even notice. Besides, you look wonderful in anything."

"Oh, Eliot, you say the sweetest things." I hugged his arm. It seemed we were back on track. My humiliating antics forgotten.

When we returned to The Bristol, I stopped by the cigarette machine. "Go on ahead, I need to grab some smokes."

He headed toward the elevator as I dug in my coin purse for a quarter. I yanked the lever for a pack of Chesterfields, which fell out with a thunk. As I grabbed it, I spotted the Lucky Strikes. I remembered all the times I'd smoked his. But I was out of quarters. I glanced up toward the front desk, thinking maybe they could make change when I saw a tall, thin woman in heels and a red wool coat talking to the man I already knew as Mr. Cohen.

I sucked in a gasp. Oh no. No. Not now. I stood frozen, unable to move, my heart revving as I pleaded, *Please dear God, don't let it be.*

As the man moved to the side to check on something, the woman turned just enough for me to see more of her face.

And there it was. The truth. The god-awful truth.

31.

I pounded my foot on the floor like an angry child who just got her candy taken away. I couldn't help it. Things had been going so well.

I was so startled I didn't know what to do. I watched the bellhop take Evaline's leather train case and lead her to the elevator.

I stayed safely hidden on the side of the machine, squeezing the cigarette packs so hard, they'd be too smashed to smoke. The minute Evaline disappeared behind the big gold doors, I rushed to the next one.

"Floor?" asked the liftman.

I was so disoriented I had to stop and think. The man stood holding the elevator door, staring at me, waiting. I recalled the day we arrived. *Lucky Seven,* Eliot had quipped. Humph, he couldn't have been more wrong. "Seventh floor, please," I said with clenched mouth.

When I got out, I saw Evaline knocking on Eliot's room door. I snuck around the corner in case she turned her well-coiffed head. When the door opened, I could only imagine Eliot's shock. "Evaline. What're you doing here?"

"Hello, Darling," she said, not waiting for an invitation before sweeping into the room. "Thought I'd surprise you."

Well, mission accomplished.

The second the door closed, I tiptoed over—not easy in heels—and placed my ear against it, wishing I had a glass, like I'd seen in the movies. But that wasn't necessary, I found, as the conversation escalated quickly.

"So where is she?"

"Where is who?"

"Oh, don't play those games, Eliot, it's getting old." Her voice trailed in and out, like she was walking through the room as she talked.

"Your constant jealousy doesn't become you," Eliot replied in an icy tone.

"Neither does your constant womanizing."

"You are wrong. You've always been wrong about that."

"So you're saying your little floozy *fan dancer* isn't here in New York with you?"

Floozy? That term was getting old.

"That's enough."

I'd never heard that particular tone from him before. The boom in his voice told me he was very close to the door. "Yes, Lydia is here." His voice had lost its volume but not its edge. "In her own room. I am not sleeping with her." I pressed my lips tight. That was all too true. "I'm working with her on a personal matter that is no one else's business. She wishes to keep it private and I am honoring that."

"Oh, aren't you the gallant one."

A pregnant pause. Then, "I think you need to go back home, Evaline. We're close to getting the information we need so I should be home by Sunday, maybe even Saturday, if all goes well."

"No. I'm here now." Her turn to pause. Perhaps suggesting relief that she had not found what she'd feared. "Oh, darling, I don't want to fight." Her voice suddenly softened to a purr. "Let's make the best of it, shall we?"

He didn't say yes or no. I imagined Evaline's lips on his now. My heart pumped harder. What did this mean, now that she was here?

Finally Evaline spoke again. "How about we go eat something, huh? I'm famished after the long trip."

"A trip you didn't have to make."

"Aw, come on, El, I just missed you is all."

The shuffle of footsteps coming closer made me jump back. I sprinted on my tip toes again round the corner to my room, dug my keys out of my bag, and once safely inside, leaned against the door, shuttering.

What to do now? We were so close to the reunion I'd long been praying for. Evaline was ruining more than just my time with Eliot, she was ruining my very life. I was so mad I could spit. What made me madder still was that I knew I had no right to be sore. Evaline was his wife. She called the shots.

There was no way I could go to The Black Cat now. Not alone. A lady just didn't saunter into a nightclub or restaurant unescorted. Especially in a big city like New York. I was among strangers here.

And how would I get home? Did this mean I had to take the train back alone?

I flung my pocketbook on the bed and sat next to it. I allowed my body to sink backward and laid there for who knows how long as a montage of scenarios played out in my head.

I held onto the faint chance that he would at least call me. After all, Evaline knew I was here. He had told her what was going on. She had to give him the opportunity to explain a change of plans to me.

Fat chance. No way would the woman let him out of her sight, or hearing distance, for the duration for this trip.

Still, guilt plagued me. As Eliot's wife, she had every right to be here. Then again, she was doing it only to spite us both. That much was clear. When the phone remained silent by six o'clock, I lit up a cig and began pacing the room wondering how I could possibly go to The Black Cat alone to at least see if Tess was there. I paused, gazing out at the skyline when an idea came.

I fished in my purse for Loretta's number and dialed, hoping her class was over. When she answered I felt encouraged that luck hadn't abandoned me completely. "Loretta, it's Lydia, we met this afternoon?"

I explained there was a change in plans, that Eliot couldn't accompany me now and would she be interested in joining me there for dinner? "It's on me, of course," I quickly added, recalling Eliot's wise offer. A college girl was always up for a free meal.

We met at 7:30. As Eliot had mentioned, it was a swanky place. I felt funny being there with another female, seeing how the romantic ambiance was more suited for couples. I couldn't help wishing Eliot was here with me. The place was jammed, but again, luck was on my side. A table was just opening up. I prayed the good fortune would continue through the evening.

The minute we were seated, the waitress—sadly, not Tess—was johnny-on-the-spot asking for our drink order. We both ordered Cokes. I was tempted to ask for some good rum in it, but I wanted to be completely sober for whatever might happen. When the waitress returned, I had to ask. "We were hoping to see Tess tonight. Is she working?"

"Tess?" The girl eyed me strangely. "Sorry, there's no Tess working here."

My heart sank. But I'd known it was a risk, hadn't I? "Have you worked here long?" Maybe Tess had been here but quit.

"About three years now."

I looked over at Loretta, who shrugged, "Sorry. That's what she told me."

"Jesus, I can't catch a break." I said, probably too loud, and fell back into my chair. I wanted to high-tail it out of there but had committed to buying this girl dinner. Now for no good reason. And what could we possibly talk about? To make things worse, Loretta ordered a high-priced steak while I asked for a salad I knew I wouldn't eat.

"Aw, don't give up," Loretta said after an uncomfortable silence. "Look how far you've already come. You met me, didn'cha?" She forced a little laugh. "Look, I promise tomorrow I'll ask around to anyone I think might know something. She must've gotten a job somewhere else, that's all. Come on, cheer up."

By the time dinner arrived I could feel the tears brimming. "I'm sorry, Loretta, I'm not good company, but you've no idea what I've been through. I've had the absolute worst day."

I ended up ordering a highball and told this stranger how my life was falling apart. Why not? I'd never see this Loretta again and I just had to voice my anguish.

I told her about my struggle to find Tess, about my hopeless feelings for the *married* man I'd come with, and how I now had to find my way back to Cleveland alone.

"I am the biggest fool." The stream of tears dripped down my face. I couldn't stop them if someone put a gun to my head. Which right now, didn't seem all that awful.

A proper lady, Loretta came equipped with tissues in her handbag. "Well, you can't choose who you fall in love with."

It was such a teenage thing to say. But right then, it sounded truer than any statement I'd ever heard. I accepted the tissues and dabbed my eyes. "You have a guy?"

Loretta shook her head. "Not yet, but I know he's out there somewhere. Just a matter of time."

Again, teenage whims.

"Do yourself a big favor. Stay away from married men."

Loretta lifted her Coke. "Cheers to that."

A Place We Belong

I gulped down the last of my drink, which tasted like watered-down Kool-Aid. After my drawn-out confession, the ice had melted from sitting too long in the warm room. Bland, diluted, and lukewarm, like my life.

I forced myself not to order another since I'd have to take the streetcar back and even then, had a bit of a walk to The Bristol. Or maybe I'd spring for a taxi. What the hell? I'd be broke by the time I paid my way home as it was. I shrugged to myself. I'd just have to work a lot of extra shifts. George would be thrilled.

After hearing repeated thank you's from Loretta, I paid the bill, got our coats from the hat check girl and reached over to grab a couple of mints. Just then, in the corner of my eye, I could have sworn on our mother's grave I'd seen Tess pass by. Was my mind playing tricks on me?

Granted, the girl in the waitress outfit was on the heavy side, and her hair was much blonder than Tess's, but that face! I grabbed the arm of another worker going by. "Excuse me, that girl over there," I pointed to where the Tess look-alike was taking an order. "What's her name?"

"Oh, that's Jean."

"Jean?"

Loretta had already walked to the door, but noticing I hadn't followed, came back to my side. "Lydia? What's wrong?"

I heard Loretta's voice but didn't answer. I couldn't figure it out—

Then it hit me. Jean. Jean Harlow! Tess's favorite actress. She'd been obsessed by the sexy blonde actress so much that when she was twelve, she began insisting everyone call her Jean. At least until it became too much trouble to keep correcting people.

215

I let out a shrill. "Oh my god." I swayed toward Loretta, held onto her arm. "It's her! Did you see her?" My knees felt so weak I was certain I was about to faint.

Loretta must have thought the same thing and held me up. "See who? Are you okay?"

I pointed straight ahead. "There. It's her! That's my sister!"

32.

*D*izzy from shock, I rushed across the room, Loretta scurrying behind me, to where Tess was taking an order from a couple who was just trying to have a nice dinner. I snatched Tess's arm. "Tess, it's me!"

Everything in my words, my expression, my very soul, expected a grand response. If not a tearful one. My heart was throttling like a race car.

My sister's eyes grew wide at the sight of me. Then squinted with hate. "Excuse me," she hissed, yanked my arm away. "You must be mistaken." She turned to the couple. "Sorry, please go ahead with your order."

I felt like I'd been slapped. "What are you talking about? It's me, Lydia. Your sister." Did she have amnesia? I spoke softly, not wanting to cause a scene. "Don't you remember me?"

I knew she did when Tess's eye twitched. That always happened when she was nervous. Tess's focus switched to Loretta, flashing her a vile look as well. "Sorry," she said to her customers, before pivoting and dashing toward the steel kitchen door.

I stayed in place, trying to process what had just happened. A minute later, the maître d approached me. "Ma'am, I must ask you to leave."

I shook my head in disbelief, which the man took as a no.

He seized my elbow. "This is not a suggestion, ma'am. You must go now." He turned to Loretta. "You also, miss."

"Come on, let's get out of here," Loretta whispered.

How can this be? Why was Tess acting like that? When I didn't budge, Loretta, with a thin smile to the maitre'd, practically dragged me outside, where she turned on me too. "What the hell was that?" Loretta's arms were crossed like an angry child. "Obviously there's bad blood between ya's, and you used me. You set me up! And now she hates me too." She flipped up the hood of her coat. "You just cost me a friend."

Friend? Tess hadn't kept in touch with her since leaving the boarding house. I wanted to remind Loretta of that, but the girl was already stalking halfway down the street.

A wintry flurry blew up, whipping around me like an enraged ghost. I let the icy flakes smack against my merging tears, praying that I'd get pneumonia and die. Life made no sense. And it certainly was not on my side.

It never had been.

The street was practically deserted. I had to figure out how to get back to the hotel and I had no idea where I was. I started walking in the black of night, ambling through the slush, feeling stupid for reflecting on the train that I'd made a good go of things. That I had won at the game of life. Ha!

In truth, I was a foolish mess. And alone. Solo, in this god-forsaken world. That much was painfully true. I hugged my fur coat tight against me. At least I had material things to keep me warm. I always told myself that I didn't need a man. That I'd learned to live on my own terms, fend for myself. And where had that gotten me?

I may not need a man but that didn't mean I didn't want one. I longed for someone who could fulfill my other needs, be my friend, stave off the dreadful loneliness I was experiencing this very minute.

Where was Eliot this lonely night? Certainly not lonely. What was he doing right now? What were *they* doing? Before I could punish myself more with thoughts of him, I caught sight of a yellow Checkered Cab coming my way.

"Oh, taxi!" I yelled, flagging it down. The man stopped and rolled down his window. "Sorry lady, I'm off shift now."

The whole awful day came rushing out of me. "Oh, please, mister. I'm from out-of-town and need to get back to my hotel, The Bristol, and I have no idea how to get there." I could hear the desperation in my voice. I wiped my wet face with my gloved hand. "Please," I choked out.

The driver shook his head but seeing me standing alone on the snowy deserted street must have swayed him otherwise. He let out a frustrated sigh. "I'm really not supposed to pick up anyone else tonight. But okay, get in."

I thanked him as many times as Loretta had thanked me for dinner and climbed into the back seat. I was thankful the driver wasn't up for chit-chat, and relieved the cab had a heater. I leaned into the cushion and let my body warm up. But my mind wouldn't shut off.

No matter how I tried, I couldn't understand Tess's reaction. What was going on inside that head of hers? Why wasn't she at all happy to see me?

Maybe the answer lay somewhere in our past relationship. That last year, in particular. After being separated, I refused to allow myself to think about the bad blood between us. My grief over losing her erased all the arguments we'd had, the verbal, sometimes physical, slinging back-and-forth between us. I had pushed it all far back in my memory bank, filing it under simple teenage sibling behavior. We'd shared a bedroom, so naturally, we fought over stealing clothes, fought over the neighbor boy's attention, fought just to let off steam. But it became more than that once Father left us for good.

His leaving had affected Tess the worst. She'd idolized him and somehow blamed Mother for his leaving. As if it was her fault that she couldn't keep her man happy. So Tess made things even harder on her. She seemed to go out of her way to defy our mother on a regular basis. Not helping with household chores, starting arguments over the littlest of things, at times going as far as demanding that Mother go find our dad and bring him home. Which, of course, was impossible.

I could have blamed Tess for Mother's heart attack, given her behavior. But I hadn't. Because we'd been left with just each other, we needed each other. I'd only realized that once the girl was gone. In the end, our bond as sisters was all that mattered. I refused to think about the rest.

But now I had to. Clearly something laid dormant in Tess's mind that had burrowed during our time apart. Or perhaps those people from the orphanage, or her adoptive family, had told lies about me to keep her from running back home?

Was that it?

As I watched the bright city lights pass by through the dirty cab window, I forced myself to face the hard truths.

"Here we are, Ma'am." The driver's voice startled me.

I looked up to see the front of the hotel. "Oh, yes, thank you." When I dug into my handbag to pay the driver, something fell out and hit my foot. I bent over to retrieve it. The minute my fingers felt the cold round glass, I choked on my tears. Tess's marble.

I sat back and stared at it. In that moment, I knew what I had to do.

33.

I paid the driver extra, thanking him again his trouble. I was half tempted to go into the Pink Elephant for a much needed night cap but was too afraid I'd run into Eliot and Evaline. I'd already had enough drama to last a lifetime.

I stopped at the desk hoping against hope that Eliot left me a message.

Nothing.

In my room, I changed into my nightgown, despite it being only nine o'clock. All I wanted was to close my eyes and get out of the nightmare I was in, if only for a few hours. I considered giving up on the whole idea and hop on the train home in the morning.

But giving up wasn't my nature. I was my mother's daughter. I would not give up on my sister.

By some miracle, it didn't take long to fall fast asleep. When I awoke, it was still dark. The sun wouldn't be up for another hour. I put my hair in a shower cap to keep it dry and took a leisurely bath before dressing in a warm sweater and wool slacks. By the time I put on my coat and wrapped a winter scarf around my head, it was getting light outside.

I decided to take a long walk, breathe in the crisp air, attempt to rally renewed strength and combat my dejected state.

The city was already in full motion with people passing by and businesses opening up. I wasn't sure how long I'd been gone, but I did return with a new attitude. I reminded myself how lucky I was to have a job I loved and friends like Frank and Helen, Kitty and Dottie—people I could rely on. I wasn't alone after all.

And my sister was alive.

Pushing through the swinging doors, I entered the lobby with one thought in mind. Nothing and no one was going to get the best of me. I would face whatever came, handle it, and move on.

I couldn't wait to get back home but there was one more thing to accomplish in New York. I stopped at the desk again to inquire about messages. My heart quickened when the young man answered yes, there was. "Just a moment." As he turned away, I had to face the truth. A note. Not a phone call. Which meant he was not coming back for me.

Mr. Cohen appeared and handed me the envelope himself. "The gentleman wanted to make sure I gave this to you personally."

"Thank you." I pulled off my gloves and grasped it, already fearing its contents. "Is Mr. Ness still in residence?"

"He is not, miss."

I bit my lip. "Mr. Cohen, I am not sure how long I may be staying." *Maybe I could wire George for emergency money to keep me here a bit longer.* "Would that be a problem?"

"We do need twenty-four hours for a new reservation, but Mr. Ness has already left instructions that your room be paid for as long as you need it."

Well. It's the least he could do for leaving me stranded.

I rode the elevator to the seventh floor, clutching the envelope to my chest. I wanted to rip it open right then but not knowing its content, it was best I wait till I was alone in my room.

So many questions raced through my mind. Now that he'd left me here, did that mean I was on my own when it came to Tess? How could I get my sister to talk to me without getting thrown out again? Was this the end of my relationship with Eliot? Despite the fact I was sure Eliot must resent Evaline for showing up unannounced, I doubted it gave him cause to leave her. He had never responded when I'd asked him if he still loved his wife. That silence had been my answer.

Was it possible we could stay friends? Even if so, I knew that every time I saw him, I would think of our time together in New York. And how it ended. The thought of no longer having him to rely on, gave me a deep sense of loss.

I took off my coat, threw it on a chair, sat on the bed and opened the envelope. The letter was brief, written on the hotel stationary. I wondered how he managed to write it with Evaline's eagle eyes always near. But then, even the divine Mrs. Ness had to go to the bathroom at some point. When I pulled out the letter, a fifty dollar bill fell to the floor.

My dearest Lydia,

I cannot describe how sincerely sorry I am for these present circumstances. I racked my brain trying to figure a way to let you know of Evaline's sudden arrival. I feared you'd think I was evading you when I failed to show up for our planned dinner but when you didn't appear at my door or call I realized somehow you knew.

The handwriting was not his usual neat penmanship. He must have been in a terrific hurry when writing it. I could only imagine.

I'm anxious to learn if you did in fact reunite with Tess, as is my deepest hope, but that'll have to wait until we can talk once we both return home. You can also guess that I'll be leaving now with Evaline at her insistence.

I have made provisions for you. Your room is paid for and I enclose your train fare here. There should be enough left over for food and the cocktails I imagine you will need. Again, I cannot express how sorry I am. The minute I learn of your return, I will stop in and see you at your place of work.

Very sincerely, Eliot

Wow. Two sorrys and a *very* sincerely—and more than enough money to get back home, and then some. He must truly feel bad. But he was not to blame. He had no idea this would happen and despite everything, I knew he held deep feelings for me. Maybe even loved me.

I lounged around most of the day, waiting for the clock to turn four. The time when I'd take a taxi and head back to the Black Cat.

I tried to time it just right. I knew now that Tess started work at five-thirty so I gave my coat to the hatcheck girl at exactly five and headed toward the bar, finding a seat that allowed me to watch everyone coming through that front door.

There were just two men at the bar and the barmaid looked bored so I decided to befriend her. Her long dark, wavy hair was styled ala Katharine Hepburn, which turned out to be her name.

"Nice seeing a woman mixing drinks for a change," I said with a friendly smile. "That's a rarity."

"Yeah, my boss is smart," Katharine said, giving me my Coke. "He knows a woman who shows a little cleavage can get men to stick around longer, buy more drinks. Get pretty good tips too."

I grinned. "Oh, yes, I am aware of that."

A Place We Belong

Seventeen minutes after five, the door swung open and Tess appeared wearing her uniform, her dyed blond hair pinned back in a tight bun. I stood immediately to stop her before she could take another step, blocking her from moving past. "Tess, we need to talk and unless you want me to make a real scene and get you fired, you'll go over to that table there and sit down with me." I pointed to an empty table furthest from the bar.

Tess gave me a wicked look, but it was no match for my intense stare. "Fine," she puffed out. "I do have some things I want to say to you."

This was not going to be the tearful reunion I'd always dreamed about. I gestured to Katharine to have my drink moved, not daring to take my eyes off Tess in fear she'd take off to avoid confrontation.

We sat across from each other, lighting up smokes almost simultaneously, an obvious attempt to calm our jitters. My lips turned upward when she noticed we smoked the same brand.

Katharine set down my Coke. "Keep my tab open," I said, "I'll be having dinner too." In truth, that would depend on how this conversation went, but no waitress wants a patron sitting around drinking soda.

"Kat," Tess interjected, "can you please tell Mr. Wiseman I have a family emergency meeting here, *unexpected*," she glared at me, "ask Susan if she'll take my first few tables. Please." Tess pleaded with her eyes, which shifted back to me. "I can't afford to lose this job so please let's make this short."

"I understand. I'm a working girl too."

"Really?" Tess gave me the once-over. "Looks more like you're a kept woman."

I straightened my spine. I'd heard it all before. "Nope. Bought everything myself, right down to my shoes." I lifted my

225

feet from under the table, showing off my maroon sling-back pumps that matched my cashmere sweater.

Before Tess could ask, I told her what I did for a living, hoping that would break the ice.

"No kiddin'?" Tess tilted her head, seemingly to conjure up the scene. "Well, good thing you didn't have me around to burden you and interfere with your swanky career."

"What is *wrong* with you? I've been a wreck since you were taken away. Haven't you ever wondered about me too?"

"Sure did, like how you rushed to get me outta that place they took me the *second* you turned eighteen, ha! They told me you'd come but you never did."

"What? First of all, I had no idea where you were, they never told me a thing once they took you away. Took me this long to get someone to help me find you." How could Tess think I simply gave up on her? "Believe me, I tried on my own and got nowhere."

My sister shook her head. "That's not what they told me. They said once you turned of age, you'd come get me. I waited and waited. Your birthday came and went and you were a no-show." She stamped out her cigarette before it was half-smoked. "Weeks later, they pawned me off to the Ginarts. And *they* only wanted me to take care of their daughter because of their jet-set life."

Noticing my expression, she added, "That's right, big sister, I was bought, *purchased*. Like a fuckin' slave." Her tone cut through me, but it was her words that burned my chest.

Tess crossed her arms and stared me down. "How I've hated you for that."

"But you can't hate me, Tess! I swear I didn't know." I had to make her understand. "They told me we had to be separated because we were orphans and you had to be placed—they wouldn't tell me where. I only recently found out that I would've been able to take you in soon as I turned eighteen." I lowered my head at the memory. "I now know that would not have happened, anyway. It's obvious they had other plans for you."

Tess stared at the floor, considering my exclamation.

"Anyway, few awful weeks at the Murphy Home, I gave up hope they'd bring you back. Plus I was afraid they'd send me off somewhere, too, so I snuck out one night and train-hopped back home."

I leaned in. "Remember Patsy? She told me once how to do it. It was crazy scary, but I made it home. Slept in that old jalopy of dad's. Mary helped me out by bringing me her family leftovers each night, got me a blanket, and actually gave me the gumption to get my job in burlesque." I looked her straight in the eye. "All this time, I've worried about you, scared to death thinking what might be happening to you. It was unbearable, but I had to go on."

Tess stared at me, like she wasn't sure to believe me. "They told me you agreed to let me be adopted because it was for my own good. After you came of age, they said you couldn't take care of me and gave up your rights so I can be adopted."

I reached for her hand. "Think about it. Who would most likely be telling you the truth?"

Tess's eyes settled on her glass in thought. Something in her expression told me she was finally convinced I was telling the truth.

Katharine returned. "Hey, Jean, you better get to work. Wiseman's not happy." Then turning to me, she asked. "So you ready to order something, Miss?"

"I gotta get." Tess was already standing.

"Go on, do your job. I'll be here when you get off."

"But that's not till round midnight by the time we do our side work in the kitchen."

"However long it takes, I'll be here waiting. I may leave for a bit, take a walk, but I'll be back." I stood too, gave my sister a tight squeeze. "I didn't leave you then, I won't leave you now," I whispered. "There's no one who can take you away anymore. We're gonna get those vile bastards." I pulled away but held her shoulders. "I know someone. A man who can bring those people down, punish them for what they did to us. What they're still doing to others."

Tess's eyebrows raised. "Oh, count me in for a little revenge." She gave me a look that I remembered from many years ago. Just seeing that spark soothed my anxiety. "I want those people to suffer dearly. You have no idea what goes on at that place."

"So I've heard. I'll be anxious to learn more."

Finally, a slight smile. "I'm sorry I didn't believe you, Lyd. I'd been convinced you abandoned me."

"I know." I took a hankie from my purse and wiped her face. "We got screwed, that's for sure." She swiped her eyes, tucked it into her apron. "We may not have always gotten along," I continued, "but if I'd known what they were doing, I'd never have . . ." Then reality set in. "Aw, hell, who am I foolin'? I couldn't have done a damn thing back then. They took you so fast. They bamboozled us, used us as pawns."

"Yeah and we weren't the only ones, I'll tell you that." Tess glanced up at the wall clock. "Wow, I gotta go." She smoothed her uniform. "But when I get off, you'll have to tell me about this guy you mentioned who can fix everything. What is he, Superman?"

"In my book, he is." I hugged her once more before we parted. "I can hardly believe I found you." I squeezed her hands. "I *found you*, Tess." I let the words sink in. "So many times I didn't think it would happen."

I turned and lifted my Coke glass. "The Swanson sisters are back together again. And we're gonna kick some serious ass."

A Place We Belong

Our laughter was loud enough to turn heads. But we didn't care.

34.

After a hearty dinner of Veal Scaloppini, I took a brisk walk, practically skipping through the streets with happiness. As I passed several shops, I realized I'd been too busy to buy myself a trinket, or some memento, of my time here. The time I had finally found my sister.

I popped into a quaint little shop called Bonnie's Boutique and laid my eyes on a gorgeous turquoise necklace. Did I dare use some of the money Eliot had left me? I knew it was more than enough to get me home. And I'd already decided to pay him back. Every red cent of it.

Feeling uplifted by our talk, I also wanted to get Tess something. But what? I had no idea what her tastes were. I didn't want to give her anything too extravagant, fearing it might look like I was being boastful about my comfortable lifestyle.

I'd almost given up when I came across a beautiful cameo pendant necklace, much like one Mother used to wear. Looking at it broke my heart thinking of all her possessions now gone. We would never know what became of any of it. Tess and I had been so taken advantage of and scarred by strangers' decisions. How many more girls and boys' lives were changed forever by those scoundrels? Lives purposely misdirected merely for profit.

Profit made at the suffering of innocent children. It still unnerved me. But right now, I had some celebrating to do.

I purchased the necklaces and had the saleswoman box them up. As I strode through the chilly streets, thankful it wasn't snowing, I thought of all the catching up we had to do. We were teenagers the last time we knew each other. So much had changed. Did I even know her anymore? Despite facing the truth about our difficult relationship, seeing her again made me forgive it all. It was time to make a brand new start. We had to get reacquainted as the grown women who now were. We'd lived totally separate lives. And once we talked everything out, what then? What would happen to us? How could I go home and leave her here?

Maybe there was another option.

Although it was dark now, my watch read not quite eight o'clock. I decided to hail a cab back to the hotel, where I gathered up my things and started packing.

It was still only eleven when I returned to the restaurant to wait at the bar. But Tess surprised me. She was already there. "Hey, slow night so I got off early and couldn't get a hold of you. I don't even know where you're staying."

"Oh, right," I said, taking the empty stool next to her. "I'm at The Bristol."

Tess told me where she was living and from there, we ordered gin and tonics (turned out we both liked gin, and Katharine ignored Tess's age) and began a conversation that filled in all the blanks of the past years.

I learned about Tess's adopted family and how she ended up in New York. "My boyfriend got a job here, and I came with him 'cause we were supposed to get married. But the bastard reneged on his promises and left me high and dry." She'd been fending for herself since then.

"And yes, I've gained some weight, but did you know all the bad stuff for you, like breads and pastry and stuff are a lot cheaper than fruits and veggies? Least I get a discount here so I eat as much as I can. Their burgers are the best!"

"You look swell, sis," I reassured her.

"Remember that delicious bakery Ma worked at?" Tess asked.

"Of course, Hough. There's one not far from where I live now." I couldn't wait to treat her as soon as I had the chance.

Deciding the time was right, I pulled the package out of the shopping bag I'd brought with me. "Happy Birthday."

Tess's glee-filled face took me back to our childhood. "You're three days early."

I frowned. "I'm five years late."

Tess held the gift in her lap, looked up at me. "I can't believe it's been that long. Seeing you now is like time stood still."

"Oh, I think we are both much better looking now," I said, patting my hair in jest.

Smiling, Tess opened the box. "Oh my god, is this mother's?"

I shook her head. "As I said, everything was gone when I got back to the house. So this one will be special, to honor her." I reached into my pocketbook. "I have something else for you. I wanted to give it to you first time I saw you, but we had to straighten out a few things first," I smiled, then took my sister's hand. "Close your eyes."

I placed the emerald marble into her palm.

Tess opened her eyes and stared at it like she was trying to figure out where she'd last seen it. Closing her fingers around the small marble, she lifted her head to meet my eyes. "Oh, Lyd. I just got chills. But how'd you—"

I told her where I'd found it and how I managed to scoop it up when no one was looking.

Tess squeezed the glass ball to her chest. "Such a simple thing. Yet it means so much."

"I know." I flicked my teary eyes.

"Thank you." Tess leaned in and gave me a squeeze." I really have missed you so," she whispered, then began to sob.

A Place We Belong

"How could they do that to us, Lyddy? Just when we needed each other the most?"

I pressed her head to my chest like a mother to a child. "That's what I'm aiming to find out."

I pulled her away now, grabbed her shoulders, took in a breath. "So . . . I was wondering. It doesn't sound like there's anything holding you down here, you can waitress anywhere. How would you feel about, maybe, coming home with me?"

"Ladies, we're closing up now," Katharine was back, scooping up empty glasses and dumping the ashtrays.

I opened my pocketbook to pay the tab. "You'll love where I live," I went on. "I have the best landlords, a truly lovely older couple. *And* I can even help get you a job."

"As a burlesque queen?"

I laughed, feeling a lightness in the air. "No, smarty-pants. There's this wonderful restaurant called The Theatrical just a block from my work and they could always use extra help. But hey, you don't need a job right away, I can take care of you until you get settled."

"Wow, uh, I don't know." She shook her head, like trying to clear a jumbled mind. She scooted off the stool. "I live in walking distance, wanna stay at my place tonight?"

I understood that Tess might not want to make a sudden decision, but then, I had to get back home soon. Still, I knew I couldn't badger her. I decided to stay the night and allow us more time to simply enjoy each other. We stayed up half the night reminiscing about good memories and telling stories from the years we'd missed out on.

Our time spent must have convinced Tess to come home because by Saturday, Tess quit her job ("I didn't like it anyway," she told me with a grin), and the day after that, we were on the train headed for Cleveland.

On Monday I took Tess downstairs to introduce her to Frank and Helen, who joined us that night at The Theatrical to celebrate our reunion. I told the owner that I'd be back performing my Roxy Wednesday shows and Helen talked the kitchen manager into giving Tess a job there. We were all in good spirits as we got up to leave. That's when I saw him.

He sat in a corner table with Evaline and another couple. By now, Tess knew the whole story about Eliot so when I elbowed her to look his direction, Tess raised her brows. "Oh my, he is easy on the eyes, ain't he?"

"Yes, he—" I stopped. As the couple got up to leave, Eliot turned to bid goodbye to someone, and I spotted his tie. It was the tie I'd bought him in New York. I put my hand to my chest, feeling a warmth inside, like an embrace that flowed straight to my heart.

35.

*E*veryone seemed happy to have Blue Satin Doll back at the Roxy, especially George. He was the first to greet me when I returned. "Welcome home, Doll." He remained the only one allowed to call me that because he said it with love and affection. And this time, with a dozen red roses.

"My word, George, I wasn't even gone the full two weeks." I leaned over the vanity displaying the vase and basked in the aroma.

"And thank God for that." He patted my shoulder. "Had to fire Gloria. She was downright awful. I lost a lot of money last week. People still come to see you more than any of the girls. You're still my number one."

"Aw, George, that's music to my ears!" I gave him a heartfelt hug.

"K, K, 'nough of the groveling. Go out there and get 'em." He gave me a wink, which made me laugh. George never winked.

Back on my home turf, I dipped, swirled, and shimmied, as I thanked my lucky stars. Being away, even for a week, gave me new appreciation. The gods, finally, were on my side. I loved where I lived, loved my job, and after seeing him wear the tie I'd bought him, I knew I still had Eliot in my life.

That fact gave me enough confidence to call his office the following week. To my relief, he was happy to hear from me. I told him about finding Tess, her coming back home, then quickly asked if he'd meet with me so I could tell him more about Tess's experience with Georgia Tann and her operation. "That is, if you're still interested."

"If you'll still have me," was the answer I wanted to hear, though I also knew he was already invested in the cause.

A few nights later, I headed to the bar after my show. There he was, nursing his typical scotch on the rocks. He looked up as I approached and saluted me with his glass.

I hopped on the stool next to him. "Thanks for coming, Eliot."

I raised a hand for Tony. "A refreshing highball, please." Then I dug into my cleavage, pulled out a hundred-dollar bill, and handed it to Eliot. I'd felt almost insulted that he had paid for practically the whole trip. I needed to stand my own ground. "Here. I didn't need your money." Saying it out loud sounded harsher than I'd intended. "I'm sorry, I'm not mad at you, just the situation."

"Lydia, I can't take your money, especially not double what I gave you."

"Don't argue with me. You've never seen my wrath, and you don't want to." I slipped the bill in his shirt pocket and gave a look that showed I meant business. "It's partly my fault too. We got in over our heads and I know it's caused you a bit of trouble."

He grinned at me. "Just a bit." We exchanged an understanding look, like the old friends we'd become. "Perhaps I could've handled it better. It's just that you are a very attractive woman, and I have a very jealous wife."

"So how did she learn I was in New York with you, any-who?" I took a sip from my whiskey highball anticipating his answer.

"From what she told me, a male friend of hers happened to be here at the Roxy and learned you had taken a vacation and mentioned it to her. She didn't believe it was a coincidence that we were both away at the same time."

A Place We Belong

"Just like it was no coincidence that a friend just *happened* to mention that to her." I was sure the woman had picked up some good spying tips from her husband.

Eliot simply nodded.

Maybe I was too harsh. "I swear sometimes I think that woman is tailing me. It's not like we run in the same circles."

He swirled the liquid in his glass. "Listen, tell me what you've learned about the Tennessee orphanage."

For the next hour I relayed everything Tess had told me of what she'd experienced and witnessed at the Home. Some of which made my skin crawl. The stories ranged from dirty conditions, lack of care for sick children, letting some go hungry at their whim, harsh beatings to those who didn't conform, to overcrowded rooms.

"Tess often slept in the attic with a few other children. As we suspected, she'd been the oldest one there and Georgia often used her as a free housemaid and someone to tend to the children." I lit another smoke right after the last one. Talking about it made me a nervous wreck, like a runaway train rumbling through my veins.

"Tess gave her a hard time, as was her way, and soon learned it made things worse for her. Georgia had her believing I abandoned her. She grew to hate me because of it. Tess believes she became more trouble for Georgia than she was worth and that's why she decided to get rid of her. For a pricey sum, naturally, seeing how she'd been trained to keep house.

"By the time the Ginarts came to see her—which was months, not a few weeks like Georgia told you—she had no more fight in her."

Eliot listened intently.

"Tess was only allowed to bathe maybe every two weeks, but soon as there was some interest in her, Georgia made sure she got a nice hot bath, spiffed her up in a new dress and a woman in her employ cut her hair. Tess had a terrible case of acne from all the anxiety she was going through so Georgia's aide put on a cake of makeup to hide her pimples. All so she'd be more appealing to the Ginarts, who, of course, bled money." I shifted in my seat. This was hard to talk about. "Tess often wouldn't eat. She'd put what she could in a napkin to later share with the children who weren't given enough. And there were plenty of those."

I pulled my embroidered hankie from my clutch, dabbed my eyes. "Broke my heart, all that she told me. Awful stories. I keep thinking about those little children. Something needs to be done, Eliot." My voice softened to a whisper. "Yet I have no idea how to go about it."

Eliot seemed somber as I told him everything Tess told me. "Although the Ginarts used her as a maid and babysitter, they didn't abuse her. They had a cook, so she ate well and gained back her weight, and then some. And being a society lady, Mrs. Ginart paid for expensive creams and treatments for Tess's acne so she'd look and feel better about herself. She also got to travel. She spent part of that first summer on the beaches in New England, then winter vacations in Colorado..."

"And she stopped missing me."

"You know better than that."

I shrugged. "I think about all those days and nights I worried about her and she was perfectly fine this whole time . . . but of course, I am truly glad about that." I sat with my hands on my lap clinging to my kerchief. "Despite the nice lifestyle, Tess began to rebel, as Mrs. Ginart told you. She didn't feel like she belonged there, or anywhere. Tess said she became angry at the world and really gave them a hard time. Like Georgia, they began to regret taking her. So when she got a boyfriend who wanted to take her to New York, they had no problem letting her go. Tess never wrote to them, though she feels bad about abandoning the girl. But she felt it was best to make a clean break."

"Anyway," I continued, "whatever can we do about that place? It's no longer about finding Tess now, I feel for those poor children. How can we expose that woman?"

"We'll find a way." He met my eyes. "I'll do more digging."

"Tess said whatever you need, she's on board."

He gulped down the last of his drink. "Right now, I need to get home."

"Of course."

He drove me home and when he pulled in the drive, I turned to him. "Eliot? Even though we'll be working together again, I promise I'll not interfere with your marriage. Our friendship means too much. I don't want to mess it up. Most of all, I don't want you getting hurt."

He wouldn't look at me, or respond to what I'd said, just stared out the windshield. "Sleep well, Miss Lydia."

I threw him a smile that he didn't catch, and headed inside.

36.

A week after our talk, I read a newspaper account about Eliot's work struggles. For the first time since the Kingsbury Run murders when he was chided for not nabbing the culprit right away, the reporters, together with his own department, had turned against him. As safety director, Eliot took pride in turning the police precinct into an honorable and well-structured district, and yet the same folks who had hailed him early on, were changing their tune. Attitudes, and loyalties, were shifting. The press—and as a result, the public—were suddenly questioning his every move.

This time, he was getting backlash for hiring and placing "two colored patrolmen in charge of a squad car, which is unheard of for the department." According to the article, older members of the force resented his attempts at changing a long-held system and were beginning to organize against him, working to unravel his other efforts as well. Ness seemed to be using more energy battling defiant officers than doing his job fighting against crime. As a result, he was accomplishing less in his position. Everything he tried to do backfired or was rejected by higher-ups.

I threw the paper down, feeling horrible. I could well imagine how this was affecting him. Rumors were circulating at the Theatrical, too, about his excessive drinking that was matching his wife's. This came as little surprise. Eliot, deep down, was a sensitive man who was used to achieving anything he strived for. But things had taken a despondent turn. And, apparently, so had his love for scotch. I was sad that this word-of-mouth gossip had even reached his favorite watering holes.

And I couldn't help but worry that this meant his losing interest in our shared mission. Should I give up on this passion for justice concerning the Tennessee Home Society? After all, if higher ups weren't doing a thing to put that woman behind bars, what made me think *I* would have any influence? Especially given my occupation. They'd laugh me out of the state.

I was well aware that power and money was king of the world, and had to remind myself of the well-known adage, "you can't fight city hall."

Still. There were innocent children involved. Not only had Tess witnessed abuse at the hands of this Georgia Tann, but I also knew first-hand how it felt to be homeless. To feel like no one in the world gave a damn about you. I may have only lived in that car for a week, but the empty, lonely emotions I felt during those days would stay with me forever.

Like Eliot, Tess, too, had other things on her mind. At breakfast with my landlord, I'd been absorbed in the paper when she suddenly shouted, "Hey, did you know there's a school for nursing near here?" She had told me of her new dream of being a pediatric nurse. If we couldn't do anything about Georgia Tann, Tess would find another way to help children. "Maybe Mushy can promote me to waitress soon and I can start saving money for it."

The only available job at The Theatrical had been in the kitchen, and though she enjoyed working next to Helen on salads and desserts, Tess wasn't into the culinary arts.

I bent over to read the ad. "If you're serious, I'll help you pay for it."

"Oh, and we will too!" Helen said, standing up and grabbing the dirty dishes. "We don't have children or grandchildren, so this can be our contribution to the world."

"Seriously, you'd all do that for me?" Tess jumped up and gave us each a hug. "Oh my gosh, I'm calling right now and get all the details about signing up." She clutched her hand to her chest. "I'm going to be a nurse!" Waving the ad in the air, she dashed upstairs.

I turned to Helen. "That's so generous of you, but are you sure Frank will be okay with that?"

"You mean Mr. Cheapskate?" Helen laughed. "He'll be fine with it. He does have a good heart, and he's starting to see her as a daughter, like he does you."

"Oh, Helen, you two are the best. We love you so." I finished my tea. "I gotta get. I'm meeting Kitty at Sullivan's later and need to spruce up a bit." We had some catching up to do. Kitty had been working less hours and I wondered how she could afford to work only part time. I guessed it helped to have a rich boyfriend.

Kitty already had a drink in front of her when I arrived. "Hey, girl!" She brightened when she saw me.

"How I've missed seeing that cheery face of yours at work," I said, taking the seat across her and grabbing the menu. "I'm starved. Didn't have much breakfast." I couldn't wait to tell her about Tess going to nursing school, but first things, first.

"Forget the menu right now." Kitty yanked it down from my face and set it on the table. "I've got big news." She leaned forward and flashed her left hand in front of her face. "Lookie!"

The diamond ring sparkled in the darkened tavern. I knew my diamonds. This rock was a biggie. "Wow," was all I could muster.

"Yes, wow. I never thought he was the committed type!" She leaned back still admiring her ring. "I'm going to be Mrs. Gary Bruno!"

A Place We Belong

Oh, Kitty, you could do so much better. I faked my most sincere smile. I wouldn't dare burst my friend's bubble. At least not today.

"My word, Kit, it's gorgeous. Looks like two full carats."

"Two and a half, but who's counting?" Kitty batted her eyes. "It is a beauty, isn't it?" She wiggled her fingers so it would hit the light.

"Congratulations. I hope you'll be very happy." I meant it, though I had my doubts.

The waitress took our order and as soon as she walked away, Kitty told me of her plans of quitting the business, settling down and being a housewife and mother. "I can't wait to stop dancing. I'm sick to death of it all."

I hid my surprise, shock, really, by picking the menu back up in front of my face. Sure, some girls weren't cut out for the long haul, but I never guessed Kitty would be one of them. She certainly had never said as much.

We clicked glasses to Kitty's future, and as we did, I felt we were also signaling an end to our friendship as we knew it. No more wild nights at the Roxy, exchanging saucy tales about men, shopping together . . . so much we had shared. I suddenly felt isolated.

"Ya know, for me, it's the opposite." I let my true feelings out. "Since New York, I have a new appreciation for our work. Not many women can have a job that pays so well, and lets us pretty much do what we want, and how we want. And get to wear such elaborate costumes."

"Yeah, and then take them off!"

I laughed, immediately feeling better. Kitty was still her witty self. More relaxed now, I told her how great it was to be reunited with Tess, and the plans for her future. Then I confided my sadness about Eliot's work problems and how it

243

was bound to affect his pursuing the case of Georgia's operation.

Kitty listened politely but her gorgeous dark eyes were distant. It appeared my once best friend didn't give a hoot about any of that.

"Hey, did I tell you the date?" she interrupted. "I've always wanted a June wedding and yes, I know that's just three months away, but Gary's aunt's church has an opening for the last Saturday that month, the twenty-ninth, so we booked it. And the Mound's Club agreed to have the reception there. And you must be my maid-of-honor."

What else could I do but smile and say, yes? It may be the last time we would share something together. I pushed away the thought as Kitty went on about shopping for the perfect dress.

Despite my misgivings about the wedding, I found myself caught up in the excitement of it all. So much so that once at home, I wondered if I'd ever know the thrill, the security, of having someone who wanted to spend the rest of his life with me.

Would I ever find a man like that? Was I destined to be alone forever? As much as I liked my job, I couldn't help feeling that there must be something more.

37.

*K*itty's wedding turned out to be a welcome reprieve, at least for a night. Gary organized a fleet of cars for the wedding party, and with his gang's connections, hired policemen friends to stand guard at the reception doors to block any visits from enemies. Tess and I shared a table with the Roxy gang and danced to many of the orchestra big-band tunes. Kitty made sure that I caught her bouquet, and soon after, the happy couple slyly made their exit. The guests, however, were in full party mood so the band played till the wee hours.

Tess and I returned to the apartment a little drunk and a lot tired. "I hate weddings," I told her, kicking off my heels.

"What? That was fun!"

"It was," I said, the exhilaration from the alcohol long gone. "I guess it makes me think maybe I'm missing out on something, though I've always doubted marriage was for me. The whole idea seems awfully restrictive."

"Yeah, and the man can up and leave anytime he damn well feels like it."

I winced. We had yet to talk about our feelings toward Father. Knowing how Tess had idolized him, I struggled what I should say on that topic when the time came. Should I tell her about when—not that long ago—he had the nerve to show his face at my work? Only to leave the worse kind of note a father could leave his daughter? I quickly erased it from my brain, leaned over and pinched my sister's cheek. "Best we stay single gals. Especially you. You'd give any guy a real run for his money." I picked up my evening's token—my acquired wedding bouquet—and gave it a shake. "But least I got flowers."

"And that means you're next."

"Ha," I laughed, heading to the kitchen to retrieve the only vase I owned. The one Bill had bought me for my birthday. I didn't want to think about him, or the only man I could envision actually marrying. The one I could never have.

I didn't bother taking the roses, lilacs and Lily of the Valley stems apart. Just stuck them in water in the container, bid Tess goodnight, and flopped into my bed. Alone. Again.

The next day's news didn't help my state of mind as world reports became exceedingly more ominous. Everywhere, from the local delicatessen, to the beauty shops, to the barroom stools, talk was amped up over the war in Europe. The "Isolationists" heartily opposed it. In fact, a group of women were actively picketing in Chicago. Then there were the "Interventionists" who felt we had many reasons to get involved in a second world war. I feared things were heading toward a bad turn.

A bright spot came in July when I, along with Frank and Helen, took Tess to the grand Cleveland Stadium to see her first Indians game. The night game was the most anticipated of the season because the famous center fielder, Joe DiMaggio, and his damn Yankees were returning to play against the Indians after stripping the Cleveland team from first place in the American League. Under the night lights—among the biggest baseball crowd of the season—the game became historic when DiMaggio failed to get a hit against the Indians, ending his momentous 56-game hitting streak.

Afterward, we all went for drinks at The Theatrical. I secretly hoped "Joltin' Joe" would make an appearance there so I could introduce him to Tess, who had never met a celebrity before and had been bowled over by the photograph of me, in full burlesque attire, snuggling up against the famous ballplayer. The snapshot was encased in a silver frame on the wall of my dressing room.

246

A Place We Belong

Sure enough, an hour after we were there, the ball player walked in, surrounded by men paid to protect him against overenthusiastic fans. I grabbed Tess's arm. "Come on, let's go to the powder room."

I knew we'd pass his table on the way there. He was talking to the waitress when we went by the first time, but luckily, on the way back, DiMaggio caught sight of me. I was thrilled to see recognition in his face. He waved us over.

I introduced him to Tess, and they exchanged pleasantries. He looked tired and spent. "I'm sorry about the streak, Joe," I said with a kind smile, "but what a streak it was! Fifty-six straight games is nothin' to sneeze at!" I glanced around the table of highballs, spotted a glass of water, grabbed it and lifted it up in front of him. "I think congratulations are in order."

He threw me a kind smile. "Thank you, Miss Satin, I guess I needed that reminder right now." I felt my cheeks flush, recalling he had called me that when we'd first met at The Roxy.

The man sitting where the glass had been was giving me the side-eye, so I set the tumbler down with a wink, turned back to Joe and whispered, "I still have your picture on my dressing room wall."

He threw me one of his famous grins. "I am honored, Miss Satin. I hope, despite my blunders, I retain that privilege for years to come."

"Darn tootin' you will, Joe." I smiled and gave him a quick squeeze. "And when my dancin' days are over, it'll be hanging on my *bedroom* wall." Everyone heard me, and the table shook with raucous laughter.

*T*he summer brought record-setting heat. Even with the additional fans that George had put in the place, the stifling air felt like I was in hell, dancing for the devil. Daytime was worse with the sun, yet this was my first summer with my sister since we were teens so I kept us busy. As children we rarely went many places, so I took Tess all over Cleveland. We visited the Zoo, the grand Art Museum, and Crane's, of course, where Dottie took Tess under her wing and helped her with books on the nursing field. But some days, the best thing to do was go to the beach so we could add some glow to our alabaster skins.

Whether it was pure luck I didn't know, but I was relieved that as many places as we went, I hadn't run into Evaline once. Perhaps the woman had stopped trailing me.

Still, I couldn't keep from missing Eliot. For months now, he hadn't appeared at any of the usual establishments. I'd heard through the grapevine that he was spending more evenings at home now. It appeared that he was indeed trying to save his marriage—and his reputation, which was teetering from admirable to questionable. He was smart to do whatever it took to avoid another scandal.

And his friendship with me, the notorious Blue Satin Doll, was one of the most scandalous. Tongues were a-flappin.' Not from a recent sighting—Lord knows there weren't any to be had—but rather, one we hadn't known about at the time. That much was clear when the *Cleveland Press* published a short article on page two in the Sunday edition—the most read day of the week—with a photograph of the two of us together.

It seems a news photographer had been at the Lake View Cemetery last autumn to cover the famous garden cemetery on the very day Eliot and I had been there. The shutterbug had been taking pictures from the balcony of the Garfield Monument, and although it showed a couple below, he hadn't given thought on who they might be.

Until recently.

"I was going through old images that I'd taken the past year," the photographer was quoted in the story, "that's when

I looked harder and recognized our city safety director. Naturally, I know what his wife looks like and his companion was not her. I became intrigued by who this mystery woman was."

Although it had been taken far away, and appeared innocent enough if we hadn't been who we were, the shot showed Eliot and me sitting together on a bench, enjoying one of the lively conversations we'd had that day.

Of course, the man did find out exactly who "the mystery woman" was and informed the newspaper, which had a field day. The article hinted that it was some kind of secret rendezvous.

Again, Blue Satin Doll made the papers unwillingly and without my permission. I wanted to write a letter to the editor defending myself and Eliot, but didn't dare. There was nothing I, being what some thought as a "woman of ill repute," which I certainly was not, could say to redeem us.

But Eliot did strike back. He told the reporters, who dogged him for days, that I was a client, and just like other clients, he sometimes met them outside the office. It was business, he insisted.

While I knew few would believe that, I was touched that he had defended me. Yet, the whole scenario concerning him hurt like the dickens. I finally broke down and called his office, crossing my fingers I'd catch him there. He answered on the second ring.

"Hi, Eliot, it's me, Lydia."

"You don't need to ID yourself. I'd know your voice anywhere. How are you?"

"I'm fine. Been thinking about you a lot lately. Are you okay?"

He hesitated before answering, perhaps choosing his words carefully. "It's been a trying time, as you can guess. I'm sorry I've had to be, well, distant. I'm mad as hell someone invaded your privacy like that, publishing that damn photo. Fine if they want to peck at me, I'm a public figure, but you shouldn't have to be subjected to that. I hope you understand I'm staying away for your own good. They can do what they want to me. Not you."

"Oh, hell with them. They should leave you alone when you're not at work."

"That's not how it goes, I'm afraid."

"No, I suppose not. But Eliot? Please know I thoroughly understand. I just wanted to touch base and tell you that I am so sorry for everything you're going through." I paused for a second before adding, "And that I miss you."

"Thank you, Lydia." There was a brief silence before he added, "I appreciate the call."

I wished he'd said that he missed me too, but he didn't.

He sounded so sad, so defeated. I fought the urge to hop right on the streetcar and go see him. *Impossible*. "Guess I'll let you go. Please take care of yourself. You know things like this always blow over, and when it does, give me a ring, okay?"

"I will. Take care of yourself."

"You, too, Eliot."

38.

*D*espite all the goings-on, the summer seemed to drag. The Roxy stayed busy, with many out-of-towners coming to enjoy what the famed nightclub had to offer. Blue Satin Doll made sure no one knew of her anxieties, her mixed emotions, the lack of love in her life.

After all, I was a pro.

But I did miss having a man in my life. Thoughts of Bill haunted me. He hadn't been perfect, God knows, but he may have been my only chance at love.

Friday nights in August were always hot, sticky, and cumbersome. Still, this night, bachelor boys packed the place. Just my luck, I was forced to give two performances back-to-back when another undependable girl failed to show up.

The humidity seemed to seep through the walls, and by the end of my show, I was a sweaty mess, despite having little clothes on. I was bushed, no doubt about it, but after changing into street clothes, I stopped to see Tony for a nightcap, hoping it would help me sleep in my stifling upstairs apartment. I'd only taken one sip when I heard, and felt, a large man pounce onto the stool next to me.

"Hey, sexy lady."

Ugh. Here we go. I turned to see Harland, one of the regulars that I disdained. The guy gave me the creeps with his sloppy bulk, straggly brows, and constant leer, onstage and off. George had always emphasized the importance of being polite to customers, but tonight I was in no mood. Since the rowdy boys had moved on to wherever young men went after one a.m., Big Joe had called it a night so my back-up was gone.

But the night wasn't over for some. I ignored the drunken man, sucked down my drink, slapped a dollar bill on the bar and dashed out the door.

Despite Eliot's warning when we first met to never take the streetcar at night, I had begun doing so with more frequency. Kitty was gone, basking in her new marital status, Tony lived on the other side of town, and George's son, Johnny, wasn't always available to drive me home. Besides, I hated having to depend on anyone for a lift. I often reminded myself to check into those driving lessons but had never gotten around to it.

On my way out the door, I glanced at my watch. The last trolley was due anytime. Hopefully I'd make it. I was mad at myself for stopping to have that drink, but it's no fun drinking at home alone. Still, I'd been foolish to risky waiting at the stop alone so late at night.

I stepped up my pace, the loud clicking of my heels echoing in the deserted night. I was almost there when I heard heavy footsteps behind me. Or was it my crazy imagination? But then they got louder. Pounding harder on the pavement. Despite the balmy air, goosebumps crept up my spine. I took a quick glance back.

Harland was right behind me.

And he saw that I saw him. "Where ya goin' babycakes?"

My heart thumped wildly. I hated feeling so vulnerable, so alone in the dark world. My eyes darted left, then right. Searching for somewhere to get away from him. All the businesses were closed and there were nothing around but those alleys. Dark threatening alleys. I knew better than to get myself cornered there.

"Where ya offta so swoon," he slurred. "Hey, hey, girly, get your sweesh ass over here. I ain't gonna hur'cha, Blue Satin baby. You know me."

A Place We Belong

I'd always been able to dodge him at the club but now I felt trapped. It was just the two of us on the deserted street and he was sloshed. Fear choked me, making me gasp for breath. I was sprinting now, best as I could in the damn kitten heels, fighting the urge to keep looking back. My fear rapidly turned into sheer terror. Harland was a big man. Even sauced, he could easily force me down. *Rape* me. I could end up like the Kingsbury victims, slashed and left for dead in a darkened littered alleyway.

I willed the images out of my head. Blinking back tears made it hard to see but I knew I was close to the stop. Could I make it? I began praying to a God I often ignored.

"Come here, ya li'l whore." His voice turned angry now. And angry drunks were the most dangerous.

Another glance back, I saw he was ambling. Attempting some swagger in his walk but his intoxication made it just look awkward. The streetlight highlighted his puffy cheeks, his sickening snarl, his wild glazed-over eyes.

"Hey, Bitch!" He lunged and caught me mid-stride. A thick, hard grip seized me.

His foul whiskey breath invaded my nostrils. He pulled me into him, wet sloppy lips smearing my cheek. I twisted and fought. Screamed and spit, yanked and pulled, feeling the bile rise in my throat. A rush of iron will pumped through my body as strong as the pounding of my heart. Suddenly, and somehow miraculously, I managed to wiggle out of his clutches. Half-crazed by the attack, all I could think was to dart.

I heard a loud clanking but my mind couldn't identify it until I saw the bright glare of lights. At the high-pitched screech of brakes, I felt my heel catch in the tracks. I pivoted to turn back, the deafening sound engulfing my ears. I got my foot out of the shoe just before I felt the cold, hard metal slam against my body that shook me into another dimension. Into instant darkness.

Act Three

39.

I awoke in horrific pain lying in a strange bed. The bright room was blinding, I tried to blink it away, clear my vision, when a hand touched my arm, startling me.

"Lydia? It's me, Tess."

I wanted to nod, assure her that I knew who she was, yet my hazy brain seemed to halt the process as I surveyed my unfamiliar surroundings. I spotted several bouquets of flowers as if I were in a botanical garden.

"Am I dead?"

Tess snickered. "My God, no. You're in the hospital, but you're gonna be fine."

The lights in the room were still too bright, burning my eyes. "Is it nighttime?" I stared at my sister like she was my lifeline.

"Uh, huh."

"What day?" Moving my head slightly felt like marbles scattering my brain.

"Saturday night."

Saturday? "Hey, I'm supposed to be at work." There! My mind was back. "Did George get another girl?" My left arm felt sore, and I saw the black-and-blue marks and how swollen it was. "Wow, did I get in a fight with Joe Lewis?"

Tess rubbed my hand, a tight smile on her face. "They'll go away in no time." It sounded like the rest won't?

I went to sit up but my whole midsection tightened when I did, I lifted the sheet to take a look and saw a large bandage wrapped around me. My eyes studied the thick bandage wrapped around my ribcage, then zeroed in on the cast on my left leg—all the way to my hipbone. I gasped. *What the*—? "Are my ribs broken? Is my leg broken?" I had to stop to catch my breath. "What the hell *happened?*"

"Calm down, it's okay. Uh . . . you, well, ya kinda ran into a streetcar."

"*What?*"

"We're still trying to figure out how that happened."

My head fell back on the pillow. I closed my eyes to force myself to try and remember *something*. I rubbed my forehead with my right hand, the one that wasn't bruised. "Let's see, I did a double last night and . . ." I kept my eyes closed, rewound events.

"Harland! Harland was chasing me."

"*Who?* Don't tell me someone pushed you into the streetcar?"

"No." I shook my head slightly, but even that hurt. My head was pounding. "No, he's a regular, a real drunkard. I got outta work and was headed to the trolley stop. He was trailing me, and I started walking faster and was almost there when he grabbed my arm, started pawin' me, fondled my breast . . . oh God, he was going to rape me, Tess. He's a big man so even drunk, he could've—"

Tess's comforting hand didn't soothe the terror replaying in my mind.

"I remember screaming, but no one was around. I fought, scratched, hollered and struggled with all my might and finally got loose. I just ran. I was so terrified." My eyes welled up with the memory. "Oh my God, yes." The fear I'd felt that night came back in a chilling rush. "My God, I ran right into it, didn't I?" The sheer memory made me shudder.

Tess touched my cheek. "I'm so sorry that happened to you. That bastard. I'll tell George right away." She forced a smile. "Ya know, I must say, much as you grumble about streetcars, I never figured you'd put yourself smack dab in front of one."

My dear sister was trying to lighten the moment, and it worked. I was hurting, but so grateful to be alive.

A nurse walked in and handed me a little cup with two pills. "To help you sleep," she said. I took them gladly and before I knew it, everything was black again.

The next morning, a man dressed in a white overcoat entered my room. I thought I was still dreaming. He looked like a movie star, like that handsome Gary Cooper. Except this man's wavy hair was blonder, with sunken cheekbones that emphasized his chiseled face. I held my breath wondering if the medication was playing tricks on me.

His bright hazel eyes practically glistened as he spoke. "Hello, Miss Swanson, I'm Dr. James Kent. I conducted the surgery and will be your attending physician."

"Lucky me." I summoned a grin.

He tried to hide his own grin but wasn't able to. "Don't try and talk too much yet. I just want to explain your condition." He told me that although my ribs were sore, they weren't broken. He was most concerned about my left leg.

"You broke your tibia, along with the fibula, which are located here," he said, lightly touching that part of my leg over the bedsheet.

"Hmmm, the tibia and the fibula, sounds like a silly melody. Will you be breaking into song next?" *The medication must be making me loopy.*

"Would that make you feel better?" His face softened.

Oh, I did like this man. I patted my hair. God knows what I must look like! "Actually, Doc, I could use the entertainment."

His grin was short-lived as he glanced back at his chart. Back to business. "Your leg took the brunt of it. The

A Place We Belong

policeman I talked to said the trolley had already slowed for a stop so luckily, that helped save your life."

His words made me shudder.

"That said, there was great force when it hit you, so there's quite a bit of damage in that leg. The cast will help maintain proper alignment during healing. I'm sure it feels tight, but it needs to be to minimize excessive movement." He pulled up a chair beside my bed. "Once the cast is off, in about six weeks or so, you'll still experience some pain and stiffness. You'll be given a special boot to wear for a few more weeks, which will support your leg as you slowly start to bear weight on it. Crutches will help you get around."

I grabbed my chest. "Oh, no. Not crutches."

He tapped my arm. "Only for awhile. We'll see how the leg looks once we get that cast off. Hopefully it'll heal just fine."

"Hopefully?"

His lips turned up. "Caught that, did ya? You're sharp."

I'd never broken anything in my life. The fear of not knowing the outcome seeped through my veins. "Am I going to be crippled? Please don't mince words, I want the truth." *As horrifying as it might be.*

"No, no . . ." he said quickly, but it trailed off. "Your right leg is fine. But I will be honest with you. Although the surgery went well, chances are that even if your left leg heals as we expect, you'll most likely have a slight disability, such as a limp."

"A limp? Like an old person? Oh, God." I pictured myself, hobbling on the Roxy stage trying to look sexy. "I can't have a limp." I paused. Might as well spill the beans. "Dr. Kent, I'm a Burlesque dancer." *Did I catch a look of surprise?* If so, he quickly recovered. My eyes grew teary. "I cannot have a limp in my business," I repeated. "I *can't*." Panic set in. "You just said I wouldn't be crippled, but that's being crippled!"

Blood rushed to my head. I wanted to scream, plead with him. *Take back the words.*

Again, with the hand on my good leg. "We'll cross that bridge when we come to it. *If* we come to it." Another little pat. Like a parent to a child. "You just need to rest now."

"No, you don't understand." I pulled myself up too fast and my ribs jabbed in protest. "Ow. *Damn,*" I called out, wincing. "You have to do something to make it normal. I can't be an invalid, I have to make a living."

"You're not going to—"

Tess and Helen came rushing into my room. "Hey, hey, what's going on? We can hear ya down the hall!"

By now I was weeping. "I'm crippled."

"Miss Swanson, please don't use that term again." The good-looking doctor frowned at me. "You *will* be able to walk, I promise you that. We're only talking a slight limp, you'll be able to do most normal activities."

"Yeah, most. Except walk normal. Except dance normal . . ."

He sighed, glanced over at Helen for help. "Are you her mother?" The innocent assumption made me want, need, my dear mother just then.

Tess made the introductions while I laid my head back on the pillow, letting the tears stream down.

A nurse came in to tell Dr. Kent that another patient was waiting to see him. He leaned into me, his earlier irritation forgotten. "We're going to do everything possible to get you up and healed properly." His voice, smooth as good whiskey. "There is always hope for the best. Please don't give up." Words my mother would have said. "I'll stop in and check on you tomorrow and we'll talk some more. I'll be able to release you soon. That is, until you need to come back to get that cast off." Even with the hard time I gave him, he managed a smile.

A Place We Belong

Tess's head swiveled, her eyes following him out the door. She raised her brows. "Wow, wow, wow, that doc is quite fetching. Mind if I sit a bit to catch my breath?" She pretended a little faint, which made me laugh. She sat on the edge of my bed, Helen on the other side. As upset as I was, it felt good to have them there. My family.

Tess raised her left hand and waved her fingers. "And no ring, I noticed."

I wanted to add that it wouldn't do me any good now that I was disabled, but Tess jumped in.

"But nah, on second thought, I think he's a bit old for ya. Looks like he might be pushin' forty."

"Well, you know I like older men." I smirked. "Speaking of which, has anyone called Eliot?"

"Yes, he was very concerned. He wanted to come see you, but he had a prior engagement he couldn't get out of."

"Evaline."

"Probably."

"Well, the man *is* married." Helen chimed in.

"I know that, Helen. Don't need no reminder."

"Sorry, but a wife will always come first, honey. You need to remember that."

"I don't have a choice, you keep bringing it up." It came out colder than I meant but I was feeling cranky.

Helen forced her lips shut to keep more words from spilling out.

"Hey, let's play some cards, shall we?" Tess, the peace maker. A definite first.

"You know I love ya, Helen," I added as a truce.

Tess pulled out a deck of Bicycle cards and we spent the rest of the day playing gin rummy. Unfortunately minus the gin, I thought with a sigh.

40.

"Good to see you, Miss Swanson," Dr. Kent greeted me, just as he'd done every day that I'd been here.

"And you," I replied, smiling sweetly. "Ya know, Doc, you sure know how to dress up a room." I gave him my best wink, getting a kick out of seeing him blush. It was better than thinking about why he was here in the first place.

"Oh, bet you say that to all the doctors."

"Well, seeing how you're my only one . . ." I snickered, held out my good arm for the daily blood pressure check.

I found it fun to be able to kid with him now that we'd gotten to know each other. Aside from talking about my injury, I'd managed to get him to open up, reveal a bit about himself. I learned he'd grown up in a small town in southern Ohio, had been a doctor for ten years, enjoyed playing golf, and best of all, to my delight, had no wife, no kids.

"Would you like to marry someday?" I knew I was being bold, but how else you going to get information if you don't ask?

He blushed again. "Perhaps. Just haven't met anyone special yet. Too busy with my practice, I suppose."

"It's harder than some people think, isn't it?"

He straightened his posture. "I need to attend to other patients now, Miss Swanson, but I wanted to let you know that you're doing very well and we plan to release you tomorrow. So please get some good rest." He placed a hand on my arm and kept it there. "You must listen to your doctor, okay?" His eyes penetrated mine. *Was he as attracted to me as I was to him?*

"I don't have a lot of choice, now do I?" My heart sank. I'd been here four days itching to leave, but now I didn't want to. I felt like the lovesick school girl I had never been. "Please call me Lydia."

He shook his head. "You're my patient," he said, taking his hand off my arm.

"But I feel like we're friends now, don't you?"

"I believe we are, but—" He shrugged, apparently out of argument. "I'll see you tomorrow . . . Lydia." He was halfway out the door before he turned and added, "But you still have to call me doctor." His boyish grin tickled me.

"Whatever you say. *Doctor.*" We shared a grin before he disappeared out the door.

A burst of giddiness swept through me. The handsome physician was definitely attracted to me. But how do you pursue a man who has seen you at your worst? Has *operated* on you? That was more intimate than making love!

I had less than twenty-four hours to figure it out. I sat back to read a book but couldn't concentrate. I was pondering my next move with the doc when a knock on the door intercepted. "Yes?"

My mouth flew open when Eliot walked in. My hand instinctively shot up to check my hair, patting the strays in place. But no need. I'd put on makeup and brushed my hair earlier to look good for my fetching doc.

"Oh, Eliot, what a wonderful surprise."

"Well, look at you. You look swell." He approached me with a smile.

He wore a neat gray suit that looked big on him. *Was he losing weight?* I was touched he came to see me. Even more so when I noticed . . . "Eliot, you're wearing my tie!" I gushed and leaned over to run my hand down its length. "I've missed you both so much."

He chuckled and set his fedora on the foot of my bed. He'd gotten a haircut. Shorter than usual, though that racetrack part remained. "Tess has been keeping me up on your progress. I'm sorry it took me so long to come."

He didn't explain further. He didn't have to. "I'm just glad you did. How's work?" I dared to ask.

"Still having some trouble making progress on several levels. Been given a hard time at every turn," he confided. "Seems I'm not as popular as I once was." His smirk was more sad than flip.

His vulnerability felt intimate and tugged at my heartstrings. "I'm so sorry, Eliot."

He shrugged it off. "On a more positive note, I've been able to turn my focus back to the Tennessee Home. I have reason to believe there are still children there from the Cleveland Murphy Home."

"What? They closed more than a year ago."

"Right," Eliot said with a curt nod. "We found a mother looking for her child who they took when she was arrested for prostitution. By the time she turned her life around and tried to get him back, the facility had shut down. She'd reached a dead end."

"That poor woman," I sighed. Just thinking of having a child out in the world with no idea where he was, or what kind of life he had, made me shiver.

"I have other suspicions, but too early to speak of them just yet," he said, gazing out the window. "Been working with my friend, Howard Nelson, remember him? The man from Chicago who knows a boy who spent time there."

"Oh, yes."

"He's been a help. I've learned more of how they operate." His gaze returned to me. "This Tann woman has connections in many states, not just Ohio. There are social workers, nurses, even some doctors, who help her place children. It's quite the operation."

Dr. Kent walked in just then and stopped in his tracks. "Oh . . . sorry, I didn't realize you had visitors. I just came by to check on you." I knew it was a ruse. He had just "checked" on me less than an hour ago. He pivoted to leave.

"Oh, Dr. Kent, it's okay. This is my friend, Eliot."

"Dr. Kent." Eliot walked towards him, extended his hand. "It's a pleasure to meet you and thank you for taking good care of Lydia."

"Aw, of course," as if he just recognized him. "You're Eliot Ness. Wow, it's a great pleasure to meet you, sir." He pumped his hand, glancing over at me. "Are you two related?"

Eliot and I exchanged looks, but it was Eliot who answered. "Longtime friends."

The doctor must have caught something in the exchange and his initial gusto faded. "Oh. Well, she's been a delightful patient." For a glint of a moment, I caught the men trade a look, as if sizing each other up.

Dr. Kent gazed over at me as if he was sorry for his loss. "Enjoy your visit." He left before anything else could be said.

"Looks like you have an admirer." Eliot raised his brow.

I cocked my head. "Eliot, he's my doctor."

"He's also human. I saw a spark in his eyes when he looked at you." *He did?*

His comment suggested they both sensed a proposed threat. Like polite sharks in water. Funny thing was, I didn't belong to either of them. Yet I had to admit, I enjoyed feeling like they secretly thought I did.

I shook off the psychology, anxious to discuss more about the orphanage. But Eliot seemed restless. After assuring me that he'd stop and see me once I got settled at home, he was out the door. I'd have to wait to learn more about that Tann woman. But there'd be time for that.

Time. I would have lots of it before I'd be able to live my life again. It's something I didn't even want to think about.

The sandman was a no-show until a nurse came in and gave me a sleeping pill sometime after midnight. The same nurse returned six hours later, roused me to take my vitals, and offered help in gathering my things to go home. I welcomed the thought of sleeping in my own bed. I ordered breakfast but it was the coffee I wanted. I felt too groggy and excited to eat much.

As the hands on the wall clock ticked on, I wondered if my dreamboat doctor was even going to stop in and say goodbye. I closed my eyes envisioning his darling face. Mental images of the two of us entwined together played out in erotic fashion, and I realized how much I missed sex. My face grew warm as the fantasies increased. My imaginary doctor lover had just lifted my face for a passionate kiss when he appeared in all his human glory, as if I had willed it.

"Oh, Dr. Kent, so nice to see you." I sat up straight, hoping my flushed face didn't give me away.

He looked even better today, and as he got closer, I detected a slight scent of a musky cologne, appealing greatly to my senses. He unwrapped the stethoscope from around his neck. "Let's take your temperature, get your blood pressure, check your heart." He was being unnervingly professional.

I opened my mouth to joke that my heart was just fine, sprinting like a race horse at the sight of him, but bit my lip.

Until I couldn't help myself. "Well, now that you're here, Doc, I imagine my blood pressure is off the charts." I leaned toward him, titled my head slightly and gave him my cutest animated smile.

It worked. "You really must stop toying with me, Miss Swanson." Then he shut me up by sticking the thermometer in my mouth.

That only encouraged me. I answered by shrugging my shoulders and batting my lashes in feign innocence. I watched him check the number. "Is my temperature high, Doc? Do I get to stay here longer?"

The corners of his lips twitched. "Afraid not. Ninety-eight-point-six on the nose. You're in good shape."

A nurse came in to take away my untouched breakfast tray and asked me if I was ready to go home. "I guess so. Though I must say, I've enjoyed my time here." I beamed at Dr. Dreamboat, who suddenly found an interest in his shoes.

"Well, we enjoyed having you, Miss Swanson. Good luck."

The second the nurse was gone, I spoke my heart. "I'm going to miss you."

"Oh, you'll see me one more time. I always make a house call, generally a week later."

My insides did a jig. "So this is not goodbye, then." I wondered if I should go further, do what I'd planned. He had to see me again, either way.

"Dr. Kent? Can you do me a favor?"

"What is it?" His professionalism was really getting on my nerves.

"Can you please get me my purse over there in the closet?" I hated the damn crutches, something I knew I'd have to get over if I was to heal. I hoped he wouldn't lecture me again on the importance of moving about.

He did not. He did as I asked. I reached in the big pocket, pulled out a pen and a stack of small cards wrapped in a rubber band. When George had promoted me to top girl, he had business cards made up with a very classy photo of me surrounded by my power-blue fans with The Roxy Theater logo at the bottom. If Doc didn't like the fact that I was a burly girl, then he wasn't the guy for me. This would be the ultimate test. I had to know.

265

I began to write down my home number on the back, but he stopped me. "Oh, I don't need your number, you'll be making an appointment with the secretary for some time next week."

Ignoring him, I finished writing the last two digits and handed him the card. He glanced at my photo. I held my breath, seeing his discomfort in the form of beads of sweat appearing on his forehead. Maybe I'd gone too far.

I sucked in a breath of courage. "Seeing how I won't be going back to work for some time, if ever" . . . the very thought gripped my throat . . . "I do hope you'll see fit to check on me more than once. To tell you the God's truth, I'm not feeling at all secure about my future." I didn't have to fake my woeful expression.

I kept on talking before he could say it wasn't professional or something. "I might be hobbling along, but I can still cook, and I'd like to express my gratitude. Maybe you can come by for a nice home-cooked meal?" My heart was pounding out of my chest. If he turned me down, I'd be crushed.

He checked my photo again, then his eyes swept the room as if he half expected the Keystone Cops to barge in and arrest him for unlawful mental activity.

That gave me a kick. That is, until I wondered if it would shame him, a professional doctor getting involved with the likes of me?

Seeing no one as witnesses, he looked back at me. "I think I would like that, Lydia."

I couldn't hide my shock. Now it was my turn to blush. I'd fully expected him to turn me down. I suddenly felt like a silly, shy teenager. "That would make me very happy, Doctor."

41.

The day after I returned home, Eliot came by for a visit. He brought me a bouquet of flowers; a colorful mix of daisies, carnations and petunias. And a kiss on the cheek. I had forced myself to move about with the damn stinkin' crutches every day but getting around in the kitchen proved more challenging. Luckily Helen had brought me ready-to-heat-up dinners, and homemade banana bread, which I now offered Eliot. Then I poured his favorite beverage, other than scotch. Black tea.

Eliot helped me settle back on the couch, placing a pillow under my leg for elevation. "You'd make a fine doctor," I teased, but the comment made me think again of Dr. Dreamboat. He was invading my every thought these days.

After some pleasantries, we got to the topic of Tennessee Children's Home Society. He confided to me that Howard wasn't just a friend interested in the agency's dealings but that he was an actual private investigator.

"Howard and I have found two well-to-do families living in the Chicago area who got their children from the orphanage. One couple, both in the theater and unable to have children, had sought out the orphanage after seeing an ad. They had no idea Miss Tann wasn't the respectable woman they'd been convinced of. We assured them that anything they told us would remain between us, and in sharing information they had, they could be helping hundreds of children's lives, if what we suspect is true."

He sipped his tea thoughtfully. "We talked to another couple whose wife had had a miscarriage that resulted in her being sterile. They heard about the place from a friend who'd also seen an advertisement. Apparently, they're running these ads in many of the major cities.

He stood up and pulled out his wallet. "I made a copy of an ad I found," he said, handing it to me. It read like a caption from a weird twist in a Grimm's fairy tale. ***Children in Need of Loving Homes – Yours for the Asking.***

Underneath the stark headline was a photo of a pretty, yet sad-looking girl that tugged at the heartstrings. The term "children's home" soured my stomach. According to Tess, it was anything but.

"One of the women confided that the girl they adopted often speaks of two younger brothers, so much so, they called and asked Miss Tann about it. Of course, the woman denied it, saying the girl had been an only child. So the parents assumed the girl was playing make-believe, like having imaginary friends. After speaking with us, they feared it might be true. We've also learned that these unsuspecting couples paid large amounts of cash."

I shook my head in disbelief.

"The agency has been known to charge thousands of dollars for out-of-state adoptions," Eliot added, "what they call delivery fees."

"Oh goodness." My hand flew to my mouth. "And no one thought that was suspicious?"

"If they did, they ignored it. When a couple wants a baby, they'll do almost anything to get one." His face fell. He was speaking from his own heart, this I knew.

We turned at the sound of the front door swinging open. It gave us both a start, given the dark conversation.

"I got an A on my first exam!" Tess yelled out as she entered the room.

After hugs of congratulations, Eliot caught her up on his news, and for the next hour, Tess revealed other details she'd kept inside. "I remember thinking it was odd that they

A Place We Belong

treated the fair-haired children much better, like letting them have second helpings at dinner, giving them the better clothes, not hand-me-downs like the rest of us." She held onto her teacup without drinking from it. "I remember how it enraged me. I'd get jealous and be terrible to them. I started fights with a couple of the girls because of it."

She bowed her head at the memory. "And the others, the Jewish and Italian kids, were often treated the worst. One little girl seemed scared to death most of the time. I rarely saw some of those kids at mealtime and wonder if they were even being fed. I snuck them food when I could."

A tear ran down her cheek. Tess checked it and went on. "Now that we're moving forward with this, you both need to know the goings-on I saw in that place." She gazed at me. "I wasn't going to tell you everything, but now . . . no child should be allowed to stay there. I don't know how she's getting those babies in the first place. It's like she somehow rounds up kids with a lasso."

I looked over at Eliot who was taking notes. "If that woman is so well connected, how are we going to get around her?"

"I'm working on that." Eliot grabbed his fedora from the table and put it on. "I need to get back to the office. I'll be in touch." He leaned over and kissed the top of my head. "Take care of yourself."

I could only nod. My heart ached at the thought of those children, and for their real parents who would always wonder what became of them, missing them with their whole being. Yet now I held hope that we could do something about it. I knew Eliot well by now. If he wasn't getting satisfaction from his present position, he'd put all his energy into this catastrophe. This well-hidden crime.

When Eliot left, Tess and I talked about Eliot's suggestion of going to Memphis together when my leg allowed it. At one point, Tess admitted, "I'm not sure how I'll handle going back there." Her pressed lips underscored her words. "But I'll do it. We need to do it."

"I know." I felt driven now. "Maybe we'll be able to right some wrongs."

In the meantime, the gang at the Roxy came to visit. George brought me a whole bag of Peppermint Patties, my favorite. It touched my heart, but they all acted as if I had a hangnail and would be on that stage again in no time. They were trying to be supportive, I knew, but it only made me sad. We all had to face the truth. My leg may heal for the most part, but I'd always have a damn limp, and limping was not what a sexy Burly girl did. I would no longer be a part of the Roxy family.

The only thing that made me happy was that my dreamy doctor paid me more than one house call. He started coming by once a week after his shift, and it was obvious to us that it was no longer a mere professional call. Each time he showed up, he stayed longer. The coffee visits turned into lunch visits and soon became dinner visits. I finally felt strong enough to make him that home-cooked meal I had promised. He helped me with my physical therapy while I kept him well fed. Cooking a full meal with a bum leg was challenging, but before long, I learned to manage three courses with little problem.

Soon, we shared stories of our similar Catholic upbringing, our parents—his Irish, mine, a mix of Irish and Italian—his now widowed mother in Toledo, childhood games we had enjoyed, schools we'd attended, music, books, art, and foods we liked. It thrilled me that I'd finally met a smart, professional man who enjoyed many of the same interests as I did. A man who made me feel like more than just an entertainer. A man who treated me with kindness and respect, who made me laugh over silly things.

A man who wasn't on the take.

Or married.

And yet, there remained the topic I was afraid to bring up but was most important to me. We never talked about the card I'd given him in the hospital and I worried he was purposely avoiding the subject. One evening after serving my best pot roast, I mustered the nerve to ask how he felt about what I did, or rather had done, for a living.

He was sitting on the sofa next to me, wearing a casual blue shirt that made his eyes look like iridescent stars. He preferred coffee to tea, so needing something to do as I waited for his answer, I reached for the pot on the table in front of us. I wanted to offer him a cigarette but the dear doctor didn't smoke. And he declined offers for after-dinner drinks saying, "I don't drink alone, and you're not ready," reminding me that it wasn't a good idea to drink alcohol when walking with crutches.

So, no smokes, no cocktails. Dr. Dreamboat was already a good influence on me.

My hands quivered as I refilled his cup and fought to steady them, fearing I'd splatter hot coffee in the poor man's lap. When I straightened my posture, I asked his honest opinion about burlesque girls, and clasped my sweaty palms together on my lap awaiting his answer.

"I will be honest," he began. "I have never met a, um, dancer. Have never stepped foot in, uh, places like that." If it hadn't meant so much to me, I would've giggled at his awkward attempt to respond. But this was no laughing matter. I recalled his initial sour expression when I'd revealed my job in the hospital. He was about to confirm we had no future as a couple, I just knew it.

I did appreciate how he looked me straight in the eye, though. Even if he broke my heart, at least he was sincere. "I must say,"—*oh dear, here it comes*— "as I've learned more about you, I've learned something about myself. You see, I meet a lot of different people from all works of life in my profession. I try not to judge, and usually pretty good about it. Though, I'll admit, when you first mentioned it, I was taken aback." He grinned sweetly, obviously trying to soften the blow. "Not so much the exotic dancing part, it was more about your face, quite frankly. You have this softness about you, a natural beauty. I can't imagine you in all that makeup, and dressed in such provocative . . .

"Get-ups?" I wanted to make this easy on him.

He lowered his head, like a shy little boy. "I supposed that would be it." He went on. "Being raised in a strict household, I was taught that women in your profession were . . ." He let out a sigh. "Well, no other way around it. Loose. Sinful, even."

And there it was. No way was there going to be a future with him. I'd lost my career along with the possibility of having this good, darling man.

He caught my tears welling up. "I'm sorry this isn't coming out right. I'm just trying to make you understand."

All I understood was that I was getting dumped.

I felt a tear escape, making its way down my cheek. He rose and got a tissue from the box that I kept on the coffee table. He wrapped it around his forefinger, leaned in and gently dabbed my face.

"Thank you." How I would hate losing this man.

"What I'm trying to say is that I've learned my parents, and others, are hypocrites. They judge people as a whole, not as individuals. And in this day and age, especially with a war looming, we need to respect other's way of life. Especially working women. I see how hard my nurses work, I admire your sister's dedication to her studies, the school teachers . . . and of course, women who work in theater, such as yourself. Women who use their brains and talents to help make the world more tolerable, enjoyable. It's quite commendable, actually. Certainly nothing to be looked down upon."

He took my trembling hands into his. "I must also admit to you that I've done a bit of research on The Roxy. I saw you in their ads. I walked past the place the other day and saw you in the window display." His face turned red, and again I wanted to giggle despite myself. "Those big fans of yours sure look heavy." That little boy grin tugged my heart strings.

He lifted one of my hands and rubbed it against his cheek. "After getting to know you, I realize that as much as I dearly love them, my folks thinking was wrong. You, my dear Lydia, are very special. You're so different from anyone I've ever known. You're a tough cookie. Not just beautiful.

"And I am completely proud to know you." He kissed the hand before giving it back to me.

I was at a loss for words. And confused. It all sounded so wonderful. Almost too wonderful. Was he still dumping me? "So, does that mean I can call you James now?"

He laughed and pulled me into him. "What do you think?" Then he kissed me. A soft, sweet, tender kiss. For much longer than three Mississippi's.

When he finally let me go, I asked, "Does that kiss mean you're sticking around?"

He cupped my face with both his hands, leaned in and whispered. "If it's okay with you, I'd very much like to stick around. If you're up for it."

The giggle gushed out with relief. "Oh, James. Yes," I whispered back. "Most definitely, yes."

*F*rom then on, my handsome doctor came over every day that his job allowed. I found myself living for those times. James made me feel like no man had, with the exception of Eliot. And this was better. More dependable, more certain, more thrilling.

We shared more, with instinctive trust and understanding. I told him about my family, my past, my crazy times as a burly girl. He never asked about my relationship with Eliot but I wanted to confide in him about that too. A part of me wanted to test James. Make sure he was the real deal. That he could accept all aspects of me.

And so, I told James how Eliot and I met. How he helped me find Tess, and our frequent meetings that had sparked an undercurrent of gossip. I even revealed our New York trip, quickly adding that Eliot and I were never lovers. The fact that I had once longed for that very thing didn't matter anymore. Our time together had turned into a deep friendship that I cherished. I dared to hope that I didn't have to abandon it because James was now my beau.

Would he demand that I not see him anymore now that we were a couple? I watched him enjoy my homemade cheesecake as I explained how much Eliot meant to me—as a friend. "After all, he's married, you know."

He took a sip of coffee. "Well, I don't know if that's ever stopped people from having affairs."

The comment took me aback. "Well, it did in our case," I huffed.

"I was teasing you." He leaned into me. "So you're saying I have no reason to be jealous?"

"That is exactly what I am saying." And to my own surprise, I meant it. I realized in that moment, my love for Eliot was separate from the intense feelings, deeper sexual passion that I felt for this gorgeous man sitting next to me. To prove my words were true, I ran my fingers through his thick hair and kissed his soft lips with all the love and devotion I felt for him. When I released him, I added, "My heart is taken."

James not only accepted me for who I was, he accepted my bond with Eliot. He did not demand that I give him up, like most men might have. Here was a man confident in himself. A man who didn't need to take bribes, like Bill had. A man who didn't have a jealous temperament, like Bill had. And didn't have a wife. Like Eliot had.

Most of all, he was a man who knew me well enough to trust me. And that meant everything.

When my cast was taken off, I was dismayed how discolored, small and weak, my leg appeared. I'd always taken pride in my shapely gams, but now my left leg looked like a boy's. James assured me that it was normal, and every night he'd return from work, fill a bucket with warm soapy water, and lovingly wash and dry it with a soft towel, then caress my leg with my SweetHeart body lotion.

Free from the constraints of that damn plaster of paris, I finally led him to my bed and made slow sensual love to him that made him call out my name, thrilling me to greater desire.

Afterward, as we lay together, my bad leg wrapped around his good ones, I marveled at the irony of fate. If it hadn't been for that awful night when that lunatic chased me down the street forcing me to collide into a trolley, I would've never met my perfect mate. A real man who respected women. A man I could confide my deepest thoughts and feelings to. A man who cared about things I cared about.

I could hardly believe my luck.

Those thoughts renewed my ardent desires, and I initiated another round of passionate love-making. Through every touch, every kiss, every soft whisper and moan in the satiny cushion of my bed, I discovered, for the first time in my life, what making love was truly about.

42.

We began taking long walks to help my leg get stronger. Autumn was a magical time to be in love. The crisp, cooler air was perfect for snuggling, for scenic drives in the country, for gazing up at vibrant trees during idyllic strolls. I had to lean on James the whole time, but I'd never complain about that.

I practically lived now in his lovely home, perched on a hill overlooking Lake Erie in a quaint village called Bratenahl. We enjoyed long evenings talking, cooking together, playing board games by his homey fireplace, making love in his four-poster bed. He taught me to play Chess, and soon regretted it when I began beating him. "That's it. I'm not playing with you anymore," he'd say every time, but the next night, the wooden figures would be set up for another round.

There was still one thing that kept me up in the wee hours, and James knew it. I'd been racking my brain trying to decipher how I could do my performances with a bad leg. How could I turn it around and make it fun? Perhaps even have my audience laugh, in a light-hearted manner, at my expense. An awful thought, really, but I was feeling desperate. I couldn't imagine myself never working again. Burlesque was all I knew.

One rainy evening James came home with a present for me. I'd been sitting in his living room listening to the big-band music I so loved, longing to get back to the stage. Back to dancing. Back to normal.

I'd been sulking again, feeling sorry for myself, when he threw open the door with gusto, carrying a long brown box. I sat up and put on a happy face.

"What's this?" My first thought was long-stemmed roses but the package was too big and too long.

A Place We Belong

He set it down in my lap, smiling with excitement. "Go ahead, open it."

The anticipation on his face urged me on. Lifting the top, I unfolded the tissue paper and stared at the thing, not knowing how to react. The long stick was beautiful, with exquisite wood craving and a handle in the shape of a shiny brass eagle.

But.

It was a cane.

My throat tightened. Instead of bringing me joy, this gift choked me with despair. I had hoped I wouldn't need this, but apparently, my doctor knew different.

"I know what you're thinking," James said, leaning over and pulling it out of the box. "But it's not a cane, not really. It's a walking stick. Or what some call a staff."

Doesn't matter what you call it. If I could walk normally, this box would contain roses.

"See the handle? It reminds me of you," James was saying. "You have the soul of an eagle. You're strong, independent, and soon you'll be soaring and spreading your wings just like a great eagle."

Oh, I did love his romantic side. "You're just saying that and I appreciate—"

"I am not *just saying* that. You are a unique and resourceful woman, Lydia. Remember when we went to that library a few weeks ago?"

Of course I did. We'd been on one of our long drives when I pointed out the window. "Oh, let's stop in there." It wasn't my local library so I didn't have a library card but the red-brick building was quaint and welcoming.

"While you were immersed in the fiction section," he went on, "I found this book on the personality of eagles and that's when I decided to find the perfect staff that exemplifies who you are. It took some detective work, and asking a few

277

coworkers, but I finally found it in this old man's shop in Toledo. He carves them himself."

"Toledo? When were you in Toledo?"

He threw me a sly grin. "When I went to visit my mother, the shop was less than an hour from her place."

He pulled the staff from the box and held it out in front of me. "Maybe you could use it in your act. They're becoming quite fashionable, you know." *In what country*, I wanted to ask, but kept the words in my mouth. "We can get you a top hat to go with it," he flashed a dimpled grin, "you know, like in that movie with Astaire and Rogers." *But Ginger Roger's legs were perfectly fine.*

I sighed. The poor man was trying. When he saw that I wasn't convinced, he took the cane and twirled it around in front of me, did a little jig. It wasn't that good but it made me laugh out loud.

His enthusiasm wore me down. When he handed it back to me, I ran a hand along the stick, feeling the grooves.

"I know you, Lydia. You won't let anything stop you when you put your mind to it. With every step you take with this, I hope you'll remember that."

As much as I wanted to hate this cane, this *staff*, I could not. It truly was an artful piece. I admired the craftsmanship, and my man's sentiment. I stood up and tried it out. It did make me feel steadier, stronger. And given the fact that it was my first big gift from James, I would cherish it always.

After walking with it through the entire first floor and back, I stood in front of him, and with my free hand, pulled his head to mine and kissed him with gusto. "How did I ever manage to snag such a wonderful man as you?"

"You broke your leg," he paused, his eyes misty. "And you healed my heart."

"What do you mean?"

A Place We Belong

He sat me down and told me about his first love and how she died from bone cancer at age seventeen. It was the first I'd heard of it. "That's when I decided to become an orthopedic surgeon, sort of a way to honor her." He pressed his lips together and I could tell he was fighting deep emotions. "My dad was a pharmacist and I planned on following in his footsteps but this job is a better fit for me." He pulled me into him. "And I've never been so thankful for my career as I am now. I truly never thought I'd find another girl to love." He kissed me, soft and sweet. "I was so wrong."

I was stirred by his admission and talk of love, yet I still couldn't help worry about my own career. In recent dreams, my leg was perfect. I'd float across the stage in my glittery costumes and beautiful swaying ostrich fans—my Dr. Dreamboat sitting front and center, clapping louder than anyone. My name, my career, bigger and brighter than ever.

But then I'd wake, and it would take great effort to get out of bed and stand without wavering. While James was at work, I spent hours thinking up ways I could still do my bits. I imagined possible new routines I could do with a cane, inspired by James's top hat routine. Maybe I'd change my name to Candy Cane. I could make red striped outfits and a red wrap for the cane . . .

Yet, once I changed my name and routines I would no longer be who I had been. My big colorful fans were my biggest attraction. I would never be able to use them now. Not with a damn cane.

One night I shot up in bed, recalling a story one of the visiting showgirls, Vivian, had told me. We'd gone out for drinks and I asked her why she never took off her gloves in public. She'd pulled off her gloves and I saw that her hands were cramped up, crooked. Vivian explained that she had crippling arthritis and told me of the time she had gone on without her gloves and a front-row customer noticed and demanded his money back, saying he didn't pay to see a "crippled strip-teaser."

After that, I stopped having dreams of returning to the Roxy. It was as if my subconscious knew what I feared was true. Despite all those daily exercises I endured to get my leg moving properly, it was clear that I would always have a limp. Whenever I walked into a room, people would turn to see me not as the striking, glamorous woman I had been, but because I walked awkwardly.

I put my head in my hands and wept.

Blue Satin Doll was dead.

"I don't know what I'll do," I told James one evening. I had just walked the length of his vast living room and fell into his arms, sobbing. I hadn't wanted to admit it. But the truth always catches up to you. "And all those outfits I made. I know I wasn't that good at it, the seams were always busting loose," I frowned. "But I enjoyed making them."

"You can always wear them just for me to enjoy." He always had a way of making me smile when I least felt like it. James would not allow self-pity. "You are smart and beautiful and have more energy than anyone I know." He gave me one of his serious looks. "You just need to discover another passion."

"Besides you?" I asked through tears.

"Well, I hope I'll always be number one." He touched my cheek. "But yes. We'll figure it out together. In the meantime, give yourself some time."

I prayed my good doctor was right.

The next morning, Tess came over and told me that Eliot had called to say he was coming by the apartment the following day. I sighed. It was time to tell him about my new serious relationship and I realized it made me anxious.

I set down my coffee cup. "Why in hell am I worried, nervous, about telling a married man that I now have a beau?"

"Because you have a relationship with that married man?" Tess raised her eyebrows.

"It's not a *relationship*. It's a deep *friendship*. Eliot and I never had sex."

"Yes, you have said that, more than once, actually. I just find it hard to believe. I've seen the way you two look at each other."

I nodded. I knew. "Yes, we do have a bond. Dare say we love each other. And maybe that's why we never succumbed. Too afraid to ruin what we have."

"But you two went to New York together. Stayed at the same hotel, for god's sakes. You can't tell me there was no hanky panky. Come on, Lyd, fess up." She crossed her arms, daring me.

I exhaled. "Okay, I admit it *could've* happened, but it didn't." I told her about the first night when I was too exhausted to do a thing but sleep. Then, that second night when I got horribly drunk and put the moves on him, but Eliot was too much the gentleman to take advantage of my inebriated state. "Now I'm glad we never did because it would make things more complicated with James. Would I have had the nerve to tell James if we'd had an affair?" I shook my head. "Thankfully, I needn't worry about that and hopefully we can all be good friends. *Comfortably.*"

"Then you shouldn't have a bit of problem telling Eliot that you got yourself a great catch." Tess said with a big ol' grin.

"You're right." I said, yet still had to wonder how this might change things between us. It felt like mourning a loss of something that never was, and never could be.

The next day, Tess came and brought me to the apartment so I'd have a chance to tell Eliot where I was really staying. We had a lovely chat over tea. When I told him about James and our new status, he seemed genuinely happy for me.

"Maybe I won't have to worry so much about you now," he said. I brightened at the thought that he worried and cared that much for me. Maybe we could manage to keep what we had between us, after all.

Especially when it came to our joint mission to bring down Georgia Tann.

A Place We Belong

43.

With the falling of the leaves, I grew stronger and more capable of accomplishing nearly any household task. Although James and I had initially agreed that I'd return home once that happened, I already had most of my things in his home. No one had to know we were essentially living in sin, except that I did need to be up front with my landlords. Tess would be taking over the rent of my upstairs apartment.

And so, James and I held our first dinner party in his spacious home for Frank, Helen, and Tess to make the announcement. I bought a new satin cocktail dress in James's favorite color of fuchsia and dug in my jewelry box for the diamond clip-on earrings I'd purchased with my first big paycheck from the Roxy. It was the first time I'd gotten dolled up since the accident and the glamourous feeling harkened me back to the excitement of my stage days. But I would not think of that tonight.

Wearing my best pink ruffled pinafore to protect the dress while cooking, I spent hours on my rack of lamb, the Theatrical recipe Helen had secretly given me. And to my own amazement, I managed to make delicious homemade mint jelly from my new Betty Crocker cookbook and cooked up perfect roasted potatoes and green beans. And because my mother was on my mind with her birthday approaching, we'd have her favorite mincemeat pie for dessert.

"I've never had that kind of pie," James said, hugging me from behind as I mixed the dried fruit, raisins, pecans and spices. "So where's the meat?"

I laughed. "I once asked my mother that and she said, 'well, that would be supper, then, not dessert, wouldn't it?'

Made sense to me." I laughed, reaching for the brandy. "Now here comes the best part." I poured some into the mixture, the rest into two glasses for the two of us.

We lifted the crystal tumblers. "Here's to a successful dinner party," I said.

"That's a given with you. Let's toast to us."

"Even better." I took a swig, then kissed him deeply until the timer went off announcing time for the pie to go in.

After dinner, we all settled in the main gathering room with the stone fireplace warming the house as well as our hearts. I told Frank and Helen of my upcoming change of residence and was pleased that they made no judgement. In fact, they seemed happy for me. They clearly liked James Kent.

James couldn't wait to try out his new Kodak camera and we all took turns posing for pictures. Tess and I hadn't any photos together since we'd been separated, nor had she any of me and James. And knowing that I was permanently leaving Frank and Helen's wonderful house, I would treasure these photographic memories of us.

Once James decided he had enough photos, he handed the camera to Tess, who got into the spirit, playing photographer's assistant, directing me and James in different angles throughout the room. They decided the best place for us to stand was in front of the roaring fireplace.

I caught James giving my sister a little smirk. What was that all about? He then disappeared into the kitchen and returned with a bottle of champagne and a tray of flutes. "My word, James, we're going all out now, aren't we?"

I was sitting in my favorite blue armchair, noticing everyone else squeezed into the gold settee. "You all can spread out," I said, laughing, "we have plenty enough chairs." But no one moved. And why was Tess still holding the camera? Something was going on. James set the drink tray on the table and motioned to me. "Come here, sweetheart."

A Place We Belong

I scanned my attentive audience, their faces lit up like a beacon. A tingly rush of anticipation swept through me.

Helen stood up and handed me my cane. "How about one more picture," she urged. "You make such a beautiful couple."

I began walking towards James, who met me halfway and led me to the fireplace. He leaned my cane against the wall and took both my hands in his. His eyes were filled with such emotion that it made me dizzy with gratitude. This man truly loved me, like I'd never been loved before. I felt it through my entire body.

"My dearest Lydia," he began. I loved how lyrical it sounded whenever he said my name. "I believe it was fate that brought us together. Ever since I set eyes on you, I knew you were the one for me. You are the most amazing woman, and I am very proud to be your beau."

He released my hand and bent down to the floor on one knee. "But I don't want to be just your beau. I want to be your husband. The man who will be yours, and yours alone. Who will be there for you whatever life has to offer. To protect you and love you forever." He reached into his jacket pocket and pulled out a red velvet box. A ring box. Now I knew what was up!

"My beautiful Lydia, will you do me the great honor of being my wife?"

I gasped when he opened the box. It was the most beautiful ring I'd ever laid eyes on. A platinum ring with diamond center surrounded by blue sapphires, what he knew was my favorite color. My favorite gemstone.

I let out such a yell, the neighbors probably heard. "Oh, James! Yes, yes, of course!" If my leg had been better, I would've jumped for joy.

James gave me a long, meaningful kiss, made all the more special because it was shared in the presence of the three people who meant the most to me. Applause echoed through the warm room amid bombarded hugs and congratulations.

    I knew that no matter what would come in the future, I would look back on this moment as the happiest of my life.

44.

*T*ess came by for a traditional Thanksgiving dinner and while enjoying my pumpkin pie—I'd become quite the homemaker—we got down to business, planning our wedding. Most men didn't want a thing to do with those kinds of details but James wanted to be a part of it all, which thrilled me.

I handed Tess a tablet of paper for note-taking as the three of us settled in the living room. The simple act of discussing my wedding seemed foreign to me. My wild childhood dreams often consisted of being a female pilot like Amelia Earhart, or a strong, intelligent first lady like Eleanor Roosevelt. I may not have reached such ambitious heights but I'd gotten much satisfaction in being a showgirl who wooed an audience, and made money all on my own.

And while the thought of never stepping on stage again saddened me, I only had to gaze at my now-fiancé to realize there was something greater in my future. Perhaps I could do great, noble things, as a doctor's wife. As *Mrs. James Kent*. I was exhilarated about this new future.

Despite my independent nature, the one thing I'd always wanted was the love of a good man. I now had that. There was nothing more I could want.

Not even Eliot Ness.

James pulled me from my thoughts when he brought his lips to my ear. "If I had my way, we'd get married tonight."

I placed a hand on his knee. "Well, it's not like we haven't already consummated it many times," I whispered back.

"Oh stop, you two," Tess interrupted across the table. "You're making me jealous."

"Oh, you'll have your turn, no question. And God help the poor man," I teased, giving us all a good laugh. "But right now, you have to concentrate on your studies." I tugged James's arm. "And our dear doctor will be here to help you along the way, won't you, dear?"

"You bet." He reached out to pat Tess's hand. "It won't always be easy getting through some of those courses, let me assure you, but you're a smart girl, like your sister, you'll get through it with flying colors."

"Ah, thanks for the show of confidence, I think I'll need it." Tess rose and gave us a hug. "You two are the best."

"Okay, now that that's established," I said, pouring cups of eggnog. "Time to set a date. I was thinking how many brides want a June wedding. I want to be different."

"How about August eighth, the day we met?" James suggested.

"You remember the exact date? And how do you know if that's a Saturday next year?"

"I've been holding on to that ring for a few weeks now," he grinned, pointing to my left hand. "I've had time to check certain details." Hearing how he'd planned this made me beam.

We discussed having the reception at the most beautiful dining place in all of Cleveland, the luxurious Hollenden Hotel's elegant Vogue Room. The room could certainly hold a large crowd, but after some thought, we decided we preferred a more intimate affair with family and close friends. Tess, of course, would be my maid-of-honor, and James's childhood friend would serve as best man. I thought about having Kitty as a bridesmaid, but after she married a known mobster, I had kept my distance. I'd had enough of mobsters in my career and wanted no part of that lifestyle. Especially now, being engaged to a prominent doctor. Still,

Kitty was dear to me so, of course, I added her and Gary to the guest list.

After settling on our attendants, James leaned forward on the edge of his chair. "You know, I never did take my vacation and need to before the year's out. I had plans to go somewhere last summer, but then a beautiful woman came into my life and I realized there was no place I wanted to be but by her side."

I'd never tire of how he appreciated me.

"So how would you girls like to accompany me to say, Memphis, next month?" We glanced at each other. "And while we're there, perhaps we can pay a little visit to the Tennessee Home Society . . ."

He explained that he had phoned Eliot because he knew how important this was to me and wanted to support Tess and me. We both jumped up at once and lavished him with hugs. James understood our desire to do something to protect the children in that woman's care, and he agreed with it all. This was his way of letting us know he was on board.

"Oh, James," I said, after giving him a grateful kiss. "I'm so glad you feel the same way we do about this." I paused. "How about I call Eliot and ask for an update so we're all on the same page?" I didn't dare suggest he go with us, though the thought was there.

"Yes, good idea." His face grew serious. "I hope he doesn't mind that I get involved too."

Tess spoke up. "Oh, he won't. Especially when he learns you'll soon be part of the family."

I suppressed a gasp. I'd been so wrapped up with wedding plans, I hadn't given thought to Eliot. I needed to tell him right away before word got out. He deserved to hear it from me.

Since learning that James and I were a couple, he had respectfully stayed away. And there was no stopping to see me at the Roxy or Theatrical anymore. I hadn't been anywhere in public since the accident. No way could I walk into those places with a cane. It was like I had a third leg.

Eliot proved hard to get a hold of the whole next week. He hadn't been in his office and I didn't dare call his home. After three attempts by me, as well as Tess, we had to stop. Rumors might begin to circulate if women kept calling him at his work place, and I had caused him enough problems for him.

I decided it would have to wait. I told James all we knew about Georgia Tann so far and we laid out a plan on how to discover more as we prepared for this rather risky trip.

And so, that first week in December, the three of us boarded a train bound for Memphis, Tennessee.

45.

The only thing that concerned me was Tess going back there. When I suggested maybe she shouldn't go, that it might bring up too many bad memories, she wouldn't hear of it. "I want to do it for the kids," she insisted. "Plus, just knowing I'm no longer stuck there should keep the ghosts away." She gave me a brave smile.

On the way to Memphis, Tess asked, as if it just occurred to her, "What if Georgia recognizes me?"

"With all the children that come and go in that place—you said so yourself—I'm confident she won't after all this time," I said. "You don't look at all like that thirteen-year-old you once were. You're taller. And ya finally got boobs," I teased to lighten the moment.

With a plan in place, we arrived on a Wednesday, settled into a hotel, and immediately went shopping for children's toys and a Santa outfit for James.

The following day, the three of us appeared on the steps of the stately brown brick house known as the Tennessee Children's Home Society. The home was surrounded by shade trees—sycamores, pine, dogwoods—and lush gardens. It did not look like a place that harbored neglected and abused children and sold them to the highest bidder. But then, that was precisely the point.

James rang the door in his bulky red suit and fake beard accompanied by Tess, dressed as an elf. Then there was me. Looking rich in my best organza blue dress, glossy black high-heeled patent leather pumps, and mink coat. This was all for Georgia's benefit, of course. And, hopefully, for ours as well.

The woman who answered appeared to be about the same age as Georgia but did not resemble the picture I remembered seeing in her advertisements for babies.

"We come bearing Christmas gifts for the children, ma'am," James told the woman in his charming way. He introduced us as members of a children's charity. "I know we're a bit early, but we want all orphans to enjoy the entire season, including the children of Jewish faith."

At least that much was true.

The woman's face brightened when she noticed the large canvas bag filled to the top with festive wrapped presents that all three had lugged up the steps. "My, that is kind of you, what charity is it again?"

James didn't miss a beat. "The Kent Children's Charity Foundation. You see, I got the idea recently due to an unfortunate family tragedy, and knowing all the good you are doing here, your well-known facility is our first stop."

"Are you Miss Tann?" I worried she might not be here and we'd miss the chance at talking to her and slyly get information.

"No, I'm her assistant, Miss Ringler. Come in, please." She looked quickly behind her before allowing us inside. "I'm afraid Miss Tann isn't here right now."

Probably busy snappin' up more innocent charges, I thought with a grimace I managed to stifle.

"We haven't had a chance to put up a tree yet," the woman said, leading us into the foyer. "We've been quite busy. We recently acquired several small waifs and they're a handful."

Waifs. I gaped with open mouth at the awful term. James—knowing me well by now—quickly said, "Can we round up the children? Tell them Santa's here!"

Miss Ringler hesitated, as if unsure if this was against protocol or not. Just then a boy, I guessed to be around six, with baggy pants and equally oversized wrinkled shirt, peeked around the corner. I caught his eye, and we smiled at each other. His red hair had been shaven on the sides but the top was just long enough to reveal a colic in front. My heart sank at the sight of him. A red-haired boy with unruly hair, long past the cute baby age, marked him as a "lesser" child in Georgia Tann's view. I wondered how long he'd been here.

I walked up to him and stooped down to his level, hands on knees. "I see a little boy over here who might be ready for presents," I said, loud enough for James to hear.

James jingled his ring of brass bells. "Well, hello, there, young man. Ho-ho-ho!"

The boy's face lit up, then shyly inched his way toward the sack of gifts.

The bells did their magic and other children came running from all directions. Tess stayed next to James as his helper, giving me a chance to take this woman aside.

"Thank you, Miss Ringler, for this opportunity," I said, walking away from the ruckus, toward what appeared to be the formal reception room. I knew the woman would follow. "We love bringing such joy to these unfortunate children."

"They are not unfortunate, ma'am." The woman gave a sour expression. "They are quite lucky to have us."

"Oh! I didn't mean no disrespect." I bit my lip. "My apologies, I'm just so sensitive about orphans." I touched her arm for a brief moment, then pointed to a large red settee. "Will Miss Tann be back soon?"

"She's out of town," the woman said with a curt tone.

Just as I feared. "Oh, well, may we sit? I'd like to talk to you." I didn't give her a chance to refuse, and sat down. Once she was settled across from me, I began. "Mr. Kent is my fiancé." waving my left hand proudly, making sure the woman saw my big, expensive ring. I switched to my most serious expression and whispered, "I will be honest with you, Ma'am. There was more than one reason we came here today."

"Oh?"

I bowed my head. "James and I have recently learned that I cannot bear children."

Miss Ringler's brows raised ever-so-slightly. "Oh, that's a shame."

"Yes, as you can imagine we are quite disappointed to say the least. Practically on our first date, we discussed how much we both wanted a family."

My eyes shifted to the other room where excited children waited patiently in line to see Santa. The boy we'd seen first stood like a little soldier behind two younger girls. He must have let them in line before him. I felt another tug at my heart.

"The doctor and I have heard what good things you are doing for these children. So much so that we've come all the way from Ohio to visit your generous home. We are thinking about adopting one for now, possibly more soon after, once we marry and get settled in our home. It's right on the lake and much too large for just the two of us." I clasped my hands tight. "I realize Miss Tann isn't here, but could you walk me through the process so I can discuss with him when we go back. For instance, how long would it take to get a child? We'll be married soon so I'm anxious to get started since James is a bit older than I, and we don't want an only child."

"I see."

I could almost see dollar signs in the woman's eyes. *She must get a healthy cut.* "The paperwork doesn't usually take long, and we do give our esteemed clients first priority." She smiled but rather stiffly. "There are some rather large fees involved, however, when dealing with out-of-town clients, such as travel expenses for delivery of the child. We will first require necessary information about you both, which includes a background check, naturally, and that runs a few hundred dollars. And of course, we can't get anything started, you understand, until we get that promissory note. Then there's the

A Place We Belong

transport fee, with you living so far away, and that can be upwards around five hundred. I tell you this all to be perfectly clear and upfront so we don't waste each other's time. And we are quite choosy who gets our poor little urchins."

I winced at yet another awful word. "I do appreciate you being forthright, Miss Ringler. And let me assure you, any child of Dr. Kent and mine will certainly be well taken care of, spoiled even." I flashed my stage-worthy smile. "My husband-to-be is a very successful and prominent doctor. We can afford whatever it takes."

I could tell by the woman's captivated expression that I was saying all the right things, along with the suitable refined language. I was glad I'd done my homework.

She stood now. "Well, then, I will speak with Miss Tann on your behalf. Soon as she returns."

"Oh, wonderful! Dr. Kent will be so happy."

I glanced into the next room again. There had to be twenty children there now. Small ones took turns on James's lap while Tess handed them each a wrapped gift as they climbed off.

"Doesn't Dr. Kent make a fine Santa?" This I meant, my heart full of pride watching James bask in this role.

The little boy who had caught my interest was opening his present now, his expression, pure joy when he found it was a fire truck. Immediately, he clutched it to his chest as if in fear someone would take it from him. He rushed toward the steps.

I pointed to him. "That boy there, running upstairs. What is his story? We do want an older child, at first. We understand they are less in demand than babies."

"Do you live on a farm?"

I tilted my head. What a strange question. "No, we're just outside the city." I didn't want to give away too much but wasn't used to being stared down. "The Cleveland area."

295

"Ah, Cleveland, Ohio. We've had success placing children there."

And have taken children from there.

"I must tell you, we do like to keep the older ones for people who live on farms. We often hear from childless farmers who are in dire need of older children who can help out as farmhands to keep their livelihood intact." The woman shook her head. "Many are still suffering from the Depression. We try and help both children and adults in need."

My skin crawled. *Bullshit.* I straightened my spine. "Children as farmhands? That boy is so young, he can't be older than six."

"Seven. And of course, they do no more than they're able. Boys, especially, do well raised on a farm." She spoke without meeting my eyes. "It builds strength and character."

I couldn't believe what I was hearing. In my library research, and talking with Eliot about the orphan situation, I'd learned about Orphan Trains. How they'd take children from big cities, such as New York, transport them to rural towns where they were auctioned off, like cattle, to work in the fields. But they'd stopped that awful practice a few years ago. Apparently, Georgia Tann had picked up on the idea. Plus, I highly doubted there were "background checks" involved in their practices.

"To be perfectly frank," Miss Ringler went on, "I don't believe Jack would be a good fit for such cultured people as yourselves." She leaned in and whispered, "He's a little hellion, that one."

A cold chill prickled along my back, but I couldn't let my distaste show. That little boy was already branded. It wasn't right. I'd seen how he acted. He was no hellion. I knew a hellion when I saw one. I merely nodded. "I see. Well, could we make an appointment with Miss Tann? Will she be back tomorrow?"

The woman shook her head. "I'm afraid not until Saturday. How long will you be in town?"

We had planned on leaving Friday, but now we'd extend it. Even if James had to leave sooner for work, Tess and I would stay if necessary. I surprised myself when I realized I was not lying about adopting that sweet boy. I recalled one night James and I had discussed the possibility of adopting "down the road." I'd never been too sure about the whole pregnancy process and never thought motherhood was for me, but after being away from my career and settling down with James, I'd discovered joy in domesticity. James and I could provide a wonderful, loving home for an underprivileged child.

The very thought warmed my heart. Now seemed as good a time as any to pursue it. If it turned out that our hands were tied and we couldn't save all these children, we could at least save one. This boy Jack.

"I can stay a bit longer, if need be," I found myself saying.

"Does your charity have a branch here?"

"Oh. Well, not just yet. As James said, we recently got this idea after reading about what y'all are doing." I almost laughed. Funny how easy it was to pick up a southern twang. "We had no idea there were so many children with no living family." I shook my head. "It's truly heartbreaking."

"It is," the woman said matter-of-factly.

Tess came rushing in. "Wow, that was a hoot, the kids are so excited."

"Looks like you had as much fun as they did," I laughed, watching the last of the children run upstairs. Which gave me a thought. "Miss Ringler, would we be able to see the children upstairs? Make sure we hadn't missed any?"

"I'm afraid that is not allowed. Miss, er, . . ." Obviously forgetting my last name, or had I even given it? The woman didn't wait for me to add it, merely went on. "I can assure you, they all came down. Word-of-mouth spreads quickly."

"Yes, I suppose it does." Rats. I really wanted to see the conditions they were living in.

James entered the room carrying an empty sack, and just like Tess, a satisfying grin. "Ho-ho-ho, ladies, mission accomplished!"

You have no idea how true that is.

"Tell you what." Miss Ringler gave James a bright smile as we put on our coats. "Y'all look like upstanding people. So that you don't have to delay your trip, let me go into the office and get you the necessary forms so we can put you at the top of the list, and you can get on your way."

James shot me a questionable glance. I gave him a quick look that read, *later.*

I had obviously pulled this off. The fact that the woman would expedite the process gave me a great sense of hope and exhilaration. I couldn't wait to tell James and Tess about Jack, and call Eliot about our experience.

"Darling, we are one step closer to becoming parents!" I announced taking James arm as we followed Miss Ringler into a separate room. "Just go with it," I whispered.

We soon left, minus a check for five-hundred dollars. And another baffled expression from James. But it was Tess who was first to drill me on the bus back to the hotel. I put my finger to my lips. "Wait till we get to the room."

46.

*T*he minute the hotel door shut, Tess blurted out, "Okay, so what happened?"

"Yes," James said, "Please tell us. I didn't know it was going to cost me five hundred smackaroos."

I grabbed his hand. "I need to talk to you in private."

Tess cocked her head. "Um, okay, I'll just go down to the lobby for, what, 'bout an hour?"

"Sure," I answered, not taking my eyes off James, secretly praying he was the man I thought he was.

The minute she left, I took James's arm and led him to the small sofa by the bed. "Honey. Remember we talked about maybe having a child after we got married?"

"I do," he nodded with a tilt of his head.

I caressed his cheek, inhaled a deep breath. "And remember that little boy we saw?"

"Which one? There were at least ten of them."

"The one who came in first. The shy one."

"Oh, with the red hair, right?" James brightened. "He was a cute fella. Do you know he let about four kids in front of him before he came to me? Though he was hesitant to sit on my lap. He just stood there and stared at me with these sweet eyes. Even said thank you when I gave him his gift."

"Yes, and did you catch his excitement when he saw it was a fire truck? Red, like his hair." I laughed, squeezing his arm, hoping I was reeling him in. "I caught him in the corner of my eye. So, you were taken by him, too?"

James was silent for a moment. "Sure, who wouldn't be? Actually all of them got to me. You have to wonder what their stories are."

"Exactly. And that's why we're doing this, right? To save these children from a harsh fate. Protect them from those who don't have their best interest at heart."

"Yes . . . *and?*" He asked cautiously, still trying to figure out where this was going. When I hesitated, he added, "Before you explain the five-hundred bucks, I will say, the place didn't appear the way you and Tess described. It was clean and seemed to be an organized institute. Besides, the woman let us in. You'd think she'd be more cautious if we appeared to be real schemers."

"You were dressed as Santa Claus."

He smirked. "Yes, and that's just it. *We* could've been schemers. We caught them unaware, no appointment, which I'm sure isn't how it's done. If someone can just show up unannounced and be let in, maybe it's not as bad as we thought." He took my hand. "Maybe the place has changed since Tess was there. After all, that was several years ago."

Leave it to James to be the devil's advocate.

"Didn't you notice the children's sloppy attire? On the way out, Tess said some looked like they hadn't bathed in weeks. And look how firm that woman was about not allowing us upstairs."

"I hadn't really thought about that, though I did look out the window and saw a swing in the back yard. I figured that's how some got dirty. Playing outside."

"James, listen. Eliot and Howard have enough reason to think they could be prosecuted, if only people stopped covering for them, which includes nurses, even doctors. I know, given the ethics of your profession, you'd want to stand against those who abuse it."

"Of course. There are bad apples in every orchard."

"That's right. And think about it. That Ringler woman seems as bad as Georgia. I was with her long enough. She didn't seem compassionate at all about those children. Did you hear her call them a *handful*? Why? Because they cry? Wet the bed? They're children, for god's sakes." I grabbed my cane and pulled myself up. "She called them *waifs*. And *street urchins*. How could she? She's hired to care and protect them!"

James took my hand and guided me back on the sofa. "Lyd, I'm sorry this is affecting you so. And I understand—"

"She called Jack a hellion!"

"Jack?"

"The boy. That sweet red-haired boy. He's old enough to know what's going on. He acted like he was deathly afraid to make the wrong move. I watched him. He hung onto that toy truck like someone was going to yank it from him and he'd never get it back."

"Honey, maybe he was just afraid another boy would take it. Kids do that."

"It was more than that, I tell you." I took in a breath. "I can't get him out of my head, James. It was obvious Miss Ringler wasn't fond of him. He's not being treated right, I feel that in my bones." I took a deep breath, tried to calm down. "You know, there was a time in my life, not so long ago, when I couldn't fathom being a wife and mother. I was happy with my life. I loved my job, making those elaborate costumes, performing in front of an appreciative audience, and yes, teasing the hell out of them." I gave a mischievous grin. "I made my own money and spent it as I pleased."

I took one of his hands and placed it on my chest. "Then you came along, with your gentle manner, your big strong healing hands, your smarts . . . and that dreamy face." I raised my brows, making him smile. "You quickly became my best friend, as well as lover. We have this connection . . .

"And when I saw Jack come bouncing into that room, I felt a similar attachment. My heart did this crazy flip-flop. It was almost like I recognized him. And those blue eyes, they just drew me in. Like they could see right through me. It's strange, I know, but I felt this pull towards him right away. I feel he needs us. Who knows how long he's been there."

"Lydia? Are you actually suggesting?"

"Yes, I am. James, I want to adopt Jack." I sucked in a breath. "And I really hope you'll think about it."

He stared at me. "You're serious."

"I really am." I leaned into his chest, rested my head into it. I could feel his heart pumping, strong and steady.

"This is pretty unexpected." He pulled away just enough to look me in the eye. "We only saw him for an hour, Lyd. How can you be so sure you want to do this?"

It was a fair question. Maybe I had a motherly instinct all along, recalling the dolls I took everywhere as a child. But this wasn't a doll. Jack was real. A bigger investment, a bigger responsibility . . . yet, one I felt ready for. But was James?

"I know it may seem a tad, well, irrational," I admitted. "But people often adopt kids they haven't met or spent much time with, you know? Of all those kids there, I felt drawn to that boy the minute I saw him peek around the corner. That image won't leave me. I can't explain it more than that. My mother always told me to follow my gut. I haven't always listened but whenever I have, it's turned out for the best."

"And your gut is saying Jack needs to be our son."

Looking directly into his eyes, I said. "I feel it in my very soul."

He pursed his lips. Still contemplating. "So the money I gave was actually towards a real adoption, not a ruse?"

"I guess so." I bowed my head, sorry that I couldn't explain it better. "You said yourself you were touched by him." I raised my shoulders and gave what I hoped was a persuasive impish grin.

"Yes, I did say that. And yes, I was. But . . . well, it is quite a surprise."

I knew I had him when his face softened. "Oh, James." I threw my arms around his waist. "This is right, I just know it." I gazed up at him. "Plus, this way, we'll have proof about how they operate. Make sure you keep that check stub."

"Oh, you know I will," he snickered. "And you realize, this might mean moving up the wedding."

"Now, wouldn't that be a shame?" I grinned.

He cupped my chin and kissed me. "You know I love you enough to give you anything you want, and I'm with you about Jack. I do feel he's special, too." He stood up. "I just ask that we learn more about him, okay?"

"From what I understand, they probably won't give us much, and it could be all lies. Let's go back tomorrow before we leave. After the money we gave, we should be able to spend some time with him. Not to mention giving them another surprise visit."

47.

I stood over his shoulders as James dialed. I'd been awake worrying half the night. *Were we really doing the right thing?* He held out the receiver enough for me to listen in as he reinforced our interest in adopting Jack. "My fiancé and I would like to take Jack out for a bit today before we return home," he told Miss Ringler. "Get to know him, and him, us. After all, this is not like it is with the infants."

I squeezed his shoulders.

"We have a policy, Mr. Kent," the woman was saying, "we just can't have people coming in and out, it would be much too disruptive. It's precisely why I should think you'd be more pleased with an younger child and one that is less, dare I say, trouble."

There she went again. What was it about Jack?

"Miss Ringler," James answered. "To be honest, neither of us have any desire to be changing dirty diapers," he said, with a lighthearted laugh. *Good comeback.* "I'm sure you'll welcome having someone serious about taking him off your hands."

The woman couldn't say much to that.

But she must have said enough to Georgia to summon the woman back from wherever she'd been the day before because when we arrived, it was the director who opened the door.

She was just as Eliot had described her. Mannish, with short cropped curly hair and wireless glasses. Her manner, all business. "My assistant tells me of your interest in little Jack," she said after brief introductions. She scanned us from top to bottom, then settled briefly on my mink.

"Yes," I answered. "We're here to visit with him so he can know us a bit before we move on with the adoption process. We want him to feel comfortable around us."

"We concern ourselves with the prospective parents first," Georgia answered curtly. "Children do not know what is best for them."

I opened my mouth to protest but James stopped me with a warning squeeze to my hand. *Play nice, Lydia.*

"Perhaps we can sit over there?" James pointed to the visiting room. "We don't want to be a bother to the others. We can have a chat with the little fellow while you go over our paperwork." He pulled out the form from his inside coat pocket. "I'm sure Miss Ringler informed you that we already provided the promissory note, in a check for five hundred dollars."

If Georgia didn't know, she was fully aware now. Did I detect a small glint in the woman's eyes?

Her demeanor softened. "The children are preparing for lunch. Why don't you come back at, say, one?"

I glanced at my watch. Almost eleven-thirty. We had planned to take the two o'clock train back home. I looked at James. "Maybe we can take a later train back?"

James didn't say yes or no.

"It's not too nippy out," I said to Georgia. "We'll just take a walk into town and come back." When I turned toward the front door, I spotted Jack, hiding under the stairwell. "Well, hello little Jack. Look, James."

"Jack!" Georgia's harsh voice made us both jump. "You get back upstairs this minute."

"Oh, Miss Tann, he's already here, can't we just have a moment with him?" I regretted saying it as soon as I saw the woman's irate face. I had crossed the line.

"Dear Miss Tann, we mean no disrespect," James gave her his most sincere smile, his charm on full display. "But I

305

really should get back to my job, and the boy is right here. Can we just have a few moments, what harm could it do?"

"The boy's already disobeyed. Children are not to come down until we tell them. We have rules, Mr. Kent. That's what keeps things running smoothly."

"I understand, Miss Tann. But please, allow us this." James soft eyes made Georgia's face soften like butter.

"Five minutes." She pivoted and headed upstairs.

I knelt under the stairwell. "It's okay, Jack, you can come over here with us." I reached out my hand, and after a brief pause, he took it.

But then, he started weeping, so soft and quiet, you wouldn't notice if you didn't look square into his face. We took him into the room and sat him down on the settee. I held him in my arms, stroked his head.

"I'm in trouble again," he whispered, wiping his eyes.

"No, you're not, big guy." James said, rubbing his back. "Say, I bet you like comic books."

James got him talking about Buck Rogers and Superman, and soon, his tears dried. James was going on about how Superman lived in our very hometown of Cleveland when Jack looked at him more intently and said, "You got Santa eyes."

We both laughed. James glanced at me as if for permission. "Can you keep a secret, buddy?"

Jack nodded shyly, and James explained he was Santa's helper. "I got permission from the big man himself to go to places while he's busy at the North Pole. I'm his best helper." He gave the boy a broad grin, then put his finger to his lips. "But you can't spoil it for the other children. You need to be our Superhero and keep this information just between us."

Jack was thrilled to do just that. When we saw Georgia approaching, James quickly said, "Say, would you like to maybe visit us someday?" I was surprised, worried it might give the

306

A Place We Belong

boy false hope. But then, I had learned that hope can be a good thing.

His little face lit up. "Yes, sir." Then he looked at me and whispered. "I don't like it here."

My heart broke into pieces. That had sealed it for me. We'd do whatever it took to get this child out of this place.

As Georgia neared, Jack waved, "Bye," and sprinted up the stairs.

James asked if we could discuss more details before we left. Georgia didn't look a bit happy about pursuing the matter, but after some hesitation, she led us into her office.

"Tell us, Miss Tann, how long has the boy been here? What happened to his parents?"

She walked over to a tall file cabinet, pulled out a drawer and retrieved a manila envelope. "Let me tell you first that he was about to be adopted by a nice couple but after a few weeks, they brought him back and chose another boy. It's why we're hesitant to try again."

"But he can't live here forever?" I was heartsick.

"Of course not." She threw me a sour look. It was clear, unlike James, I had not earned any points with the stern director. "But we are very good with matching the right people with the proper child. That boy has been here nearly a year now and does not follow direction well. You saw him sneaking around the corner, as he does often, eavesdropping when he's supposed to be upstairs playing with the other children. It's taken us this long to teach him simple instructions, like how to make a proper bed, and good manners. He has never appreciated all we've done for him, giving him a roof over his head, food to eat. After speaking with Miss Ringler, a couple of your status should have a child that is easier to manage. We have a lovely little girl about four, a well-behaved child that would be a better match for you."

I could not stay silent a minute longer. "Miss Tann, we appreciate your judgement, really we do. But considering we have expressed our intention and met your initial fee, we should be the ones to decide. We understand your fear that we may bring him back, but I assure you, that will not be the case." *No way would we bring him back here.* "We'll even sign a waiver, if need be." I sucked in a breath. "Now, please tell us more."

"Very well," the woman said, exasperated. "We got him around this time last year," she began. "The parents were quite poor. There was a fire in their shack. Electrical, caused by bad wiring on their Christmas tree. It happened in the middle of the night so by the time they woke, the place was in flames. Both parents perished."

James and I linked hands. This was worse than we'd imagined. "How did Jack escape?" James asked.

"He was staying overnight with another boy down the road, fortunately."

I recalled how Jack let other kids go in front of him in line for Santa. This boy had experienced horrible tragedy and yet was not bitter or hardened.

I stood up. "We want Jack, Miss Tann." I looked over at James, who added, "And we will marry as soon as possible, so that won't be a problem." I could've jumped in his lap and kissed him all over.

Georgia's resolve was weakening. "I will tell you that normally we give prospective parents thirty days to see if the child works out. Our main concern is the effect on the child should he be returned. They often are adversely affected and he's already proved to be difficult. If you are set on Jack, we'll draft a formal agreement that if you take him, you cannot bring him back."

My mind was racing. Were we getting in over our heads? What was it about this boy I felt so strongly about? Yet, besides being drawn to him intuitively, the fact that they

308

A Place We Belong

viewed him as "difficult" and a "hellion" brought out those maternal protective instincts even more. I believed children were a product of their environment and felt compelled to save this boy from his.

James stood now too, wrapped his arm around me. "That won't be a problem, Miss Tann. Also, it won't be necessary for you to deliver him. As soon as the necessary requirements are met, we'll return for him." He took out his wallet, wrote another check. "I'll give you half the money for the transportation fee for good standing."

The woman was speechless. But satisfied. She took what he offered.

48.

James ordered a bottle of champagne for the three of us as the train rumbled toward home. After catching Tess up on our success, I expressed what was foremost on my mind. "James, I'm a bit worried. I know we can afford, as you say, to pay what's necessary, but in doing that, are we no better than those other rich folks? Are we aiding and abetting their criminal behavior?" Even as I asked, I knew that since we were attempting to adopt from the agency, we were closer to proving their shady dealings.

"Obviously, things have taken a turn we hadn't expected. But this is still part of the investigation, and why we must speak with Eliot and Howard immediately. Now that we'll be directly involved, we need their counsel." He leaned over and kissed me. "I can't believe we might be having a child. Life sure is full of surprises, isn't it?"

I laughed. "You can say that again. And if we can get Georgia's operation shut down that'll make all the difference. We'll make sure Jack's adoption is legal, then get that money back and use it to help the other orphans, somehow."

The *somehow* lingered in my mind, but I had to stay positive. It was all so complicated, but I suppressed my worries. We would fight and we would win. I couldn't allow myself to think otherwise.

Tess refilled our flutes. "I'm going to be an aunt!" Her eyes brimmed with tears. "Have I ever thanked you, Lydia, for not giving up on me?"

"Come to think of it, no," I smiled. "But the person you should really thank is Eliot. If it wasn't for him—"

A Place We Belong

"Yes, and speaking of which," James interrupted, "We'll have him and Howard over for dinner soon as possible so we can go over our next steps."
I hugged his arm, relieved that he genuinely liked and respected Eliot. "That's a wonderful idea."
And yet, I couldn't help wonder, would it feel awkward to have Eliot in his home? The home where James and I were now living, together?
Sunday afternoon a more immediate crisis came into our living room. I'd been ironing James's shirts for his return to work. He was napping, exhausted from the trip. As always, I was listening to big band music on the radio when suddenly a man's voice broke in.
"We interrupt this radio broadcast for a special news bulletin. President Roosevelt has just released a statement that the Japanese have attacked from the air and all naval and military activities of the island of Hawaii, the principal American base in the Hawaii islands.
"I repeat, the White House has announced that Japanese forces have attacked Pearl Harbor, the naval base in Hawaii at precisely one-forty-seven p.m., Washington, D.C. time. Stay tuned for further developments. . . ."
"James! James!" I rushed into the bedroom and shook him awake.
The rest of the day and into the night, we clung to each other hearing the startling news that America would now be involved in the war we'd all hoped to avoid. Sitting near the fireplace listening to commentators, we wondered what to expect of our lives.
Although James would now have to register for the draft, at age thirty-seven, and having what was called a reserved occupation as a medical doctor, chances were slim that he'd be called to service. The news was debilitating, nonetheless. As the shock settled in, I worried this war might change all of our plans. Everything was now uncertain, and Georgia hadn't yet

311

gotten back to us on matters of the adoption. How long would we have to wait?

I was surprised to see that despite the boys going off to war—and what that meant to every American—people still wanted to make the best of the holiday season. Wreathes hung cheerily on resident doors, Christmas trees were being bought, and departments store window displays were all a-glitter with gift ideas.

As if the world was still normal.

But this was sure to be no ordinary holiday and I couldn't help wonder if James and I should be so concerned with a celebratory wedding when so many were heading towards the unknown, fighting a war no one knew they'd return from. We'd already planned to move up the date for Jack and now there was another consideration.

It was James who mentioned it first. "With everything going on, how would you feel if we just made our ceremony simple?" He asked one night as we cuddled by the fire. "Would you be terribly disappointed if we just went to city hall and got married? Just us and our wedding party? Maybe in a week or so? It might help get Jack sooner."

"Oh, James, I was thinking that same thing." But hearing him say it aloud sparked a twinge of disappointment. Since our engagement, I indulged in daydreams of a big, fancy wedding. Now that we were going to church regularly, I envisioned walking down the long aisle of the grand Old Stone Church in the heart of downtown Cleveland in a beautiful white gown and long veil. Then again, the sooner we married, the sooner we'd have our boy. *Hopefully.* "I agree we need to move fast and send that marriage certificate to Georgia to sway her to speed up the paperwork."

"So what new wedding date should we toast to?" James asked, setting down his hot cocoa.

"Are the offices open on Christmas Eve?"

"Doubt it. But I just thought of a more perfect place for us to say our vows." He squeezed my hand. "How about right here? In this room, where we spend each night to unwind, to kiss . . . enjoy our amorous pleasures." He raised his brows in a Groucho Marx way that made me burst with laughter.

"And where we got engaged." I kissed his cheek. "Yes, it's perfect."

The next day, James contacted his friend, Judge Shubert, and arranged all the details. We spent the next week revising a smaller guest list, got our blood test and marriage license, then I grabbed Tess and we shopped for the perfect wedding ensemble. We found it all in downtown's Halle's department store. A brocade mid-calf, off-white dress suit with a fitted jacket that gave it a posh look. Tess spotted a peach colored fascinator with netting that dropped over the eyes, in place of a veil. To complete the look, I purchased a gold velvet brocade purse.

Next, we hit the perfume department where I walked past my standard Evening in Paris and went straight to the counter displaying the more expensive Joy, by Frenchman Jean Patou, with its trademark jasmine and rich rose scent. The name was apropos for how I felt.

"Ooo, la-la!" Tess said when she saw the price. "I guess you really are a doctor's wife now."

"Don't try and shame me, sis. I've always loved this scent. Every time I pass this counter, I give myself a little spritz from the sample." I did this time, too. "As a newlywed, I want to smell as romantic as I feel."

"Fair enough."

I told the saleswoman to give me two bottles." Wrap up one for this girl," I said, getting a kick out of seeing my sister's delight. I wanted my good fortune to be hers too.

On the way to the escalator, I heard children. Lots of them. "Aw, look," Tess pointed to the long line of children waiting to see Santa. There were mothers holding babies while older kids chatted excitedly as they inched their way to the jolly man that represented goodness and light.

An unexpected memory clutched my belly, recalling what had once been an idyllic childhood. "Do you ever think about Dad?" I asked out of the blue.

Tess did a double-take. "Sometimes, why?"

"We need to talk."

During lunch in the department store restaurant, I told her about when our rat of a father came to see me at work, and the note that he left. I recited every word from it as I knew it by heart.

Tess sat quiet, took a sip of her Coke, then anger colored her face. "*You're* the disgrace to the family?" She shook her head. "He got it wrong, Lyd. Any man who abandons his wife and kids is the real disgrace."

If we hadn't been in a public place, I would've gotten up, walked over to my sister in that busy restaurant and squeezed the hell out of her.

Instead, with teary eyes, I added, "His loss."

I spent the night before my wedding with my sister. I awoke to her throwing open the curtains. "Look, Lyd, it snowed last night." I rushed to the window and was relieved to see a mere light dusting on the lawn. I didn't want anything to spoil this day.

I'd barely had my coffee when there was a light knock on the door and in walked Helen, who handed me a wedding bouquet of red and white carnations surrounded by holly, leafy greens and pine cones. "Just big enough to hold in front of you," she said with a smile. "After all, you're getting married on Christmas Eve."

Kitty arrived soon after. I hadn't seen her in eons. When we changed wedding plans, I sent out no invitations, just called the small group we had decided on. I didn't want Gary there so I didn't call Kitty. But Tess must have. And somehow convinced her to come without her husband.

I wrapped my arms around my dear friend. "Thank you for coming, Kit," I whispered in her ear. "I'm really happy to see you."

"Me too, girly. Us girls need each other."

"Now that's a fact," I brightened. "You look great."

"And so do you, Lyddy."

"Ha! In my nightgown? You *are* just saying that." It was as if nothing had changed between us. "I'd look better if not for this damn limp. Some days I feel fifty years old."

"Oh, honey, don't even think about it, you can't even tell."

"Yeah," Tess was quick to add, "and you wouldn't be marrying a doctor had that not happened. Just remember that."

"You got me there, sis." Every time I wanted to complain, I'd remind myself of that.

"I brought your something blue," Kitty exclaimed, holding out a small package.

I unwrapped it and pulled out a blue satin garter belt. Kitty grabbed it and wiggled it around her fingers as we all let out jubilant giggles. The gift could've made me sad at the reference because I was no longer Blue Satin Doll. And yet this gift was completely fitting. I would be throwing away my old life in exchange of a new one. One that, I prayed, would last through old age.

We arrived at James's house an hour later at the home I would share with my new husband. I was greeted by our closest friends and family and was so pleased to see Dottie from Crane's Book Shop there as well.

"I closed my store for the entire day so I can see this for myself," the self-proclaimed spinster joked. "One of my best customers and the most eligible bachelorette getting married."

I turned to see James's mother, standing near Tess. Although we hadn't met in person, we'd become fast friends on the phone. At sixty-five, she had lovely silver-white hair, but hardly a wrinkle on her soft face. As I hugged my soon-to-be mother-in-law, I spotted the mantle. James had added beautifully framed photographs taken when he'd proposed to me with lit candles in between, creating a romantic atmosphere.

Now, facing each other in front of the judge, with Tess and James's friend, Robert, next to us, we vowed to love, honor and cherish each other till death do us part. And like a divine plan, the winter sun made a grand entrance through the open curtains just as I became Mrs. James Michael Kent.

After hugs, kisses and congratulations, we all headed to The Theatrical where Mushy closed the restaurant early so we could have a private reception. We dined on prime rib with lobster bisque while listening to a lounge singer that Mushy hired for the occasion.

"What? You couldn't get Dean Martin?" I teased.

During the traditional bridal dance, James held me up so well, I didn't need my cane. As my new husband and I swayed to "Cheek To Cheek," I couldn't help thinking of where I had been a year ago this very day. Lying on the bathroom floor completely beside myself. Feeling abandoned by my family, abandoned by Eliot. Abandoned by life. With no hope of finding my sister.

Who could've imagined where I was now. A newlywed dancing with my handsome doctor who loved and understood me better than anyone. "Funny how life is," I whispered in his ear. "I would never have guessed that I'd be married to the most wonderful man on earth. I feel I don't deserve you."

He moved his head back to look at me more intently and lifted my chin. "Promise me one thing," he said, "Never say you don't deserve something. You deserve the world. I'm just the lucky man who is happy to be in that world." Just as he said it, the music stopped and we kissed long and sweetly to the applause of everyone in the room.

"Thanks for making an honest woman out of me," I whispered.

"My dear Lydia, other than my mother—who you've charmed completely, by the way—" he grinned, "you are the most genuine, upstanding woman I've ever known."

And I, Lydia Swanson Kent, finally believed that too.

49.

*T*he last week in January, Kitty called and invited me to lunch and I happily accepted.

At her suggestion, we met downtown, at Higbee's popular Silver Grille restaurant on the store's tenth floor. We ordered gin highballs, like the old days.

"I'm glad you called," I began. "There's something I've been wanting to tell you." The day before, Miss Ringler had called to assure us that the adoption process was going well. It was time to tell her about Jack.

"What, you pregnant already?"

"Well, not exactly." I laughed, looking at her and remembering our dear friendship. "Look at us. Two respectable married ladies out to lunch. What would the Roxy girls think?" I took a sip of my drink, thinking I should ask about Kitty's life before jumping into my big news. "We didn't get a chance to talk much at the wedding, how's married life treatin' ya? How's Gary doing?"

Kitty rolled her eyes. "Gone a lot."

"Oh. Business?" What kind of business, I was afraid to ask.

"Yep. Sometimes I don't even feel married." Kitty leaned in to whisper, "We haven't had sex in three months." She paused in thought. "Well, unless you count a drunken rendezvous on New Year's Eve. Which I don't." She leaned back, her face sour.

I began feeling uncomfortable. As single gals, we often talked about sex freely. Now, as wives, it seemed too personal.

I was also surprised. Since our first time together, James and I made love several times a week. Did sex go by the wayside that soon after marriage? Kitty and Gary had only been wed seven months.

The appearance of the waitress kept Kitty from going further and by the time we ordered, she had, thankfully, changed the subject. "Forget him, tell me what your big news is!"

I took a hearty sip of my drink. "Well, remember me telling you about that adoption ring in Memphis?" I told her about what Tess had relayed to us, our trip to Memphis and our discovery about the organization. "The more we find out, the more we know something needs to be done to protect those kids."

As I went on, I caught Kitty's troubled expression. By the time I got to my news about adopting Jack and exposing the agency, Kitty's face had turned ashen.

"What's the matter, Kitty? You feeling okay?"

"I thought once you found Tess, you'd forget about that place."

"Oh no, especially not after seeing the children myself. Eliot and Howard have suspected all along that it's a black market business, and well . . . that's what I want to tell you. Falling in love with little Jack has us smack in the midst of it all."

Kitty looked like she was about to be sick. "Oh, please tell me you're not."

Our salads had arrived, but we hardly noticed.

"What do you mean?" I sat forward. "I know it must seem surprising to you, seein' how I never spoke much about kids, but I always loved them. I just never thought that was my fate, ya know? Not with our career. But now I feel in my gut that this is the path I'm meant to be on. It's like every circumstance has led me to where I am now. My friendship with Eliot, discovering Tess had been sent to such a place, then meeting the man of my dreams to make all this happen."

She was moving the lettuce around on her plate. Was she even listening? I sensed something was off, but I needed to finish. "James has been so supportive . He gives me confidence in myself, allows me the freedom to pretty much do as I please." I clutched my glass. "*And* although it took him a minute to realize it, he wants Jack as much as I do."

"Lydia. You don't know anything about this strange boy."

I was shocked by her reaction. Shocked by her use of the word, strange. "But we do. They told us how he lost his parents. It's heartbreaking. You should see him. Kit, he's precious. He's got this red hair with this little colic in the—

I trailed off, put off by the look on her face. "What? Why are you looking at me like that?"

The waitress returned to ask if everything was okay, but pivoted after seeing we were deep in a conversation I now wasn't sure I wanted to have.

Kitty grabbed the waitress's arm before she could get away. "Give us another. Please."

I got a chill. Something was definitely up. "Kitty, what's—"

Kitty raised her hand. "Wait till we get our drinks."

The dining room had emptied, we were alone, and the silence was palpable. My heart quickened. The waitress set the drinks down and left abruptly.

Kitty took a healthy swig. I followed suit.

"Okay, now, what the hell is wrong?" I crossed my arms in frustration. I couldn't imagine why Kitty seemed to have a problem with my good news.

"God damn it, Lydia, this is not easy for me. You have no idea what you're getting into. Gary would kill me if—" She took another look around to make sure no one was in ear shot. She leaned so close, I could smell the mixture of booze and cigarettes. "Listen, you gotta keep this under wraps, what I'm about to tell you. Especially where you got this information." She was visibly shaking as she reached for her smokes. Then she slapped the pack down. "Ah, hell, Lyd. I know James is involved, too, so I won't tell you not to tell him. Because well, you have to. But please—"

"God, just tell me already." The dramatics was making my skin crawl.

She exhaled heavily, looked me straight in the eye. "That Memphis place? It's part of the business."

"What business?"

She closed her eyes, and in a hushed voice, said, "Gary's business."

50.

I couldn't believe what I was hearing. "You know your husband's involved in selling children and that's okay with you?"

"Aw, Christ, Lyd, of course not!" She looked around for the millionth time. "And keep your voice down." Kitty downed her drink. "I had no idea what I was gettin' into with Gary. I admit, I was swayed by his money and big house and lifestyle. And, sure, I knew he did underhanded things, like the gambling, but I had no idea all he was involved in. No way did I ever fathom children were involved . . .

"I swear I didn't know." She started to sob, frightening me all the more. The poor thing was miserable, and scared.

The waitress took notice again, but thankfully didn't approach us so Kitty went on. "He doesn't tell me nothin' but I sure have learned a lot about being a gangster's wife. We are to be seen and not heard. We are not allowed to voice our opinions, especially when it concerns their business." She took out a hanky from her beaded clutch, dabbed her eyes.

"So how'd you find out?" My skin prickled.

She leaned back, inhaled. "He's been gone so much I suspected an affair. I mean, even when he was home, he wasn't there, know what I mean?"

"I gathered that when you mentioned the lack of sex."

"Exactly." She blew her nose, replaced the hanky and leaned into me. "You know how much we used to go out. All those swanky places. Laughing it up. Jokin' around, havin' fun . . . well, lately, he's all secretive." She shook her head. "We never go out anymore, and you know me, that was pissing me off. You know how I like to get out and carouse. So yeah, I started sniffing his clothes for women's perfume and going through his wallet. I even tried listening in on conversations, but one time he caught me and smacked me good."

"Oh, God, Kit, he's beating you?"

She shrugged. "Naw, I mean, it's not a regular thing. Only when he wants to make sure I understand he's not foolin' around."

This was a whole other side of Kitty I never saw. One who had been brow-beaten into a submissive life. I never thought I'd see the day.

"Anyhow, I started going through his things when he's out of town. Last time he left, right after Christmas, I searched the whole damn house with a fine tooth comb, I tell ya."

The waitress was back, this time with the bill. "Honey, we'll let you know when we're done," Kitty said sharply. Catching herself, her voice softened. "Sorry. I don't mean to sound harsh. Just give us another highball, please." She let out a half snicker. "Good thing we're both taking the streetcar."

"None for me," I told the girl, who nodded and walked away. "I really don't drink much anymore. Two is plenty for me," I said, turning back to Kitty. "Plus, I need to process what you're saying."

"Suit yourself." She shrugged. "Anyway, I looked everywhere in the house for the key to his file cabinet. I didn't think I'd really find any proof of an affair in there—he's too smart to save receipts or whatever—but by then, I was damn curious about his business activities."

Another pause at the presence of her requested drink, then Kitty leaned in again, whispering as if the room might be bugged. "One of the Mob guys, not saying his name, worked for that Murphy Home you mentioned. Apparently, he was in charge of transporting kids to foster and adoptive parents. When that orphanage went under, they got more involved with the Tennessee place." Before I could ask how she discovered

323

that, she added, "I found contracts, Lyd. They all had that woman's name, Georgia Tann, on them. I found documents. Placements for children from here to Memphis, and New York too. It's quite the setup." She wouldn't look at me, talking to her drink instead. "I suppose he's keeping it all for blackmail, if it comes to that. You know, protection."

She lit another cig, took a puff, blew it toward the ceiling. "I don't know what Gary does for them, exactly, but he's definitely involved or he wouldn't be retaining those papers. No surprise he keeps it all under lock and key."

I stared at her. "Oh my God."

"Yeah, and if Gary gets wind about what y'all are up to, well—" She downed her drink, she didn't have to elaborate.

My mind whirling, I wanted to fly out of there to tell James. And Eliot. But between the awful shock and the drinks, I feared standing up too fast. Leaning on Kitty would be of no help, what with her cocktail consumption.

As upset as I was, I felt horrible for Kitty. Under normal circumstances, I may have said I told her so. After all, I never liked the man to begin with. But there was no crossing that bridge now. I felt awful that I'd once wanted to push Kitty out of my life. It took a true friend to tell me what she knew.

Despite my objections about Gary, I had believed that he was so crazy about Kitty, that he'd protect her no matter what. I thought she was safe with him, mobster or not.

We were both fools.

The ride in the elevator down was eerily quiet. We walked together arm-in-arm to the stop, like the friends we've always been. As we waited for the trolley, I almost asked her to stay with us but thought better of it. James and I were already in deep. We couldn't possibly have a mobster's wife at our house. Not with what I now knew.

324

But I had to break the god-awful silence as we rode in the half-empty streetcar. "What do you do all day when Gary's out of town?"

"Besides snoop?" She shrugged. "Well, I tried knitting for a time but do you know how damn boring that is?" She forced out a laugh. "Now I just shop. One benefit of all this, he lets me spend the hell out of his charge plate." Her stop came all too soon.

"I'll call ya." She jumped up and was out before I could tell her how much I still cared.

Once home, my head was pounding from the drinks and the trauma of Kitty's revelation. My body wanted to slip under the covers and sleep away this reality, but I had to organize my thoughts, and James wouldn't be home for three more hours.

I dialed Tess. "Oh, sis, I gotta talk to you. In person. It's very important. Can you come over, right now?"

"Now? What's wrong? Are you okay?"

"It's about Georgia, that's all I'll say till you get here."

"Oh, wow, okay. I was just doing homework but that can wait. I'll be there in fifteen." Luckily Tess had a car now. It was pretty beat up, but good enough to get her around town.

When she arrived, I sat her down and spit out everything Kitty had told me. I emphasized the need to keep it among ourselves, though I knew I didn't have to. "I realize this makes everything even more complicated, and dangerous, with those thugs involved, but we need to get Jack here soon as possible. I need to call Eliot and Howard right away." I pointed to her bag. "Got a smoke in there?"

She even lit it for me to keep me from having to get up. "Maybe we can manage to get proof now of their operations. Get the place shut down for good. These people need to be arrested and prosecuted. Imagine the Mob being involved! Making money off innocent children. Homeless children. It's beyond my comprehension."

"Calm down, Lyd, one thought at a time. Listen, I know what they're doing is horribly wrong, but you must consider that some of those children may have indeed been from bad homes, or even the streets, and being adopted by well-to-do families is probably a blessing, ya know? I may not have appreciated my time with the Ginarts, but they provided for me very well."

"The Ginarts! Do you think we can get them to testify?"

Tess let out a brisk laugh. "Oh, Lydia, you're getting nuts now. You're getting way ahead of yourself."

I sank into the sofa, forced a faint smile. "Yeah, I am. I'm just haunted by those kids. Seeing them in person made it all too real for me. I can't get those faces out of my head."

"I know." She walked over and hugged me.

"Tess, you were there. You know they're not all being saved. What kind of people are they selling those children to? Especially the less desirables. Children like Jack, who aren't blonde. Not cute little babies . . ."

"Yeah, I wish I'd paid more attention back then," she sighed. "I'm anxious to get Jack in our family too, but we can't save them all. We can't risk lives if those men get wind of us getting nosy."

"It's risky, but that's just it, maybe we *can* save them all. We need to save them all."

Tess was looking at me like I'd lost my good sense. But I was overcome with an idea that had been brewing in the back of my mind for some time. It was too early to speak of it yet, but I felt sure I could make it happen.

With Tess and James on my side, I now had the ways, the means, and the power.

And a very special agent.

51.

When James came home, I took his coat, made fresh coffee and served tea biscuits because I hadn't a clue what the hell to make for dinner. It was furthest from my mind as Tess and I set him down and told him about Gary.

"We need to get back there, James. I don't trust them. We need to call Eliot and hope he and Howard can come with us." It was the first time I lit up a smoke in front of him but once he heard this, I knew he'd understand.

I hadn't heard from Eliot since before James and I were married, but this new development involving the Cleveland syndicate was his jurisdiction, maybe something Eliot already knew about. I was sure that once he learned of our personal involvement concerning Jack, Eliot would help us.

"Lydia," Tess interrupted my spiel, "You know, Eliot has problems of his own right now. Did you see that article a few days ago? The department isn't pleased with him. He's even taken a part-time position as a consultant for some federal program. Sounds like he's got enough on his hands."

"That's just it. If he brings down local thugs involving the abuse and sale of children, it will assuredly redeem him in the public eye. It's a win-win." I noticed James was pacing. "James, you haven't said a word. Please, tell us what you're thinking."

"I'm thinking we might be getting too entangled in police matters. It's more than any of us bargained for."

My heart dropped to the floor.

He caught my forlorn expression, halted his marching. "But yes, I want Jack enough to do what's necessary."

I grabbed his neck and pulled him to me. "Oh, I love you so. We'll be doing such good all around."

Now it was a matter of setting plans in motion. "One request." I wrapped my arm through his. "Would you mind terribly if I met with Eliot first, alone? He has no idea about our trip, or Jack. That ups the ante considerably. I feel we've been friends for so long, and with him having a time of it lately with his job and reputation, he might be more comfortable catching up with all our news with just me there. A simple lunch, that's all."

Tess found this a good time to go into the kitchen to rustle up something for us to eat.

"We'll have him and Howard over for dinner soon as possible." I smashed out my cigarette and held my breath. Would he insist on accompanying me?

He looked at me, contemplating, then said, "What's marriage without trust? Do what you feel is best. I trust your judgment."

I squeezed his hand. "Oh, what did I ever do to deserve you?"

"Get hit by a streetcar?"

That made me chuckle. "Well, if that's all it took, I should've done it years ago."

It was wonderful that we could joke about it. I hated the limp that I'd have the rest of my life, and yet, I'd been blessed with great luck finding James as a result.

I could hardly sleep that night, reviewing all the changes in the past year. I was no longer a Burly Girl. I no longer spent hours practicing new routines for my shows. In fact, I no longer worked at all. Despite my grand new life, a part of me missed my Roxy world. Not the mobsters who frequented the place, though some weren't so bad. Or the backstage johns—especially not the one who chased me down that fateful night. But I missed George, Big Joe, the chorus girls, my fellow burlesque queens. And I missed the excitement of being on stage with my colorful fans and beautiful costumes I'd so proudly made—all which now hung in the back of my old closet where Tess now lived.

But now I found myself on an important mission. One I had no idea how it would play out, but would be the greatest act of my life.

*F*irst thing Monday morning, I dialed Eliot's office at exactly nine a.m.. The third ring proved the charm.

"Eliot! It's Lydia, how are you? It's been so long since we've seen each other." I wanted to tell him how often I'd wanted to call but that seemed pointless.

"Lydia, what a pleasant surprise. Yes, it has been too long." He explained that he had just returned from a vacation with Evaline but did not elaborate.

"Oh, how nice. Ya know, I, too, recently came back from a vacation and I have such news for you."

"Really? Are you going to join in the war effort?" He sounded good. Relaxed. Like the Eliot I knew, and missed. We talked a bit about the jarring current events, such as First Lady Eleanor Roosevelt summoning women to get involved in various programs. He asked about Tess and James then I veered him toward the real purpose for my call.

"I know this is sudden but could we meet for lunch today? I'm sure you must be terribly busy but it's about Georgia Tann. And well, we all got ourselves pretty involved now. I can't say anymore until we meet."

"Oh?"

"Can we lunch today at Sullivan's?"

I placed a grateful hand to my chest when he said, yes.

52.

*I*t took all the gumption I could muster to walk into that place with a cane, but that was precisely why I'd chosen the two o'clock hour when the tavern was less crowded. The cold weather had made my leg stiffen up more, but I told myself—for the hundredth time—it was something I'd have to deal with.

I walked in hoping no regulars would recognize me. Chances were good they wouldn't. They may look twice at the cane, but I no longer looked the part I used to play. Gone was my bright peachy blond hair. It was more subtle now—less peachy, more sandy blonde, and worn down instead of in an upsweep. I was also minus the full makeup, save for lipstick. I'd never go without that.

I wore a plain beige wool coat, and because it was slushy out, fur-lined boots over a pair of flats. Underneath, I had on a simple navy blue frock, but at the last minute decided to dress it up a bit with a rhinestone trimmed belt. I couldn't help add a little pizzazz, it was still my nature.

And I wore no jewelry. Except my newly-acquired wedding ring hidden inside leather gloves.

Eliot had beaten me there, sitting at his old corner table. The cane was the only thing keeping me from sprinting towards him. It felt so good to see him again. When I reached the table, I wrapped my free arm around him for a hug, before leaning my cane against the empty chair.

He gave me a peck on the cheek, pulled the chair out for me. "You look wonderful, Lydia. More beautiful than ever." Before I could respond, he added, "So what'll it be?" He had started without me, a half empty glass in front of him that was surely scotch.

A Place We Belong

"Honestly, I don't know. I don't drink much these days." *Except when I was with Kitty, and for damn good reason.*

"No?" His chin lifted. "Why is that? Doctor's orders?"

"Oh, no orders. James isn't much of a drinker. We really only drink on special occasions." I said, offhandedly. Then I smiled. "But this *is* a special occasion, isn't it? So, yes, I'll have a Pink Lady." Anything stronger might make me wistful, being with him again. My feelings for Eliot would never change, though our circumstances, our relationship, had.

He waved the bartender over. "We'll take a coupla menus, as well," he told the man I had never seen before.

"New barkeep?"

"Oh, Ronnie's been here since summer."

"Oh my, has it been that long since I've been here?" I looked down at the checkered table cloth. "I can hardly believe the accident was, gee, a good six months ago." I sighed. "I'm sorry I haven't been in touch, what with the holidays, the war news . . ."

"I understand. And I'm sorry I haven't been in touch either. Our investigation on the Tennessee Home had to take a back seat."

I straightened my spine. "Actually, that's what I wanted to discuss with you. A lot has happened since we talked."

"Oh? Everything okay?"

"Well, before we get to that, I have a few other updates." I lifted my cane. "I'm afraid I need this dreadful thing all the time now." I immediately felt bad mentioning it, recalling how pleased James was in giving it to me. "Though, it is lovely, isn't it?"

Eliot took it and turned it around in his hands. "It is. Beautiful craftsmanship. Wherever did you get it?"

"James found it in a shop in Toledo."

331

He stood up, crossed his hands over the brass eagle head, and struck a pose. "I'm tempted to get one myself. Makes me look rather distinguished, don't you think?"

I laughed. "Well, you already have that worldly gentleman air about you."

Ronnie brought our drinks. "Ready to order?"

I shook my head. "Give us a few more minutes, please," though I'd need more than that. When he walked away, I took off my gloves, placed my hands on the table. "There is also this."

"Oh my," Eliot reached for my left hand. "Is that a wedding ring, I see?"

"It is." I smiled. "It was rather sudden." I hoped he didn't feel bad for not being invited, or even told about it. "We had a very small ceremony on Christmas Eve, just immediate family."

"I see. And is there a reason for the speedy nuptials?" His eyes lifted in suspicion.

I let out a light laugh. "I am not with child, if that's what you're getting at." *But maybe soon.*

He let go of my hand, but not his gaze at the ring. "Your doctor has exquisite taste."

"That he does," proudly staring at the ring.

"I meant that about you, also."

I felt my face flush. "Aw, Eliot, you're sweet."

He clicked my glass. "A toast to you. Congratulations to you both."

"Thank you, I'm very happy."

"I can see that. And it's what you deserve. He seems like a great fellow." He pulled out a cigarette, lit it, pointing the pack towards me. "Would you like one?"

I shook my head. I'd just promised James I'd quit for good. "As I mentioned on the phone, there's an important matter I need to tell you." I took in a breath. "The reason James and I married so quickly was, well, something happened when James, Tess and I went to Memphis last month."

"Memphis? You went to the Tennessee Home?"

"Yes."

Over the next half hour, I talked and he listened. As we lunched on tuna sandwiches and chips, I told him how James dressed as Santa, and Tess as an elf, to fool Georgia's staff in order to see how the place was run.

"Well, that's resourceful." He grinned, seemingly impressed.

I was about to tell him about Jack when the conversation took a turn.

"James is a special man to take on your cause." Eliot said, reaching for the hand without the ring. "I'm sorry I wasn't there more for you, Lydia."

I turned my hand right side up and squeezed his. "Oh, but you were. You certainly couldn't do any more than what you did at the time. I never expected you to shirk your other responsibilities with my personal mission."

"It was my mission, as well. I hope you know that."

"I do. But you also had to do your job. That had to come first." Not to mention—but I did—his marriage. "And a wife must always be a priority," echoing what Helen had said to me not so long ago.

He suddenly looked sad. "Both are getting perilously close to extinction, I'm afraid."

"What do you mean?"

"The vacation I just returned from? It was more of a request from my boss, to get away for a bit." He pushed away his near empty glass as if just remembering the culprit. "They say I drink too much."

I'd read the papers, and heard the gossip one day at Dolly's bookstore. There was nothing I could to say about that. He didn't need a lecture from me.

333

"I've taken a small position to help out at the Federal Social Protection Program." His face turned almost crimson. "Seems the military has a problem with an increase on venereal diseases."

I winced. "Oh, dear."

"It is an important health issue."

"I can imagine." Time to get off that topic. "Eliot, I need to get back to why I'm really here."

"Yes, sorry. I thought we'd covered it. A surprise marriage, a new sleuth partner—"

"I need to tell you something I've just learned." He didn't look surprised when I told him about Gary and the Mob involvement with Georgia. As I suspected, he already knew.

"We can't do this without you and Howard." I pleaded with my eyes. "I know you have a lot going on, but well, there's this boy."

I told him about Jack. How could he refuse me now? "Will you and Howard come over for dinner so we can discuss it together?"

I waited, letting him gather his thoughts. "I must say, I'm sorry to hear you got yourselves so heavily involved. This is serious business." He nodded. "But of course I'll come. And I'll contact Howard. We need to form a team, keep you safe."

We made a dinner date for the following night, then I stood, reached down and hugged his neck. "This means the world to me, Eliot. As much as Tess did." I kissed his cheek.

I was about to turn, put on my coat and bid goodbye when he added, "I envy you, Lydia. You have your whole life ahead of you. Husband, children. A real future."

What was this? I tried to wave it off. "Eliot, you're not exactly an old man. You have a brilliant future ahead whatever you do. You're the best."

He gulped down his last drop of drink. "I'm sorry. I don't mean to sound maudlin. Maybe it's the war—of which

A Place We Belong

I'm too old to fight in—but things seem very dire to me lately." His stare was so direct it startled me, stabbed at my heart.

"Aw, come on, you must know things'll get better. And we'll win the war, that I'm sure of." My face brightened. "And we will always be the best of friends. Just with new missions. And now that I'm all respectable and domestic, I'll keep us both outta trouble." I threw him my showgirl wink.

That got a laugh as he stood now too, and I was grateful I'd eased his solemn mood.

"You will never lose me, Eliot," I whispered, gazing into those blue-gray eyes I had always loved. "No matter what happens in our lives, you'll always hold a special place in my heart."

"Thank you for saying that. I think I needed it."

"I have to go now, it's getting late." How late I had no clue, but the tavern was filling up and neither of us could risk another damn rumor.

He helped me with my coat. I put on my gloves, grabbed my cane, and bid him goodbye. As I walked out the door, I could feel a wistful tear trickle down my cheek.

53.

*O*ver after-dinner brandies, we learned Howard had discovered more disturbing details about Georgia Tann's operation. "She was ousted from the Child Welfare League of America years before she became head of the orphanage," he told us.

I gasped. "What? Why? And more important, how could she then be assigned to operate the Memphis Home?"

"Normally those would be fair questions," Howard said. "But given her tight association with Ed Crump, it's not surprising that incident was swept under the rug."

It was Eliot's turn to elaborate. "Crump was Memphis mayor for an unprecedented three terms. He's no longer mayor but has influence in everything in the state—so much so that he's known as the Godfather of Tennessee politics. Since no one knew about her past dealings, Georgia managed to get a public reputation for doing good by taking in orphans and finding them homes. To this day, no one questions her methods. She basically does as she pleases."

James squeezed my hand as Eliot walked over to the fireplace. "With the help of men from various organized crime units, it's become an extremely profitable business." Eliot shot a look at Howard. "And this is the most disturbing part and may be hard to hear . . . but some of these children are not orphans at all."

I felt faint.

Eliot went on. "I paid a visit to Angelo Parrisi, one of the goons I sent to jail last year."

I turned to James. "He and his girl, Thelma, were regulars at the Theatrical," I explained.

"Yes, and he's now doing time," Eliot added. "He helped us with another investigation hoping to get his sentence reduced so we've become fairly friendly." He flashed a crooked grin. "I asked him point blank what he knew about members of the syndicate involved with the Murphy House and what's happened since it shut down. We know several are working for Georgia, but he confirmed some of the children she's acquiring are actually being stripped practically from their mother's arms."

It was James's turn to stand. "How's that?"

"As you all know, Georgia works with some underhanded folks in medical and social services. When someone calls them, for whatever reason, Georgia gets wind of it and sends one of her employees to show up at their door. Especially in instances when a mother, often with absent fathers, calls about a sick child, a woman in nurse's garb will appear at the door, check the baby, then say they need to take it to the hospital immediately, that they'll handle everything. Mind you, these are people who are poor with no transportation and welcome any help for their sickly child, although it's often simply a bad cold or flu. The next day, they tell the mother their child has died. The parents are too bereft to question it."

He went on to tell us how Georgia hires men often connected to the mob to find unattended children living in shanties along the river, often called "river rats," and take them to the Home to be sold to wealthy families. "Parrisi admitted, too, that one of his old pals is on Georgia's payroll." Eliot lit a cigarette and if James hadn't been there, I'd have grabbed one myself.

This was all so inconceivable. I was grateful Tess was at work and didn't have to hear this. "This confirms everything you suspected, Eliot," I said. "They take children from their parents under false pretenses." Chills crept up my arms like tiny insects. I tried to rub them away to no avail. Had Georgia lied to us about Jack's past? If he was one of the children stripped from his parents, I determined that—no matter how much it would hurt—we'd do the right thing and reunite them. Either way, Jack must be saved.

"My God." James shook his head in disbelief. I was certain he was thinking of Jack too. "So apparently, Georgia Tann is a reverse Robin Hood. Steals from the poor and gives to the rich. And in this case, it's the giving of human lives." He reached for my hand. "The children are merely commerce to them."

"Yes," Howard said. "The irony of it all is that in some of these cases, these kids end up with better lives, with rich folk who can give them everything. Except their real parents. Who will never find them."

James and I spent a restless night worrying about that little red-haired boy. When morning broke, James got Georgia on the phone. He told her we had married and would like to come get Jack. We prayed that between our new marital status, and stable financial standing—and the fact that we'd already given her money—Georgia would expedite the process.

Once again, I stood over his shoulder to hear every word. "Oh, yes, we have you at the top of our list," the woman assured. "And great news. We just received a sweet four-year-old girl, so no diapers—"

"Miss Tann, we've already told you—more than once—we want to adopt Jack."

The silence made us both think we'd been disconnected. "Hello?" James clutched the receiver, forgetting to lean it toward me. I moved the receiver closer just in time to hear, "I'm sorry, Mr. Kent, but that child is no longer available."

"No, that's not possible!" I screeched.

A Place We Belong

James put his finger to his lips to quiet me. "Excuse me for being blunt, Miss Tann, but we gave you a promissory note, and then some, in good faith. We were very clear about our intention for Jack."

"I'm afraid that doesn't guarantee one particular child. We know the children best and we are the ones to make those decisions on where a child is placed."

"Well then, we want our money back," James said through clenched teeth. My heart raced. Had Jack been adopted, or about to be?

"Be reasonable, Mr. Kent, we have other children and you've already signed the request forms," the woman said in a clipped tone. "Everything is moving along, and as I said, we have the perfect child for—"

James slammed down the phone. "Pack your things. We're going to Memphis."

I called Eliot immediately, praying he'd be able to accompany us. "Well, since I'm already not on their good side these days," he said, referring to his job, "a few days off for an emergency won't make much difference."

"Oh, Eliot, are you sure? I don't want to get you in trouble."

"Truth is, I've been considering leaving the department anyway. I've got another offer on the back burner. And I want to do this, Lydia. Give me one day."

Eliot got back to me the following evening. "It appears the Memphis police department has been trying to get Georgia closed down for some time. They're conducting a state-wide investigation and once they have enough proof, that judge protecting her can't stand in the way. He will assuredly be disbarred and arrested." I heard the shuffling of papers. "And that's not all. I talked again to Angelo Parrisi, who's been singing a lot these days, still hoping to get his sentence reduced. Said Georgia's groundskeeper, guy named Cal, happens to be a former associate of his and wants out of the whole mess. According to Angelo, he's become touched by the children and willing to do what he can to get the place shut down. I have his number and we're making arrangements to go down there."

The next morning, Tess, James and I piled into our Roadmaster that was roomy enough for us and overnight bags. Eliot and Howard followed behind, assuring us they had back up for whatever may happen. We had no idea what to expect but were determined to find out where Jack was, first and foremost, and if luck was on our side, bring Georgia's operation down, then deal with the children's welfare. A lot was riding on this trip.

After an overnight stay at a nearby motel, Eliot arranged for Cal to meet us that morning so we'd be amply prepared before arriving on Georgia's doorstep. Over breakfast at a mom-and-pop diner, we met Cal.

He was older than I'd expected, though with a mobster's stocky build and full mustache. He quickly gave us a rundown of the organization's comings and goings, and best of all, we learned that Jack was still there.

"They have plans for the boy," Cal said. "I'm gettin' old and can't do everything I used to do, so they got that kid doing stuff, like weeding, fixin' things 'round the mansion. He even had to fix a toilet once," the man shook his head. "Work no seven-year-old has any business doing."

I glanced at James. "So that's why he's not available."

"Miss Ringler's off today, which should help our cause," Cal added. "They're tough broads and they stick tight. Together they'd be a handful."

And so, we devised a plan.

An hour later, Georgia answered the door to me, James and Tess facing her. Catching her off guard, we stormed in like militants, not waiting for an invitation.

A Place We Belong

"What is this? You can't just barge into my—wait. *You!*" Georgia grabbed Tess's arm. "You look familiar."

"I should." Tess stood her ground, not letting Georgia intimidate her. "Your crooked staff took me from the Murphy home in Cleveland seven years ago when our mother died. Separated me from my sister, then used me to do your dirty chores and care for the children until you sold me to the Ginarts. Now you remember?" She raised her hands. "I'm all grown up now and this is my real family."

Hands on hips, Georgia yelled, "Get out or I'm making a phone call."

"Go right ahead, Miss Tann, we can round everyone up at the same time." Eliot and Howard's timing was perfect. They entered the room now, confusing Georgia even more. Her eyes narrowed and fastened on Eliot. "You've been here, too, asking about a girl . . ." Her eyes flashed to Tess, trying to put the puzzle together.

"Yes, but my name is not Samuel Swanson. I'm Eliot Ness, a special agent, and this is my partner and lawyer, Mr. Howard Nelson. We represent this couple." He took off his hat but didn't bother shaking her hand. "We don't want trouble but Mr. and Mrs. Kent requested a particular child who you initially said was available, and now you've told them he is not. We have proof of their promissory note, and the extra good-faith money in the form of a check. We demand you proceed with their wishes."

I squeezed James's hand. Eliot was being vague yet threatening at the same time. And it seemed to be working. Georgia's cheeks burned. She looked rattled.

"I'm afraid what's done is done. The child has already been given to another couple."

"*Given* is hardly the word I would use, Miss Tann." He stepped closer, inches from her face. "Besides, we know you are lying."

341

With Georgia's attention fully on the others, Tess snagged her opportunity. She backed away slowly toward the stairway, then swiftly but quietly took two steps at a time, from the first floor to the second, to the third. The attic. The dingy room she remembered staying in.

Dark memories flashed back to her as she entered the dim hallway but she willed them away as she creaked open the door. "Hello? Anyone here?" Again, she struggled to stay focused, not succumb to the past. She couldn't let memories or emotions get in the way. She may not have been able to help these children back then, but she had the means to now.

She crept inside and saw a small girl peeking from the shadows. She was thin, scrawny even, with dark stringy red hair, who looked to be around five years of age.

"Yes, ma'am?"

Tess wanted to weep. The child's face looked fearful and yet, she remembered her manners.

"Hi there, what's your name?" Tess whispered, making sure the girl saw her gentle smile in the poorly lit room.

"Molly."

A boy stepped forward from behind the girl, wearing a wrinkled plaid shirt, saggy dungarees and suspenders.

Tess inched closer to him. "Jack?"

"Who are you?"

He didn't seem to recognize her without the elf costume. She wanted to hug him but feared she would startle him. Seeing the two standing next to each other, her mouth dropped. "Is this your sister, Jack?"

The two of them held hands, clearly scared and confused. She bent down, palms on her knees. "Jack, do you remember when Santa came around Christmas time? I was the elf who helped him." When their eyes met, he knew. "And

A Place We Belong

remember that nice couple you met, they came to visit a few weeks ago and told you they'd like to adopt you?"

He looked at the ground. "I thought they lied."

"No, no they didn't. And guess what? They're here, right downstairs." His eyes widened with hope. "But they didn't know you had a sister." She glanced over at the small girl standing there, clinging to her brother. How would James and Lydia feel about her? She had no time but to go on instinct. "But it's okay. You both can come with me."

She spotted a small raggedy doll in the corner. "You can bring your doll, too, Molly. And Jack, go get that fire truck Santa gave you."

He rubbed his eyes. "I don't have it anymore. Miss Tann took it away 'cause I was bad but I don't know what I did." He was on the verge of crying.

She threw her arms around them, squeezed them tight. "Don't worry, we'll get you a brand-new one."

"Like the other one?" Jack whispered in her ear. "I really liked that one."

Tess thought her heart would break. "Yes, of course. And other toys too."

As they headed toward the stairs, loud voices seemed to shake the walls. Georgia's was the loudest, shouting to get off her property. Tess turned to the children. "Stay right here. Don't move." She inched her way to the bottom of the stairs where she stopped and watched the scene.

Eliot was calling Georgia's bluff, saying his G-Men were at this very moment rounding up the Cleveland men who worked for her. "We already have proof that you get these men to rip children from their parent's arms and sell them for profit. We have the means to shut you down right now. You'll not only lose the agency but this very house you live in. Your connections mean nothing. They are not as loyal as you presume."

"If you cooperate," Howard added. "We'd be happy to have you work with us for a possible lighter sentence."

Tess rushed into the room. They seemed shocked to see her approach, as if wondering where she'd been. "While the men hash out the details, I need to speak with both of you." She gave Lydia and James a desperate look. As Eliot kept Georgia at bay, they followed her around the corner, where Tess pointed to the stairs. Jack stood there, one hand on the railing, the other holding the girl's hand as she clung to him.

Tess leaned in and whispered, "That girl with him? She's Jack's sister."

Lydia's eyes flashed to James. "*Sister?*"

"Her name's Molly. I'd say they're a package deal." Tess raised her brows in a hopeful expression.

James and Lydia stared at the girl whose red hair was just a shade darker than Jack's. "Oh, James. Look at them." She gave him a pleading look. Could he possibly be ready for not just one child, but two?

Without taking his eyes off the children, he murmured just two words. "Get them."

54.

*E*liot did not lose his job at the department for leaving work without due notice. When the press got wind of his part in bringing down the notorious illicit adoption ring that involved several Cleveland gangsters, he was back to being the town hero. Eliot and Howard had rounded up more men, unearthed more damning evidence, and investigations were underway to get the Tennessee Children's Home Society shut down permanently.

The newspapers also praised the work of James, Tess and me, in a full article that featured "Dr. Kent, his wife, and their instant family."

I was not surprised they again mentioned my former risqué occupation, but this time, I didn't mind. I was a part of a hero's story. I had been redeemed. "The former Roxy burlesque dancer," it read, "best known as Blue Satin Doll, has traded in her flamboyant fans for apron strings." It made me laugh. *Funny, how life turns out.*

At least they hadn't mentioned my limp. When the reporter was at the house for the interview, I remained seated, and when James brought my tea, the man simply took it as a loving gesture.

Meanwhile, James and I kept busy decorating our extra bedroom, putting up bunk beds for Jack and Molly and enrolling them in school, all while adjusting to our sudden role as parents to two small children. The story Georgia had told about the fire turned out to be true, their parents were truly gone, but the circumstances paved the way for a smooth and rapid adoption. Especially in light of how we rescued them. No one knew yet what would be Georgia's fate, but our own group of Untouchables had succeeded beyond our mission. We had given two needy children a wonderful new life.

And now, we hoped to do more on that end.

The fact that there were twenty-two children left in limbo reinforced the idea I'd been keeping inside since I'd first laid eyes on Jack. After putting the kids to bed one night, James and I were relaxing on the sofa when I decided it was time to share my inspiration.

"James?" I gently lifted his Agatha Christie mystery and set it on the table. "Remember when I was feeling down about my limp, and you said I just needed to find another passion?" I was surprised how nervous I was and took his hands in mine to stop my own from shaking. "To my own great surprise, I've found how much I care about children, and it's only quadrupled since becoming a mother. Everything about Jack and Molly amazes and delights me, frightens me and amuses me . . . all I want to do is make life good for them. And, I want to make a difference in all children's lives.

Please be up for this. "I think about the other abandoned children, and it keeps me up at night. At first, I thought this idea of mine couldn't possibly bear fruit, but now—"

James gave me an anxious look. "Lydia. Just tell me what's on your mind."

A forthright man, James always did want to cut to the chase.

"Okay. I realize it may sound crazy, but what do you think about me starting an adoption agency?" I held my breath, watched him intently.

"Wow." His deadpan expression, and hesitancy, sank my heart. "Have you given this complete thought? I mean, it would be a huge undertaking."

"I realize that and it's why I hadn't brought it up sooner. But the more I think about it, I almost cannot *not* do it, you know?"

A Place We Belong

We discussed all the logistics that would be involved, and the next evening, I invited Tess to dinner, hoping she, too, would be on board. After discussing Tess's forthcoming RN degree, I revealed my idea.

"There simply aren't enough good agencies out there for these children left behind," I began, knowing Tess was well aware. "So imagine this . . ." I inhaled a breath of hope. "We can start our own adoption agency. With you as a nurse, and James with his additional medical knowledge, and me, with my good business head, we can do amazing things."

The spark in Tess's eyes encouraged me to go on. "We can save so many orphan's lives. And I'm sure Howard and Eliot would advise us on all legal matters. It'll be a nonprofit foundation to help place orphaned children with good families." I stopped and took my sister's hand. "We can call it The Emerald City Adoption Agency. The public will relate to it from the 'Wizard of Oz,' but for us, it'll represent that emerald marble I carried around for so long that kept my hope for you alive."

Tess was not one to get teary eyed so seeing it happen confirmed my answer.

Before I could approach Eliot on this exciting new venture, however, fate had turned on him once again.

*M*arch 1942 had come in like a lion with a pronounced blizzard and swept the city safety director into its wrath in the form of more bad publicity. James had just gone to work and as always, I began my day reading the morning paper after seeing the children off on the school bus. At the bottom of page one, a headline grabbed my attention.

"Ness Cover-up?"

347

This could not be good. What did the fickle press have to say this time?

```
It has just been revealed that three
nights ago, Mr. Ness and his wife, Evaline,
were involved in an automobile accident as
they headed home from the Hollenden Hotel
after a late night of dancing and drinking.
Due to icy, snowy conditions, Ness's car
apparently swerved sideways and straight
into the path of an oncoming vehicle driven
by a twenty-one-year-old man, whose name is
being withheld at this time.
```

The article went on to say that no one was seriously injured and that the young man hadn't recognized Mr. Ness, who had made sure everyone was okay, then went to the hospital. It wasn't until a reporter discovered that the license plate number belonged to Eliot, and that the report had been left unfiled. The safety director was now accused of hit and run.

"Oh dear Lord," I exclaimed out loud. Not only was I alarmed that he'd been in an accident, but the press was making him out to be a drunken criminal.

The next few weeks, it was all you heard on the radio, and in newspapers, alongside continuing updates on the war. People turned on Eliot right and left, accusing the man, once referred to as a "boy scout," of using his position to try and get his name stricken from the accident record.

James even heard the gossip at the barber shop. "I wanted to defend him," he told me. "It's not right to kick a man when he's down, and he's our friend. But I realized nothing I could say would change their minds at this point."

"You're right," I said, equally disappointed. "I admire that you always think before you act. That's not my strong suit."

"No, it is not," he said, making me laugh. "But that's one of the things I admire about you. You're not afraid to speak up, speak your mind. And it's why we now have two beautiful children in this house where, for years, I spent many nights alone. Thank you for loving us all."

His words brought me to the verge of tears. "It's actually been the easiest thing I've ever done."

A week later, Eliot called. "I want you and James to be one of the first to know that I'm resigning from my position." It was a Sunday evening and I'd just put the kids to bed. "I've taken a full-time job in Washington, D.C. I'll be director for the Federal Social Protection Program."

I couldn't blame him for wanting to start fresh somewhere else but my heart hurt for him. And for our loss. Would we ever see him again once he left town? "James and I would love to have you over for dinner before you go," I offered. "Bring Evaline."

"Thank you, Lydia. That is kind, but I start my new job on Thursday."

"*This* Thursday?"

"Yes."

"Oh, my." It was so sudden. "Will we not see you at all before you go?"

There was a pause. Then a sigh. A sigh that spoke volumes. "I'm afraid not."

It would be five years before I would see or hear from Eliot Ness again.

55.

On August 14, 1945, President Truman announced that the Japanese agreed to surrender. It was Victory over Japan Day, forever known as V-J Day. World War II was over.

James and I, along with eleven-year-old Jack, and nine-year-old Molly, huddled around the fire listening to the happy news on the radio. A few years earlier, I would've been among the mass of revelers celebrating in the streets of downtown Cleveland. But these days, my focus was on family. And the many children who depended on me now to give them good, decent homes.

The Emerald City Adoption Agency had opened two years before and quickly became a godsend to the community, as well as hundreds of needy children. That same year, James started his own practice, and along with Tess, now an RN and executive director of the company, the three of us were able to give our young charges quality health care until finding them suitable homes. I basked in my role as president and CEO of a children's foundation that was both legitimate and respected.

Our biggest regret was that Georgia Tann died before ever being prosecuted. But at least the men who had helped her were doing time, including Kitty's husband, Gary, whom she divorced soon after he got sent up. Although I had offered her a job at the agency, Kitty decided to start a new life in Chicago and was now happily remarried to a successful restaurant owner.

I felt bad upon learning that Eliot and Evaline's marriage did not survive their move to Washington DC. Evaline had left him for the model from her life-drawing class, confirming those long-ago private rumors. That affair didn't last, but Evaline went on to a rich career in New York City as a fashion illustrator for the prominent Saks Fifth Avenue department store. She would also realize her dream as a children's book author, while never having children of her own.

Eliot remarried just three months after their divorce, which came as no surprise. He liked being married. This I always knew.

When I heard about Elisabeth, wife number three, I recalled the names of all the Mrs. Nesses: Edna. Evaline. And now Elisabeth. Maybe if my name had started with an E, I might've had half a chance. It was a silly thought, but it gave me a giggle.

Eliot had not stayed in touch during his time away. He did return to Cleveland in 1947, following through with those earlier thoughts of becoming Cleveland's mayor, but lost to the incumbent Mayor Burke. Apparently, the public had not forgotten the controversy over that car accident.

More years went by when, out of the blue, I received a phone call. Eliot said he needed *my* services this time. He and his wife wanted to adopt a child.

They arrived on a Saturday. He introduced her as Betty, and like the other Mrs. Nesses, she was a looker. But in a quiet, understated way. I felt instantly comfortable with her.

"Please sit down." I motioned to the two chairs facing my desk. "I want you to know, Eliot, that James and I are indeed sorry you didn't become our mayor," I said, hoping it wasn't a sore subject.

"Oh, who wants an honest politician anyway?" he quipped. Eliot seemed back to his old self.

The couple sat in my office for more than an hour. I served up tea, remembering Eliot's preference outside of scotch, and we caught up on each other's lives. I learned that, like Evaline, Betty was an artist, a sculptress. Eliot stated

351

proudly that she'd had an exhibit in the 1939 Cleveland's World's Fair.

Observing the two together, I determined that Betty was a good match for Eliot. Or maybe it was just that I liked this woman who seemed to just want to make him happy. And he certainly seemed to be that now. And content.

Contentment, I now knew, was a gift.

A few months later, the couple returned to sign papers to adopt a dark-haired little boy they named Robert. As I summoned my assistant to get the child who would become Eliot's son, I was filled with great delight to be the person who made Eliot, finally, a father. I knew he would be a great one.

When Betty and the boy bid me goodbye and stepped out of my office, Eliot did not follow. Instead, he held back, came to me and took my hands. "How can I ever thank you enough?"

"Eliot. You know you changed my life. And now, I'm happy to be able to change yours. Congratulations on becoming a father." I managed a smile, but it was bound to be a tearful goodbye despite our business-like attempt. "I hope you'll keep in touch."

He said that he would, though his shoulders shrugged as he said it. "I'm proud of you, Lydia, you've done well for yourself. You're making a difference in people's lives."

"I learned from the best." I reached out and touched his cheek. "You took down a lot of bad guys, Eliot, you have much to be proud of—and somehow, along the way, you managed to make me a better woman." My hand remained on his face as I gazed into those eyes I remembered so well. It had been ages since we'd touched, and when I felt the heat of his blush, I let my hand fall. "Your wife seems to fit you well. She's quite an accomplished woman."

A Place We Belong

"Well, you know, I always go for the smart ones," he said with a soft grin. He walked back to the door, then turned and added, "It sure was good, you and me, wasn't it?"

"Best relationship I ever had with my clothes on!" I quipped, giving him my best wink for old time's sake.

He chuckled, loud and hearty, walked back towards me and sealed our bond with a light peck on my cheek. When he turned to leave, I opened my mouth to speak, but shut it just as quickly. There was nothing more to say.

We had no idea—though we might have guessed—that our lives would never merge again.

Fate had other plans.

So perhaps it really was true. That life paths were destined. Not chosen.

In the end, we had all found a place where we belonged.

September 10, 1997
Lake View Cemetery, Cleveland, Ohio

*T*ess arrived in the nick of time.

She rushed over, heels digging into the grass as she reached my place on the bench, and gave me a quick hug. "Sorry," she whispered, "traffic was terrible, didn't think I'd make it." *You could've left sooner*, I wanted to say but through decades of working side by side, we had learned not to push each other's buttons.

And how the years had flown. Our children were adults now, living their own lives. "I wish Jack and Molly could've made it," I said in a soft voice. They had grown up hearing all about the great Eliot Ness. Not the mythical character, but the real man who had helped them escape the unsavory orphanage that only Jack remembered. If it hadn't been for Eliot Ness, who knew what their lives would've been like?

To my delight, the children had turned out exceedingly well. My only regret was that they lived so far away. Jack had followed in his father's footsteps, becoming a doctor, and because of his childhood experience, chose to work at a children's hospital in Boston. Molly was married with two children, and was an elementary teacher in a small Michigan town.

How I wished James was by my side, but we'd lost him to cancer five years before. The kids had urged me to move closer to one of them, but I couldn't bring myself to leave the elegant home that had been mine for more than fifty years. The house was filled with memories, mostly happy ones, and I was certain it was what kept me going. And then, there my driver, Edward, who in the past year had become more than just a cherished friend.

A Place We Belong

I had stepped down from my role at the adoption agency ten years before, and Tess and her husband followed suit shortly after, turning it over to their son, Jonathan, and his wife.

So yes, I, Lydia Swanson Kent, the former Blue Satin Doll, had much to be grateful for.

A large crowd had gathered on the hill near the pond where he and his family would be put to rest. I recalled reading that Robert, the boy they'd adopted from my agency, had died far too young, at age twenty-nine, from leukemia in 1976— nineteen years after his father. Betty had passed one year later.

At the sound of bagpipes, I turned my head and marveled at the long procession. The Cleveland Police Mounted unit riding on beautiful majestic horses. The Fire Department Honor Guard. The Greater Cleveland Pipe and Drums. Seemed all of Cleveland had come to honor the man who was not just a folk hero in books and movies, but the man who had fought for important changes in the city.

The Pennsylvania State Police Honor Guard was there too, representing the place where Eliot and his family had spent their final years. The Pipes and Drums of the Chicago Emerald Society were also present because that's where Eliot's renowned crime fighting had begun.

Eliot would be mightily impressed. A moment he long deserved.

As I grabbed the memorial pamphlet the older man was passing out, my hands began to shake. On the front of it read,

In Remembrance of Eliot Ness
And his family
Elisabeth Ness
Robert Eliot Ness

355

Now the parade halted as the 1938 Buick Century came to a stop in front of the pond, practically right in front of me and Tess. We clasped hands.

A police commander's voice echoed through the quiet as he welcomed the crowd. "For all the positive changes implemented by our former Safety Director Ness during his tenure with the City of Cleveland, it is only fitting that he be laid to rest here in Lake View Cemetery."

Fitting, indeed.

After the speeches, a lieutenant and police officer rowed out into the middle of the pond to the sound of "Amazing Grace" and dispersed the ashes. The leaders then unveiled the memorial monument that would be placed up the hill to physically honor Eliot's presence in the garden cemetery.

"I'm losing so many people I love," I whispered to Tess. Before she could respond, the hum of Taps resonated through the air, shaking my very core. The man honored today had been, in a sense, my first real love. He had propelled everything that made my cherished life what it became. And I proudly gave back by presenting him and his dear wife with a child they had longed for.

"You know, Tess, I do believe we end up with the people we are supposed to be with," I said, squeezing her hand. "The people to whom we truly belong."

Tess gave a squeeze back and the ceremony concluded. As the crowd began to clear, Tess stood. "I have to go now. Will you be alright?"

"Yes, I'll be fine," I answered, watching Edward approach.

I stood now too, steadying myself with my cane.

"Ready?" Edward said, his hand on my elbow.

I'd been the first one here, and the last to leave. And rightfully so.

A Place We Belong

"How 'bout we go to that nice Italian restaurant in Murray Hill?" Edward said as we headed to the car. I glanced over at him and felt a deep yearning for this man to finally know everything about me. I had never mentioned exactly how Eliot and I had become such dear friends. I'd kept my past secret all these years, mostly because of the children.

But what the hell did I have to hide anymore? I had been a classy dish back then and I suddenly wanted the world to know.

"That would be lovely, Ed," I smiled, feeling giddy for the first time in forever. "In fact, let's have a cocktail. I have a story to tell you."

"Oh?"

"Damn straight. It's a li'l tale about that famous crime fighter, and the best burlesque queen this town had ever seen."

He looked over at me like I'd already had a cocktail or two.

Then I flashed him one of my fabulous winks.

I simply couldn't help myself.

Afterword

As promised, here are a few more facts you might be interested to know.

In my Author Note, I thanked Rebecca McFarland. She was the librarian who played an integral role in getting the ashes of Eliot Ness, wife Elisabeth, and son, Robert, returned to Cleveland and their final resting place at Lake View Cemetery.

Eliot and his wives lived in several Cleveland-area residences during his twenty years here. He and wife, Evaline, lived in the Hampton House apartments, before moving to an apartment on E. 9th street, across from City Hall. The couple also lived for a time in a converted boathouse at Clifton Park Lagoon in Lakewood, which is mentioned in this book. For an interesting list of other places Eliot and his wives lived in during his time in Cleveland, as well as intriguing facts on his life, see www.clevelandpolicemuseum.org.

As most know, Cleveland has had its share of powerful crime syndicates throughout the early twentieth century. I chose to mention two notable ones that were active in the time period that I wrote about. However, I did make up some details to best fit the story that I was telling.

Also, it is true that in 1942, Eliot left Cleveland for Washington, D.C. to work as National Director for the Federal Social Protection Program. The purpose was to control the rampant spread of venereal disease in communities surrounding military bases. The program ended with the end of the war.

Eliot and his wife, Elisabeth, did indeed adopt their son, Robert Eliot Ness, through a Cleveland-area adoption (an orphanage in Ashtabula, Ohio). And so, I thought it made perfect sense that the fictional Eliot would use Lydia's agency for that adoption.

And that bridge on the cover of this book? You may be interested in knowing that it is the Sidaway Bridge, Cleveland's only suspension bridge, which spanned Kingsbury Run ravine where the torso murders took place. The bridge still exists, however, has not been used since 1966. It was listed on the National Register of Historic Places in 2022. Big thanks to my graphic artist, Janet Sipl, for adding that fascinating detail on the cover image.

Lastly, readers may notice that I did not focus much on the Torso Murders. So much has already been written about it and I did not want to distract readers from the real topics of this book.

Acknowledgments

I am so blessed to have such wonderful people and talented writers in my corner. They continue to add much to my writing life in many ways. Big thanks to my Beta readers, Erin O'Brien, Barbara McDowell, and Edward Buatois and Kim Wuescher (who also served as editors).

Special thanks to these amazing friends and authors, Kylie Logan, Shelley Costa, Marsha McGregor, Geri Bryan, Miriam Carey, Mary Ellis, Don Bruns, Abby Vandiver, Scott Lax, and K. Zonneville, for their support and contribution to this book.

And to Janet Sipl for creating the most fitting book cover design. Thank you for your insight and talent, and for reading the entire story in order to capture those wonderful details that made the perfect cover for this book.

Lastly, big hugs to the entire Cleveland writing community. We are tight, we are supportive, and we are needed!

Reading Group Guide – Questions for Discussions

NOTE TO READER: Since there are some spoilers below, please consider reading the book before looking at this guide.

1. In the beginning, Lydia resents her "son-of-a-bitchen father" for leaving. Yet when he shows up at her workplace, she allows herself to be hopeful. Until he disappears again, leaving her a note demeaning her. Do you think his harsh words helped her to finally come to terms with his void in her life? Or leave her with a permanent sense of loss?

2. Do you think Lydia was insecure or a confident person? How did she change through different events in the book?

3. Was Lydia fond of men or distrustful of them? What changed by the end of the book?

4. What did you think about Eliot and Lydia's relationship? Do you think, given different circumstances, Lydia and Eliot would have ended up together?

5. How did the streetcar accident, and the loss of her career impact Lydia? Do you think it made her more vulnerable, or stronger? Do you think she jumped too soon into her romance with Dr. Kent?

6. Do you believe men and women with a strong bond can remain friends, like Lydia and Eliot managed to do?

7. Do you think Lydia was being hasty in her sudden impulse to adopt Jack? Or was it, as she said, an immediate strong emotional connection?

8. Were you surprised at Lydia's decision to start up her own orphanage?

About The Author

Deanna R. Adams is a multi-genre author, speaker and instructor. Her love of history, music, pop culture, and her native town of Cleveland, Ohio, is the inspiration and driving force for all her books. Deanna is the longtime coordinator of the Western Reserve Writer's Conference, is the "Book Whisperer" for The Cuyahoga County Library's Writers Center, and teaches online writing courses for the Pennwriters organization.

Find her on Instagram@Deannaadams_author, or Facebook.com/Deanna Adams Author. Or see her website, www.deannaadams.com

Printed in the USA
CPSIA information can be obtained
at www.ICGtesting.com
CBHW031314161024
15953CB00012B/53